When Two Worlds Collide

By

Joan B Pritchard

www.publishnation.co.uk

CONTENTS

Did She Fall or Was She Pushed?

He could see her pink shoe quite clearly – the buckle, shining in the moonlight. It seemed to be clinging to the crest of a wave, but just for a few moments, before disappearing beneath the choppy surface of the ocean. Is that what had happened to her – was her body now slowly sinking through the icy sea to the bed below? Would it reach the bottom of the ocean, or would a shoal of hungry fish find her soft flesh too tempting and bit by bit, gobble her up? It didn't bear thinking about – except he found himself doing just that.

"Mr Parker, what are you doing? It's too cold to stand out here in the night air, especially in your night clothes. Come along now, let me take you back to your cabin – your wife will be wondering where you've got to."

"But…..but….." he started to speak, but couldn't find his voice, " She's down there, down in the water. I arrived just in time to see her hanging half over the ship's rail but I was too slow getting to her too slow to save her." Now, his voice was just a whisper and he reached out beseechingly to the man, whose face he recognised but whose name he'd forgotten.

"Come on old man, let's go back to your cabin." And the man took hold of Tom Parker's arm and began to lead him below deck. As Tom took a step forward, he tripped over something lying on the deck and bent down to pick it up. It was a lady's pink shoe, with a shiny buckle still attached to the front. It was his wife's shoe, the one that hadn't gone into the water. He stared at it, looking quite confused, "That's Judith's other shoe – she was wearing her pink shoes tonight – they matched her dress, you see. The other one's down there – gone forever, I should think." He cradled the shoe in his arms as if it was a baby, and stared at the man, as though daring him to touch it.

"No, I can't come with you, I mustn't leave here in case she comes back – and she'll be so afraid. She's always preferred to have people around her you see, like a crowd – yes, she always preferred to be in a crowd." He realised he was gibbering by the man's puzzled expression.

Soon however, the good Samaritan had his way and Tom was standing outside his own cabin door. The man knocked on the door and waited for Judith to answer. She'd be relieved to see her husband back safe and sound, but there was no answer to his knock. The cabin door was slightly ajar and he pushed it open slowly. It was very quiet and obviously empty.

"Why, your wife's not here. Where on earth can she be at this hour? Did she tell you where she was going? Is that why you were on deck – were you looking for her?" He was even more concerned now – what was the couple up to? And where was she? He looked at Tom, who was still cuddling the pink shoe. "I told you – she's in the sea. I saw her shoe floating on the surface and then it disappeared beneath the waves – just as she must have done. Don't you understand, she must have fallen overboard – she wouldn't have jumped – I know that because she couldn't swim. She never learned, you see." He sat down on one of the bunks and placed the shoe carefully on the pillow.

"Look, you stay there old man, I'm going to get someone to help you. Do you hear me – I'm going to find an officer who'll soon sort this out – he'll find your wife?" Richard Smith left the cabin then – in fact, he was glad to get away as he didn't want the responsibility of the man and his wife. He knew he was panicking as he ran back along the corridor and up to the ship's deck. The helmsman would be there all night, ready to deal with any emergency that occurred in the wee, small hours of the night. This emergency was really going to surprise him though.

And so, the story had soon spread around the ship like wildfire. 'A passenger had gone overboard in the middle of the night! No, it was a woman, not a man! You know the couple, yes you do, you'll have seen them at dinner – I think they're called Parker – he's Tom and I think she's called Judi My God, how did such a thing happen? Do you think he pushed her or did she jump?' Yes, it's bound to be the latter – it's got to be a suicide!'

As the news was spreading, Tom was with the ship's captain, who'd left the bridge to deal with the situation. There were two other officers present– one a doctor and one his second-incommand. The atmosphere was intense as no-one knew what to say to the bereaved man. A complete search of the ship had taken place in the early hours, after all, the woman could have fallen over someplace and was still lying there hidden from view. Despite a thorough search however, she couldn't be found – and with Tom's description of what he'd seen the night before, it seemed more likely that she had indeed gone overboard. Several lookouts had been instructed to search the horizon, but nothing unusual was spotted. A small rescue vessel had been detached from the main ship and had sped back to where the ship had been the night before. It was all useless however, there was no trace of Judith.

"We'll be back in port in two days Mr Parker and I'm afraid the police will be waiting to speak with you then. We've already radioed ahead and told them what's happened and they've promised to contact your son and daughter with the bad news. In the meantime, the doctor will give you a sedative to help you sleep. You must be exhausted." The captain was trying his best to reassure the man but it wasn't easy.

Tom took the sedative and returned to his cabin, where he threw himself onto his bunk, thinking the world had suddenly gone mad. Judith's clothes and make-up were still lying around the cabin, upsetting him afresh. Even her shoes were there – but not her pretty pink ones of course! The sedative began to work and his eyes slowly closed – sleep had never seemed so welcome as it did that day. 'I'm a widower now – I have no-one,' was his last thought before oblivion took over and he slipped into welcome oblivion.

When the ship finally docked two days later, the passengers began to go ashore but Tom was asked to stay behind until the police had boarded the ship. They wanted to speak to him before he went home as there would have to be an investigation into Judith's disappearance. Tom was still in shock as he waited patiently in the captain's cabin. He was alone of course, as the ship's officers were on deck to say goodbye to the passengers. Tom was tempted to light up a cigarette – a dirty habit he just couldn't shake – but no, he'd wait until after he'd spoken with the authorities, then he'd be able to enjoy his one indulgence. Actually, it had been about his smoking habit that they'd had words about two nights before, when she'd rushed out of the cabin, screaming that she 'just had to breathe fresh air.' But she'd done more than that, hadn't she? He was still confused over her disappearance – had she fallen overboard or had she jumped into that icy water? Surely a smoking habit wouldn't be enough to drive someone to take their own life! Of course not, he reassured himself. The words, 'Did she fall or was she pushed' came unbidden into his mind and for a moment, he felt like laughing but that was probably hysteria. Was it time to try to stop smoking, he wondered? He knew the answer though – maybe in the future!

"Mr Parker, I'm Chief Inspector Harding and this is Sergeant Jones and we've come to discuss the terrible experience you've just been through. First though, we'd like to express our condolences for your loss – you must be feeling extremely upset." The tall, dark-haired Inspector sat down in the captain's chair and Sergeant Jones hovered behind him, notebook in hand.

"In your own words – and I'm aware you've already told the captain – can you please talk me through what happened that night when your wife disappeared from the deck. Did you actually see her, see what she was doing – or did you arrive too late?" He turned to the Sergeant and asked him to find someone who could make a cup of tea. Jones sighed and put his notebook in his pocket, then left the cabin. The Inspector drew his chair around the desk to be nearer to Tom and waited patiently for him to speak.

Tom didn't speak however. Instead, he burst into tears and reached into his pocket for a hanky. He had none, so the policeman handed him a box of tissues from the captain's desk. "It's all right Mr Parker – we're not here to grill you – just to get things out into the open and square away what's taken place. Do you understand – please, just talk to me."

The Sergeant returned with a steward carrying a tray of cups and saucers. "That was quick Jones." Inspector Harding reached for the tea pot – it looked like he was the one eager for a brew. He handed Tom a cup, first putting in lots of sugar.

Tom gulped down the hot, sweet tea and then began his story. "We'd had a nice dinner – the food is lovely on this ship – and Judith and I were very tired – it had been a long cruise after all.

We went straight to our cabin, not even bothering to take our usual stroll around the deck – we agreed we were both too tired. I took off my tie and lit a cigarette – I sat in the one armchair in the cabin. Judith didn't make any move to get ready for bed – in fact, she sat on the bed fully-clothed and stared at me. She seemed to change suddenly once we were in the cabin – and I knew she was going to start a fight. When you've been married as long as I have Inspector, you know the signs." Harding just nodded his head as though he understood exactly what Tom was saying.

Tom suddenly became agitated, "Then for no reason, she flew at me and snatched the cigarette from my mouth. Then, she was screaming at me - going on the way she'd done so many times before. It was the same lecture about my filthy habit and how I'd never had any self-control or I could have given up the filthy habit years ago. She usually went on about how much she'd suffered and how selfish I was. It was the same complaint I've had so many times before." He paused and looked thoughtful, " I suppose my reaching for another cigarette was a bit antagonistic in the circumstances but I really needed one – there's no smoking in the dining room, you see, so I really needed one. She screamed at me and rushed out of the cabin, swearing like a trooper as she closed the door."

The Inspector reached into his coat pocket and produced a packet of cigarettes. He lit two of them and handed one to Tom, who accepted it gratefully. The other, he put into his own mouth and immediately had the look of a contented man. "Jones here doesn't smoke – but unfortunately I do and I could see you really needed one. Please go on with your story – your wife had left the cabin. What happened then?" Tom decided the Inspector was a saint – or at least a normal human being!

"Well, as I said, we'd had this argument so many times before, so I knew she'd soon be back and we'd both act as if it had never happened. I changed into my pyjamas and dressing gown and sat back in the chair and waited. I waited and waited and I was tempted to get into bed, so tired was I – but I didn't, as I knew that would be another wrong thing in her eyes. I was on the point of falling asleep, when something awoke me and I realised how much time had passed since she'd left the cabin.

She'd been gone over half an hour and it was then very late and dark, I knew something must be wrong, so I went up on deck myself. I was too late however and my last sight of her was as she disappeared over the rail. It all happened so quickly Inspector, I wasn't sure what I'd seen exactly. I never saw her again, although I did spot one of her pink shoes still floating on the water, but it soon sank and disappeared. I knew that must have happened to Judith as well, but I didn't know for certain." He paused again, before adding, " I never knew if my wife was in that deep sea cause I wasn't sure exactly what I'd seen. She must have gone over though because she was nowhere to be seen. Having said that, I can't really believe she'd have jumped over deliberately – it just wasn't her style. She didn't really like the sea and I had quite a job to get her to agree to a cruise in the first place. Obviously, I wish now I hadn't been successful." He was crying again and the Inspector handed him the box of tissues again.

The Sergeant had been writing furiously in his notebook, then he looked up and paused. He was fast coming to the conclusion that the man seemed genuine enough – he looked like someone who'd just lost his love – and in what a terrible way? He closed the notebook and waited for his boss to continue.

"Thank you for that Mr Parker and for being so frank about what happened. I should tell you now what we're going to do. The captain has already explained how he immediately ordered a small boat to return to the area where your wife disappeared - but nothing was found. He also contacted the nearest life boat station, several fishing boats and along with them, the air rescue helicopter – searched the area. Again, they found no sign of your wife. In the circumstances, I can't fault the captain's actions, which were quick and far-reaching – I'm afraid he couldn't have done more. Unfortunately, we're not yet able to declare your wife a missing person - her disappearance doesn't constitute a missing person's status – not yet anyway."

Sergeant Jones coughed politely, obviously having trying to tell his boss something. Chief Inspector Harding nodded to him, "Yes I know Jones, I was coming to that. A report of what's happened will have to be forwarded to the Crown Legal Service as your wife will have to be declared as being lost at sea, but we'll contact you at home once this has been done. Now, is all that clear – have I explained it satisfactorily?"

Tom nodded. The Inspector had been rather nice in the circumstances and he appreciated the man's kindness. He asked, "What happens now – can I go home? My children will be waiting for me?"

"Most certainly Mr Parker, you go home now. Do you have transport? If not, I'm sure we could do something to help." Tom said his own car was still parked where'd he'd left it on arrival at the port, so that wasn't a problem.

And that was that! Tom found himself walking down the gangplank, first shaking hands with the captain and saying goodbye to his officers. 'Funny, I came here with my wife and we had a lovely cruise. Now, I don't have a wife and I must go home alone.' One very unhappy man got into his car and began the journey home.

Right from the start of the long, curving drive, he could see his daughter and son standing on the doorstep, as though they'd been waiting for him – but that couldn't be – they hadn't known he was on his way home. As always, the old house had a welcoming look and he realised how glad he was to be home at last. Three weeks at sea with a wife who was often unhappy, had been too long a time. The trees along the drive were in leaf and cast a cooling shadow over the ground. The house was Elizabethan – well it had been built as such, but had been renovated at least three times that he knew of. It looked exactly what it was – a fine old house ready to welcome him home. The heart of it was still mainly Elizabethan however and Tom was proud to live there. It had actually been in Judith's family for at least three generations - maybe even four. Either way it had belonged to Judith when they married and he'd moved there without question. She may have owned the house, but he'd always been the bread winner and paid for everything both inside and outside. There's been many renovations and alterations, so he felt it was just as much his house as it was hers.

Ellie came rushing over to the car – he could see she'd been crying. Of course, she'd been crying! Thomas, made of sterner stuff, followed slowly behind her. "Dad, what the Hell happened? We had a call from the police saying mother was missing at sea. That can't be right surely?" But when the young man looked into his father's eyes, he knew the answer to his question. Well, Mum wasn't with him, was she?

Ellie, who was only eighteen, wrapped her arms around her father and told him to come inside the house. "Thomas, fetch Dad's bags, will you?" And he did as he was told, bringing mother's bag as well – but unfortunately, no mother.

Ellie forced her father into his armchair, the one he always used when he and mother would sit there, chatting over the day they'd just had. The room was so comforting – the 'familiarity' of it helped, especially after the last two days. For just a moment, he thought he could smell Judith's perfume – she always wore the same one – but he knew it couldn't be. He was imagining things!

Thomas left the bags in the hall and went to the kitchen to ask the home help to bring some tea into the sitting room. Mary was just about to leave for home – she'd been there since early morning – but when she heard Mr Parker was home, she took off her coat and made up the requested tray. She already knew what had happened to Mrs Parker and still felt very upset by the tragic news. She'd been the family's daily help for many years now and was fond of the whole family.

As she placed the tray on the coffee table, she suddenly raised her head and sniffed the air. "Why, that's Madam's perfume I can smell!" She spoke without thinking, then realised she shouldn't have said that – was it insensitive and would it upset Mr Parker?

"It's probably the bags in the hall Mary – I thought I smelt it too when I came in." He sighed deeply and Ellie poured him a cup of tea, "You can go home now, if you like Mary. We'll manage the supper, won't we Thomas?" A grunt was all she got from her brother – but she was used to that. He'd always been a man of few words – or a total ignoramus – whatever! But now, the young man sat down opposite Tom and asked, "What happens now Dad? There must be something we should be doing. Mum just can't disappear off the face of the earth – and then nothing! What kind of search did the captain organise to try to find her?"

Tom explained everything yet again – he was becoming quite used to telling the story. He told them how their mum had been arguing with him about his smoking."

Ellie butted in with, "Oh no, not that old chestnut again. You're always arguing about that."

"I know that dear, but it was different this time – she seemed more angry than normal and was almost goading me. She just stopped shouting and then rushed out of the cabin. I didn't follow her of course, because I'm used to those tantrums – but after half an hour, I went on deck to find her. I never did find her though. I only saw her one pink shoe in the sea. No sign of your mother I'm afraid." He reached down into the small bag he'd brought with him and produced the other pink shoe – the buckle was still shining.

"Oh Dad, that must have been awful. What a dreadful experience." Ellie was crying afresh but Thomas asked, "Is she a 'missing person' now? You know, she can't be declared dead for at least seven years – unless of course, she turns up one day and I hope to God she does– or they find her body!" His voice broke on his last words.

Tom Parker sat there in the comfy armchair and listened to his children arguing with each other. He was used to that and knew he just had to let them get on with it. They'd always argued and fought with each other, it was quite normal.

He broke into their argument suddenly with the words, "Seven years – it takes seven years before a High Court can declare Judith dead – the police Inspector told me that. He'll also be writing a report for the authorities to register what's happened and record the date mum disappeared – and I've already signed a statement, confirming all I know."

"So, there's nothing we can do now? It doesn't seem right somehow, that someone can just disappear out of all our lives – and we do nothing. How will we grieve for mum and without a body, there can be no funeral? Our bereavement is going to be even stranger than most." Thomas was working himself up and becoming angry at the injustice of losing his mother in such a sudden way.

"Right, that's enough – you're being too pragmatic in the circumstances – too logical and practical. We've got to grieve first, before we discuss what is and what's not possible." Ellie was furious with Thomas, "Dad needs to rest now. Come on Dad, let me help you to your room and you can have a little nap. I'll start preparing supper – and you can help me Thomas."

And that was Tom Parker's first night at home. His first night in the house he'd shared with Judith for more than twenty-five years. Now, there was no Judith – my God, that was going to be hard - he felt as if he'd lost his right arm. Who would he discuss things with now –there had been the news, the villagers, next year's fete and most of all, what Thomas and Ellie would do next in their lives? And what would happen to his business – he always liked to talk with Judith about that – it helped him make what he thought were the right decisions? His business was in tracing, buying and selling antique books – he'd been doing it for a long time and he managed to make a very good living from it. Judith had been a silent partner – she benefitted from many of the benefits, but was never an official business partner –the business belonged completely to Tom. And lastly, who would he argue with now – they'd always had a lively relationship but very different points of view – their arguments had eventually become a way of life.

Sleep came quite easily to Tom. Maybe it was the familiar surroundings that did it. His dreams were vivid however and when he awoke, he wondered how he was going to face the rest of his life.

"Dad, Dad – supper's ready. Now, don't jump up, take your time and don't hurry. It's a cold supper, so it'll keep." She left his room, the room he'd always shared with mum and went back downstairs. There was no mistaking that perfume now – it was Judith's favourite. It wasn't surprising that it would be lingering in the room and even along the corridor, but it did remind everyone that its wearer was gone – and gone for good.

The next day was almost normal, except for the arrival of a neighbour who lived a short distance away. The woman had actually called to see Judith and was astounded at hearing what had happened. "But Judith was our committee chairman and she made all the important decisions. What are we going to do now?" She seemed more upset at losing a chairman, than she did at losing a friend, but then, Marjorie was known for her selfishness. She was very self-serving, so Tom wasn't in the least surprised by her attitude. He soon feigned a migraine headache however and the woman went off to spread the word around the village. "We've lost our chairman – what are we going to do now? And we've lost her in an incredibly dramatic way! Marjorie would enjoy embellishing that story.

Walking in the garden later, he came upon a sad-faced Ellie sitting under the ancient, gnarled tree – always a favourite place for the family. "Oh Dad – it's all so sad, isn't it? My poor mum had a horrible death and I'm going to miss her so much." He crouched down beside her and for a moment, allowed himself the luxury of smelling the newly cut grass. "Come on Ellie, you'll soon be back at university and you know mum wanted you to do well there."

"No Dad, I'm not going back there, I'm going to stay here and help you in your business – and before you start lecturing me, you should know I've quite made up my mind. I've told Thomas and he understands – he's going to go ahead and get his Masters, but after that, he's going to come back here and do the same – help you in your business. Between us, we'll make it grow even more." She stood up and looked down at her father, but he was staring hard at the front of the house.

"Look Ellie, can you see that curtain moving – the curtain in the fourth bedroom from the right. It's as though someone's watching us. It can't be Thomas – he's over there reading by the pond. Strange really!"

Ellie had seen nothing and told him he was imagining things, "Mary's already left for home, so there's no-one in the house. I'd better get back inside and see what she's left for dinner – I said I'd cook it, if she prepared it." And she ran off across the garden, leaving a puzzled man behind. *'I was sure I saw the curtain move – it couldn't have been the breeze as the window's closed. Ah well, Judith always claimed the house had a ghost – in fact, more than one usually. He laughed at the direction his thoughts were taking. 'I've certainly never seen one – but perhaps I have now and he looked up at the window again.'* He had to do something he was dreading but perhaps he'd ask Ellie to help him. He had to empty Judith's travelling bag – it would bring it all back to him.

At dinner, he asked his daughter the question, "I don't think I can do it by myself Ellie – it'll make me think of that last night onboard ship." Ellie suggested they'd do it after dinner.

In the bedroom, they were working together, "Look Dad, her favourite cocktail dress – and it still smells of her." And although she held it out to him, he didn't move to take it. "Put it on that pile over there dear – I plan to take those things to the charity shop in town." Ellie held onto the dress tightly however, "No Dad, I want this one – it really was her favourite. You don't mind, do you?"

'Of course he didn't mind. He was glad she wanted to keep her mother's dress and he told her so. He reached then for Judith's jewellery, the pieces she always took with her. "There's some nice pieces in that," he said as he passed the box to the teary-eyed girl. Your mother would have wanted you to have them." Ellie was touched but said she'd give some pieces to Thomas, "After all, he might get married one day – if anyone will have him – and he should have some of mum's personal things too." Tom thought, 'those two argue all the time, but deep down, they're really fond of each other

The bedroom was full of the smell of Judith's perfume now – it was as though it exploded from the bag - Ellie leaned her head against her chair and breathed deeply. "It's just her, isn't it? And look!" she pointed to the dressing table, "There's a half-empty bottle still there – as though it's waiting for her to come back." She sprayed some on her wrist and then ran from the room, leaving a bewildered Tom alone.

He could hear the shrill ringing of the downstairs telephone and quickly jumped off the bed. Thomas's voice called loudly, "Dad, it's for you – a Chief Inspector Harding."

The report had been written and the Inspector wanted to deliver a copy himself. "May I call on you on Friday?" he asked. Tom said that would be fine and he looked forward to seeing him again. "I also need to go over your statement again – the one you signed on the ship – just in case you've remembered something new. Sometimes that happens when the initial shock of such a thing wears off."

That night, Tom had been reading until quite late but sleep had overtaken him and the book fell to the floor. He woke with a start and for a moment, was unsure where he was. *'How silly, you're in your own bed in your own house. And yet you heard a noise, an unusual noise, didn't you? It came from the corner over there where the wardrobe is. My God, the door is wide open – I'm sure I closed it before getting into bed. Now, how could that have happened – it had to be one of Judith's ghosts finally come to visit him. Well, it was high time it happened.'* He got out of bed and crossed the room and having closed the door a second time, he glanced out of the window into the dark garden below. There was a flash of white flitting across the lawn – then it disappeared behind a tree. He kept staring into the garden but the white shape never reappeared – everything was still and silent in the dark. *But I did see it, I know I did. It looked like a woman, a slightly built woman, dressed in something long and flowing. She seemed to be wearing a hooded shroud or something like that – it hid her face completely. Am I making all this up, he wondered – it had happened so fast, just a glimpse of something white. But no, I'm sure what I saw was a woman. A ghostly figure, that's what it was, or else my imagination's working overtime. Maybe what I've been through recently has affected my mind!*

Back in bed, he began to read again, but couldn't concentrate. He kept seeing the white woman in his mind and with that thought still niggling him, he eventually lapsed into a welcome sleep that lasted all the way through until the next morning.

Chief Inspector Harding arrived at ten o'clock on Friday morning as he'd promised and rang the very old doorbell. Mary, the home help opened it immediately and invited him inside, "You're expected Sir – please come in."

The first thing the Inspector noticed on being shown into the sitting room, was the great stone fireplace, which must have been there since the house was first built. To say it was grand, was an under-statement - it really was magnificent and very much in the Elizabethan style. What he also noticed was the lady's pink shoe sitting on the mantelpiece, bang smack in the middle of several rather expensive-looking china ornaments. He knew the shoe had been important to Tom Parker but it seemed a strange place to keep it. He knew too, if his Sergeant had been there and seen the shoe, he'd have had some psychological explanation to do with a guilty conscience or even evidence of self-blame. But Jones was a young man and full of modern detective traits, which Harding had no time for. He still used his nose and gut for detection work. Still, where Tom Parker chose to keep his wife's shoe wasn't police business – he'd come to go over the man's statement, that was all.

The two men greeted each other – almost as if they were old friends, but not quite! Tom knew he was still under police surveillance and it affected the way he felt. After all, he couldn't prove Tom hadn't pushed his wife overboard – not yet anyway. And afterwards, he pretended to be a broken man. Tom was only too aware of this, *'I'm not stupid – I know how it must have looked at the time. Harding might suspect that Judith's shoe had come off in the struggle – the struggle when I forced her body over the ship's rail. I must make sure I stick to my statement, but that should be easy as it's the truth!*

The two men chatted for a while, going over the statement in detail and soon, an hour had passed and Mary was at the door, asking if the gentleman was going to stay for lunch.

"Yes Mary, I'm sure the Inspector would like that." He turned to Harding waiting for his response. The Inspector hesitated at first, but when Tom added, "Our Mary's a very good cook and she'll do you proud," he knew he had no choice." It had been a long time since the Inspector's breakfast.

Later Thomas and Ellie joined the two men at the dining table and Thomas immediately began to ask the Inspector about the rules that applied to 'a missing person.' "It's not easy Inspector, "he explained, "with no body to bury and being unable to say goodbye to Mum, we're all feeling rather lost and confused."

The Inspector explained that a report of the incident had already been sent to the Home Office and, "You now have to wait seven years before Mrs Parker can legally be declared dead."

Ellie pushed back her plate away and stood up, "It's been nice meeting you Inspector, but I can't stay here any longer and listen to my mother's death being referred to as an incident. She was one of the nicest people you could ever meet – certainly not an incident." She left the dining room and the Inspector looked towards Tom, his hands held up in apology.

"It wasn't your wife I was referring to when I called it an incident – rather it was the fact of her going overboard and being lost at sea. Please will you explain that to your daughter for me?" And he left the Elizabethan house faster than when he'd arrived. He'd got what he'd come for and the man's recent statement was exactly the same as his first. It had obviously been just one of those terrible things that happened from time to time. In his job, he'd seen many!

Out of the blue, Tom suddenly asked, "Thomas have you ever seen anything odd around here, or heard any strange noises?" He couldn't get the white lady out of his mind.

"Dad, you're not going all spooky on me, are you? I know mother believed in those things, but I never suspected you of the same. It's an old house Dad – a very old house, so there's bound to be noises and sounds that can't be explained. I often hear things I don't recognise but I'm sure it's nothing – and certainly not ghosts." Tom could see his son was amused by the thought his father was beginning to hear things 'that go bump in the night.'

"It's not a joke Thomas, I definitely saw a strange figure in the garden one night – just after I'd been awakened by a loud creaking. And the wardrobe I knew I'd closed earlier was wide open." Thomas just laughed again and went upstairs to his room. He turned at the door and added, "Don't tell Ellie about this, will you – or you'll scare her out of her wits."

Tom was in his study two days later, sorting through some very old, first editions. There was no question as to their value and he made sure he wore protective gloves when handling them. He was admiring a small number of Dickens' books that stood along one particular shelf, when he suddenly noticed something odd. Two books – ones he knew he definitely had in his collection – were missing. He frantically looked around but couldn't see them anywhere. The books were of course first editions and worth quite a bit of money. *'Now, don't panic, there's bound to be a logical explanation. Perhaps Thomas or Ellie have borrowed them and forgotten to bring them back – or they've brought them back and mis-filed them. They've always been told not to do it – without asking first, but you never know.'*

He went into the sitting room where they were both listening to some music – but no, both emphatically denied touching the books. "We know not to do that Dad – we'd never move your books without asking." Tom was puzzled.

Going to bed that night, he was surprised to find one of the missing books lying on his bedside table. When he picked it up, he saw that many of the pages had been turned down at the corners – one of the worst things you could do to a book – particularly with books of this value. He tried to undo the damage by folding the corners upwards, but the damage had been done and the pages would never be the same again. *'What's going on? Thomas and Ellie swear they've not been near my books, so it wasn't them. I know I didn't do it and Mary has never shown any interest in the things in my study – she'd never touch my books.'*

He had a quick shower and changed into his pyjamas, closing the wardrobe door yet again – although he knew for definite he hadn't opened it in the first place. But, worse was yet to come! He spotted the edge of something sticking out from under his bed. In fact, he stubbed his toe against it. It was the other missing book. Relieved at first, he reached down thinking 'Thank God, this is one that's worth a great deal of money - except it wasn't worth any money now – someone had torn out almost half of its pages and hadn't even had the decency to leave the torn bits alongside the book. It really was a disaster! He was shocked beyond words – who would do such a thing? It wasn't just the lost money caused by the destruction that upset him, but the disappointment at losing such a wonderful work of art. So few of such books had survived the ravages of time and those still in existence were becoming fewer as the years passed – and now there were two less for the world to admire. His love of old books was very real and he almost cried at their loss. He didn't cry however, he just climbed into bed and pulled the covers over his head. There was nothing he could do about it that night – or even tomorrow, so he lay down, feeling properly miserable.

There it was again! It sounded like a woman crying! But Ellie was the only female in the house and it certainly didn't sound like her. Who was it – and where was it coming from? He sat up and switched on the lamp, listening closely. He thought it was coming from overhead, but it was only the attic up there – and certainly, no-one would be there at this late hour. Then, he thought he actually heard the words, " It was you! "You did it!" And the words were repeated over and over again.

'What could it mean? Was someone talking to him – and accusing him of doing something they didn't like? Perhaps it was about the torn first edition - but no, it couldn't be that – everyone knew he'd never harm his own precious books. The sobbing voice stopped suddenly and he heard nothing else that night.

Next day, he took the two books downstairs, intending to show them to the children, although he'd already accepted they'd had nothing to do with it. Both of them were as shocked as he was. "What a terrible thing to happen Dad." Ellie was first to speak. Thomas lifted both books from the table, "My God, who would do something like this? Everyone knows such books are valuable – and more to the point, irreplaceable." Both were as shocked as their father. *'What's happening to me? he thought. First Judith's death – then the white lady in the garden, the ever-open wardrobe, the accusing voice of a sobbing woman and now my first editions. Ah, the first editions had truly broken his heart – not as much as losing Judith of course! But the destruction of the books felt like the straw breaking the camel's back.'*

Everything had been so normal before the cruise. Yes, he and Judith had had their ups and downs throughout the years, but no more than any other married couple of twenty-odd years. For the first time since it happened, Tom wondered if he could have saved his wife – had he just gone after her sooner. *But I didn't, I took the time to change into my night clothes and have another cigarette before leaving the cabin. Had I been quicker, could I have saved her? But then, I don't know whether she jumped, fell or was pushed. I like to think she fell, yes that was it, somehow she'd fallen over the rail. She was always staring into the deep ocean – it seemed to hypnotise and hold a fascination or her – she probably leaned over too far and lost her balance. Of course, that's what happened!*

Before this moment, he hadn't admitted to himself that maybe he could have moved faster and perhaps saved her. He'd loved his wife but now guilt was taking over – could he have moved faster? Why didn't he? 'Oh, what a twisted web we weave.' It was that damned voice he'd heard the other night that made him feel this way – the voice accusing him of he knew not what. Was it accusing him of failing to save his wife? Or God forbid, was it accusing him of pushing her over? His mind was in turmoil and he knew he had to supress his own damned conscience.

He went back into his study the next day and began sorting through his manuscripts. He planned to re-organise and catalogue them, something he'd put off more than once. Mary brought him some tea and cake in the afternoon, which he thoroughly enjoyed. That woman really knew how to bake a cake! Judith had always oved Mary's creations – especially her baking.

Thomas wandered into the room and grabbed at the last piece of cake. He was carrying a large leather-bound book, which he was obviously enjoying.

"Dad, did you know that houses like this one – as old as this one – had hidden priest holes where the Catholic priests could conceal themselves and give the family communion when they wanted it? It was mainly when James 1st of England became King, after the death of Queen Elizabeth. James was apparently scared of his own shadow and greatly feared witches and wizards. He was a staunch Protestant and didn't like the Catholics, but most of all, he feared witches.

"Okay, okay Thomas – you're lecturing me and anyway, I already know most of that stuff. I take it it's a good book." Tom had to smile at his son's eagerness. "Any way, your point was about a secret priest's hole here in the house, wasn't it? Well, I've certainly never seen anything like that and I don't remember your mother ever mentioning it either." As he spoke, he pulled the mobile step ladder along the shelves of books, "I'm going to clear out this top shelf and see what I've got hidden up here – it's been years since I last did it." And he began to work his way through the accumulated dust of many years – a smell he loved and it stopped him thinking about potential ghosts.

The job was taking longer than he'd anticipated and he was still clearing the top shelf two days later. He wasn't sleeping well and by mid-afternoon, he was feeling quite tired. Thomas had helped him for a while but then lost interest, as he tended to do, and had returned to his fascinating book. Ellie was in the kitchen, working alongside Mary and trying her best to produce a cherry cake – her dad's favourite.

"It's odd Mary – odd how life goes on as if mother never was." She said sadly as she spooned flour into a bowl.

"Yes Miss, I'm afraid that's true, but it's how life is. The world can't stop every time someone dies or it would be stopping every two minutes." Usually a woman of few words, that was quite deep thinking for Mary and she nodded her head, as though in agreement with herself.

"Yes Mary, you're right of course – but it's still hard to get used to mum not being around." She turned her attention to the task in hand and said, " Now for the cherries – I should cover them in a light flour first, shouldn't I – so they don't sink to the bottom of the cake." The girl had learned a lot from the older woman, whom she regarded more as a friend, than a domestic. Mary had been around for a long time and had known the children from the day they were born.

When the finished cake finally came out of the oven, it had risen beautifully and Ellie stood back to admire it. Mary was in the utility room overseeing a washing and Ellie had turned her back for a moment and missed seeing the cake, still in its baking tin, move off the top of the stove and hover in mid-air, before falling to the floor with a loud clatter. The girl looked down on the smashed cake, which had half fallen out of its tin. She looked around for Mary, but the home-help wasn't there. Ellie was the only person there and she hadn't been anywhere near the cake when it fell. How bizarre was that?

That was the first time she'd ever thought about ghosts. But how else could a solid object have moved and crashed onto the floor? *That cake was for dad – his special favourite! It's as though it's damaged to spite him. She told herself, ' Don't be so silly Ellie, you're just trying to find a logical explanation for something that's completely illogical. '*

She did however manage to save half the cherry cake – the half that had stayed in the tin, so dad would still have his treat for tea. *He doesn't need to know it's been on the floor – and no-one but me actually knows it has – so what the eye doesn't see, the heart doesn't grieve over. A pretty silly saying and totally untrue – after all, she didn't see her mother fall into the sea, and yet her heart ached every time she thought about it.*

The wardrobe door in Tom's room was open every night now. He'd checked the hinges and the lock but could find nothing wrong. Maybe the floor was uneven and the door couldn't stay closed – yes, that was certainly a possibility in a house of this age, but he couldn't recall it happening before. Under the carpet, the floor on the landing area – and in all the bedrooms - was still the original oak boards, a few of which had been replaced throughout the centuries – but there were still enough in-situ to claim the floor was original – and perhaps not as even as it should be. The wardrobe however had always stood in the same place and uneven floorboards had never been considered.

He went into his garage-cum-workshop and fetched some tools – and a new, but simple, lock, which he fitted to the wardrobe. *There now, let's see 'the things that go bump in the night' open that door. I'll be a monkey's uncle, if they can! A strange saying that, I wonder where it comes from.*

Thomas was packing his bags to return to university to complete his Master's Degree – something he'd always promised his mother he would do. His room was in a complete mess with clothes strewn all over the place and books lying everywhere.

"Thomas, this will never do – what a disgrace you are." Ellie looked around his door.

"Butt out Ellie, I know exactly where everything is – don't you touch anything." He was very defensive about his catastrophic belongings. They were his after all!

She asked if she could just tidy away the things he wasn't taking and he grudgingly allowed this. "Not that one Ellie, I'm taking that with me."

"But it's full of holes and hasn't been washed for ages." She began to roll up the sweater to dispose of it later.

Thomas grabbed it from her, "It's got character girl – can't you see that?" And he gently packed the smelly sweater into his bag. In doing so, he saw a piece of paper fluttering to the floor. Before showing it to Ellie, he read aloud, ' He didn't help me – although he could have. I was left on my own.' It was in his mother's handwriting – undated and unsigned but definitely written by his mother. He handed it to Ellie, who read it quickly.

"What does it mean Thomas – and when was it written?" she asked.

"More to the point, how did it get here? Mind you, I've not worn that sweater all summer – maybe it's been there a long time." They stared at each other but could think of nothing.

They took the note to dad's study and showed it to him. Tom said he had no idea where it had come from – but it did seem to be accusing someone of something. "It's not referring to me – I never left Judith alone when she needed me." He looked surprised and upset, especially by the expression on both the children's faces. "I can see what you're thinking - you think it's got something to do with your mother's drowning? I assure you it hasn't – I would have saved her if I could – but there was no sign of her when I got on deck – except for her shoe of course." *For one split second, he saw her going over the side – he pink dress floating in the breeze. But no, that couldn't be!*

He desperately wanted to change the subject, so he asked, "By the way, have either of you moved the shoe from the mantelpiece – I see it's gone from there." He looked at them questioningly. The words 'Me thinks the lady doth protest too much' crossed Thomas' mind when he heard his father's desperate tone.

"Perhaps it's an old note and has been there for a long time. I mean Thomas doesn't exactly take care of his clothes and he might have missed it. As for the shoe, it's been moved to the sideboard – I thought you must have done it." Ellie the peace maker, didn't like the way the conversation was going.

"I didn't move it – why would I? I put it there when I first came home – somehow it looked right there, reminding us of her every day." Tom was feeling rather aggrieved and felt as though his children were putting him on trial. He was feeling guilty and yet he'd done nothing wrong – except perhaps insisting on a cigarette at the wrong time.

He was left alone in the study to get on with his cataloguing and Ellie reminded him there was cherry cake for tea, so he wasn't to get too involved in his work - she'd made it specially for him. She didn't mention she'd only managed to salvage half of it – the other half having been on the floor! That would be her secret!

Later, Thomas came rushing into the study, "Dad – Dad, I've seen your white lady. She was running through the trees on the edge of the garden. I ran after her, but she was too quick for me – and disappeared." He was breathless and Ellie arrived behind him, "Don't listen to him Dad, you know how he imagines things. I was looking out the window, standing right beside him and I never saw any white lady." She had come to tell him tea was ready and was waiting for him in the sitting room. "I thought we'd just be cosy tonight and have tea where we're most comfortable."

Between munches, Thomas couldn't stop talking about what he'd seen. Mary had gone home and the three of them were in the house alone. Tom believed his son – hadn't he seen the woman himself? "Don't worry son, I believe you, even if Miss Dubious here, doesn't. I guess we'll just have to accept there really are such things as ghosts.

And so, the sobbing came again that night and Tom left his bedroom and began to look around the house. Of course, all the rooms were empty. The atmosphere upstairs had been quite different from that on the ground floor. He stood in the hall and could smell a strange dampness in the air. *What is it? I know I'm not alone down here – but I can see no-one. What was that noise – suddenly he heard someone move around in the sitting room – and then something drop onto the floor. Crash! I've got to go in there – there's probably an innocent explanation - granted his thought were more from bravado, but he had to psych himself up somehow.*

He pushed open the door, summoning up courage he didn't really have. *Could it be the white lady herself? Had she come into the house now?* He reached up and switched on the ceiling light – it was the brightest – and quickly, but carefully looked around the room.

There was no white lady of course, nor any other lady for that matter. The sitting room was empty, but he could still sense a presence. The shoe had been moved from the sideboard this time and lay upside down on the hearth – it looked as though it had been thrown and landed that way. Cautiously, he picked it up and reverently placed it back on the mantelpiece.

I can smell it – it's stronger over here by the fireplace. The smell filled his nostrils and almost made him choke. Bile rose in his throat and 'I'm going to be sick' thought was upper-most in his mind. Where was that smell coming from? Was it perhaps Judith's perfume – no it was actually quite foul. There was nothing to be seen.

Back in his bedroom, he felt safer – until that is, he spotted the small padlock lying on the floor. The wardrobe door was open again and this time, he knew someone, or something, had been in the room – the padlock couldn't have broken itself. He didn't even close the door this time, but just dived under the bed clothes and squeezed his eyes shut. *Let the morning come soon! What an experience – now I know there's something odd going on here – and I'm beginning to wonder if it's Judith, come back to haunt me. If it is, she's driving me mad and I don't know how much more I can take.*

Next day Thomas left for university. Tom drove him to the station and slipped him a few notes for a meal or two. He had a bank account of his own of course, but it was often empty and Tom knew it. "Take care Dad – at least Ellie's staying with you and I'll be coming back every now and again to check on you. Keep looking for that elusive priest hole – I'm sure the house must have one." And he was gone to catch the next train.

He was day-dreaming, sitting in a garden chair. The weather was mild and the clouds had disappeared to make way for some watery sunshine. He'd brought a book with him – something he'd read before – but something he'd enjoyed. He often read a book more than once – and often picked up something he'd missed the first time around. He rubbed his tired eyes and let his head drop against the back of the chair. For a few moments, he stared at the house upside down - it really was a magnificent building. The frames of heavy vertical timbers were supported by diagonal beams and the wattle walls had been daubed with fresh whitewashed mortar. It still reflected the Elizabethan architecture of the sixteenth century. Inside the house, there were still the original – and very large central fireplaces in the main rooms – and there were even candle sconces still affixed to the walls, but nowadays for effect only and not for any practical reason. He smiled as he looked at the garden ornaments dotted around the lawn, some of which must have been placed there a very long time ago. Yes, the house was a real original and now it belonged to him alone – and not to his late wife! *Am I allowed to call her that I wonder – she's not been officially declared dead yet, but as her spouse, the house would naturally pass to me. I don't need a lawyer to tell me that – it's common knowledge. I wonder how she'd feel about that, were she alive – she'd always been very protective of the house, after all it had passed down through her family for generations. She could be quite snobbish about that and regularly reminded him that she was the sole owner. My God, I sound quite unfeeling, don't I? I'm not unfeeling though and I really do miss her – but I wonder now just how much! The thought came unbidden into his mind.*

Mary called from the doorway, "Dinner in ten minutes, Sir." And disappeared back inside.

His thoughts returned to the house. Now Judith wasn't there, he would make changes to some of the furniture. She'd always wanted to keep it as authentic as possible, whereas he'd always thought it rather ugly and heavy. He decided the bed would be the first thing to go – it was typical of the medieval style, large, solid with a canopy overhead and exaggerated carved legs. Its hangings were dark red velvet that sometimes, made him think he was being suffocated. *All that will go, but I mustn't be too hasty or it'll look unfeeling – and I have the children to think of. I'll start the changes in a couple of month's time. I'll make the inside of the house lighter and a little more modern – it'll be much more comfortable that way. Authenticity was one thing, but Judith was far too preoccupied with it – I'm a modern man and I like my home comforts. God, I remember the time she insisted on Mary bringing ewers filled with warm water to the table, so we could wash our hands before eating. I managed to win that one however – affected, or what?*

He jumped up then and made for the house. He didn't want to be late and upset Mary – she was much too precious for that. Ellie was already at the table, looking rather tired, he thought. "Are you sleeping all right dear? Or have you had a few wakeful nights?" He was genuinely concerned about his delicate daughter.

"Oh, I'm all right Dad but you're right, my sleep has been broken for a few nights lately. Can I tell you something? Something very odd that might upset you?" She paused and looked embarrassed, "I keep hearing noises in the night – sort of banging noises, as though furniture's being moved about. It sounds crazy I know, but I've never heard those kind of noises before."

My dear, don't feel foolish, you're not imagining things – I hear them too and although I've searched throughout the house at night, I've never found anything unusual – except perhaps one night, when I went downstairs. That damned shoe belonging to your mother had been moved again and I distinctly smelt a strange and unpleasant odour. *Now, who's sounding foolish, he thought? But at least I'm not the only one hearing strange noises.*

"I'm sorry to hear you're having disturbed nights, Ellie. I wish I could help. What do you think we should do about it? It's not as if it's an invasion of flees or mice or something like that – then we could just call Pest Control and have them removed. But this is something quite different – sort of spiritual or super-natural or some such thing – it has to be a ghost, doesn't it, or even two?" He paused at last and waited for Ellie to speak.

"I think we'll have to approach a vicar or a priest – and have him perform an exorcism. I don't understand why it's all just begun. Could it be something to do with mother's passing over – maybe she has something to tell us – and what better way than through the house she loved so much? Again, I know how crazy that sounds, but I really don't know what else to suggest." The young girl looked pale and afraid. She'd never experienced such things before and had never even considered the age of the house as being relevant – it was just home to her, no matter how many generations had lived – and died – there.

"Let's do it Ellie – I think it's a very practical suggestion. I'll see what I can find out tomorrow. With a bit of luck, we can get everything back to normal before Thomas comes home next time." And they both began to tuck into their meals, feeling relieved as though they'd just reached a summit. At least, it was a plan!

That night in his bedroom – and after he'd closed the wardrobe door – he remembered his decision to get rid of that monstrosity of a bed. He took the bedside lamp under the canopy and pulled back the heavy drapes. The headboard was actually built into the wall itself and was decorated with several intricate carvings. Odd, he'd never really looked at the headboard closely before – and yet, he'd slept in that bed for decades. When you see something every day, you stop really seeing it. There were carved flowers, roses in particular, but also two or three cherubs with their plump faces and hands held up for all to see. It really was quite a work of art. He sat down on the bed, putting the lamp back on the table and in a sudden bout of enthusiasm, he pulled the red drapes from the canopy and threw them on to the floor. Immediately, he felt free – the air was less suffocating and he decided to give the drapes to Mary next day – she would know of a jumble sale where someone would buy them. Now, he felt tired and couldn't be bothered to read - but as usual, he was soon awoken by the sobbing sounds of a woman in distress. He was almost getting used to it now!

Next morning, he and Ellie drove into the nearby town. They agreed it wouldn't be wise to go to the local, village vicar to ask for help – as the village community would soon learn of their problems. It was well known that even the vicar himself was prone to gossip.

The day for the exorcism was set for the following Thursday and Reverend Thompson arrived, bible and small black bag in hand. These were obviously the tools of his trade and he did look very business-like – but a bit like a doctor on a call-out.

"Some tea Vicar – or would you prefer something a bit stronger?" Tom invited his visitor into the sitting room, where Ellie was waiting. Waving away the offer of alcohol, the small man accepted a cup of tea from Ellie – and also a slice of cake, made especially by Mary for the holy man's visit. Between mouthfuls, he explained this wasn't something he did very often, but he would do his best to rid them of any unwelcome spirit who was hanging around the house – and causing them distress. It was their home after all and not a place where spirits were supposed to linger. He did stress that he could offer no guarantee and that sometimes the spirits just wouldn't budge. Having made it clear that one exorcism may not be enough and there might have to be more, – and after having demolished a second slice of cake - he reached for his small bag and took out two brass candlesticks. He fixed cream-coloured candles into them and placed them on the mantelpiece, like an altar. He removed the lady's pink shoe he found there and offered it to Ellie. She looked at her father with a question in her eyes. Tom quickly explained the shoe might be relevant to the exorcism as it had belonged to his late wife – and that she was one of the spirits they suspected was in the house. Of course, he'd already told the vicar of how she'd died and of how the family repeatedly smelt her favourite perfume, especially after 'an incident' had taken place.

"Interesting!" Reverend Thompson rubbed his chin thoughtfully, "May I ask if the ghostly happenings are a recent phenomenon – or have you experienced them throughout the years?" Tom said the incidents had only begun after his wife's death – the family had never noticed them before.

"That's not unusual Mr Parker – the arrival of a newly deceased's spirit has been known to evoke other spirits who've been dormant for many years. This could explain why there seems to be more than one spirit here." He lit both candles before kneeling down in front of the 'altar.' He raised his arms heavenward in prayer and proceeded to invoke God and his son, angels and archangels and two saints, whom Tom and Ellie had never heard of before – to aid him in removing any earth-bound spirits who were lingering around this home. Three times, he said, "Help me to cast out these spirits and return them to their eternal rest – I ask this in the name of Jesus."

He continued to kneel at his 'altar' and repeated the same request to the Holy-of-holies. All in all, he was in the house for just over an hour – and must have repeated his plea three or four times before standing up abruptly and beginning to pack away his bits and pieces.

Tom wasn't sure what to say or do, he'd never been in this situation before. *How did you thank an exorcist? It wasn't as if he'd just done them a normal favour, like offering them a piece of chocolate or a drink of milk. Thank-you just didn't sound right somehow!*

Reverend Thompson saved Tom's embarrassment by saying, "Well, I've done my best Mr Parker – Ellie. I hope I've been successful in helping your lingering spirits. That's what my intentions are, you know – it's not just to help you – but also to help the lost spirits who've found themselves 'stuck' between Heaven and earth – in a permanent limbo, to be exact. They are as unhappy here, as you are to have them here – I'm sure they'll welcome eternal rest, just as we would in their position."

And with that, he said his goodbyes and left the house, but not before asking Ellie if she could get him the recipe for that cake. "I'll give it to my housekeeper at the vicarage – it's the most delicious cake I've ever tasted." His request helped bring some normality back into the room – and Tom and Ellie smiled at the unexpected request. Exorcisms and cake didn't seem to match somehow, but Ellie promised to send him the recipe.

"We'll just have to wait and see what happens now Dad." Ellie was his practical child, who'd always been more sensible than her brother. "Tell you what, why don't we tell Mary not to bother with dinner tonight and we go to the village pub and have a slap-up meal – just to celebrate the fact we've done something at last about our problem?"

She didn't have to ask twice and father and daughter spent a pleasant evening in the company of the villagers, many whom they knew well. A couple of the locals offered their condolences at the loss of Judith, but returned to their own table, murmuring 'Lovely lady – always kind. A great loss.' They were nice, but Tom didn't know how to answer them. If he tried, he found himself welling up with unmanly tears. Ellie said thank you for both of them.

Always the practical one, my dear girl! That's the second time I've thought that today.

When they got back that night, there was a scribbled note on the hall table. A Chief Inspector Harding had called to speak to Tom and he would call back the next day – he might even have to visit the house again. Apparently, he had some news!'

Harding didn't ring next day, he turned up in person on Tom's doorstep. "I've decided what I have to tell you is too important to do on the phone. I hope you don't mind my turning up uninvited. This time, he had Sergeant Jones with him. *I wonder if that's an ominous sign – but no, the worst had already happened, hadn't it?*

"You see Mr Parker, a woman was picked up by a deep sea fishing vessel near the spot where your wife went missing. The boat had been at sea for a month and couldn't travel unnecessarily to take their 'passenger' back to shore. The woman they picked up had to be very patient and just wait until she could be brought back. They say she didn't know who she was and could remember nothing before the intense cold of the sea was all around her – unfortunately, she has completely lost her memory and can't even remember her name.

"She'd been in the cold sea for many hours you see, and shock and hyperthermia could have affected her mind." The Inspector was obviously upset at having to give such news – especially when he had no idea who the woman was. He didn't want to give the family false hope – after all it could be bad or good news. Either way, they had to be told.

Sergeant Jones took up the story, "The captain of the boat has confirmed the woman speaks English – English without an accent, so it's very likely she is English. She's in hospital in Southampton now and being treated for hyperthermia and loss of memory. Apparently, other than that, she has no injuries – and her age is around forty to fifty." Jones too, looked apprehensive waiting for the Parkers' response. Was the woman this man's wife – or wasn't she? Tom and Ellie just sat there very still, both too shocked to speak. Eventually, Ellie moved closer to her father and took his hand in hers.

"Dad, what do we do now? Could it be mum?" She gulped suddenly and swallowed hard trying to with-hold a choking sound, then she started to cry. In fact, she cried harder than she'd done on first hearing her mother had drowned – it was like a flood-gate bursting open and a delude of water escaping. Tom knew it was something she needed to do.

The sergeant involuntarily moved forward and knelt in front of the distressed girl. His boss said nothing, although it wasn't usual for a policeman to show such compassion for a member of the public. *Well, they were both young! he decided.*

"Let it out Miss – just let it out. You'll feel better in the end" He paused before going on, "You shouldn't get your hopes up – not yet anyway - this woman might not be your mother and might be a total stranger. People fall off boats more than you think."

His boss nodded his agreement. "Mr Parker, the police in Southampton are preparing for your visit – and they'll take you along to the hospital where you can meet this unfortunate woman. Will you make your own way there – or would you like us to arrange police transport?" Harding asked.

Tom said he and Ellie would drive to Southampton and go straight to the police station. The two policemen then left the house to allow the news to sink in and anyway, they'd done what they'd come for. Tom and Ellie continued to sit there, saying nothing to each other. *I can't take this in, Tom told himself. It's just not possible – could Judith just turn up out of the blue? I've reconciled myself to her disappearing out of my life – and now this!* His mind returned to that night on the cruise ship. He found himself standing on the deck, staring down at the pink shoe. *Did I see her bending over the ship's rail? I can't remember! If I'd moved forward, could I have saved her? Don't be silly Man! You're beginning to imagine things again– you know you didn't see her that night – she'd already disappeared over the side before you' even arrived.*

The man's memory was playing tricks on him – he found he couldn't shake off the picture of Judith hanging over the ship's side, but no, he couldn't have seen that or he'd have run forward and held onto her. *But that's not what happened – she had already gone when I arrived on deck. I really did love her – sometimes more and sometimes less - but I'd never have watched her fall to her death. I couldn't have done that, could I?*

"Right Dad!" Ellie was back in control of herself, "First thing tomorrow morning, we'll set off for Southampton. Agreed?" She was wiping the tears from her eyes and Tom thought how young she looked. She was his little, motherless girl again. He knew he had to pull himself together, "Yes my dear, that's what we'll do and we'll go straight to the police station. Best tell Mary what's going on." And he went off to the kitchen to find the home help. "Just some sandwiches tonight Mary – it's been such an exhausting day, both Ellie and I are shattered and couldn't face a cooked meal." He explained that both he and Ellie had to go someplace the next day and that they'd probably be away for a night – it would be too long a drive to get there and back the same day.

Before going to bed that night, Tom noticed the pink shoe had moved yet again – it was back on the sideboard now. *What was going on with that silly shoe? Yet still, he couldn't bring himself to get rid of it – it would feel like losing Judith all over again.*

He closed the wardrobe door as usual and crossed to the bedroom window. Staring into the darkness, he searched for the woman in white – but there was no trace of her. Perhaps the Reverend Thompson's mumbo-jumbo had worked after all – but he thought that was too much to hope for. He closed the bedroom curtains before switching on the bedside lamp – somehow, he managed to trip over the edge of the rug and fell headlong on top of the bed. He wasn't hurt but one arm hit the headboard hard and out of the darkness, he heard a clicking sound. He realised his hand had landed on a raised shape - a shape carved as a small, rosebud. It turned out to be a well-hidden button that opened a secret panel beside the bookcase, at the side of the bed. In fact, the bookcase was as old as the Elizabethan bed itself. The open panel revealed a dark passage inside, that led into a small room behind the wall. The walls were solid stone, very bare and the room had no windows. It smelt dank, dark and very un-inviting.

My God, what have I found? How could I have slept here for so many years and never known this was here? Had Judith known about it – if she had, she'd never mentioned it to him?

He stared into the dark room and knew he couldn't bring himself to go inside – not just yet anyway. His investigation would have to wait until the next day when it was light – and make him feel braver into the bargain. Could this be Thomas's 'priest hole' he'd kept on about – it seemed larger than how priest holes were often described - maybe it was meant to conceal more than one person at a time? Tom wondered how many poor souls had hidden there throughout the centuries – hidden in a desperate attempt to save their lives. And for what reason? They'd obviously been persecuted by someone. And they might not all have been holy men – maybe Royalists or Roundheads or just Protestants whom Bloody Mary had detested. There'd been so many times throughout history when persecuted men had to hide from the authorities.

The actual walls behind the bookcase and into the room beyond, must have been about three feet deep – a stronghold if ever there was one. No living sound could ever be heard outside that dark, secret place. He told himself he had to be brave the next day – he might find something that had lain there for a very long time. What a gruelling thought!

Could the priest hole be the reason for the unusual sounds he'd heard in the night? The vicar had said the arrival of 'a new, restless spirit' could evoke other spirits who'd gone on before. Could it have been Judith's spirit that had 're-started the hauntings.' She'd always liked to stir things up, had Judith.

Tentatively, he touched the rosebud on the headboard again and the bookcase panel slowly moved back into place. Tomorrow was another day and everything would seem less daunting in daylight.   And after all, he'd have Ellie to hold his hand!

But I have to leave early in the morning to drive to Southampton. I'll say nothing to Ellie about the secret room until we come back – what we find in Southampton might affect how we deal with the 'priest's hole'! Should the woman in Southampton turn out be Judith – everything would have to change again.

They could smell the fresh sea air long before they arrived at their destination. Tom breathed deeply and told Ellie to do the same. The sounds of the seagulls were deafening – their high-pitched squawking reminded Tom of his time on the cruise – the cruise when he'd still had a loving wife – well, he thought she'd been a loving wife. They'd been together for so many years, maybe they'd just gotten used to each other – and they'd loved the children – oh yes, they'd both loved the children.

They arrived at what was obviously the police station. They knew they were expected – Inspector Harding had arranged it – and they found a safe place to park. It was difficult to know who was the most nervous, the girl or her father. A policeman was waiting for them, to take them to the hospital. Apparently, she hadn't been told some people were coming to see if they knew her – Tom and Ellie had agreed to pose as hospital visitors, should they be spotted by her. She was still under the hospital's care and not yet recovered from her ordeal, so everyone had to be careful.

"Just leave your car there Sir – it'll be quite safe – and I promise you won't come back to a ticket on your window. I'm responsible for taking you to the hospital, so, shall we go?"

It was a modern building with many windows shining in the sunlight, like lots of prying eyes. The Ward Sister rose from behind her desk and came forward, her hand outstretched. "Hello Mr Parker – Miss Parker – I'm very pleased to meet you. How was your journey? At least the weather is on your side. Now, before I take you along to meet Elizabeth – we're calling her Elizabeth until her memory returns – would you care for some tea or coffee perhaps?"

They declined her kind offer – they were both eager and hesitant at the same time. It was a big moment for them and the Sister knew it. She led them along a corridor towards a private room at the end, but before opening the door, she turned, "I should tell you again that we haven't told her the reason for your visit, as we don't want to raise her hopes unnecessarily. You do understand that, don't you?""

Tom assured her they'd been told that already, "The last thing we want to do is upset someone who's been through such a terrible time. My daughter and I have come a long way, hoping she is our loved one, but having said that, we're quite prepared for 'Elizabeth' to be a stranger. We're just hospital visitors, that's all."

The Sister looked thoughtful at his words, "Your attitude does you proud – you're obviously thinking of her and not just yourselves and I thank you for that. There is another way we could deal with this, but only if you're happy." She pointed to a small window a few feet from the door, "That's how we keep an eye on some of our patients, especially those who've been through such trauma – Elizabeth is one of those. You could just view her through that window and she wouldn't be able to see you – the glass has been specially treated so she can't see through it from her side. She understands it's that way for her own safety – we don't tell her we can see through it. Well, what do you say?"

Both Tom and Ellie agreed – that was the best solution. Ellie said, "And we won't have to disturb the woman unnecessarily – unless of course, it's mum."

Through the 'magic' window, they stared at the woman in the bed. She had long. blond hair that hung in curls about her face. It was a rather round face and as she smiled at the Ward Sister who'd gone in on some pretext or other, they saw two large dimples appear in either cheek. Her eyes were blue and sparkly – but she wasn't Judith! In fact, she looked nothing like Judith. Tom and Ellie turned away – he was disappointed but she was very disappointed. The woman had been about the right age but with looks very different from Judith's own looks.

"Mum had such lovely hair – shiny and black. In fact, she had the profile of a model, I always thought – granted an aging model in the last few years. That poor lady must feel so lonely and lost – my heart really goes out to her. Amnesia must be an awful thing, mustn't it?" Ellie was devastated – she'd convinced herself the woman was going to be her mother – although she'd never actually said it. Now she felt lower than she thought was possible.

The Ward Sister and the policeman had both been lovely, but Tom couldn't wait to get to the hotel where they were going to spend the night. It really was too late to start back on the road at that time, so they'd made the right decision to stay overnight.

"Tell you what Ellie, let's go down to the pier before settling down for the night. Fish and chips followed by ice cream are called for in that order– we mustn't miss the opportunity of spoiling ourselves, must we?"

"Making ourselves sick you mean, don't you? But yes, I'd like that Dad – let's go." Ellie laughed.

And that's what they did. They had a good time on the pier, playing the slot machines and firing blanks bullets at moving targets. Two candy flosses later, they sat down to a meal of fish and chips – but the ice cream had to wait. It would have been just too much.

They arrived at home late next afternoon – it had been a strange forty-eight hours and both were sad and yet, happy at the same time. The hospital had been sad, but the pier had been happy. Having said that however, home was best and Mary was glad to see them. She'd made a special supper to welcome them home. They were glad they'd not told her why they'd gone to Southampton – she would have been disappointed, just like them.

"By the way Ellie, after we've had this superb supper, I've got something upstairs to show you. No, I'm not telling you what it is – it's a surprise. By the way, will you remind me to telephone Inspector Harding tomorrow – it's too late to do it tonight?" And he began to tuck into his special supper, forgetting all about his promise to show Ellie his 'surprise.'

"Perhaps you could invite him to come and see us again – and bring along that dishy Sergeant." She was joking of course – at least that's what she said.

The night time noises started again but not until the early hours of the morning. Now Ellie too, could hear the sobbing woman and she went to her father's room to ask if he'd heard her. He told her it had become a regular occurrence, as had the banging sounds of something heavy being moved around in the attic. "We'll go up there tomorrow and see what's been happening – I'm afraid it seems the Reverend Thompson's exorcism hasn't been successful."

She wished she was a child again and she could climb in bed beside her dad – but of course, she couldn't. She was a young lady now – but just as scared as she'd been after a nightmare. But at least the banging had stopped for the night.

As she left his room, Tom mumbled in a sleepy voice, "Close that wardrobe door, will you Ellie?"

He'd not been asleep very long, when something new awoke him. The grey light of dawn was just beginning to creep into his room through the shutters and he could see strange shaped shadows forming in the half light. He sat up in bed and peered into the greyness. There she stood in front of the wardrobe. It was Judith just as he remembered her on that last night on board ship, only this time she was dripping wet. Her black hair clung to her head and her pink dress was sweeping the floor and clinging to her body. In the greyness, she looked pale and quite threatening - and in her hair he noticed small pieces of seaweed. Those added a touch of realism to the silent apparition, who just stood there – intimidating and accusing. She looked angry with him and her very white skin glowed in the eerie half-light.

He rubbed his eyes, but she didn't go away – in fact, she actually took a step closer to the bed. Like a child, he pulled the covers over his head – he couldn't bear to look at her. He knew she wasn't real but she was real enough to scare him out of his wits. Lying under the bed covers, his thoughts went back to the night on board ship. *I could have saved her – I've just blotted it out of my mind. He could see her again, leaning over the ship's rail. Had she really been so upset and unhappy to think of ending her life in such a horrible way? Did I really just stand there and watch her? I remember now – I remember quite clearly. I did let her go over - perhaps her foot slipped at the last moment and she hadn't really intended to go all the way – but either way, I didn't try to help her and now I know what the note Thomas found really meant - I did turn away from her when she needed me most!*

When he felt brave enough to bring his head from under the covers, the figure had disappeared. In the increasing light, he stared at the carpet where she'd stood and saw no water marks, although he'd actually seen the drips fall to the floor. The carpet looked bone-dry but he wasn't going to get out of bed to check. *Anyway, could a ghost leave water marks?*   *Luckily, sleep overtook him – the utter exhaustion of the last two days had worn him out. He slept the sleep of the dead – a pun which, in the circumstances, would normally have made him laugh – but not after what he'd just been through.*

Working in his study, he remembered he'd forgotten to show Ellie the secret priest hole. He'd keep that surprise for a little later – anyway, his bedroom wasn't the most inviting place since Judith had visited him there.

God, I feel peckish – I wonder if Mary's left anything tasty in the kitchen – she sometimes does when it's her day off. I feel just like a naughty school boy he thought as he crept along the corridor towards his own kitchen, glad that Ellie wasn't at home to see him behave like a naughty child. She was visiting an old school friend and wouldn't be back until evening.

And there it sat in all its glory! A magnificent cherry cake – his most favourite cake in the whole world! Mary had excelled herself this time – Ellie's cake had been good, but not a patch on Mary's. A glass of cool milk made it perfect and he cut himself a generous slice – Mary always packed her cake with the maximum number of cherries possible. Ellie, not so much! He sat at the kitchen table and cleared his plate, right down to the last crumb. He looked greedily at the rest of the cake but immediately turned his back muttering, "Get thee behind me Satan."

Back in the study, he found he was feeling tired and put it down to the enormous slice of cake he'd just had. Grabbing a book from the shelves, he settled down in an old – but very comfortable - armchair and didn't get beyond the second page before his mouth fell open and he was sound asleep. Although he was a self-confessed snorer, he didn't do it this afternoon. He just sat there as the book slipped from his hands onto the floor.

Tom Parker was dead! He'd felt a few pains in his stomach, but nothing too bad – his mind had wandered in that pleasant way it sometimes did just before sleep. He was back on board the cruiser, sitting in a deckchair on deck and the warm sun was making him feel drowsy. All was right with the world and everything was just as it should be. *As he breathed his last however, he realised Judith wasn't with him. Where was she? Ah well, she'll soon reappear!*

After half an hour, an unknown figure came through the kitchen door. She was wearing rubber gloves and a plastic cape – very unusual clothes. She began tidying up the kitchen and worked fast – but carefully. She removed the rest of the cherry cake and placed it in a small rubbish sack she'd brought with her. That would go on a fire in the woods. She wiped the table clean of any stray crumbs and thoroughly washed the glass clean. She stood back and admired her work. Everything looked fine. She went out the back door and returned with a wheel barrow – luckily the gardener usually left it just outside the back door. She wiped its wheels before pushing it into the study where, using all her strength, she dragged Tom's body from his chair and dumped him into the barrow. Someone from a previous generation had fitted a lift in the house – but it was never used after the invalid had passed away. It still worked however -a bit rickety but usable - the woman, if it was a woman - took Tom's body upstairs to his bedroom and pressed the carved rosebud on the head board. Unceremoniously, she dumped his body inside the priest hole and left him there – a crumpled heap on the floor. For good measure and to add insult to injury, she bolted back downstairs and returned carrying the pink shoe from off the mantelpiece and threw it inside the little room so it landed on top of Tom's body.

No-one else knew about the secret hideaway – but she obviously did! And the secret would remain safe with her and he could lie there for years and no-one would ever find him. A job well done, she told herself – and she pressed the rosebud again, this time to close the secret room – for ever, as far as she was concerned.

Before leaving the house, she filled two suitcases with Tom's belongings and took them out of the house in the wheel barrow. She also found his passport which she'd burn later with the cherry cake. The room was cluttered and untidy with various bits and pieces strewn around – things he'd left behind in his haste to leave - a sudden on-the-spot decision to get away in a hurry. *Tomorrow, I'll empty his bank account, the woman told herself - I've been forging his signature for long enough, so that won't be a problem. She was actually sorry that it had come to this – she'd have preferred him to take his own life, but oh no, Tom was too much of a coward to do that. The cherry cake was the only answer!*

As she carried out the rest of her plan, she couldn't help thinking of how hard she'd tried to push him over the edge. All that ghostly sobbing every night, the banging noises to keep him awake, the white lady running through the garden and that damned wardrobe door – she'd had to open it every damned night. Then her piece- de-resistance when she visited him from a watery grave with bits of seaweed still in her hair. That should have worked – it should have put the fear of God into him and made him think suicide was the only answer – but he just pulled the covers over his cowardly head and lay there like a great dummy. The man obviously had no conscience. Still that was all in the past now. She'd dealt with the matter!

The afternoon faded into early evening and Ellie arrived home, "Dad, I'm back. Have you had a good day – I certainly have! Maggie was such fun!" She hung up her coat before wandering through the house in pursuit of him. He was nowhere to be seen. She checked the car was still on the drive so he hadn't gone out, so, where was he? After half an hour, she decided to ring Mary in case she knew where he'd gone. Mary was not only her home help, but a friend as well. She'd always been a presence in Ellie's life – as long as the girl could remember. Mary knew nothing however, but asked if Ellie would like her to come over

- she wasn't doing anything important. Gratefully, Ellie accepted and within ten minutes, Mary arrived. Together they searched the house - but had no luck. It seemed Tom had completely disappeared. They checked his bedroom and found evidence of a hasty departure – bits and pieces all over the place and Ellie noticed that two suitcases had been removed from the top of the wardrobe. My God, what was going on? He hadn't mentioned he had to go away.

"It certainly looks like he left in hurry, but why? Where could he be going, and without telling anyone? He never mentioned anything to you Mary, did he?" Mary assured her he hadn't. "Let's give him 'till tomorrow, shall we – and if we don't hear anything, I think you'll have to contact the police, although I'm not sure how long a person has to be missing, before they'll do anything." Mary didn't want to leave the girl alone in the big house – especially after she'd heard the family discussing strange happenings and noises around the place. Ellie reassured her she'd be all right – in fact, she was planning to ring Thomas and tell him about recent events. "He's not been home for three months now – so maybe it's time he paid us a visit. I've got quite a lot to tell him."

On her own, the house seemed so quiet that she had to switch on both the radio and the television at the same time – she needed the comfort of sound around her. That night, she slept the sleep of the innocent and heard no sobs or bangs in the early hours. She was really worried about dad of course – this just wasn't like him. Normally, he'd never be so inconsiderate as to leave without a word – no indication of when he would be back.

Thomas turned up next day, haversack hanging off his shoulder and a bulging bag of dirty laundry. Ellie gave him a quick update of all that had happened since he'd last been home. It was a lot for him to take in, but he managed in the end – and then he did something completely out of character – he reached over and cuddled his little sister. The family had never been one to show much emotion, but on this occasion, it seemed the right thing to do - and Ellie had been through so much, whilst he'd been posing around at university, without a care in the world. Ellie laughed and pushed him away, "Stop being so soppy Bro." But she liked it all the same. "I'm sure Dad will be back soon with a perfectly good explanation for his sudden departure. In the meantime, we should contact Chief Inspector Harding and tell him what's happened now. He'll be sick of this family!"

However, Harding wasn't sick of this unfortunate family - and he turned up at the door the very next day with Sergeant Jones in tow. He listened to what had happened and how Tom had just upped and left the house – with no warning. He told the brother and sister, "I'm truly sorry to hear this, but we'll make it our business to find him for you. He's a very rational man – I'm sure he had good reason for what he's done. Leave it with us, but in the meantime, I have some surprising news for you."

The other half of the duo took over then and Jones said, "We've been notified by the local police that a woman has turned up at their station, claiming she's been suffering from amnesia for about three months. She woke up this morning and suddenly remembered who she was. Apparently, it all came flooding back to her and they couldn't stop her talking in the end." He was smiling as he spoke and Ellie knew what was coming was good.

Thomas however, still looked puzzled, "Well and what has this woman to do with us?" he asked impatiently.

"Oh Thomas, can't you guess what's coming?" She looked at Jones and waited. The Sergeant couldn't conceal his pleasure as he said, "The woman claims to be called Judith Parker – your mother." He paused then to let the news sink in – and the Inspector took over. "Obviously, we have to be careful. The story of her death was in all the newspapers at the time and this woman could know you own a beautiful house, worth a lot of money. Becoming Judith Parker – your Judith Parker – might be very advantageous for her. There's much to do before we allow you to meet her.

"Does she look like our mother? Is she the right age? Does she know anything about our family?" Ellie was excited and afraid both at once – after all, she'd been through this once before with the woman in Southampton.

"Well, as I explained, a lot of information was in the papers at the time – so people would have learned a lot about your family. We'll have to tread carefully and speak with her at length. Of course, the final piece of the puzzle will be when you meet her." He stood up and indicated Sergeant Jones should do the same. "If I could ask you to be patient now and allow us time to interview her more. She claims to have been sleeping rough in the streets for months – she's haggard looking, dishevelled and is wearing dirty and torn clothing but I would expect that – living in the streets can be rough. She also has no money and no valuables – so you can imagine how claiming to be part of your family would be an attractive proposition."

When the two men finally left, Thomas said, "He's right of course – it could be just a big con, but you and I will know – I think it's a safe bet that we'd recognise our own mother. Whilst we're waiting Sis, there's money to consider – bills, groceries and of course, Mary's wages. How will we manage 'till Dad comes back?"

Ellie told him not to worry, it wasn't a problem. She had a joint account with dad and could draw money when needed. "I'll get some cash tomorrow and let you have some of it," she promised.

What a shock was waiting for her! She called into the bank in the next town and tried to make a withdrawal. The bank clerk looked embarrassed as he said, "I'm sorry Miss – there's no money in your current account – your father emptied it two days ago." She told him that couldn't be – her father would never do that. "May I speak with the manager please?"

Unfortunately, the manager repeated what she'd already been told – he too looked embarrasses. He went on to soften the blow however and mentioned her father's savings account. "If you could just get your father to sanction a transfer of funds, we could move some money into the current account – and then you'd have access to money." His eyebrow was raised questioningly and he waited. Ellie couldn't tell him Tom Parker was temporarily missing – not yet anyway. She told him she'd speak with her father and arrange what he'd suggested.

My God Thomas – he's left us with no money. I'd never have believed it of him. It must be a mistake – I'm sure it's a mistake." Ellie was crying. What a lot of crying she'd done over the past few months. Between sobs, she asked, "Thomas, do you think dad's run away because it's all been too much for him? I always sensed he felt guilty at how mum died – I think he couldn't forgive himself for not saving her and apparently, their argument was all about his smoking – or rather the fact, he couldn't stop. So, in a way, he caused what happened. That must have added to his guilt, mustn't it? He's wrong of course, I'm sure he'd have saved her if he could."

"Come on old girl, chin up – we'll sort all this out. Let's just take it step by step. Dad will come back, just you wait and see and we'll all be fine again. I have no doubt he'd have saved mum if he could – we both know that!" He changed tactics then and tried to be positive, which wasn't easy in the circumstances. "Tell you what Sis - why don't we do something practical in the meantime and sell a couple of bits and pieces? That'll give us some ready cash – it'll help until things calm down again." He liked the idea and was already appraising the room for potential valuables. "I'll even have a rummage around in the attic to see what I can find. There's bound to be things up there worth a bob or two."

He was as good as his word and climbed the steep steps into the attic the next afternoon. *God, life is funny – whatever next? His thoughts were all over the place – things were changing so quickly, he could hardly keep up. He was the man of the house however – at least 'till dad came back – and he had to take care of Ellie.*

The attic was dark and foreboding – he hadn't been up there for years – but he remembered where the pull-light was and soon, 'there was Light'. That's much better, he thought. God, there was so much stuff up here – many generations' worth, he thought. He wandered around slowly, picking up and putting down several things, some of which he immediately decided were genuine antiques. *We should be able to get a few bob for some of these. He had to move a dressing table, at least he thought it was a dressing table – and in a small area to its rear, he saw a couple of bed blankets and a pillow. Had someone been sleeping here – and when? Had they had a visitor they didn't know about? It seems they had – and not all that long ago as the bedding was quite new. There were two large church candles as well – thick stemmed and only burnt half way down. Should I tell Ellie about this, he wondered – or would it scare her even more?*

Whilst Thomas was investigating the attic, Chief Inspector Harding and Sergeant Jones were interviewing the alleged Judith

Parker. As far as she was concerned, the time had arrived for her to tell the truth – well, her version of the truth anyway.

"I remember it all now – I'd grown to hate my husband throughout the years we were together. I know the word hate is a terrible word to use, but you want the truth, don't you?

He irritated me beyond words – all he cared about were his books and his cigarettes - the first smelly and musty and the second just smelly. He didn't love me – he did nothing for me, not even leave me, something I told him to do many times. He was too comfortable though – living in the house my parents had left to me. To me – not him! He had a good life with me and he knew it. I was desperate on that last holiday we had together – the cruise in the sun was fine – but our cabin smelt overpoweringly of tobacco and he refused to smoke in the open air. The smell made me sick all the time. I swear he just wanted to annoy me – and he succeeded. I know this must sound trivial to you – but believe me, it's not." Harding and Jones exchanged glances but said nothing – she was in full flow and they didn't want to stop her. Things had obviously built up inside her to such a pitch, she couldn't control herself. And it all helped with their investigation.

"I had to get rid of him out of my life – but how? On board the ship, I formed a plan – if I fell over board and he hadn't tried to help me, my drowned corpse would surely play badly on his conscience. I even planned how to make it happen. He'd feel so guilty – he'd decide his only option was to end his own life – and I'd be shot of him forever. Then I'd be able to live in my lovely home with my two lovely children." She stopped talking and stared at the two men's impassive faces, "Oh, I know what you're thinking – callous bitch – but I'm not you see – you don't know what it's like having to live each day with someone you hate – and who probably hates you."

Harding said, "Please Madam, go on with your story. Jones and I are here to listen – not to judge. Where did you go after you'd pretended to fall into the sea?"

"I hid in an empty lifeboat – and when I saw Tom come on deck, I threw one of my shoes into the ocean – I'd left the other one beside the rail, as though it had fallen off when I clambered over the rail. The ship was still at sea and I had to stay under that tarpaulin for two days – until the ship docked and I could escape in the midst of the passengers. I'd changed into the casual clothes I'd hidden in the lifeboat several days before and that's how I got ashore safely, without anyone spotting me. I was just another passenger amongst so many." She stopped talking and asked if she could have a glass of water. Jones fetched it and told her to go on with the rest of her story.

"To cut a long story short, I was mugged by two men soon after leaving the ship – they smashed my head with something iron – God it hurt – and they took my bag and purse. I think they were disappointed because I had nothing else of value. They left me lying in a pool of blood in a back lane and I must have passed out. When I woke up, I couldn't remember who I was or anything about my life. I didn't even know I'd just been on a cruise with my husband. I was just another down-and-out, with no money or belongings – and that was when I started living on the streets. There was always a corner where I could hide – and then I met up with people like myself – and I stayed with them, sleeping wherever they slept and stealing what I could from the shops. I must have been with them for at least three months – although it felt a lot longer. One thing I will tell you however, is that I'll never again walk past a street person, without giving him something, because that person could have been me."

The Sergeant asked her, "Did anything out of the ordinary happen that might have jogged your memory – something that triggered the realisation of who you were?"

"Nothing I was aware of," she told him, "but something must have happened – one moment I was a down-and-out and the next, I was Judith Parker, who'd just been on a cruise with her husband. That shook me a lot."

And that was the story she told the police. And that was the story the police believed in the end. They subsequently judged the woman was indeed Judith Parker, the woman they'd believed had been lost at sea for three months. But there was one further question that needed an answer.

"Just out of interest Madam, will you be going back to your husband now?" He didn't mention Tom Parker had gone missing and that no-one knew where he was. Official identification was still needed and only her close next-of-kin could be relied upon for that.

Back in the house, Thomas and Ellie were furiously polishing two old lanterns he'd found in the attic. They were brass and of a style probably used in the seventeenth or eighteenth century.

"Worth some money, if I'm not mistaken." Thomas predicted proudly – although truth to tell, he had no idea. "I'll take them into town tomorrow and get what I can for them. That'll keep us going 'till dad gets back."

Ellie was admiring her handiwork but suddenly said, "By the way Thomas, have you moved that pink shoe from its usual place on the mantelpiece? I noticed it's been moved again? But I don't see it anywhere."

"Why on earth would I do that Sis – one shoe's not much good without the other – and I'm not into women's styles anyway, "was his disinterested reply – he wasn't even curious about why the shoe kept moving about the house.

The shiny police car drove slowly along the drive. It stopped outside the front door and two men and a woman climbed out. It was Chief Inspector Harding and Sergeant Jones and with them, there was a middle-aged woman with dark hair. She was quite thin – almost scrawny in fact, although from an upstairs window, Ellie had no problem in recognising her mother. She ran down the stairs where Thomas was standing in the hall.

"It's Mum, Sis – it's definitely her. She's come back to us," and he opened the door to the visitors. Without hesitating, he threw his arms around the woman's neck and held onto her for several moments. Ellie came up behind and he released Judith Parker into her daughter's arms.

"Oh Mum, Mum, so much has happened since you left for the cruise, "Let's go into the sitting room and Mary will bring us some tea – and cake. When she brings it, you must make a fuss of her – she's missed you as much as we have." She turned to the two men, "And you gentlemen, please come into the sitting room – wait 'till you taste Mary's special cake!" She was bubbling with excitement – her mother really had come back from the dead and she just couldn't believe it.

Inspector Harding first had to say his piece however and so, "Mrs Parker has been charged with wasting police time – she has caused the country significant financial losses, not to mention the great distress to you, her family. However, the Crown Prosecution Service and the Police have agreed not to award the usual six month's prison sentence– as this would merely cost the tax payer even more money. Instead, she is to be given a Fixed Penalty Notice under the Criminal Justice and Police Act 2001 – the sum yet to be decided."

Having carried out his official duty, both he and Sergeant Jones changed from being policemen to cake worshippers and joined in the family celebration, to welcome the woman home. Both had been involved in the case since the beginning and felt they'd got to know the family a bit more than was usual, so they were almost as delighted at Judith's return than her family was.

Judith Parker spoke at last. She was uncomfortable, unsure, and wondered just how much the children knew about what she'd done – about how she felt about their father – and to what incredible lengths she'd gone to get him out of her life. He was their father after all! She looked questioningly at everyone and her eyes filled with tears until Ellie said, "It's all right Mum, we know everything – but we didn't know how much you'd grown to hate our dad."

Thomas joined in, "Ellie's right Mum – we had no idea. It's only right that both Ellie and I love our father and we're looking forward to his coming home. How do you think you're going to cope with that – us all back under the same roof?"

Judith looked puzzled and Inspector Harding coughed to cover the awkwardness, "Your mother doesn't yet know Mr Parker is missing – and that he seems to have gone away suddenly for some kind of holiday. He must be planning to be away for some time as he's also emptied his current bank account."

Judith Parker was even more confused, "I was expecting him to come into the room at any moment," she admitted, "I had no idea!" She looked at Ellie and Thomas, "How have you two been managing with no money?"

Thomas explained how they'd started a little business and had been selling things from the attic." He looked very proud of his entrepreneurism – he liked that word and grinned widely at everyone in the room.

"Well done Thomas!" Sergeant Jones couldn't help saying, "That was thinking on your feet!" Harding looked at him with a furrowed brow but could only smile at his young Sergeant's eagerness to please the Parkers. 'Or was it just Ellie he was trying to please?' the Inspector wondered

The police were leaving but first, they explained they'd had no luck in tracing Mr Parker's whereabouts, "But we're still on the job." Jones added and received a big smile from Ellie. Those two really seemed to be getting on well.

When they'd gone, Judith stood up and said she was going to the kitchen, to congratulate Mary on the cake. "It'll allow me to have a chat with her as well – and to thank her for looking after you and the house over the past three months." She was beginning to sound more like the mother they remembered – and from here on in, it could only get better.

If only dad would come home!

The next few days and weeks passed and the family adjusted to the different atmosphere in the house. Judith put on a little weight and began to look even more like her old self. She insisted in sleeping in her old bedroom, although Ellie thought she'd be happier in another room. "No, my dear – I have to get back to normal – and that has been my room since I came home as a young bride and started married life. Before that I'd slept in the room on the top floor. One thing however, I'd like to have the hangings back around my bed – it's what I was used to but Tom obviously didn't like them – although in all the years we slept there, he never mentioned it."

The ghostly noises had all stopped – the wardrobe door stayed closed and the white lady was not seen again. Life was getting back to normal, except for Tom's disappearance. Ellie helped around the house as she'd done before and she also took up where her dad had left off – she began working on cataloguing his books. She even began dabbling in the buying and selling of the masterpieces and found she really enjoyed it – in fact, she began to make good money for the family. But she was doing it all for dad – for when he finally came home again. Thomas was also busy, continuing his clearance of the attic – finishing his Master's Degree was a thing of the past and studying for him was over. He was a business man and like Ellie, starting to make money, which he enjoyed. That attic had many surprises and he was given a free hand to buy and sell the bits and pieces he found. They were his family heirlooms after all.

What did amaze him however was how the bedding in the attic had completely disappeared and there were no signs of anyone sleeping there now. He decided to say nothing to the others, as it would only worry them needlessly. Judith began to look and act more like her old self – in fact, she seemed better and happier than ever before, so perhaps Tom's absence from the house had a positive effect on her.

Time passed and after a couple of months, Ellie and Jones slowly but surely, became an item. She still called him Jones as it seemed right somehow – she thought Malcolm didn't suit him at all. Two years later they were married and the reception was held in the house – a reception in an Elizabethan house was such a good start in life. Jones actually decided to give up his job as a policeman and joined Ellie in her enterprise with antique books. The family was growing but there was still no sign of Tom – and his absence ensured a sadness that just wouldn't go away.The family grew even more when Eliie and Jones had a little boy exactly one year later – all was well in the Elizabethan house – except for that one fly in the ointment – where was Tom and why had he never come back?

"Oh Mary, you can't retire – how will we cope without you?" Judith was genuinely upset at hearing Mary's plans.

"I'm sixty years of age Madam – I think it's time, don't you? It'll give you the chance to employ someone younger, with more energy and perhaps someone with a liking for babies, who can help Jones and Ellie. Not that I don't like babies, I do – but I did my bit with them a long time ago."

"A nanny, do you mean – but what about all the other things you do? We'll never find anyone as talented as you – and don't think I don't know how you already help with little Paul. Please reconsider – if it's money – we can pay you more money/" Judith was almost pleading.

Mary said it wasn't anything to do with money and she already loved Ellie's son Paul– it was just her age and how she felt she needed to slow down a bit. Judith had an inspiration, "Well, stay on Mary and we'll employ someone else to support you and to help with the baby. You can do whatever hours you want and we'll work around you."

And that was how they agreed to leave things. Mary stayed - on reduced hours and duties and a young nanny came to live in the house. She was a live-in nanny and in due course, she also looked after Ellie's second child. The new nanny was called Charlotte and she became very friendly – very quickly with the young entrepreneur, Thomas. When she had some free time, she loved wandering around in the old house's huge attic, trying to find objects for sale – she and Thomas were like kindred spirits and loved what they were doing. There were two lucrative businesses working from home now and Judith was happier than she'd ever been before. She had her ever-growing family around her – and no Tom to spoil it.

"Yes, the house is big enough – there's no problem with that – and if you and Charlotte want to marry, you're both more than welcome to live here. Personally, I'd love to keep all my family close to me, so what could be better than your coming here as a married couple?" Judith had somehow managed to put what she'd done to Tom, completely out of her mind. She rarely thought of him these days – in fact, unless one of the children mentioned him, she didn't think of him at all. *I surprise even myself sometimes at how I can justify killing my husband, lying to both the family and the police, and finally, convincing myself that he deserved what he got. I do wonder if he'd just done what I asked and given up those damned cigarettes - he might still be alive today. But then, it wasn't quite as simple as that – I'd fallen out of love with him not long after we'd married and that's the real truth of the matter!*

Thomas and Charlotte married and continued to search the old rambling house, looking for they knew not what – but convinced they'd find something unique one day – and something worth a great deal of money! They both lived in hope! Thomas still had his theory about the priest hole that **should** have been in the house and never gave up his plan to find it.

Fifteen months passed and one morning, Judith woke up feeling quite unwell – she had to stay in bed all that day. Thomas took his young son upstairs to visit his Grandma and cheer her up. Little Georgie had been born just after his mother and father married - a strange occurrence, which no-one ever mentioned. He could walk now and wandered around Judith's room before climbing into the bed beside her. He liked the pretty flowers carved on the head board behind her head and touched them one by one.

"Is he bothering you Mum – shall I take him back downstairs?" Thomas realised no matter how cute a toddler was, he could also be annoying, especially if Judith was feeling unwell.

"He's fine Thomas – let him be – he loves his Grandma!" She smiled down at the child, but then it happened. The chubby little hand moved across a particular carving – it was a rosebud, near the top of the head board. The bookcase suddenly slid open, revealing the elusive priest hole. Thomas was astounded! He'd always known it was somewhere.

Judith Parker sat up very straight. What she'd dreaded for so long – and what she'd managed to forget ever happened – was finally here. "Take Paul downstairs Thomas, you can look in that place later – but not now, not with the child here." She sounded so desperate that Thomas did as she asked and took his son downstairs to Charlotte. However, he was back with his mother only moments later. He'd brought a torch this time and made straight for the secret opening in the wall. Inside it was dark and smelt musty - a heavy dampness hung in the air and as he stepped slowly forward, his foot hit something on the floor and he stumbled. The torch had a strong light and soon showed him what he'd tripped over and it was horrific!

At first, he thought it was just a pile of bones but as his eyes adjusted, he realised it was actually a complete skeleton – a skeleton bent double, as though it had been dragged there and thrown carelessly in a heap – as indeed it had! Thomas stumbled backwards into the bedroom and saw that his mother had left her bed and was standing there, in her dressing gown. She had her hand across her mouth and her eyes were round and staring.

"What is it Thomas?" she asked. "Is it really a priest hole – I never knew that was there? Is there anything inside it – perhaps some valuable antique?" She sounded desperate, even to herself and quickly added she was going downstairs to find Jones. "He'll come up and help you."

"Yes, please Mum – I'm going to need him – once a policeman, he'll know what to do. I'm afraid there's something very unpleasant in there – something he should see."

Strangely, Judith didn't ask what it was and quickly left the bedroom.

"Touch nothing!" Jones had been inside the priest hole and cautioned Thomas that it might be a murder scene and Forensics would arrive soon – along with the police. "I've already rung them and now, we'll just have to wait. By the way, what did you make of that odd -looking thing on top of the skeleton – it looked like an old shoe to me?"

Thomas knew he'd seen it before – some place, some time – but he couldn't remember where. Then it hit him, "My God, the colour's faded but I think it's the same shoe that used to sit on our mantelpiece – the shoe my mother left on deck before she hid in the lifeboat. You remember, don't you – I think it was you who actually handed it over to us as a keepsake – that was just after Mum was declared missing, lost at sea." The two young men stared at each other and all Jones said was, "Bloody Hell – what's going on?"

"I think it has to be a stranger, who somehow knew about the priest hole." Everyone was in the sitting room and Thomas was talking, "I never told any of you this, but a few years ago when I was first searching the attic for things to sell – it wat at the time our dad chose to disappear and leave us with no money – I actually found evidence of someone sleeping in a corner of the attic. There were blankets and pillows and candles. Somebody had definitely been living there."

Ellie interrupted, "Why didn't you tell me Bro'? We were so close at that time, you could have shared it with me."

"Don't you see, that's exactly why I kept quiet – you already had enough on your plate, what with mum being dead and dad running off – I didn't want to make things worse."

Judith couldn't conceal her shock at the news, "Do you mean we were sleeping in the house and a stranger was coming and going - and sleeping just above my bedroom – and neither Tom nor I knew anything about it? We might have been murdered in our beds."

"The person might not have been sleeping there before you went on your cruise – in fact, I doubt they were. Remember I discovered it after dad disappeared – and later I found the blankets had gone along with the intruder." Thomas could see how upset his mother was and tried to reassure her.

"Considering what was going on in the house at that time, being murdered in your bed was certainly a possibility. Ironic or what?" Jones couldn't help sounding like a policeman, even when he wasn't trying. Just as he finished speaking, the shrill sound of the telephone was heard.

Jones went into the hall and answered it. He talked for a short time only and when he returned, it was obvious he'd heard something he didn't like. Ellie put her hand on his arm, "What is it darling? Don't make us guess."

"You may as well hear it from me, although the police will be visiting tomorrow – to take our statements. Forensics have had the time now to examine the bones and the teeth. The results are one hundred per cent conclusive – the skeleton is Tom Parker, your father and husband." He looked around the room and waited for someone to speak – but no-one could. The news was shocking and soft-hearted Ellie immediately began to cry – great, deep sobs came from the pit of her stomach. She'd been holding out for confirmation that her father was never coming back and yet she dreaded hearing it at the same time. All she could say was, "Oh Dad – my poor dad."

"I don't believe it," Judith blurted out, "I just don't believe it. How could Tom have got himself stuck in that terrible place – like me, he didn't even know it existed."

"You don't have any choice Mum – you have to believe it. The police don't make mistakes in such matters. They'd never have released the news, if they hadn't been sure it was dad. And you know, strangely enough he and I used to discuss such things – we were both interested in history and we suspected there would be a priest hole in a house like this. I bet he was investigating one day and got lucky. Well, not lucky exactly, I just mean he bumped into it – probably the day he pulled down all the bed hangings from the bed. Remember when he gave them to Mary for a village jumble sale? Funny though – he never mentioned he'd found it!"

Jones explained the police could find no reason for Tom's death – the bones wouldn't be enough to give up that particular secret. Thomas interrupted him, "I accept that and I accept he blundered into the room by accident – I even accept the door could have closed behind him and no-one was able to hear his cries – the walls are so thick. What I can't accept though, is why mum's shoe was with him – why on earth would he have taken it in there?" As a policeman, Jones had seen some terrible things, but what had happened to Tom had to be one of the worst.

Everyone in the room was quiet. It was all too horrific to contemplate, so they desperately tried not to picture it. As luck would have it, one of the children chose that moment to wake from a dream and start to cry. "It's Paul – I'll go to him." Charlotte jumped up, she was actually glad to leave the room. She felt an invasive newcomer – after all, she hadn't even known Tom Parker. Ellie told her mother she mustn't sleep in that bedroom – not now – and she went off to make up a bed in the last spare room in the house.

The local police took statements from all the residents of the house – but there seemed no crime to investigate and they put Tom's death down to 'unknown circumstances'. There was only one person who did actually know what those circumstances had been – and she certainly wasn't going to say anything. *Finally, I've got away with it, she told herself. My secret will go with me to the grave – and why shouldn't it? Even after all this time, I still believe what I did on that cruise ship was justified. He was slowly killing me! Since it happened, my life has been just as I wanted it to be – my loving family around me, children and grandchildren, but with no irritating husband to spoil each day.*

"I'd rather sleep in my own room Ellie, it's where I feel most comfortable. Your father's no longer there and I've arranged for a local builder to come in and brick up the priest hole- so what happened to Tom can never happen again." Judith was quite emphatic although her daughter didn't think it a good idea – but she always liked to agree with her mother – after all, the house still belonged to her and she could sleep where she liked.

What was really odd however, was that the strange noises began all over again - the 'things that go-bump-in-the-night' noises. They didn't happen every night, but they always came at night. Sometimes, the children woke up crying – the sudden noises scared them and they sometimes suffered from nightmares.

Judith woke suddenly one night – she didn't know what had awakened her. The door of the old wardrobe hung open - she knew it had been closed when she'd gone to bed. Her mind raced back to the times when she used to open it every night – just to scare Tom.

Then the sobbing sounds began and at one point, they reached such a crescendo that she had to hold her hands tightly against her ears to shut out the noise. It didn't work though and she spent the rest of the night downstairs in the kitchen – the cosiest room in the house. Mary had died the previous year but she'd left behind the safe, warm atmosphere she'd created when she'd worked there.

Jones contacted a well-respected medium in the town and made an appointment for him to call at the house and meet everyone. For a fee, he was willing to attempt to chase the ghostly presences from the house and settle them where they should be. He turned up one evening – a rather arty, flamboyant chap, but one who seemed to know his calling. Nicholas the medium, preferred to call it 'his skill.'

He explained to everyone that he had a regular spirit who often came when called. Jones was surprised to hear the contact was a woman, but surprised himself as he couldn't say why.

Ellie told him to be quiet, he was being sexist!

Nicholas continued, "Sometimes, she likes to behave coyly and won't come, but I can usually persuade her on the night. It might also help you to know that the ghostly visitations you've been having and the unexplained noises you hear, are usually visited on the home by one particular person in the household. It's never possible to know who that is – but sometimes, you can find out on the night of the seance. You don't really need to know more than that – just leave everything to me and in the meantime, perhaps you'd be kind enough to pay my fee up front. On occasion and when my spirit guide fails to appear, people refuse to pay – and I've wasted my time and expertise for nothing." Jones quickly took the agreed payment from his wallet – and handed it to the man. Ellie found the manner of the exorcism very similar to that of the Reverend Thompson from many years before – and therefore she doubted it would work. However, it was certainly worth a try – and those noises were driving them all mad!

They were all sitting around the large table in the dining room. The lights were low and a candle stood in the middle of the table – a round table of course – a séance demanded that. Nicholas had instructed them to spread their hands on the table so that the tips of their fingers touched. Every face looked apprehensive in the eerie glow of the candle light and Thomas felt a sudden need to laugh at what was going on – but of course, he couldn't.

Soft music played in the background and Nicholas leaned back in his chair and closed his eyes. Then the words they'd been waiting for, "Is there anybody there?" His voice sounded strange but demanding, as he added, "Is there someone there who has a message for someone here?" Silence! Nicholas asked again, "Is there someone there who has a message for someone here?" This time the table began to shake and Charlotte pulled her hands away in fear. "Do not break the circle please or the spirit will depart and refuse to come back." Charlotte did as she was told and put her hands back on the table.

"Is your message for a man or a woman – knock once for a man and twice for a woman." The table bumped up and down twice and that simplified things for Nicholas and he asked, "Is your message for Judith, Ellie or Charlotte? Speak up Bethany, I can't hear you."

Bethany's childlike voice was faint but quite clear. "The oldest one!" Nicholas told the child not to be rude and asked, "Is your message for Judith?" The table shook again before the voice continued, but this time, it was deeper, more gruff – it was a man's voice.

"You were never in the sea – you planned to make a fool of me.

Now I'll scare you 'till you die – whilst the others wonder why."

A deafening silence filled the room – Bethany had obviously gone now. Nicholas's head fell forward and Jones jumped up and switched on the light. "Somebody get him some water – he's passed out."

Now, seated in comfortable armchairs in the sitting room, they all waited in silence. Nicholas had already left almost immediately after the séance, saying he was exhausted.

Ellie asked, "Who do you think the message was from – and why was it directed at mum?" But before she could say more, Thomas spoke out, "Oh Sis, don't be so naïve – the message was for mum because it came from dad. You don't have to be Einstein to work that out."

"Leave her alone, can't you see she's upset? If you were normal Thomas, you'd be upset too." Jones defended his wife. "The medium was only successful in contacting a spirit, but he didn't seem able to chase away the ghost that's annoying us all. A pity that, as it's the reason I paid him."

Judith stood up and said she was going to bed, "Stuff and nonsense – that's what it was. I only agreed to take part because you'd have made a fuss if I hadn't. As for the spirit's message, that was just the medium being dramatic – he had to say something, didn't he and what better than a question with no answer.? I think the gruff voice we heard was his own, not Dad's." And on that note, she it was swept from the room and went upstairs. She'd had enough for one day.

In bed that night, she tossed and turned until the early hours, when she finally forced herself to get up and close the wardrobe door. 'This bloody door will be the death of me!'

Getting back into bed, she told herself the wardrobe was old and rickety and the floor was uneven – that's why the door kept swinging open. But Tom had thought that too at one time, and she'd known better then. After all, she knew the truth!

The noises continued and the family told themselves they had to learn to live with them. They didn't hurt anyone, so it was just a matter of getting used to them. Not an ideal situation but an inevitable one! And if some objects moved around the house, so what – they could always be put back? Strange how they managed to convince themselves that living with ghosts was okay, but then what option did they have? Even the children had stopped being scared by 'the noises. In fact, they even managed to ignore the man's sobs in the end. No-one mentioned it was now a sobbing man! They daren't!

The sobs however were what Judith found hardest to take – they broke into her sleep regularly and she hated them. There was no doubt in her mind as to who was sobbing - she knew exactly who it was and what he was trying to do. He wanted her out of the house, so he could claim it as his own and haunt the place freely. Well, she wasn't going to allow that to happen – she'd live to a hundred, if she had to.

Charlotte had taken to preparing mugs of cocoa last thing at night- the women preferred that to the whiskies the men swore helped them sleep. She came into the sitting room, carrying a tray of steaming mugs and placed it on the sideboard saying, "Give it a minute ladies – it's boiling hot." Judith was last to pick up her mug and she noticed some of it had spilled down the sides. She wiped it clean and said she was going to take it upstairs to bed, "I don't know why but I feel particularly tired tonight." She disappeared, leaving the young folk to chat about the events of the day. In the room, she closed the wardrobe door, smiling at the inevitability of it. Would that man ever give up?

Once ready for bed, she remembered the cocoa and took it to the bedside table. Her pad and pen lay there too -she'd left it earlier, meaning to jot down a list of essentials needed for the house. She relaxed against the pillow – yes, she really was tired tonight – too tired it seemed, to either write her list – or drink the cocoa. She did try however as she didn't want to upset Charlotte, but managed only half of the drink in the end. Anyway, a thick skin had formed on the top and looking at it, made her feel quite sickly.   She pushed it to the back of the table thinking, *I really can't finish that. 'I know I'll offend Charlotte, but what can I do?* She knew the girl would come upstairs to collect the dirty mug before she went to bed herself. The girl was so fastidious – sometimes Judith found the trait rather irritating – but then, so many things seemed to annoy her these days. What would especially annoy her tonight was, if that damned man started his dreadful sobbing again.

Hastily, she scribbled a few words on the pad and left it on the table for Charlotte to find.

She didn't want to seem churlish, so she wrote:

'Sorry -I just couldn't go on. I did try – honestly – and I am grateful for all you do for me.'

She didn't realise it sounded like a 'goodbye for ever' note. But then her attention shifted and she heard the first sobs of the night. *God, he didn't even allow me ten minutes sleep.*

He thinks I don't know where his sobs are coming from – well, I'll soon show him. Getting out of bed, she put on her dressing gown and reached to the top of the bed's head board – the little rosebud was waiting and asking to be pressed – and that's what she did. Of course, the priest hole was revealed immediately and the angry woman marched boldly towards it. Inside it was dark and musty, but she knew that's where Tom was hiding. She stepped inside, finally ready to confront her tormentor – the man she'd murdered. There was no sign of him, so she felt her way along the sides of the wall and knew she'd reached the end of the room, when the wall suddenly turned at a right angle. *God, I feel tired – what's the matter with me? My mind feels so fuzzy – I think I' m going to pass out. Why am I so tired?*

A dizziness overwhelmed her and she hit the hard floor with a thud. She just lay there in the complete darkness of the secret room.

What she didn't know was that some of her belongings – jumpers, skirts, shoes and even jewellery – had come flying out of the wardrobe at that moment and the whole pile landed inside the priest hole – right on top of the drugged woman on the floor. A ghostly hand, the same hand that had put a sleeping draught in the cocoa, spilling some over the side – was now emptying her clothes from the wardrobe. The same hand found the rosebud button – it knew exactly where to find it – and the door of the priest hole swung closed once more.

Finally, Tom had achieved it – achieved the thing he'd waited so long to do – and he'd managed it in style. He'd wanted her to suffer and know what was happening, so when she came around, the full horror of being shut away would hit her. That was what he called revenge – but there was more - he knew too that Old Peter was coming at the crack of dawn tomorrow to do a job for 'the Mrs.' He was coming to brick up the priest hole on the 'Mrs's instructions - and he always turned up for work at the crack of dawn. *Tom thought, 'My God, I feel wonderful – magnificent. I got my own back at last!' Old Peter didn't know quite how much he was going to do for the Mrs.*

The old builder arrived at five o'clock next morning, before the household was even awake. He knew where the spare key was kept, so he filled the wheel barrow with bricks and cement and trundled it up to the 'Mrs's old room. The lift was handy for moving the heavy bricks and he worked quietly and quickly – but was careful not to go inside the horrible room. He was superstitious and wary of such scary places and he'd heard from the villagers recently that seances had been held in the house. Seances to get rid of unwelcome spirits. So, the wise old man kept well away from the inside of the priest hole. And who could blame him? It wasn't any of his business after all. 'The Mrs' had shown him where the secret button was, so he just got on with it. He had other jobs that same day, so he wanted to finish and be out of there before anyone else was around.

He stood back to admire his work and tidied the floor around the bookcase – he was an old-fashioned craftsman and tidiness was all part of a job. "Yup, a good solid job," he told himself and took the empty wheel barrow back along the corridor and into the old lift.

The first thing Charlotte did in the morning, was to go upstairs to fetch Judith's dirty cocoa mug. She was actually surprised Judith hadn't come downstairs yet – she was usually an early bird, but she had seemed extra tired the previous night. The bed had obviously been slept in – the covers were tousled – but there was no sign of the occupant. *I wonder where she is! She can't have gone out yet, can she? I would have seen her.* She checked the other upstairs rooms and even the bathroom, but Judith wasn't to be found.

Then all Hell suddenly broke loose when she ran downstairs to tell the others. In her hand, she held the note Judith had left on the bedside table.

"My God, she's run away – she's actually run away from home." Thomas was aghast. His mother wouldn't have done that,

"I know she's never been the same since that incident with dad – but leaving the home she loved – no, I don't think so."

"Check her wardrobe Ellie – see what she's taken, if anything. Maybe she's just gone out for an early morning stroll and we're all getting excited over nothing." Always the optimist and the policeman, Jones kept his cool.

The days passed and Judith never did reappear. Of course, they reported her disappearance to the police but with the family's long- established reputation for people coming and going, all the stops were not pulled out by the police this time. The woman was an adult after all, she had a history of lying and creating havoc for her family – and she'd taken all her most valuable jewellery with her. Much of her clothing was missing and she'd left behind a 'goodbye, can't cope any longer' note. Secretly, the police suspected she was probably stretched out on some beach in sunny Spain and didn't want to be found.

Now, the family continued to live in their Elizabethan manor - they settled down to live their lives as best they could. They were after all, the next generation. Ellie however, was never convinced about the Spanish theory – and felt it in her bones, that Judith was actually dead, perhaps someplace far away. As it was impossible to prove this and because of the family's history of people going missing, the coroner waived the necessity for the seven-year rule for missing people – and so the house now belonged to both Thomas and Ellie, and presumably to their children after them.

It wasn't the last of Tom and Judith Parker that the family heard. The voices continued as did the moving of furniture, but there was no sobbing ever heard again and everyone in the house agreed they could live with the odd 'thing that went bump in the night.'

One thing however, they did find difficult (and this was what finally convinced Ellie she was right about her mother's death) – were those sounds of voices raised in anger and coming from the master bedroom, where they the sounds of parents who hated each other?   Coming from the room where no-one ever slept now. Were they coming from the room itself or were they coming from the bricked-up priest hole? Who could tell – and no-one ever tried to find out. None of the family ever went near that room, after all it was obviously already occupied.

One thing that did irritate them however, was that on the odd occasion, when the sun was at its brightest and the fluttering butterflies added to the beautiful scenery – a man and a woman could be seen sitting on a couple of sun chairs in the garden, berating each other in angry, loud voices. Both seemed to be claiming something belonged to them, whilst each in their turn, called the other a liar and shrieked 'It's mine, damn you. It's mine!' None of the family ever learned what 'it' actually was.

As they sat in the garden however, Tom and Judith knew exactly what 'it' was. The Elizabethan manor could only ever belong to one of them and they'd never agree to whom that was!

Cluedo – or Whodunnit

Maggie looked over her glasses, her very blue eyes sparkling with triumph, "Miss Scarlett, with a gun, in the conservatory." And she looked around the table at the others waiting for them to scoff 'rubbish' or 'try again old dear' but the room was silent. None of them had worked out an answer of their own. Liz reached for the envelope in the middle of the table where the correct answers were concealed and shook out the culprits' picture cards.

"Miss Scarlett with a gun in the conservatory!" Liz repeated incredulously, "She's absolutely right would you believe? I hadn't even worked out one answer! You're just a smarty-pants Maggie." All six of the players relaxed back in their chairs – a couple of them sighing with exaggerated relief, after all it took a lot of concentration to play this game!

Maggie couldn't conceal her feeling of superiority and looked very smug indeed. She liked to think herself a super sleuth – in the style of Miss Marple. She busied herself tidying the cards, ready for a second game – if there was time. She was still an attractive woman although she was knocking on the door of fifty. Her hair was still very blond – something her lady friends couldn't understand as she always swore 'she put nothing on it.' She had to admit she'd 'd gained a few pounds, especially after the children were born, but as she liked to believe 'she could still get a wolf whistle from a group of builders.' Mind you, she hadn't tried that out for a few years. She had a son and a daughter – Tom and Bethany, both in their mid-twenties and both living and working in the city.

Bill stood up saying, "I think we all deserve another drink after that sound thrashing," and he crossed to the sideboard where there was a generous selection of spirits, beer and soft drinks. He was a well-built man who'd played rugby in his younger years but he too had gained a few pounds over the years and could be accused of perhaps letting himself 'go to seed' just a little. But he still had a shock of blond, wavy hair of which he was blatantly proud.

"Don't overfill the glasses Bill - you always do and make such a mess." His wife Jenny admonished him before he'd even started to pour. She was the careful one whilst he was always in a rush to get things done – and inevitably made a mess.

"Yes dear. No dear. Three bags full Dear." He mimicked her cautionary words and the others laughed.

Now as for Jenny his wife, she was a brunette. She wore her hair in a long page-boy style and didn't mind admitting its rich, dark brown colour came from a bottle. Whether it did or not, she still looked good for a middle-aged woman – God, how she hated the term 'middle-aged woman' but unfortunately, she knew that's what she was. She and Bill had one son – Ben – the apple of both their eyes. He'd just completed a university degree and was apprenticed to a large bank in the city – Bill especially was very proud of him – his son, the professional banker! He smiled every time he thought of the rhyming slang!

Maggie's husband was Peter and he was a doctor – a GP, who was the senior partner at his own surgery. He was tall and slender – he'd never carried much weight and liked to think it was because of his hard work and having to run around the park every morning – but as Maggie often pointed out to him, it was probably because of his inherited genes. His father had been built like a whippet as well. Peter wore horn-rimmed glasses – in fact he'd began wearing them even before he needed them as he believed they helped give his patients confidence in his medical skills. Anyway, he thought he looked smart in them.

There were another two players there – friends of everyone – Liz and Dominic. Like Bill, Dominic was a lawyer and ran his own practice in town. He was quite a slim man – almost frail in fact - and very fastidious in his dress sense. He'd once been described as having a rather effeminate dress sense. He hadn't cared for that. It didn't let it bother him however – he knew the insulting remarks came from pure jealousy. He was a manly man he told himself and that was what he preferred to believe.

Finally, and last but certainly not least, we come to Liz - or Elizabeth to those she didn't like. She too was a fifty-year old blond but her hair colour definitely came from a bottle as it tended to change over time - something she kept very quiet about. There was absolutely no argument, she was the tart of the group and her hour-glass figure was regularly draped in very provocative clothes. But for all that, she had a kind heart and her sharp wit always amused people, so she was popular amongst her friends. The greatest sadness she and Dominic shared, was that despite trying every possible solution available on the market, they'd never managed to conceive a child. Rich, attractive and very comfortable they may have been – but without a child, they often wondered what life was all about. This failure may have been the reason Liz tried so hard to enjoy life – a subterfuge to pretend everything in the garden was rosy. Either way, she certainly managed to fool everybody – but not her real friends – they all knew how much she had wanted a baby.

In all, there were six of them and they'd all been friends since their university days. They'd returned to their home town about the same time, some setting up their own businesses and some pursuing their chosen professions and some, a combination of both. For a few years they'd lost touch with each other and gone their different ways, but now in their late forties/early fifties, and with their families grown up, they re- formed the old friendship and now met regularly. They had so much in common with each other and this served as the basis for their enduring friendship.

Three men and three women who'd known each other for a very long time and whose relationship was as sound as ever. The strangest thing of all was their fascination with the game of Cluedo, something they played regularly at each other's homes. Tonight, they were at Maggie's and Peter's home, which they all considered was just right for a game of murder.

Liz and Dominic lived in the same road as Jenny and Billi – their new build home was very similar to others in the row – they were all luxurious and large, full of every mod-con. Like others in the road, they were people who'd obviously 'arrived' - not the kind of place affordable by first-time buyers. The gardens were extensive and well looked after by a young gardener called Jonathan, whose services they all shared.

The third couple in the group lived on the edge of town in an old Edwardian house which they were continuously renovating – a costly pastime they would tell you it was a labour of love for both of them. Any time, one of the others in their brand-new homes bragged about a luxury item, they liked to say their house was built to last and would certainly out-last anything built in the present day. The old house did have large, spacious rooms with high ceilings decorated with elaborate corniches, something always admired by visitors. They much preferred the older style of property, claiming it had much more character than new builds. Of course, this was disputed by the others but always in a friendly way – never confrontational.

As was usual and it being Saturday evening, they were settled in the dining room around a large circular table. They were in the Edwardian house of Maggie and Peter. Liz sat beside Dominic, her husband – and Bill was beside his own wife, Jenny. As hostess, Maggie had just won the last game – something she thoroughly loved doing. She also liked to claim the atmosphere in the old place actually added to the excitement of the game of murder. It was easy to imagine ghosts and goblins in the high-ceilinged rooms with shadows cast around the walls. Who had lived there before – what catastrophes had happened – the house was a place that could tell stories if it wanted to? It was probably full of ghosts, something they'd never seen however, but they liked to dream. Everyone sat wherever they landed with no formality whatsoever – they were very comfortable in each other's company.

"I could have sworn the murder was going to be in the kitchen, judging from the things some of you said – but I was wrong. But then, I'm a man – I can take it." Peter lied badly. He much preferred to win – but then they all did. Although friends, they took the game very seriously and gave no quarter when success was so hard to achieve.

"Who's turn is it to host next weekend?" Dominic asked, knowing full well it was his. Liz raised her eyebrows and confirmed it was their turn."I enjoy our evenings no matter whose home we're in, but I have to admit this one is perfect for a murder game. It's so old and sometimes scary – oh not in a horrid way, just in a cosy comfortable way." She realised what she said could be construed as criticism, something she hadn't meant that at all.

"I mean there's a library, a party room and a conservatory – as well as all the more usual rooms – that's what makes it so perfect. It's as if we're right in the middle of the murder scene itself." She was getting quite excited and Dominic told her to calm down. "You're beginning to scare me, darling – and you know I'm easily scared," he joked.

"Yes Liz," Maggie was looking rather impatient at her friend's enthusiasm, "I know what rooms I have! There's no time for another game, is there? I suppose it's quite late." Everyone agreed but insisted they wouldn't leave until they'd finished their drinks. It had been another enjoyable evening spent with friends and they were already happily contemplating next Saturday's game.

The two visiting couples left the old house and drove home to their shared road. Peter began to put the game away- they'd all agreed it was easier for each couple to have their own game. It made things simple – less moving of the box from house to house. He suddenly dropped down on his knees and began to move his fingers across the carpet, as though looking for something under the table.

"What are you doing?" Maggie asked impatiently and was told he was looking for a piece of the game, a character seemed to have disappeared. He said finally, "Professor Plum has upped and gone, I'm afraid – I can't find him anywhere." He was puzzled but too tired to do anything about it then – and he had an early morning appointment the next day – his surgery was always busy and as the most senior partner, he took his responsibilities very seriously. He stifled a yawn, "I hope I don't get a call-out tonight – I fear I've drunk too much." He said he was going to bed and didn't wait for Maggie's inevitable lecture about not drinking when he was on-call. He'd heard it many times before and certainly didn't want to hear it again.

Before bed, Maggie popped into the kitchen where Martha was still washing up the supper dishes, "When you've finished those Martha – there's nothing else to do – you can go home." The home-help was a local woman who lived in the town and on the nights of the 'Cluedo' parties, she'd visit whoever's house was hosting, to serve supper and clear away afterwards. She never said much, just got on with her duties. When the couple had both gone upstairs to bed, they left her to lock up, which was quite usual. In fact, she had a key to all the friends' houses, so trusted was she.

A local woman, she'd never had much and had grown up in a deprived and run down area of the town, always having to strive just to put food on the children's table – but she'd managed this from sheer hard work and always holding down more than one job at a time. Her family were now grown up and had left home some time ago, so she was alone now, her husband dying two years before. She was so quiet and unassuming that sometimes people forgot she was there which was a great way for her to eavesdrop and hear things perhaps she shouldn't have - but she was always discreet and made a point of keeping what she'd overheard to herself. She really was the ideal home worker.

Once upstairs in the bedroom, the telephone rang and Peter mumbled in his sleep. "Hello, Maggie speaking," she whispered into the mouthpiece.

"Mum, it's your best loved daughter – more accurately your only daughter. Sorry to ring so late but I need a favour." Bethany's loud tones almost shattered her mother's eardrums.

"Are you ringing from a party by any chance Bethany – is that what all that noise is?" Maggie spoke quietly so as not to wake Peter. "Speak quietly darling, daddy's' asleep. Only you would ring from a party!"

"Yes, but that's not why I'm ringing. I need a small loan Mumsy and I know you'd want to help. It's my rent on the flat, I've not got enough to meet it this month. Can you transfer a couple of hundred by tomorrow?" Some voices could be heard singing in the background – in fact they all sounded pretty drunk. But then, what could Maggie say about that – she'd been young once herself.

"Really girl, money doesn't grow on trees and dad and I have just had some unexpected repairs to pay for. You know this house just eats up all our spare money. I really don't know whether I can help you this time."

Bethany began to wheedle and she began to sound distressed, but her mother knew what an actress she was. "Please Mum, you don't know how serious it is – if I don't pay the rent tomorrow, I'll be evicted – and then I'd have to come home and live with you and daddy – and you wouldn't like that, now would you?"

Oh, she knew how to turn the screw and put the pressure on. Maggie thought quickly. She didn't want a disgruntled twenty-five-year-old on her doorstep – not again anyway. Inevitably, she capitulated and gave in to Bethany's demands. She usually did when either of her two children were concerned.

"This will be the last time Bethany – I really mean it. You can't go on flogging a dead horse you know. Leave it with me and I'll see if I can do it tomorrow but I won't be able to let you have as much as two hundred as I just don't have it."

"Mum, it's got be two hundred as that's what I owe and if you can't let me have it, I'll have to go to someone else and you won't want me to do that."The girl did sound desperate, but then she knew how to do that. She was a good actress.

"You'll get what I can afford Bethany, that's all I can say." And she quickly hung up before the girl could argue more. It meant another trip to the bank in town tomorrow, but she wouldn't mention it to Peter yet – let him see it on the bank statement. He'd deal better with it as a fait-accompli.

On reaching home, Liz and Dominic soon began to have an argument which was quite common hen they'd both been drinking. The first jibe he made was, "I saw you snuggling up against Peter, pretending you were straightening his tie. You're so obvious my darling, it's sickening. When will you get it into your mind that he's not interested. Now, Bill's a different kettle of fish altogether! I think you could reel him in quite easily." He threw his jacket on the sofa and kicked off his shoes. He always enjoyed winding up his wife.

"Don't know what you're talking about. I think you must be seeing things. I'm not interested in old Peter." She poured herself a glass of wine and slumped down on a chair by the fire. How dare he criticise her behaviour when he was no better around Maggie!

But then, he usually started to accuse her of such things when he'd been drinking – in 'vino veritas', she thought, 'he's on his old hobby horse again.' No matter at whose house they'd been, he always found something to criticise – he was obviously quite insecure.

"Let's face it Liz, you've always been a bit of a tart – you just can't help it." Dominic seemed really upset with her this time and enjoyed the opportunity to let her know it - one of the few pleasures he had left in life. "I'm going to bed – you can sit there and finish off that bottle of wine." And he left the room, banging the door behind him. As usual, all was not well in the Collins' household and Liz did just as she was told and drained the wine bottle to its very last drop. It was how they ended most nights when they been drinking at friends' houses.

Next morning, everything was again pristine and Bristol fashion – everything in its place and tempers gone with the wind. There was no trace of the argument of the night before. Dominic left early for work as he had an early meeting that morning. As a busy lawyer, he enjoyed the challenges of his work, not to mention the lucrative fees he could charge his clients. He was a delicately boned-man, handsome with a shock of brown hair, just turning to grey. He'd been called a distinguished gentleman, which he knew really meant he was getting older.

He and Liz had once been very much in love but with the passage of time and frequent disappointments when no children arrived, they'd drifted into independent lifestyles – and realised their interests weren't similar at all.

That morning in the Edwardian household, Maggie dressed smartly – she always did when visiting the bank. Her blue suit was a snug fit these days, but she knew she still looked smart. She threw back her long, blond hair and draped a blue matching scarf around her neck. She'd always believed it was wise to show the bank how affluent she was, especially when she wasn't at all affluent - or when she needed a loan for renovations. This meant that she had to dress smartly more often than she liked and this was because of her beautiful Edwardian home.

Before the bank, she went shopping as was her practice and also visited a couple of charity shops on the chance that someone with more money than sense had donated some valuables. She'd picked up a few nice pieces in the past and paid only pennies for them. She was pleasantly surprised to bump into Jenny in the first shop.

"Hello dear, great minds think alike – are you hoping to find some bargains as well? Jenny was pleased to meet her friend and knew they'd end up having a chat and a coffee together.

Maggie's blue eyes twinkled and she surprised Jenny by saying, "I'm hoping to find a game of Cluedo – so I can replace our Professor Plum figure which mysteriously disappeared after last night's game. You didn't relieve us of the card by any chance?"

She asked the question seriously but Jenny looked quite offended. "Certainly not – why would I do that – we have a game of our own?"

Unfortunately, Maggie had no luck in finding a Professor Plum card and both women left the shop together. "One of the others must have taken the figure home but for what purpose, I can't imagine." She shrugged her shoulders and immediately suggested coffee in a nearby teashop. They sat there, quietly comfortable in each other's company. They had a window seat and just across the road, they spotted Liz coming out of a Pharmacy. Maggie banged on the window in an attempt to attract her attention and was given a disapproving look by the waitress. Liz did glance in their direction but didn't react. She quickly hurried off and disappeared up the street in the opposite direction

"Well, I never,' Jenny said, "I swear she saw us." Then they saw her meet a man who looked remarkably like Bill. "He doesn't just look like Bill – he is my Bill." Jenny gasped. "Do you think she might have some legal business to discuss with him? But why would she, her own husband's a lawyer. I wonder what they're talking about."

Maggie said nothing but she lowered her eyes, then Jenny couldn't see what she was thinking. Jenny continued to watch the man and woman closely, but they turned away and walked out of sight. For a moment, Jenny was tempted to follow them, but thought better of it. Maggie would find that very odd – and suspicious. And she didn't want to give her any grounds for gossip, did she?

The women's conversation seemed flat after that and they quickly said goodbye with Jenny calling over her shoulder, "Hope Professor Plum turns up soon!" She was met by a second look of disapproval from the waitress – which she chose to ignore – and she decided to leave no tip. She felt rather disgruntled – she usually liked to know where Bill was and what he was doing

– but then Liz was a friend after all and not some wanton woman. Having said that however, she had to admit that sometimes she did act like a wanton woman – and she did love the men more than most women. She shrugged her shoulders and tried not to imagine things but her mind was full of disquiet and she wondered afresh what Liz was up to.

That night, after dinner, Jenny was sitting by Bill and they were watching a film on television. They'd seen it before, so neither was truly interested. ''I saw you meet up with Liz this afternoon – what did you need to talk to her about? Surely, you could have discussed whatever it was it after the game last night.'' She tried hard to conceal any suspicion from her voice, but probably failed.

He cleared his throat – rather nervously she thought, "It was about some of her stocks and shares – she wanted advice and didn't want Dominic to know how much of an investment she'd made. It wouldn't have been right to discuss it last night in front of everyone. I am bound by client confidentiality, you remember."

"So, Liz is a client now – I never knew that!" Now she really was suspicious and said,

"Still don't see why you couldn't have discussed it last night – we're all friends together, aren't we?" But she stopped talking and tried to control herself when Bill tutted to remind her they were watching a film – a film neither was interested in. To change the subject, he asked, "By the way, did you know that Maggie's Professor Plum figure disappeared after the game last night?"

She looked surprised and asked, "How did you know that – I only learned about it this morning." He just smiled and tapped the side of his nose. "Ah, that would be telling and it's for me to know and you to find out." He continued to pretend to watch the film, but Jenny wasn't ready to let the subject drop, "Perhaps someone took him home with them, did you do it and that's how you knew about him? He didn't grace her question with a reply, just a disdainful glance and a grunt. He knew she speaking to herself however and went right on watching the film – he wasn't going to let her annoy him so he just pretended he couldn't hear her. Best way to deal with an upset Jenny!

She chatted on however, more determined to annoy him. "I must remember the window-cleaner's coming tomorrow – I want the inside windows done as well as the outside, so I must leave a key in the usual place for him – it's so good to be able to trust tradesmen, don't you think?Bill had given up pretending interest in the film and had apparently – and suddenly - fallen asleep. ' I know you're not asleep husband dear but I'll bide my time' she thought. She knew she was right and he did have something to hide.

Winter had really arrived now and the walk to Dominic and Liz's home that night, although only a short distance, was difficult under foot as the snow was quite deep – and still falling heavily. Nothing however and certainly not some pretty snow, could stop Jenny and Bill from their weekly game of Cluedo. Maggie and Peter would have a difficult time coming from the edge of town – but their car would make it. It always seemed to hang on although its days were numbered and it had seen better days. The couple really liked to get their money's worth out of anything they possessed. Jenny clung tightly onto Bill's arm, as she slithered and slipped all over the ground.

"Thank God, they live so close." An exhausted Jenny said as her friend's big house came into view. It looked so warm and inviting with lights at every window and its mock-Georgian style of architecture helped make it look even more grand. As it was nearing Christmas, the windows were more brightly lit than usual and a wreath of green foliage and red berries adorned the big front door – pinned to it was a large and shiny red ribbon hanging there in welcome. A magnificent Christmas tree stood in the window, shedding a cascade of twinkling coloured lights over the blanket of snow. My God, it was beautiful! And they hadn't even put up any decorations yet!

"Isn't it a picture – a beautiful picture! But ours will look just as nice once you get your finger out and bring the decorations down from the loft." Jenny was still gripping her husband's arm but made him stop to admire the view. "See what can be done with a little imagination and hard work."

"Yes, it's incredibly beautiful, "he agreed, "Well, you should get on with it Jen – everything manual doesn't have to be done by me, you know! I just wonder how Dominic managed to do it – so much work after all – and him a busy lawyer."

"You're a busy lawyer too – but I have every confidence once you get into that loft, our house will look just as lovely. Mind you, all those lights must have cost a fortune. Can we really afford so many lights?" Jenny looked pensive.

"We have no option dear – remember Ben has promised to come home for Christmas – so we have to afford the burning of the lights, we can't let him down." Ben was their only child and was the centre of their universe. Bill realised she was right and promised himself he'd get up into that loft the very next day. Thinking about it however, he added, "I do agree though that financially, Dominic has been luckier than most people. He inherited a fortune, didn't he?"

Jenny nodded her head, "Yeah, he's been a lucky man indeed!" she reached out and rang the doorbell. "It was his father, wasn't it – don't you remember? The old chap died when Dominic was a teenager and then his mother passed away a few months later. He inherited everything, so he's never known what it's like to be short of a bob or two. When Liz married him, she knew she was onto a good thing – but then, she had money of her own as well– and with no children, they never had to meet the expenses we've had."

She had to shut up quickly as the front door was opened by an over-dressed Liz. Or should that have been an under-dressed Liz who always believed in high hemlines and low necklines. At least she was consistent. She always ensured that she looked her best when it was her turn to be hostess. Bill had just been on the point of saying that the couple had wanted children, but unfortunately had had no luck. Liz's arrival stopped his words! He felt quite defensive of the couple's childless marriage and knew how much Dominic would have liked to have a family. Before they stepped inside the house however, they heard their names being called from behind. It was Maggie and Peter, holding on to each as they climbed out of the car. If anything, the falling snow was getting even heavier.

"Wait for us - we plan to beat you soundly tonight." Peter called out and all four of them fell into the hall together when Liz held the door open. They took off their snow-covered boots and rushed into the sitting room in their stockinged feet - a glorious fire burned in the hearth and called out a welcome to the visitors. They playfully knocked each other out of the way to get the most heat from the flames, "Now, that's what I call a fire!" Bill won the place at the front of the group – his rugby playing body still came in handy on occasion – and anyway, he was bigger than most people.

Liz re-appeared in the doorway with a silver tray holding 6 goblets of hot mulled wine.

"Now there's a pretty sight, if ever I saw one." Peter elbowed his way towards the hostess and took the tray out of her hands. He placed it on the coffee table, saying, "This is grand Liz – where's yours? I hope you've got something stronger for later."

"I've always admired that fireplace, you know – how old do you reckon it is?" Maggie liked the new house and all its mod cons but she especially loved the fireplace which had come from an old derelict house. She thought it would look even better in her own old Edwardian house. Dominic didn't answer her question – he knew she coveted his fireplace, she'd said it often enough.

They all settled around the flames and enjoyed the warm wine, "That fireplace is 250 years old, I've seen the Deeds of the house it came from." Liz knew Maggie loved the fireplace and decided to put her out of her misery. Dominic got up to put another log on the fire, knowing he'd have to change the subject as Liz and Maggie could fall out over the fireplace. They were both fiercely competitive – but deep down, he knew they were also good friends - but even the best of friends could sometimes envy each other's possessions.

Maggie's attention had moved on however and she said, "Why Dominic, you're very smart tonight – I don't think I've ever seen you looking so smart." Everyone's eyes turned to the host, who was wearing a plum-coloured smoking jacket and a white cravat. "Thank you, Maggie, – you always say the nicest things." Bill grunted and coughed out, "Bit poncey, if

you ask me."

"No-one's asking you Bill, "Maggie started to say but Dominic defended his dress sense, "Nonsense old man, this is how a gentleman should dress when hosting his guests." And he admired his reflection in the mirror above the fireplace. He knew he looked the smartest man in the room.

"I've just heard Martha arrive in the kitchen – I'll just pop in and make sure she knows what's needed for supper – I've left it all ready for her." Liz hurried from the room, first quickly gulping down her mulled wine. The others moved 'the playing table' into the middle of the room, so they could play Cluedo beside the wonderful fire on this exceptionally cold night, "We can't play anywhere but near that!" Maggie pointed to the fire as she spoke – she liked her comforts did Maggie.

Soon spread over the table, the board displayed all the rooms in the game, as well as the secret passages, where someone could slip secretly from one room into the other to commit a dastardly deed - that someone being the murderer of course. Tonight, Professor Plum's face smiled from the board and he lay amongst his usual companions. There was Miss Scarlet, Mrs White, Mrs Peacock, Reverend Green, Colonel Mustard and Mr Boddy. Maggie admired the full set and now, as well as the old fireplace, she coveted Professor Plum as well. "We'll just have to use an ordinary playing card until we find a replacement." Maggie pouted, "Unless whichever one of you took him last week, would like to return him." Of course, everyone claimed emphatically that they weren't guilty of the crime.

"Let's call Martha in to do her duty, shall we – and then we can start playing." Liz called out to the home help, who was used to waiting patiently for the summons. She came in, dressed in her usual floral pinny and chose 'in secret' the murderer, the weapon and the location cards and placed them in the special envelope, which she then placed in the middle of the board. Saying nothing, she returned to the kitchen to continue her work and soon came back carrying the finished dishes. As usual, the food was delicious and was soon gobbled up by the hungry group. A spectacular pudding followed the savoury – in fact it was a choice of three spectacular puddings. And as usual, most of the players had 'Seconds'. Bill often had to be stopped from having 'Thirds.' But they weren't successful in stopping him every time.

The six players began the game with serious expressions – they always played as though their lives depended on winning.

Speculation was part of the excitement of the game and Maggie soon suggested an answer, but he was wrong on this occasion and so she was out of the game. It was a harsh punishment for guessing wrong but it was the rule and they honoured it. She retired from the table and languidly stretched herself along one of the sofas. Ah, the luxury of having a whole sofa to oneself and that in front of a blazing fire.

Bill suddenly called out, "Colonel Mustard in the library with the dagger." He was wrong and he too, had to leave the table reluctantly. He didn't mind though – he could have an extra drink that way. Alas, the spirits had dried up, as had the wine.

" Does anyone mind if we make this a natural break and I nip down to the cellar and fetch a couple of bottles of wine?" Of course, no one did, so he left the room quickly. Bill wasn't shy of asking for what he wanted – and he wanted more of Dominic's excellent wine. As he left the room, he said to Liz, "That was a great supper Liz – please give my compliments to the chef, will you?" Promising to do that, she cleared away the empty crystal bowls and took them back into the kitchen.

Jenny stood up and asked if she could use the telephone in the study. She'd promised to check on a neighbour who'd been ill in bed for a while. And she disappeared from the room as well.

Dominic jumped up and said he would fetch some more logs from the garage as the fire was beginning to burn low. It was great to have a regular delivery of logs from the local farm and the wood always smelt so lovely. He only had to leave the garage open for the farmer and he'd deliver them without disturbing the house – everyone was so friendly and trustworthy he always thought. In fact, one of the farm workmen, Jonathan, was also Dominic's own gardener and he could be trusted as much as his dad. Jonathan sometimes worked on the farm for his dad, but gardening was his favourite pastime – and he was paid for doing it. His dad sometimes forgot that part of their arrangement. Dominic thought the house always ran so smoothly and that was because of the great local people, like Jonathan and his dad.

Peter took advantage of the 'natural break' and excused himself to use 'the facilities'. With the drink and the warmth of the fire, Maggie had fallen asleep on the sofa. She was actually snoring, although she'd have been mortified had she known. Luckily, she was all alone in the sitting room by this time, so no one did hear her. A lady never snores according to Maggie! And she certainly was a lady!

First to return was Liz who smiled at the rumbling noise coming from the sofa. Peter came back from having done what was necessary and Liz asked him, "Does she make that noise in bed, Peter?"

"I'm afraid she does – but always denies it the next day." He sat down at the table again and waited for the others to return. Next came Bill back from the cellar and he was still busy removing cob webs from the two bottles he was carrying. He plonked the wine down on the sideboard. "My God, I envy Dominic that cellar. Lucky Blighter!" He failed to conceal his envy!

Jenny came back then, telling everyone her neighbour was fine - but no one was particularly interested and so no-one acknowledged her statement. She still went on, "She's got a carer, but I promised to check on her tonight." Again, no one paid any attention to her words.

"My God, he's taking his time." Bill crouched down in front of the fire and rubbed his hands together. "That was one cold cellar. Can we get on with the game – I want to know who did it and with what. Dominic will be back in a moment." He stood up and stretched his hands above his head. He was a tall man and although getting older now, he still looked like a slightly heavy but handsome rugby player. His wife watched him – she was always anxious about how he came across to women, but there was nothing she could do about that. He was a natural flirt and never missed an opportunity to praise the opposite sex, which some women might misunderstand.

"Be patient Bill – we can't play without the host, that wouldn't be right at all." Jenny's dark hair fell across her face and she brushed it back with an elegant hand. She too was good looking – at least for her age, she was. In fact, they were a very attractive couple.

Liz jumped up, "I'll go and find him," I know his routine – he'll be coming back through the conservatory, dropping lots of wood as he does and making a proper mess." She left the sitting room and the four friends continued to wait patiently.

Moments later, she came back with her handkerchief stuffed in her mouth. "I've found him – he's in the conservatory as I thought – but I think he's dead. Please come and help me – see for yourselves! Maybe one of you can bring him around." She was clearly very upset and shocked – she quite obviously didn't know what to do next.

They all crossed the hall together and went towards the conservatory. Dominic was lying on the floor just inside the door which was still wide open – the basket of logs had spilled across the floor and amongst the wood were clumps of snow and grass. It looked a muddle as if a struggle had taken place. There was no doubt someone else had been with Dominic and had now fled the scene. Peter rushed over to his friend, dropped to his knees and felt for a pulse, but could find no signs of life. The dead man looked pitiful and was lying on his side – crumpled and twisted – Peter knew he mustn't move him but by pulling back his lovely, plum coloured jacket, he saw a knife protruding from the man's stomach. The shaft of the knife shone brightly in the soft light of the conservatory. It had an elaborately carved handle and looked very old – obviously someone's heirloom. Dominic's pitiful body was lying in a pool of oozing blood and his mouth hung open as if he'd been trying to say something when he died. Also, there looked like what could only be described as surprise in his open eyes, as though he couldn't believe what – or who – he'd been looking at moments before he was struck down.

Bill rushed into the hall and the others could hear him on the phone, "Yes – ambulance please. No, it's not a life and death situation, the poor man's already dead. You'll also inform the police? I see, that would be helpful." He knew of course that para-medics couldn't help Dominic but he didn't know what else to do. When he put the phone down, he just stood in the hall, repeating again and again, "Who could have done this – he was the most likeable of us all – a proper gentleman. Who could have done it?" Jenny brought him back to the sitting room. "There's nothing more you can do Bill – just wait here with me." And she made him sit back down at the table. He just stared at the Cluedo board – a game set up for play, something that wouldn't happen now. It was strange but now he looked closely at the cards, he saw that Dominic had been dressed exactly as Professor Plum himself – and seemed to be mocking him from the middle of the cards.

The ambulance came and the police were at its heels. A plain-clothed detective immediately took charge of the situation and ushered the people together into one room. Maggie was crying – in fact, she couldn't stop. She'd been no closer to Dominic than any of the others were but she was perhaps the most sensitive one and she was known to be a 'cryer.' She wasn't hysterical but couldn't control her sobs.

Inspector Morrison separated Maggie and Peter from the others and began to take a statement, but not before he'd arranged for a young policewoman to fetch a tray of hot drinks from the kitchen. Tea for everyone was requested. Martha was still in the kitchen, clearing away the dishes and she prepared the tray for the policewoman. She knew she'd have to give a statement to the police as well, but she'd been in the kitchen the whole time and knew nothing. Coming from a pretty rough part of town, she was nervous around the police, and dreaded the thought of being interviewed by one of them. But she'd been in the house when the murder took place, so she knew she'd have to do it.

Peter and Maggie sat together and looked like naughty children, who'd been caught with their hands in the cookie jar. They didn't know why they felt like that, but they did. Peter put his arm around his wife in an attempt to stop her crying, but she shrugged him off saying, "Why shouldn't I cry – he was our friend and now he's dead? Why would anyone want to hurt someone like Dominic? He was so gentle."

Peter told her Dominic had been his friend too and that she had to pull herself together. "The Inspector needs to talk to you." He'd tried sympathy which failed, now he adopted a more controlling tone.

"Can't I finish my tea first?" she asked petulantly and was told by the Inspector that she'd have to drink it whilst she talked. She calmed down then, feeling as though she'd been told off and paid more attention to what was going on.

Statements were taken about who was where at the time the death occurred. Who knew what? Did anyone see or hear anything unusual? The questions kept coming until all six people had eventually been interviewed. No-one could help the police much as they'd all been someplace different when it happened. It must have sounded odd however that all six people had separated for the same few moments and not been in each other's company. They'd only been separated for a very short time, but quite long enough for a man to be murdered.

When asked the same question by the Inspector, Maggie ticked them off on her fingers, "Liz had gone into the kitchen to speak to Martha, I had fallen asleep on the sofa and was apparently snoring loudly, which I dispute by the way, Peter had gone to the toilet, Jenny was in the study telephoning her neighbour and Bill was down in the cellar choosing the most expensive wines he could find. I believe that's right – I've already double-checked with the others. No-one had even gone looking for Dominic, but then they hadn't known he was missing – he was just taking a long time to come back.

Bill felt certain it had had to be a casual intruder – after all Dominic had gone outside to the garage to get the logs and someone could have been waiting for him there. He said, "They could have followed him back into the house – after all, we mustn't forget the muddy grass and snow on the conservatory floor. He'd obviously struggled with whoever it was. Yes, someone had definitely come from outside – anyway, no-one here would have hurt Dominic, we all loved him." Tears were gathering in the corners of his eyes and he rubbed them away, looking very embarrassed.

Detective Morrison nodded and said it was certainly a possibility, even likely. Then, he asked Liz to check around the rooms to see if anything was missing, but Peter quickly intervened, "She can't do that just now Inspector – she's distraught – and obviously in deep shock. Can't that wait until tomorrow?" His doctor mode had kicked in. He was agitated himself but knew Liz was much worse. Morrison took the GP's advice and agreed that would have to do, but he was adamant he'd have to leave a couple of men in the house to investigate the scene thoroughly, to search for clues and also, to make Liz feel safer, knowing she had police protection. And Liz did feel reassured knowing she would be safe.

Jenny also volunteered to stay overnight at the house, "We can't leave her on her own, can we?" She looked at the others, who were relieved that she'd offered her services before anyone else had to. They were all shook up and desperate to get home where they felt safe. But then, Dominic had been at home and look what had happened to him. Suddenly, home no longer seemed such a safe bet!

The house was empty, except for two policemen who continued with their investigation. The silence was deafening and the two women just sat by the fire, which had gone out due to the lack of logs – but that wasn't something either women wanted to pursue. They didn't know what to say to each other – what words were there? Liz looked up suddenly, "Oh my God, I forgot to tell Martha she could go home. She must still be in the kitchen."

Jenny put her hand on her shoulder and made her sit down again. "Don't worry dear, the police told her she could go a long time ago."

Bill had told them he'd come back next day to check on Liz and he left with the others, first kissing his wife goodbye. Liz smiled and thought how reliable Bill always was – he'd always do the right thing. The police had of course arranged for Dominic's body to be removed – but not before the specially dressed forensic team had done their work around the actual murder scene. Earlier in the evening before everyone had left, something odd happened when one of forensic team suddenly held up a small object in his gloved hand. It looked like a slip of paper but it wasn't that.

"Look at this." he said to his colleague and placed the small object in a plastic specimen bag. It was a picture card with a characterture drawing of a pompous-looking man. In fact, it was Professor Plum from the game and it had lain hidden in the folds of Dominic's cravat.

On closer scrutiny, the words 'Professor Plum' could be seen clearly written and it made Maggie react strangely. "Why that's our missing card – it's from our Cluedo game – it disappeared last weekend after our game. How very strange – does that mean that Dominic had taken it? But why would he – he had a game of his own – and his Professor Plum is still there on the table?"

She knew her words sounded silly and Peter put his finger to his lips to stop her talking. "Maggie, let's not go into that just now. It'll upset Liz even more." Everyone did agree however that it was strange and in an odd way, it helped solve the mystery of the missing card. 'My God, had Dominic really stolen it – how crazy!' What would he have wanted an old card for? No, that couldn't have been it they all agreed!

Sitting on the sofa together, Jenny and Liz discussed the surprising discovery of the card inside Dominic's jacket – but of course, there was no answer and they just stared at each other blankly.

"Out of interest, do you mind if I check again your Cluedo, just to make sure the card didn't come from your game, rather than Maggie's? I know it sounds trivial, but it'll only take a moment." She went back to where the game was still spread across the table – just where they'd left it before the tragedy occurred.

"Yes, here he is, safe and sound in all his glory. Funny, that means there's been two of them in the house tonight. Crazy or what?" She'd brought the complete game back into the room - Liz took it from her and put it on the coffee table. "Why, that's even more odd – look who's missing now. There's no Miss Scarlet – could you perhaps have dropped her on the floor when you collected the game?"

Jenny darted back into the other room and searched the floor. Nothing! So, the mystery deepened, but it was only a game after all and the missing cards could just be coincidence. However, the game seemed to have taken on a sinister, rather. creepy implication. Two missing figures – and one murdered man!

Exhausted after a weird evening, the two women agreed it was time for bed. They'd reached the point where it was pointless to go over things again – but both knew neither of them would get much sleep that night.

The mystery just wouldn't go away and it actually deepened when Bill called at the house next day to check on the women. Now he learned that, not only were there two Professor Plums in existence, but Miss Scarlet was now missing.

He had to laugh, "Girls, really! Your imagination is running away with both of you. So, an image of one of the game's characters is missing – what does it matter, we'll soon get another one." He was too cavalier about the coincidence however and the two women remained unsure looking at him with raised eyebrows. He was only a man after all – he'd never understand the significance of such strange happenings, especially when coupled with a murder.

The next couple of weeks passed for Liz as if in a dream. She remained in a state of shock for days, continuing to turn to her husband for comfort and realising afresh that he'd gone. The dream was really a nightmare and he really was dead. She kept going over it in her mind, thinking of why it had happened in the first place. Dominic had no enemies – in fact, everyone liked him. He was one of nature's gentlemen after all and although they didn't always see things eye-to-eye, she'd loved him in her own way. There was no answer to be had and she just sat there, staring at the wall and thinking more.

It wasn't unusual that he'd gone to fetch more logs that night – the fire was certainly low, but why had he waited until the guests had arrived? Now, that seemed odd - normally he'd have done it before they came, always ensuring everything was perfect for his guests. That was Dominic's way. This time however, his timing was off – a burglar must have been waiting by the conservatory! Perhaps on the point of breaking in, when Dominic appeared and startled him - then the frightened man had hit out blindly without thinking. He could never have wanted to hurt her husband – why would he, Dominic was too nice. She still felt bitterly cold and knew it was the shock lingering on - she had to stop going over it again and again in her head. She went up to her bedroom and fetched a woollen shawl. She had just come back when the doorbell rang. Jenny had been home for a change of clothes and had come back to help her. She tried again to comfort her friend and provided the inevitable deluge of tea in the process, throwing in a couple of brandies for good measure – and also to help with the cold and shock of course. Nothing helped however, it was too soon and the newly-bereaved widow remained in a state of shock for some time to come. Of course, the rest of the Cluedo group rallied around her and were always there if she needed them. For that, she was eternally grateful!

Even Jonathan the young gardener, knocked tentatively on the door two days later to say how sorry he was about Dominic. "And he was fetching our logs when it happened?" he asked incredulously. Somehow that made him feel involved and Liz had to tell him not to be silly, it wasn't about the logs. Over a cup of coffee, Jonathan told her how he'd had several talks with her husband about how he planned to set up his own gardening business and how Dominic had promised to leave him something in his will to help make it happen."

"He was a lovely man and said he'd help me because I should go on reaching for the stars. And I believe he would do it as well."

Liz could have sworn she could see tears in his eyes – whether because of her loss or because Dominic hadn't had the time to add the gardener to his will, she couldn't tell but she was touched by his sensitivity. To change the subject she asked how his dad the farmer was and the awkward moment soon passed with tales of the farm. She said goodbye and closed the back door, leaving Jonathan to his pruning of the hedges and trees. As there was still so much snow around, his job really consisted of general tidying up. She found chatting to him helped – it made her think of something rather than herself. The human contact had been reassuring, although some of the silences had been awkward, after all what do you say to a woman whose husband had just been found murdered?

"I think we'll soon have to get a new Cluedo game – or we'll have to call it 'The Snap game' now that the main figures keep disappearing. We'll have to use Mr Bun the Baker and his daughter Miss Bun to make up the missing cards. The police want to hang onto Professor Plum, until the case is solved, so Maggie is still short of the chap." Bill could always be relied on to see the funny side of things.

"And that's probably some way off," Jenny replied. "What are we going to do about the next night we're due to play – it should be at our house – I think I'll ring Maggie and see what she thinks. We can't just play a game after what's happened but it might be better to act as normally as we can – for Liz's sake."

Bill looked unusually sad, " It seems wrong to play a game when Dominic is lying dead, but it might be the right thing to help all of us feel more normal, and Liz is of course a priority." Yes, speak with Maggie – see what she thinks and we'll take it from there. Let's face it, we'll be damned if we do and damned if we don't. "And with that wise remark, he left for work, planting a kiss on Jenny's head as he went.

"I think we should go ahead with it," Maggie seemed convinced it was the right thing to do, "Peter will fetch Liz and take her home afterwards." She thought for a moment, was she right – she hoped so – yes, it still seemed like a good idea. " At least, you still have a full game with all the cards intact – so far at least." And the decision was made. Jenny was to tentatively suggest it to Liz and see if she felt up to it.   She hung up then and left the window cleaner in charge. He'd only just arrived at his usual time. She went into town as she had some things to do for Liz and as she left, she called to the chap, "Don't forget to lock up and hide the key in the usual place. Remember, I want the inside windows cleaned as well." It was nice to be able to trust people, she thought.

Bill had been the solicitor to draw up Dominic's will and that gave Liz the excuse to visit him in his office in town – something she'd always tried to avoid doing. There were many issues to discuss and she was grateful she had a friend in Bill, who was always ready to advise her on her stocks and shares as well any other matters that needed attention. With Dominic's murder hanging in the air between them the whole situation seemed surreal as she sat down on the other side of his desk. Everyone's status had changed somehow and they both felt it. When the secretary had brought in two coffees however, the atmosphere became less tense. As the couple had had no children, Liz was the sole beneficiary, except for some bits and pieces Dominic wanted friends to have – small gifts just to thank them for their friendship throughout the years. They were all old friends however and not recent acquaintances. His will therefore would be quite straightforward.

Once the secretary had closed the office door behind her, Bill came from behind his desk and swept the recently-bereaved widow into his arms, "Oh my darling, you've been through so much." And he kissed her passionately. He held her close for what seemed like a long time – but was only a few moments.

"Bill, Bill – I'm free now, but you're not, so we still have to be careful. I wouldn't want to hurt Jenny for the world – she's been so good to me since it happened." Liz moved away from him and sat down again, lighting a cigarette and crossing her legs. "At least, you'll be able to come and visit me openly now – you're my solicitor after all, not just my friend."

"Yes of course, but I didn't expect this to happen – not to poor old Dominic. He was a good chap!" Bill had the good grace to look embarrassed at the mention of his friend's name – especially in the present circumstances.

"I know how good he was, no-one knows better than I – I was married to him for fifteen years – but I think I fell out of love with him some time ago and was too comfortable to do anything about it. He looked after me well and I wanted for nothing. But you know that, don't you – and we can't help who we fall in love with." She spoke these words softly, knowing how awful they sounded. She stubbed out her cigarette on her saucer and immediately lit another one.

"You smoke too much, my darling." Bill rebuked her, but she ignored him and inhaled deeply, blatantly showing herself as the femme fatale she knew she looked. "You know Bill, for a moment I thought it was you who'd killed him - to get him out of the way. You know – for us!" Bill started to protest, but she shushed him, "But when I saw how shocked you were, I knew it couldn't be so." The two had been having a relationship for a few months now and felt secure that no-one suspected a thing. Now Liz was at a crossroad in her life and knew things could change – well at least as far as she was concerned they could.

Suddenly the secretary knocked at the door and immediately came inside. It was her usual way, but it startled Bill, who darted back around his desk and almost fell over his chair. The secretary's expression didn't change – it remained impeccable and disinterested but she'd certainly witnessed her boss's speedy dash around the desk.

She looked Bill straight in the eye and said, "Excuse me Sir – but you have another visitor. Your wife's popped in to see you." For a moment, Bill thought her expression was one of gloating but no, that couldn't be, she wasn't like that. At least he'd always thought she wasn't.

The two culprits could do nothing and he told the secretary to show Jenny in. Surprise was evident on his wife's face - Liz being the last person she expected to see there. For a moment she didn't know what to say and so she stammered, "I brought you a chocolate éclair to have with your tea dear – sorry if I've disturbed you. She turned to Liz, "If I'd known you were going to be here, I'd have brought you one as well." The remark sounded lame and really rather sarcastic but she'd been caught on the hop for a moment.

 She looked again at Liz, "You're looking well – better than when I last saw you." She crossed the room and sat on the edge of the desk. It seemed necessary to stake her claim on her husband's office – she wasn't sure why but she did it anyway. The situation was embarrassing but she knew she must brazen it out and make it clear to Liz that she had more right than her friend had to be there.

The newly-widowed femme fatale rose from her chair, "Well Bill, I think we've covered everything. Will you bring me a copy of Dominic's will tomorrow – there's a few things I know he wanted to give to give to people, but I'll need the will first – and he never gave me a copy. I think there'll be a few disappointed people after the reading – you know he had a habit of promising things to all kinds of people with no intention of honouring them. He promised money to anyone and everyone. I think at the time, he did mean it, but forgot immediately afterwards. I'd also like to discuss changes to my own will as I'm now unfortunately on my own."

"I didn't realise Bill had drawn up Dominic's will – so, that's why you're here. Now I understand." She looked relieved and to cover her earlier sarcasm, she asked Liz, "How do you feel today- are you feeling stronger?"Liz just nodded her head. Jenny looked again at her husband, "Have you told Liz we're having a game of Cluedo at our place next weekend? We've all discussed it and agree it might help lift your spirits. How do you feel about it, dear?" She was her old, sweet self again and smiled at her friend – but no matter how hard she tried, the smile just wouldn't reach her eyes.

Liz turned at the door, "That'll be a couple of days after the funeral, so it'll be fine. I know I'll see you all at the funeral of course- it wouldn't be right if I didn't, he was your friend too. But goodbye for now – I have an appointment with the Funeral Director and I'm already late."   She closed the door, leaving a heavy atmosphere in the room, which Bill immediately tried to dispel by offering his wife some tea. A weak gesture but at least it was something.

Jenny wasn't quite so naïve however, "No thank-you dear – you keep your tea. I'm not sure how much I believe what you and Liz were saying. You must allow me time to think about it." She stood up to her full height, which wasn't very tall, and left the office, first saying goodbye to the secretary, whom she'd always assumed was her ally, after all 'we girls have to stick together.' What a strange afternoon it had been.

Next day, Bill asked Wilma his secretary, to deliver the will to Liz as he just didn't have the time – a poor excuse and no mistake. With pursed, disapproving lips, Wilma agreed and by her expression, he was even more sure she'd seen something when she'd burst into his office the day before. Now Wilma may only have been the secretary, but she was a smart secretary. She suddenly realised she hadn't had a rise in salary for quite some time now. Perhaps now was the time to ask for one - and something told her she would get it!

The funeral for Dominic was a really sad affair. How could it be otherwise – they'd all known him for such a long time and he'd died still a comparatively young man. Forty-Seven years was too young to 'shuffle off this mortal coil.' The little circle of mourners agreed this was so and walked slowly away from the graveside. Liz did hang about a little longer than the others just to say goodbye again. It was the least she could do and she knew how pitiful, yet glamorous, she must have looked, standing there alone by the graveside.

After the funeral service, most of the mourners were invited back to Dominic's home – that is to Liz's home now. There were three distant relatives and only very few friends who gathered in the sitting room. A caterer had been hired to provide a buffet and drinks. As she surveyed the buffet and saw how much food was left over, Liz wondered what she was going to do with it and idly considered offering the leftovers to Martha to take home. Yes, that's what she should do – Martha was always grateful for anything that came her way.

Dominic had been an only child and his parents had died when he was young, so close relatives had been a luxury he hadn't enjoyed. There were a couple of teachers from the university where he'd studied – chaps he hadn't seen for many years but who'd been his fellow-students and friends at the time. The two men stood together and didn't mix very well – but they did enjoy chatting about things they'd all done in their youth at uni. A very closed conversation built on old memories, so no-one else could join in.

Looking completely ill at ease, Jonathan the young gardener was in an ill-fitting suit which he obviously rarely wore. He stood quietly with his back to the wall and beside his father the farmer, who'd always known Dominic as a long-standing customer for his logs. Both men felt they had to come and pay their respects but were surprised to be invited back to the house. But here they stood, both wishing they were someplace else. Dominic had always been a kindly employer and customer, so they believed they'd done the right thing. Jonathan had confided in his father that Dominic had promised to leave some money in his will to help him begin the business he dreamed of, which was of course a gardening firm of his own. His father had told him not to count his chickens – sometimes people said things on the spur of the moment but never got around to doing them. But Jonathan believed Dominic had meant what he said and would wait patiently for the reading of the will.

As is usual on such occasions, everyone stood around, not knowing what to do or say. Liz tried to be a good hostess and made sure everyone had a drink and something to eat, but it was hard work. Martha had answered her call to come and over-see the caterers - and of course to help with the clearing away afterwards. She hadn't been invited to attend the funeral – but she'd come in any case – it felt right and Dominic had always been a decent employer. Liz thought her home help looked different that day and then realised what it was – she'd never seen Martha without a pinny before!

As soon as Martha arrived at the house, Liz had sought her out and had a whispered conversation with her, "By the way

Martha – would you like to look through Dominic's clothes and see if there's anything you, or your family, could make use of? I don't have to show you where everything is as you already know. I do mean it Martha – take what you want, I have no further use for men's clothes." As she talked, the bereaved widow paid more attention to her reflection in the hall mirror than she did to Martha, who knew fully well that she was being patronised, but then she was used to it especially from the 'Cluedo' group. And Liz had never been known for her generosity. She thanked her employer and accepted the offer gratefully, but said she would show Liz what she was taking – just in case. Had Martha been asked, she would probably have said she thought it was all a bit too quick and insensitive – to get rid of Dominic's clothes on the day of the funeral, but of course she said nothing. It wasn't her place.

Dominic had promised her too that she'd be pleasantly surprised when his will was read out as he planned to leave her a little gift to say thank you for all her years of dedicated work. So, she too would wait patiently for the reading of her old employer's last will and testament. She'd learned how to feign patience a long time ago!

The afternoon passed smoothly. It certainly wasn't enjoyable, but then it was a funeral. One by one, people began to drift away, leaving only the closest friends – the rest of the Cluedo group actually. Bill and Liz kept well away from each other but made sure they mingled with everyone else. Jenny was keeping a close eye on both of them - perhaps a closer eye than was necessary but it did no harm and she was aware that Bill was watching her watching him. Now, why was that, she wondered? Overall, it had been an odd occasion but then funerals were odd – especially when the deceased was young and the death so sudden and unexpected. The friends felt the loss of their friend and Cluedo member, whose unexpected death made them aware of their own mortality. Not a very happy thought!

The following Saturday was to be a normal evening – as normal as possible in the circumstances - this time it was at Bill and Jenny's house, so when everyone left after the funeral, they promised to see each other in a couple of days – and Peter reminded Liz he'd pick her up at seven o'clock. "I'm your chauffeur and I'm quite a safe driver. You can always trust a doctor, you know." He laughed at his own lame joke and added, "Oh and by the way, I'll also drive you home afterwards." He really was trying to help Liz thought and she kissed him on the cheek – just a peck of course.

However, as things turned out, this was not to be. At 6.55pm that evening, Peter drove into her drive and rang the doorbell. Standing there in the bitter cold, he wished she would hurry up and so he rang the doorbell again. Still no answer. 'Funny', he thought, 'All the lights in the house are switched on.' He decided to walk around to the conservatory at the back of the house, which might be unlocked and he could get in that way. But he didn't get that far – before he reached the big glass door, he tripped over something lying on the stone patio. At first, he thought it must be a dog and then he looked closer.

He recognised her immediately – she was lying in a crumpled heap with blood oozing from a horrific gash on her forehead. The blood was still flowing freely so it must have happened recently. Her arms were stretched wide and her legs were twisted to one side. He bent down and shouted her name, he shouted it more than once and then he felt for a pulse in her neck, but there was none. Although he'd experienced many deaths in his work, to see such a close friend lying there made him shiver. He knew his friend Liz was well and truly dead.

Automatically, he looked upwards to the balcony which was directly outside her bedroom but there seemed nothing unusual there, except perhaps that the light from her bedroom was still shining brightly into the darkness as though she'd been there just a few moments before. Was that significant – he didn't know? For a moment he froze, thinking furiously – what should I do next? He told himself, 'My God, you're a doctor man – get your act together' but his brain just wouldn't function properly. He stood up slowly, stumbling a little when he noticed something from the corner of his eye and recognised a Cluedo card – this time of Miss Scarlet – the card was lying at the side of Liz's body. Picking it up, he saw what it was and immediately dropped it on the patio but then picked it up again almost immediately. He was aware he shouldn't have touched it at all – he'd watched enough TV Police dramas to know that – but he just didn't think.

His brain was working in a very muddled way and something told him if he left the card there, it would implicate the Cluedo group, so he slipped the card into his jacket pocket. He told himself the card probably had no significance at all.

Sometime after the police had arrived and the ambulance had taken away Liz's broken body, a police inspector cornered him. But there was nothing he could tell him – he'd arrived at the time he'd agreed with Liz and after failing to get an answer at the front, he'd walked around to the back and almost fell over her body. He hadn't gained entrance to the house at all, "I just stood there like a moron – I didn't know what to do – it was the last thing I had expected to see." The inspector asked if he'd be willing to come down to the station, so they could talk some more and he could make a formal statement. He'd also be asked to provide names of other people who worked around the house - perhaps a housekeeper, char lady or gardener. Peter went with him, leaving his own car in Liz's drive – he could certainly provide that information as he probably employed most of the same people.

It felt odd to be in a police station and being questioned. He should have been used to it as he'd been a police surgeon for a couple of years but hadn't enjoyed the work. This was different though. He was the one being questioned in a murder case.

He told his interviewers that he'd been picking her up to take on to a weekly game with five friends. He explained they'd all been meeting up for a long time - to play Cluedo and of course to have a drink as well. Also, he told of how long they'd all known each other. He was kept there for at least two hours and after they'd talked at length they said he was free to go but that they'd be calling on him the next day.

"Can you run me back to my car please? My wife will be frantic by now – the last thing she knew was that I was collecting Liz. God only knows what they'll say when I get home. It's going to be such a shock – especially so soon after Dominic's murder."

Having been dropped off in a police car, he found Maggie and the other two still waiting to begin the game. "Where on earth have you been, Peter – we've been waiting ages." Maggie was cross with him, supper would probably be spoiled by now and

Jenny and Martha had spent a lot of time preparing it. In fact, Jenny had already sent Martha home as it was so late and now Maggie would have to stay behind and help Jenny tidy up.

"You found what?" Bill was the first to speak, "but I saw her just today – she came to my office. We had some things to discuss about Dominic's estate. After our talk, we had a cup of tea together – she seemed fine then.' He was obviously more upset at the news than he could show. He'd really been fond of her and perhaps even looking forward to a future with her. My God, he thought I'm going to throw up! Dominic's will had actually been drawn up by his assistant Malcolm as, being a beneficiary himself, Bill knew it wouldn't be ethical for him to do it. "We did discuss her own will as well and I suggested Malcolm should formalise the draft paper. He did it quickly and she actually signed it today, asking my secretary to witness it for her. It was a very simple will just like Dominic's own. And that was the last time I saw her." His voice wavered as he spoke and he looked pleadingly at the others. "You all understand, don't you – I was the last person to see her alive but I'd never have hurt a hair on her head. You know that!"

Jenny quickly interrupted him in an attempt to stop him from blabbing on. She saw his mouth was running away with him and he was in danger of saying something that might be incriminating. She did think however, 'Methinks the lady doth protest too much' – but she didn't voice her thoughts. She couldn't help wondering that the two had been together again that day – and he'd never even mentioned it. "Nobody's asked you to account for your movements Bill – do stop going on so." She smiled at him, but the smile was frozen on her lips. She turned to Peter and asked, "What do the police think happened to Liz? Have they got any leads yet?"

"They won't commit themselves – anyway they'd never confide in me, a humble GP. They're still in the process of looking around the house and garden – but I did pick up that their first thought is it was suicide. They checked the balcony from where she'd fallen and said there was no sign of a struggle, which seemed significant to them. The forensics team were still working on it when I left. I've been to the police station for a couple of hours, you know." Peter thought some sympathy should have been directed towards him after what he'd just been through – but it seemed that wasn't going to happen. He went on, "It certainly looked like a case of suicide – it seems there was no-one else in the house with her, so it's possible she actually threw herself from the balcony. Apparently, it's not uncommon for someone recently widowed to contemplate such a thing – but Liz – I ask you? It doesn't seem the kind of thing she'd do, she was too confident and full of life."

In his turn, he looked pleadingly to the others, willing them to agree with him – but all eyes remained lowered.

He hesitated for a few moments before adding, "Oh and by the way, I found this beside her body." And he held out the Miss Scarlet card in the palm of his hand. Everyone's gasps filled the room and no-one could speak for s moment. They all just stood there - frozen in the middle of the comfortable room where the game of Cluedo was still lying - ready for the next game.

Slowly, Peter stepped forward and gingerly laid the card beside its twin on the board on the table. Jenny spluttered, "Now, that really is odd. That card was definitely missing from Liz's game the other night – I know cause I looked everywhere for her." She stared at the two identical cards of Miss Scarlet before saying, "What's going on -if any of you are playing a joke on the rest of us, speak up now cause it's just not funny. It's not funny at all." She started to cry and Bill put his arm around her shoulder – but she pulled away from him. She was annoyed with him and she was angry, but she wasn't sure why. Deep down however, perhaps she did know why!   The words 'deluding oneself' and 'denial' came unbidden into her mind. Had her husband been having an affair with Liz – well if he had – it was certainly over now.

Much later that night and after a few stiff brandies, they'd talked the subject to death. Liz was the last person they'd ever expect to end her own life – they decided unanimously that she was too full of vitality and energy. " And of selfishness – let's face it, she was very spoilt and what she wanted, she made sure she got." Maggie surprised everyone by adding her negative two penny worth. "Don't get me wrong, I loved her dearly and wouldn't ever wish her harm, but you've got to admit she was quite a madam. Anyway, I don't believe it – not her - she'd never commit suicide."

"Well, that leaves us with another murder – and possibly a new fear for our own lives. For whatever reason, the characters from Cluedo seem to play a part in the murders. Therefore, which one of us could be next? And just a thought – you say Liz had everything to live for, but is that really true? She'd just had her husband murdered and had to bury him. How did that make her feel I wonder – how distressed she must have been. All she had to look forward to was playing Cluedo with us – not much of an enticement to live really." Again, the words 'Methinks the lady doth protest too much' came unbidden into Jenny's mind. Bill seemed to be arguing with himself but was he trying to conceal how he really felt about Liz's death?

"Well, I don't think I can believe it. Not her, I still think she had everything to live for." Jenny was thinking aloud, but Bill answered, "Is that true though? Dominic was dead and she had no children to lean on or offer support – not much of a prospect!" Bill wanted to make sure his relationship with Liz would be well hidden and remain so. It was quite clear he preferred the option of suicide. Who would want to murder her anyway?Although saddened by her death, he was well aware that she'd been guilty of being clingy and would probably get more so, whereas all he'd wanted was a little dalliance – an innocent little bit on the side. He'd certainly had that but had never wanted his marriage to Jenny to be placed in jeopardy.

Jenny turned on him, "Mind you, you say she completed her last will today - she could have been putting her affairs in order, all the time planning to end it all. "She bit her lower lip in thought and then added, "No, that's too horrible to think of and she was never capable of such a selfless act, it just wasn't her. She'd always been a very selfish woman. When she left your office, she went home to get ready to play Cluedo with us – no, none of that fits in with a woman planning to take her own life. And she wouldn't have chosen such a messy way of killing herself – it might not have worked and she'd be crippled for the rest of her life. And I truly believe she was too vain to crush her body in that way." Very different opinions of husband and wife – in fact they were almost arguing with themselves, rather than each other. Confusion reigned and no-one spoke, they had no words left.

Peter stood up and fetched his wife's coat, "Let's go Maggie, there's no more to discuss tonight." And for once, Maggie obeyed with no argument. They went out the door, leaving Bill and Jenny staring into their empty brandy glasses.

The days passed but the world would never be the same again. The ever-decreasing group kept in touch with each other of course – they were like family – dammit they were a family.

For a few days – more than a week in fact – they kept their distance from each other. They were lost in their personal misery and being in each other's company was just too sad - and trying to make normal conversation was just too exhausting. Maggie asked her children to visit home, she felt she had to see them. The events of the past few weeks had made her aware of the uncertainty of life and she needed to see her kids – just to be sure they were all right. And so, one afternoon Bethany turned up, closely followed by her brother Tom.

"Mum, what on earth's been going on? Are Auntie Liz and Uncle Dominic really dead? But they weren't old enough for that surely?" The young woman was distressed at the news. "Why didn't you tell Tom and me, you know we'd have come home for Dominic's funeral?"

Maggie said sadly, "There's no age limit for murder, dear and yes, I'm afraid they're both gone. It was all so unexpected and the police still have no idea who did it – they're not even sure if the murderer was one and the same person. They just don't know."

Tom asked if the police had considered that it might have been someone Liz and Dominic had known. "After all, in Aunt Liz's case whoever did it must have been inside the house already before making their way upstairs. So, she must have let them into the house herself – it had to be someone she knew." Tom was genuinely upset to hear of the couple's death. He had been fond of the aunt and uncle who'd always remembered his birthdays. "Were there no signs of a forced entry perhaps? If not, that proves she must have definitely known her killer."

"We just don't know Tom. It's in police hands now and we must just wait for news." Maggie was becoming upset and Bethany knew it was time to make some tea.

"What about the time of death? Do they know exactly when she died? They must know that surely – so they must have checked the alibies of the people who knew her. Especially anyone who might have had a grudge against her."

"I don't think she had any enemies Tom – she didn't move in those kind of circles – I mean circles where real enemies exist. Sometimes, she did upset people by her manner but she was never that bad, just a bit insensitive." Maggie felt guilty saying these words as she knew her son was only trying to help. "Oh good, here's Bethany with the tea." And for a short time, the subject was dropped and the small group chatted about family affairs. It was a merciful relief! But Tom had the bit between his teeth and couldn't let the subject drop, "And what about Uncle Dominic's murder – who on earth could have done that? He was such a nice man. I can't imagine him having any enemies either. He was always good to us." And he looked at his sister for her agreement.

"He seemed so happy the last time I saw him," Bethany blurted out, without realising what she was saying. Her words brought a sudden blush to her cheeks.

Maggie looked up surprised, "What do you mean – you can't have seen him for several years, in fact since you first left home five years ago? It is five years, isn't it?

Bethany was still chewing nervously on her lip, wishing she hadn't mentioned her uncle's health. "I've seen him more recently than that Mum – you know I have. It must have been last Summer - remember when I arrived home unexpectedly?"

Even Tom was looking at her curiously, "You little sneak - you never told me you'd been back home then – if I'd have known, I'd have come too." He was told by his sister that it wasn't any of his business what she did and whom she visited. "He wasn't just your uncle, you know," she finished lamely.

Maggie was feeling uneasy. The conversation had taken a strange turn and she suddenly felt her hands go clammy. She was concerned at what her daughter was saying, "Did you visit Dominic last Summer, Bethany? You certainly didn't visit your father and me then unexpectedly or not. Oh, you were always on the phone, usually looking for another handout – but a visit, no I don't think so." She watched her daughter's face.

"Well, I suppose I'd better come clean." She sighed and mumbled something about 'Me and my big mouth'. "I did visit last Summer but it was only a flying visit – I didn't want to worry you at the time, so I just visited Uncle Dominic and Auntie Liz. You and dad were having money problems with the house renovations – you remember? This old house seems to eat up all your money – so I went to them to ask for a loan. I was in desperately need of money and I knew how well off they were." She had the grace to look embarrassed.

"As I said before, you little sneak Bethany – you went crying to Mum's friends to ask for money! You should be ashamed of yourself – I wouldn't have done that." Tom couldn't hide an air of superiority.

"You're not so perfect Tom – you've had little handouts from Uncle Dominic before – and I bet you never told mum or dad. Anyway, last time I saw Uncle Dominic, I learned something to my advantage – and to yours for that matter. He promised me he would leave me a nice sum of money in his will – and the same to you. So there!" Bethany couldn't conceal her smug expression.

She didn't realise what she was saying until Maggie put her hand to her mouth in a gesture of disbelief and said, "So you knew to expect money when Dominic died, did you? If I were you, I'd keep quiet about that – it gives you a reason for bringing about his premature death. I hope you didn't visit him a few weeks ago as well?" She looked expectantly at her distraught daughter and waited for her to answer, but Tom butted in first, "My sister – the police suspect! Well, I never!"

Maggie stood up, saying this had gone far enough and whilst disappointed by her daughter's duplicity, she was sure she wasn't a murderer. As she left the room however, she turned at the door and looked straight at Bethany, "Having said that, I'd still keep quiet about knowing you expected money from Dominic when he died – the police might find that very interesting."Tom and Bethany just sat in the room not talking to each other. What was there to say now that Bethany had spilled the beans.

It was another funeral on another cold and rainy day. It was as if the weather was in tune with the reason for the gathering. The small group of mourners stood around the graveside where Liz had now joined Dominic. Husband and wife were together again but their loyal friends could find no comfort in that thought – not in the dank and damp weather that made them feel even more miserable. The number of people at the graveside was similar to those who'd attended Dominic's funeral a few weeks before- very few but very genuine. Peter and Maggie's son and daughter had come with their parents as they'd both known the departed since they'd been children. Bethany had kept quiet about Dominic's promise to leave her money when he died. She did grieve though, she'd been genuinely fond of her aunt and uncle – but Maggie wondered if that had been enough. However, she knew she must say nothing!

Bill and Jenny's only son, Ben was also there as he'd also enjoyed the generosity of his aunt and uncle when he was a child – and Jenny was proud to see the young man standing there, tall and handsome, paying his respects to the couple. Jonathan, the young gardener was also there, as was Martha, the home help – both stood well back from the chief mourners but both were determined to pay their respects to Liz.

Bill turned to his son, "You'll be coming home with Mum and me to stay for a few days, won't you? We don't see you often enough and I know she'd love it. I know you were here for a couple of days at Christmas but that was a weird Christmas and best forgotten." He knew Ben would be champing at the bit to get back to his office in London, but the young man really didn't come home much - and Jenny missed him something awful. He was her only child after all – although she'd always wanted more, that was just something not meant to be.

"Oh Dad, you know how busy I am." Ben looked doubtful for a few moments, but looking at his mother's tear-stained face, he knew he'd have to agree. He promised to stay for two days and Bill had to be content with that.

Slowly, the group moved off and a small sea of umbrellas floated towards the waiting cars. Everyone offered each other a lift but some insisted on walking back to the now-empty house, waiting there on the posh estate – the house where Liz and

Dominic had recently lived and of which they were so proud – in particular the old mantelpiece.

It had been another funeral! Another dear friend gone! What was happening in the world? Everyone sat in the comfortable sitting room and exchanged stories about the deceased couple – some were funny, some sad, but all entertaining. Peter acted as host although it wasn't his house – well, someone had to. Martha and Jonathan were the first to leave- as they obviously felt out of place amongst the others.Maggie remonstrated with them, trying to get them to stay longer, but secretly relieved when she no longer had to look after them – she could relax with just her Cluedo friends and really mourn the loss of two good friends.

Feeling embarrassed, and rather guilty, Peter had told the police about finding Miss Scarlet's card on the patio - lying beside Liz's dead body. He explained that he thought it was just a trivial thing of little significance but his white lie fell on deaf ears and the police gave him a proper telling-off.

"You may never know how much your decision to withhold evidence has damaged our enquiries and I must stress your action might result in a charge being raised against you for hindering our investigations." The inspector's expression left Peter in no doubt that he'd done something very wrong. The GP was rarely talked to like that, but he took it on the chin like a man. He'd known when he pocketed the card that he shouldn't have done it, but more so now with the benefit of hindsight.

Bill had just arrived home for the evening, when the doorbell rang. "Get that, will you Tom?" he called out from the kitchen and was surprised when the police inspector and a burly constable walked in. They didn't look like casual visitors and refused to sit down.

"I'm afraid I must ask you to accompany me to the station Sir – there are some questions I'd like you to answer." The constable stood by the door as though to stop him from leaving the room. Tom stepped in front of his father in an attempt to protect him but Bill gently moved him aside and went to fetch his coat.

"What on earth do you want me for – and why me?" Bill felt himself begin to sweat, but knew he had no option but to do as he was asked. He wasn't actually being asked - he knew it was really an order.   The three men left the house together and Ben went into the sitting room to tell his mother what had just happened. She was sitting on the sofa, a glass of wine in her hand.

"Why Dad?" Jenny asked him, "What on earth reason can they want to speak to him for?" She was suddenly upset and again reached for the bottle, "Shouldn't we have gone with him – or should we follow behind him?" She didn't know what to do.

"Let's not rush into anything just yet. Remember he is a lawyer, so he knows his rights. We should give him an hour or so, before we do anything." Ben suddenly realised he was acting like the parent in the room and talking to his mother as if she was a child. He went to fetch her some hot, sweet tea. He'd heard it was good for shock.

Two hours later, they heard Bill's key turn in the lock and both jumped up from the sofa. He came into the room, looking tired and haggard. Ben decided to leave the room to allow husband and wife to talk in privacy – he'd come back later to hear about everything.

Jenny was the first to speak. She stood by the fire as Bill threw himself into an armchair.

"I won't beat about the bush Bill, I'd begun to think lately that you and Liz were thick as thieves – I even thought you might be having an affair - but not for a moment did I think you'd killed her – that's not your style at all. You're far too much of a coward to do something like that." She was almost ranting and didn't even ask him how it had been at the station – for the moment, she seemed to have lost control.

He just sat there quietly in the chair, looking as if he had no energy left. He didn't speak! He looked exhausted! His head had fallen onto his chest and he looked as though he craved sleep.

Ignoring how he looked, she went on, "Now Dominic's death is quite another matter – he never was your bosom friend. But, having said that, I don't believe you'd have the courage to stab anyone." She was enjoying firing the tirade at him as she still believed something had been going on between Liz and him. It was time it was all brought into the open. She waited for him to speak. In fact, she had to wait for some time.

"It's not what you think – they wanted to speak to me because Liz left everything to me in her will. I remonstrated with her at the time and told her it wasn't a good idea – everyone would find it very odd – especially you. She wouldn't listen – and that was the main reason my assistant Malcolm had to draw up the papers rather than myself, as it wouldn't have been right for me to do it. She said if I didn't do as she asked, she'd just go to another solicitor, so what could I do?" Jenny sat there flabbergasted at the news – she really hadn't expected that. Her first thoughts were that there had to be something between them – otherwise she wouldn't have left everything to him. It just served to strengthen her doubts!

His long speech obviously left him feeling shattered and completely unlike a man who'd just been left a fortune. "I like to believe I was thinking of you and Ben when I let her do it – you'll all benefit from her decision as much as I will." He dropped his head into his hands and just sat there. It all sounded so lame – yet it was all true.

The police could prove nothing against him, although he'd been the last person to see Liz alive – except for her murderer of course. Since she'd left his office that afternoon with the actual time confirmed by Wilma, she'd seen no-one else and Bill had remained in his office for some time. Wilma watched him closely and times and this was her speciality. She knew all his movements. After that, he'd been with Jenny until they both went to Maggie and Peter's house – for Cluedo. There was no time he could have visited Liz before that, let alone roughed her up and threw her from a balcony. He was shocked to learn from the police that Liz's stomach had contained a heavy sedative that could easily have knocked her out – at the best, it probably affected her balance and made her dizzy. She'd drunk a glass of warm milk that had made the sedatives work on her system very rapidly. She could have passed out but of course she didn't – until she hit the ground. She probably went onto the balcony for fresh air and staggered towards the edge – or she could have easily been pushed over by someone. Now, it was being treated definitely as murder and not suicide. He was even more relieved that his alibi had been sound and that the police had believed him.

Jenny and Ben had listened to his words in silence. They were both shocked. Then Ben said," So, someone drugged her and then pushed her over the balcony? That has to mean it really wasn't suicide – if she'd been going to do that, she wouldn't have drugged herself first, she'd just have done it. You don't have to be Einstein to work that out. " Ben spoke as though he'd solved the crime all by himself, but Jenny said nothing.It was all too much for her.

Next morning, Tom telephoned Ben and asked to meet with him for a pint. The two young men who'd always seemed more like cousins, drove to a village on the edge of town. They'd both agreed it was best to keep their meeting low key, considering what was going on.

"I'll get the first round in Ben," Tom was in the chair and delighted to see Ben whom he'd not met in person for a number of years. At first, they chatted about something and nothing – small talk that helped break the ice. Tom was impatient however to get down to the nitty gritty reason for the meeting. "I wanted to talk with you as it seems some of us have been led up the garden path somewhat – I'll come right out with it, did Uncle Dominic leave you anything in his will?"

Ben was surprised by the question and raised his eyebrows questionly, "Why do you want to know that?"

Tom told him about Bethany and how she'd been promised some money by Dominic – and of course how she'd been told he would have some money too. "But the will has been read now and our names weren't even mentioned – not a trinket for old time's sake even and definitely no money. I just wanted to know what happened in your case." He looked rather embarrassed as he didn't want it to sound as though he was criticising his late uncle – but then that was probably what he was doing.

" A couple of years ago, I admit I had a letter from Uncle Dominic, promising I would be a beneficiary in his will – but I'm afraid he must have forgotten cause my name wasn't even mentioned in his will. I'd forgotten all about it but when I heard of his death, I have to admit I pricked up my ears."

"So, what you're saying is that like Bethany and myself, you were expecting something from Uncle Dominic?" Tom relaxed on hearing the news as until then, both he and his sister were clearly in the spotlight with a vested interest in the man's death."

Ben looked confused, "What exactly do you mean Tom? I don't understand." Ben looked most uncomfortable.

"Oh, come on Ben, surely you see what I'm saying. Look, I'll spell it out for you – 'Uncle Dominic was murdered and we three had a vested interest in his death. From the police's point of view, we might have decided to hasten his death so we could get out hands on our benefits even sooner. Is that clear enough?" Tom spoke quickly, obviously beginning to lose patience with his friend.

There was tension now and neither of them spoke for a few moments, then Ben stood up. He hadn't finished his pint but clearly wasn't going to do so. "I'll see you Tom – probably not for another few years of course. I don't like what you're implying, in fact I resent it. I don't know what you and Bethany are capable of, but you should know I wouldn't ever have hurt a hair on Dominic's head – next to my father, I was very fond of him." He left the table and then the pub – the evening hadn't been as pleasant as he'd hoped. As he got behind the wheel, he was angry – he hadn't been waiting for his uncle's money – he was doing all right in the city. He drove back to town rather recklessly but crept quietly into his parents' house - he didn't feel like talking to anyone after the conversation with Tom.

Tom finished his pint and then jumped into his car and took the same road back to town. He'd had his answer from Ben and was left in no doubt that his cousin had nothing to do with Dominic's death. But the question had to be asked although he wished he'd done it better. He hadn't wanted to fall out with Ben.

During the next week, the police continued to question everyone in sight and for a while, they held onto Jonathan at the station, only releasing him after 6 hours. Young Jonathan had made the mistake of telling them how much he'd admired Dominic and of how he'd promised to leave him something in his will. His forthright honesty however high-lighted his innocence – he was obviously speaking the truth. On releasing him, Inspector Morrison said to his colleague, "No, he's not guilty. He's just a simple soul who believed a man's casual promise – probably a promise that man had no intention of keeping."

They'd even interviewed the regular window cleaner to check if he'd seen anything that might help. When he finally left the station after the interrogation, he bumped into Jonathan and they talked about what they'd just been through and about the strange murders in the house. Both agreed it must be a stranger and probably not someone local – no-one local would hate the Dominic and Liz enough to kill them.

The window cleaner said, "As if any of us would ever hurt that lady – or her husband! She was always nice and friendly and he was a gentleman. Mind you, I suppose she could be quite a madam when it suited her and she liked me to tug my forelock." He laughed as he spoke, "All I do, is clean windows. Okay, sometimes I see things I shouldn't – but that's not my fault, is it?" Jonathan laughed as well and thumped him on the shoulder, "The perks of the job, Mate! The perks of the job!"

In the local pub in town, Maggie and Peter had met up with Bill and Jenny. "What on earth are we going to do now – there's so few of us. Should we play again in loving memory of our two friends – or should we never play again? I think we should vote on it. Peter looked expectantly at his friends.

To break the uncomfortable silence Maggie said, "I think we should play again in memory of Liz and Dominic – we've now buried both of them and we should do something to make sure we never forget them – although I know we won't of course. Going on playing the game however, will make sure we remember how good things used to be. We could ask Martha to come in and prepare the food and drink - and we could make a special night of remembrance. You both must come to our house next weekend and we'll really push the boat out." She raised her glass in salute to her lost friends. Unsurprisingly, Maggie again had tears in her eyes!

And that's exactly what they set out to do– Peter had already set up the board game, ready for his guests and he could smell the delicious aromas coming from the kitchen. Martha was already on the job. Neither Maggie nor Peter mentioned Bill's recent good fortune as that seemed too awkward – and anyway, Jenny had told them in confidence. They sat there sipping their drinks and trying hard to pretend everything was normal. Of course, nothing was normal and they all knew it.

"Sorry to bring this up Bill – but we're all friends here. Did Liz leave anything to Martha – she'd been her home help for years? Maggie and I were just wondering." Peter looked uncomfortable but he was right, the home help had worked for all of them over many years.   He'd known Martha had been questioned, just as they'd all been – but questioning little, meek Martha must have been a fruitless exercise. She was just a little lady who kept in the background and did whatever she was asked. In fact, none of them ever remembered her asking for something. Really – Martha – quite ridiculous!

Bill knew the topic had to be raised and he explained, "The will is to be read on Tuesday 10.00am at Liz's house – and I think we should all attend. I know you're both astounded at Liz for leaving me the house and the rest of her estate. I don't know what to say except that I honestly tried to change her mind, but she was insistent. She said she had no relatives and only us as friends. That's all I can say at this time – but everything will be revealed on Tuesday." And he made it obvious he was going to say no more on the subject. Jenny stared at him as he spoke, wondering why she'd chosen Bill as the sole beneficiary, after all they'd all been her friends. Deep down she knew the answer but couldn't bring herself to speak the words. But it was out in the open at last and everyone felt relieved - especially Bill.

Maggie said, "Let's get on with the game now, shall we?" And they did. They enjoyed a good game, and in the end, Jenny chose the correct murderer, the weapon and the location.

"Well Done, Old Fruit." Bill had been stumped himself and was glad his wife had won. Jenny was a smart cookie and he knew it. Martha had produced a tasty meal and a lovely, calorific pudding which went down very well. "Seconds. Please?" Bill was first to say, but they all eventually followed him. In silence, Martha had brought in the 'seconds.'   She still looked upset about what had happened and she'd found being questioned by the police very upsetting.

Game over and stomachs full, Peter began to put away the board game, suddenly stopping with a question on his face, "Well I never did! Another card's missing – how can that be?

We've all been here and none of us have seen anything. That's right, isn't it?"

Bill walked over to the table and searched the table and the floor thoroughly, "It's Mrs Peacock that's missing. Peter's right, I know it was there whilst we were playing, but now it's completely disappeared."

Come on now chaps, let's not be paranoid, so we've lost a card, so what? These things happen and it's only a card after all." Maggie's words were brave, but she didn't sound convinced, even to herself.

"Mrs Peacock – I wonder which one of us she is. And that's two cards missing from your set now – stranger and stranger." And with Jenny's daunting words, the party broke up and went their separate ways. Secretly all four of them were taking the loss of Mrs Peacock seriously, but what could they do?

Early next morning Peter was dressing, "Maggie darling, are you planning to go into town today by any chance?" If you are, would you mind depositing this cheque in the bank for me – I have a meeting that could last most of the day, so if you could do it, it would be a tremendous help." Peter was obviously in a rush and tutted at having to re-do his tie. He was all fingers and thumbs this morning.

"Of course, darling – no bother! Give me the cheque now. I'm going to town to get some ingredients for the quiches and pies I'm going to take along to the reading of Liz's will – I think one of us should make the effort and it would be wrong to depend on Martha to do everything. She won't be there in her usual capacity, will she? She'll be there as one of us, won't she?   I know Bill said he got everything – but a small token for Martha wouldn't be out of the question."

"That's kind Maggie – trust you to think of the 'eats. There'll be plenty of drink for everyone – Bill knows his way around Dominic's cellar, that's for sure – although perhaps I should say his own cellar cause that's what it is now."

"Don't be sarcastic Peter, it doesn't suit you – even if it is true!" she responded.He kissed her cheek and handed over the cheque before disappearing. Maggie had a quick cup of coffee before leaving for the shops. Jonathan was working in the garden as she left and she shouted out. "Good Morning Jonathan – just help yourself to coffee – the kitchen door is open." Jonathan was used to making his coffee in the kitchen.

It was a very cold morning and she wrapped up well, pulling on her favourite blue woolly hat, a present from Liz. She had to push away the sad thought that came unbidden into her mind. Just over a month ago, both Dominic and Liz had been alive and part of the gang. But she'd already shed many a tear thinking of how much life the couple should still have been looking forward to. What a waste! And if they were both murdered, who on earth could have done it? She wasn't surprised that the police had questioned Bill – his position was turning out to be pretty suspicious - but then, they'd let him go so he'd obviously not done the deed. Or had he? Everything was still so open! She forced herself to stop thinking of the mystery – she'd done enough of that.

The bank was busy as it was lunchtime before she got there and people were obviously on their dinner breaks. She took her place in one of the queues – and of course it turned out to be the slowest one – she always picked the slow queue. She moved forward very slowly. Suddenly the front door of the bank was thrown open and a man ran in carrying a gun. 'Funny,' she thought, 'I've never seen a gun before!' A strange thought in the circumstances. Another man stood at the door to stop more people coming in – or going out.

The man with the gun wore a mask that covered the lower part of his face. He pointed the gun and shouted to all the cashiers, "Pass over the money from your drawers and don't take too long about it – you've only got one minute. I know you'll all be pressing your panic buttons, so when I say one minute, I mean one minute." He looked directly at the customers and waved the gun in the air. He told them to lie flat on the floor and people quickly obeyed, although some more elderly ones found it difficult. Maggie lay there, her first thought being about dirt getting onto her best blue coat. Her woolly hat had slipped to one side and she tried to push it upwards. As she got down, someone jostled her from behind and made her slip further forward but she hadn't seen who it was – probably just someone as scared as she was.

As soon as he had some money, he began to back away towards the door, where the other man was still waiting. He seemed to aim the gun at the customers and fired once to make sure they kept back. Everyone thought he'd fired into the air, but he hadn't – he'd fired at the woman in the woolly hat, who'd already got onto her knees. The wrong movement at the wrong time – it seemed to draw unwelcome attention to her. The two men ran from the bank and quickly disappeared up the street. Someone outside the bank had obviously rung for the police and they arrived within minutes. Two of the customers, on their feet now, crossed to see if Maggie was all right – but she wasn't. The blue clad figure lay still and unmoving – she was dead! Her cherished blue woolly hat lay on the floor beside her and the contents of her shopping bag had spilled across the floor. Bright red blood was oozing from the hole in her warm coat, a hole where the bullet was still lodged.

Amongst the bloodied contents of her bag, a local farmer who'd come in to pay a bill spotted a card. It was the same farmer who'd supplied the logs to Dominic, so he recognised Maggie straight away. The card looked out of place amongst the items of food and he gingerly picked it up, immediately dropping it again as his fingers became smeared with her blood.On the card was a woman dressed in white and underneath the figure, it said, 'Mrs Peacock.' Mrs Peacock's white dress had spots of blood across it. 'Had the figure always been in the bag, or had the robber thrown it there?' 'Either way, it was odd. '

The police were now mingling with the bank customers – everything was confusion and the para-medics had arrived to see to Maggie. There was nothing they could do for her however and they gently took away her body from the bank. Everything had happened so quickly and when the police spoke with several of the customers, there were many and different accounts of what had happened. Even the farmer who'd known Maggie told a garbled story. The Mrs Peacock card was bagged however and when Inspector Morrison learned about it, he'd sure to be very interested.

There were no quiches or pies at the reading of the will. In fact, it turned out that there was no will reading that day. Everyone was in a daze – it seemed that people were dying all around and everyone was scared and confused. Needless to say, Peter was devasted, "She wouldn't have been in the bank at all, if I hadn't asked her to go there. My God, that makes it my fault." He was inconsolable and wouldn't listen to anyone who tried to comfort him – all he could see were his wife's lovely blue eyes – eyes he'd never see again. 'God, how was he going to tell Bethany and Tom?' He genuinely didn't know the answer although he'd often dealt with death in his line of work – but this was his Maggie!

Now there was only one Cluedo couple left intact – and they'd never be able to play the game again – but then, would they ever want to? There was no doubt now that the game had something to do with the recent deaths. Their appearance at the death scenes proved their significance – but why?

Before he contacted his son and daughter, Peter made a decision. He knew it was the coward's way out, but so what? It was easier this way. Before Maggie had even been buried, Peter went home with a bottle of whisky and a large bottle of sleeping pills. He felt he had nothing more to live for and believed indirectly he was the reason for her death. He poured the whisky and swallowed a handful of the pills – then he did exactly the same again. In a strange way, he actually felt relief - he'd paid for what he'd done. He'd never have been able to forgive himself and knew others would feel the same, no matter how much they denied it. If only he hadn't' put his meeting before his wife's safety – he should have gone to the bank himself, but he hadn't and that was that. As he saw it, he took the only decent way out and punished himself for committing the worst of crimes. He was absolutely convinced it had been his fault and couldn't see any other way out. The result was inevitable!

And so, Jenny and Bill had to attend a double funeral this time. "That is one of the saddest things I've ever had to do – and those two young people looked so alone and scared. At least once the house is sold, they'll be comfortably off but I'm sure that's no consolation." Jenny couldn't stop the tears and added, "Oh Bill, there's only you and me now – our lovely circle of friends have all gone."

They stood together by the newly dug grave and looked at the wreath they'd sent lying on the grass. It was made up of yellow roses – Maggie's favourite colour - four large blooms amongst white ones, a yellow bloom for each of their friends. Of course, there was a card there too, in fact there seemed to be two cards and Bill bent down to read them. Printed on the card, clear as crystal was the name 'Colonel Mustard'. Now who had put that there? He questioned the funeral director, but the man claimed to know nothing about it. The irony was that Peter had served in the army as a Medic for twenty years. He'd never reached the rank of colonel but the little Cluedo card now gave him that status.

Jenny turned ashen, "Oh Bill, this is uncanny – who's doing this? That's four Cluedo characters – and four unexpected deaths. Someone's playing a cruel game and our little group are the victims. I think we should ask for police protection, don't you? I'm more scared than I've ever been in my whole life. Do you agree we should speak to Inspector Morrison?"

"I don't know what this card means Jen – maybe it's just someone playing a sick joke. Remember Peter's death wasn't the result of murder – he took his own life." But now for the first time since he'd heard what Peter had done, he found himself doubting his friend's death as suicide – the card on the wreath had done that. He told himself to stop imagining things, Peter had taken the pills with the whisky – there was no question about that – but he'd left no suicide note to say goodbye. Everyone was confident however that it was the act of a broken-hearted man, who'd just lost his dear wife. Or was it? Bill's mind was

They spotted Martha and Jonathan the gardener, walking towards the exit and Bill stopped to offer them a lift. "No thank you Sir, the walk will do us good." Martha answered for both of them, "We just had to say goodbye to our employers!" And she pulled her coat tighter around her slight form and walked on. Touchingly and despite the difference in their ages, Jonathan took hold of her arm and guided her over the rocky surface of the path. He'd always been a nice young man!

When they got home, Ben was there. He'd just arrived from the city and was disappointed he'd arrived too late to attend the funeral. He kissed Bethany on the cheek and shook hands with Tom, "I'm so very sorry about your mum and dad. What a double whammy that must have been – one dying so soon after the other.

I don't suppose you know what you're going to do now." The young man was obviously upset – he'd been fond of Maggie and Peter. He knew it was too soon for the brother and sister to know what they were going to do, but it was all he could think of to say." He was pleased to find there was no animosity between himself and Tom.

"Let's not go into that just now, there's no rush and they're both welcome to stay here with Jenny and me if they're not ready to go home yet." Jenny brought in some food from the kitchen – just some sandwiches and crisps. She hadn't had the nerve to ask Martha to prepare some eats – poor Martha seemed to be suffering as much as everyone else. The three men enjoyed the sandwiches but Bethany and Jenny couldn't stomach food yet.

Tom asked, "Do you really think it's all had something to do with Cluedo? I can't see any sense in that – it's only a game after all."

"Don't speak with your mouth full Tom – you're covering me with crumbs." His sister couldn't resist telling him off the way she always had. It broke the tension and everyone smiled. No-one could actually laugh yet, but the hesitant smiles were encouraging.

"Yes, but Tom's got a point. Of course, Cluedo's just a game but someone is using it to show there's a connection between the deaths – someone's using the character cards to show that connection. I think we've got a serial killer on our hands – oh, I know as well as the two murders, Maggie died in a bank raid and Dominic took his own life – but is that what really happened?Surely that's enough for the police to work on – they've got to find one killer who knew you all played that stupid game every week?" Ben looked hopefully at his father, but Bill just shook his head. "They don't seem to be getting anywhere with the cards and yet a different one has always appeared around the deaths, either at the time of death or just after it. I know they play a part in the whole sorry mess."

He turned to Jenny, "And I've thought about what you said darling, I am going to ask Inspector Morrison if he can provide some form of protection for us – of course, we mustn't become paranoid but out of the six of us, there's only two left." He could see he'd scared her and put his arm around her shoulder, "As they say in the movies Jen – to get to you they'll have to go through me first." Again, everyone smiled but it wasn't really funny and Jenny looked frozen with fear. How did she know she could trust him?

To break the suspense, Bethany asked, "Are there any characters left in the game? Four of them have appeared I know, but does that leave anyone?"

Bill said, "There's still Mrs White and Mr Boddy, who've not yet been involved in things. I suppose for argument's sake, that could be you and me Jen." Her eyes filled with dread and he quickly added, "Darling, I'm only joking, don't take any notice of me."

But the die was cast – and all five people were thinking the same thing. 'Bill was quite right – more vigilance was needed – and most definitely, police protection.

To change the subject, Bill reminded them, "There's still Liz's will to be read, let alone your mother and father's and that's something I'll have to arrange. It seems so long ago that Peter was stabbed and the whole thing began – but it's actually been only three months. I find that amazing – so many changes in such a short time and so many close friends gone out of our lives. Ben was looking thoughtful, "Look Mum and Dad, I think perhaps you should come up to the city and stay with me for a few weeks – just to break this awful cycle. What do you say?" Jenny thought what a kind son she had and Bill just said, "We'll see Son, but thanks for the offer. Once I see to my friends' estates, I'll be able to relax – and then the city might be just what Mum and I need."

The police were continuing to question as many people as they could. The newspapers were regularly full of the story, mostly criticising the police's tardy action – and why not – it must have been like manor from Heaven to thirsty journalists. So many murders and a suicide in such a short time and the added bonus of secret little messages beside the bodies. An imaginative journalist could make a meal of that and no mistake. Suddenly, it seemed the game of Cluedo was being talked about and apparently the sales of the game had gone through the roof. Yes, the newspapers continued to write up the story with great gusto.

Bill could feel people were looking at him suspiciously and he tried to keep a low profile. Considering what had happened, it wasn't easy. He dreaded the moment it became public knowledge that Liz had left her entire estate to him – and that she'd died shortly after doing it. My God, then they'd really look at him suspiciously – they'd have a field day.

"Close the curtains, there's a good boy Ben, I know it's still early but I feel safer away from prying eyes." Jenny lay back against the cushions and closed her eyes.

Ben did as he was asked and stared down at his mother, wondering how she'd got to look so much older. Was it really the last few weeks that had done it - he didn't remember her looking like this just before Christmas?

"Mum, you know you're being ridiculous – there's no prying eyes out there. Anyway, what have you done that could possibly interest strangers?" He covered her knees with a woollen shawl. "There, you're nice and cosy now, why not have a little nap? Dad will be back soon and then you know you won't have the chance." She thought afresh what a nice son she had until he added," I'll have to go back to the city soon – my boss has already been very understanding about giving me extra bereavement leave."

"Oh Ben, not just yet surely, especially as you still have that dreadful head cold- or 'flu, if I'm not mistaken." Ben laughed and said it wasn't 'flu but just a little cold.

"Yes, but it won't shift, will it? Your system's obviously run down and you need a pick-me-up – why don't you go and see the doctor? You're still registered here, aren't you?"

"I have seen a doctor – I saw Uncle Peter just before he died and he gave me a clean bill of health." The change in his expression showed her he hadn't meant to tell her that. She hadn't known he'd seen Peter so recently. "Some tea Mum? Shall I make us a pot, just you and me?" He darted from the room before she could say anything else and left her there under the warm shawl - but also with a puzzled look on her face. She hadn't known that. She wondered exactly when he'd seen Peter – could it have been on the day he killed himself? Surely not or he would have mentioned it before. She soon drifted off however, the warmth of the fire and the thick shawl soon worked their charms.

The next couple of days passed and Ben phoned his boss to ask for another few days' leave. His mother was in such a state, he realised he couldn't leave her – and as for Bill, he'd lost so much weight, he didn't look like himself. The build of the rugby player had changed drastically and he thought his dad seemed older by the day. No, he couldn't leave them, it would be heartless to do that.

Tom and Bethany had left home already - there was nothing left for them in the town. Their mum and dad had gone out of their lives so suddenly, they were still reeling from the shock. It was less sad to be away from their home town for a while and anyway they'd still have to come back later, as their parents' bits and pieces had to be sorted out. The house was already on the market however, so their futures were looking good, but only financially good, not emotionally. Despite their ages, they still felt like a couple of orphans.

Bill and Jenny knew they'd never feel the same again. Bill continued to go to the office however which was really a Godsend as it kept his mind focussed. And he still had to make public Liz's will – God, her death seemed a long time ago now, but of course it was nothing of the sort – just a matter of a few weeks. The reading was in 2 days and it was to be held at Liz's home, its being more personal than his office. He was dying to get that over and done with but also dreading it for obvious reasons.

Jenny obviously didn't know what to do with herself but she did make a concerted effort to pull herself together. When the morning broke sunny and bright the next day and she could see the glorious daffodil blooms reaching from the ground, she decided to dress in her best clothes and go into town. She'd get something really nice for Bill and Tom's dinner and open a bottle of special wine – she'd even light some candles and prepare a really calorific and yummy pudding for afters. Yes, that's what she'd do.

Her little run-around car wouldn't start however, but undaunted, she checked the bus timetable and waited at the bus stop. It was only a short journey and she wouldn't have any parking problems, so she joined the queue and watched for a Number 37, which would drop her right in the middle of the High Street. She thought how well British people queued, so organised and patient. She soon reached town and found everything she wanted so she had a quick cup of coffee – but found the experience upsetting as she'd always had coffee after shopping with Liz or Maggie. Memories too sad to bear!

Re-joining the bus queue to get home, she watched again for the Number 37. She was standing in the middle of a large queue of people, including several noisy school children when she suddenly felt someone jostling her from behind. Glancing back over her shoulder, she saw it was a little old man. She rewarded him with a withering look before realising it couldn't have been him – he looked so innocent and disinterested. It must have been someone else. Then she spotted a double-decker bus coming but she couldn't quite make out its number. Was it the Number 37 – she hoped so as the children were becoming more boisterous and pushier. She couldn't quite see and strained forward. Suddenly she felt something prod into the small of her back – it felt sharp and pointed and made her lose her balance. She tripped into the gutter and fell right into the path of the double decker – which inevitably turned out to be a Number 37.

Luckily, she knew nothing after that shove in the back – the one that propelled her into the path of the oncoming bus. Splattered across the ground were her prized steaks intended for dinner – a treat for Ben and Bill - but now a bloody puddle of gore. The lower part of Jenny's body protruded from under the bus and although several people reached out to help her, it just wasn't possible. The queue of people, including the now subdued and scared children, were bumping into each other in confusion but someone had the presence of mind to ring for an ambulance. The paramedics soon arrived and lifted Jenny from the ground, whisking her away to the hospital.

As bad news usually does, it travelled fast and soon reached Bill at his office. A young policewoman had asked to see him and despite Wilma's reluctance to let her past without knowing the reason she wanted to see her boss, the policewoman pushed her way past and knocked on Bill's door. When he saw the uniform, his first thought was 'What now?' but then he saw the serious expression on her face. He went with her, not knowing much but fearing it nonetheless. As he left the office, Wilma's curiosity was in over-drive.

He was taken straight to the emergency ward at the hospital. He knew Jenny had been involved in some sort of accident, but he didn't know how serious it was. A white-coated doctor and a nurse were waiting for him and before he was allowed to see his wife, they prepared him for the worst – and the worst it was. Jenny's head was completely covered in bandages and deep red and blue bruises were beginning to form under her swollen eyes. They left him with her for a few moments and then took him into a side room, where it was explained it was unlikely that she'd last until morning. Her injuries were very serious -many he couldn't even see and several of her internal organs were damaged beyond repair.

"She's in no pain now, we've seen to that – but I'm afraid there's nothing we can do for her – except make her comfortable for the time she has left." The nurse brought him a cup of hot, sweet tea and said he could sit with his wife for as long as he needed. He took his cup of tea back into her cubicle, but saw from her grey pallor that the next morning was here already – and she'd passed away in the short time he'd been with the doctor. Like his friends, he too, now had no partner. His Jenny was gone and he was alone.

There was no-one to gather around him, offering sympathy and support – all his close friends had gone. As he prepared to leave the hospital, all he could think of was, 'How do I tell Ben – he loved her so.' He bent forward to kiss her forehead and his eye fell on her coat and scarf that still lay on a chair where they'd been hurriedly placed. He picked up the scarf and immediately smelt her familiar perfume, the one she always wore. Somehow the smell seemed so alive – and yet she was gone. He knew he wasn't thinking straight and placed the scarf reverently back on the chair. Then he spotted a white piece of paper sticking out of her coat pocket. He took it out and saw it wasn't paper, but rather a card – and there staring boldly up at him was a picture of the Cluedo's Mrs White in all her glory. As he stared at her, he could have sworn he saw a smile on her pinched little her face.

What did it mean? It had been an accident, hadn't it? There was no question about that – or was there? He decided he would take the card to Inspector Morrison – my God, that was five characters from the game and all found by the bodies of his friends – and of course his Jenny.

The inspector certainly thought the new card was important and he added it to the others. His team immediately set about contacting anyone who'd seen the accident to check on what had really happened. It was all so odd because everyone said the woman was just standing there one minute and the next, she was flying under the wheels of the bus. She hadn't staggered or looked dizzy. In fact, as one woman said, "It looked as if she was suddenly pushed from behind – she didn't seem to fall over at all."

It was an even smaller group of people who stood around Jenny's graveside one week later. They'd come to say goodbye to a lady who'd always been popular. The vicar gave a beautiful sermon in her honour and described her perfectly – a good wife and mother, a good friend and neighbour. He said sadly, "It was a terrible accident that took her away from us – one of those things in life we can never understand." Bill thought the vicar's words rang true – he would never understand what had happened to Jen, she just wasn't the sort who fell in front of buses.

The vicar's voice awoke him from his reverie. "A lovely lady whom we shall all miss but who will live on in our hearts forever.God Rest her Soul."

The few sad mourners broke away from the scene and Bill and his son walked off alone to think about Jen and to curse whoever had pushed her under the bus – because they were both convinced that's what must have happened. She'd always been such a careful, cautious person.

Turning the key in the lock, the two men were met with the delicious aroma of roast chicken. What on earth? Bill rushed along the hall and found the kitchen table set for two. Cutlery and place mats had been laid opposite each other and a tureen of cooked vegetables sat on the side unit. A bottle of wine had been uncorked and two sparkling glasses looked very welcome and inviting.

"Martha – it must have been Martha. What a thoughtful thing to do. She must have let herself in and arranged the meal." Bill felt tears come into his eyes and Ben took his arm, "Well, let's not let it go to waste Dad, let's enjoy it. She went to all this trouble after all." He took the perfectly cooked chicken from the oven. "Look, she's even left us a note saying not to clear up as she's coming back in the morning to do it. She thinks of everything, doesn't she? And the two men started eating the meal, only realising then how hungry they were. It was odd but kindness could say more than many words of sympathy.

Slices of succulent chicken with plenty of different veg and a perfectly cooked mushroom sauce were washed down with the excellent wine. For afters, Ben looked in the fridge and returned with a Baked Alaska covered in thick cream and extra strawberries – a meal fit for a king - and boy, did they do it justice.

But Bill had never felt so alone in his life. It was almost as though he'd died himself – odd moments had him not only missing his dead friends, but also envying them their inability to feel so sad and alone. 'Where were they all now – perhaps playing Cluedo together and looking down on him from above - after all it was quite possible, wasn't it?' Now his mind really was playing tricks on him and he had to stop imagining such things. He felt exactly what he was – the last of the Cluedo enthusiasts, and knew then he'd never play the game again.

He knew he'd have to get the reading of Liz's will out of the way before doing anything else. Her death now seemed so long ago and yet it wasn't – just a few weeks really - but then so much had happened since she died. Maybe after that, he'd be able to pull himself together properly and get on with his life. But he also knew that wasn't really likely.

The house was empty now. Ben had gone back to the city and the house was eerily silent. He still hadn't bought any food – it all seemed such a waste of time and so mundane. However, Martha had also left a home-made beef pie in the fridge – just waiting for him to pop it into the oven. What a treasure that woman was! He'd have to try and see her soon, he must owe her back wages. He went to bed that night, if not a happy one then certainly a full one - the pie had been very tasty and he was glad he'd not had to share it with Ben.

God, everything had been so exhausting lately and he let his head sink gratefully into the pillow when just as he was about to drop off, his drooping eyes caught sight of a card peeping out from under his bedside lamp.

Just for a moment, his eyes widened and he started to get up again, but the need to sleep and close his eyes was overwhelming and he just couldn't do it. The writing on the card was quite unclear but he could still make out the bolder letters and he saw the name Reverend Green. 'So that's who I am to be.' The thought made him try to get up again but he couldn't and fell back onto the pillow. My God, why was he so exhausted? He couldn't understand it at first – then everything suddenly became clear – the card was his warning that he was close to death.

Whoever had left it there was the same person who'd left all the others. The murderer was one person – but who? And why? He couldn't think any more, everything was so hazy – all he could do was allow himself to sink into the warmth of the bedcovers and let the comforting sleep claim him. Claim him forever it seemed. He was the final Cluedo player and he was slowly in the process of joining the others. Perhaps there'd be room for him at the game being played in Heaven. He'd soon know!

At five o'clock next morning when it was still dark and no window lights could yet be seen, Martha used her own key to open the front door. Even if she'd been spotted by anyone, they wouldn't have thought it odd – she was a familiar figure to the neighbours after all. Quietly, she climbed the stairs and tapped softly on Bill's bedroom door. Inside, she saw what she'd expected to see – what she was relieved to see. The big man was curled in a ball, still covered by the warm bedcovers, except they weren't warm any longer. They were cold, just as he was cold. She looked at the Cluedo card of Reverend Green and contemplated removing it – but decided to leave it, after all the police would almost expect a card by now – in line with the other deaths. The serial killer had struck again! The rest of the room should be just as Bill had left it and she made sure it was so, even leaving his clothes lying on the floor where he'd dropped them.

Before closing the bedroom door, she put on rubber gloves so as to leave no fresh finger prints. She was being extra careful although she needn't have worried as her prints were probably all over the house. Still, best to be careful in what would soon be the crime scene.

Downstairs, she quickly helped herself to some valuables – ones she'd always coveted. She'd already gathered the best pieces of Jenny's jewellery and had them safely tucked up at home. She'd taken them one at a time, as she'd done with the other two bitches. She'd really collected some lovely pieces, but she'd been careful not to take anything traceable – or that might have been missed because of its size. No, she'd been very selective – and these latest bits and pieces would sit nicely with the ones that had belonged to Jenny's friends, Liz and Maggie. What a good thing, they'd all been so well off and liked to spoil themselves with expensive treats. What a fortune she was soon going to have!

In the kitchen, she tidied away every scrap of food and all the utensils Bill had used – she wiped the kitchen table until it was spotless, washing up everything and putting it away in its proper place. Whoever found him would believe he'd come home from work and gone straight to bed, not wanting any supper. He'd been through so much of late, he'd probably lost his appetite. Yes, that's what they would say. Everything was cleaned and polished to her exacting standards and she used a heavy-duty black sack that she'd brought with her to tidy away any evidence of food – food that she'd brought with her, such as a half-eaten loaf, a dish of butter and the pie crumbs he'd carelessly dropped under the table – she'd dispose of everything before she reached home, dropping it into several street bins. It wouldn't do if any scraps were found in her own bin. She'd picked that up from the many crime dramas she watched on television.

Looking around carefully, she was pleased that each room was immaculate and just as it should be – being a stickler for detail, she checked everything a second time and was happy there was absolutely no evidence of her having been there when Bill died. No, that would never do.

She was pleased with her morning's work - everything had worked according to plan. Now she would keep well away from the house and leave the discovery of his body to someone else. She had plenty of other clients with whom she could be busy. Fingers crossed, he wouldn't be found for at least a couple of days, by which time the cyanide would have left his system – something else she'd learned from the TV programmes. There'd be no proof left to show he'd been poisoned. The poor man must have died of a broken heart, she could hear the police say. And even if the worst happened and a trace of poison was found - well the Cluedo card by his bedside would cry out 'The Serial Killer strikes again!' Yes, timid little Martha would never be suspected of such a cruel – and clever - act– she was after all' just everyone's little home help.' It was still dark when she closed door and walked quickly down the garden path, her flat pumps making no noise in the morning air.

No-one was too surprised when Bill didn't turn up for work for the next couple of days. If a needed to rest and not to face the world, it was him. Anyway, Wilma had noticed he was starting a cold when she last saw him and with that and Jenny's funeral, he was entitled to stay away from work.

Bill's colleague Malcolm took over the reading of the will and when he saw who wale beneficiary, he was glad Bill wasn't there. He would know anyway as he'd been involved in drawing it up. Everyone assembled in Liz's sitting room and Malcolm's rather pompous voice called for silence, something that wasn't really necessary as only three people were there. Normally he'd have mentioned the smaller bequests first with the larger ones to follow but on this occasion, that wasn't necessary. The whole of the Estate and the big house itself, with all its contents and a car, had been left to Bil – as had the rights to all stocks and shares in her possession. Malcolm was rather embarrassed by this as the three people who were there, had obviously expected something – or they wouldn't have come.

He cleared his throat and added, "I'm afraid Bill is unable to attend this reading as he's apparently come down with a heavy head cold or even 'Flu. In fact, he hasn't been seen for a couple of days now – but Wilma his secretary has gone around to his house to make sure he's all right, so no-one need worry. It didn't look as if anyone had been worrying anyhow."

And that was the reading of Liz's last will and testament. The three others in the room just sat there, saying nothing. There was Jonathan the gardener, his father the farmer and Martha the home help. Three people who'd obviously been told something was coming their way. There was no mention of anyone other than her friend Bill. It had been short and to the point, with no mention of the farmer, Jonathan or Martha. Mind you, in Jonathan and his father's case, it had been Dominic who'd promised 'some little inheritance.' Liz could of course have honoured her husband's promise, but she didn't and there was nothing that could be done about that. The two men rose from their chairs and quietly left the office, 'no use crying over spilt milk son,' Jonathan's father told him, 'You win some and lose some.' Come on, I'll buy you a pint.' And they left the building in a dignified manner.

Martha however, just continued to sit there, hands clasped on her knees. She daren't say anything or the lawyer would have heard a mouthful of profanity. Liz had promised her so many things and yet, she hadn't even left her a single penny – or a small keepsake. She sat in silence, both sad and angry at the same time. She reached for her bag which was resting against her chair and she took out a large white envelope. She handed it to Malcolm who'd been studiously avoiding her eyes and asked him to read it. "Read it aloud if you would. I'd like to be sure you I did understand it." Malcolm unfolded the document and was surprised to see it was another will, dated several months before the one he'd just read. He checked that it was duly signed, dated and witnessed. The witness had been Martha herself.

He read aloud,

'To all concerned. I leave my house, its contents and my entire Estate to my close friends Bill and Jenny, then Peter, and Maggie - to inherit in that order. They have always been good to myself and my late husband Dominic and always treated us kindly. I wish them great happiness in the future. Should however, these friends die before the reading of this will, my house, its contents and the rest of my Estate, should automatically pass to Martha, my loyal and hardworking home help who has looked after me for many years. In this legal will,

I attest my wishes to be honoured and acted upon as I have directed. I declare I am of sound mind and body.'

Liz's signature was perfectly clear and unequivocally identical to the one in the more recent will. The date and Martha's witnessing signature were also clear. The date was several months before the date of the other will, so making the one Martha had produced, invalid, null and void. Liz had obviously done the dirty on her and failed to tell her she had changed her mind. Malcolm looked thoroughly embarrassed but, in his experience, such things often happened. Martha snatched the will from his hands and tore it into little pieces so angry was she. The tiny pieces of paper fell on the floor, but mostly in the bin and she made sure the pieces were very small indeed. The man felt sorry for her and offered to get her a cup of tea. She declined and moved quickly to get out of the office before that secretary came back with news of Bill's death. No, that would never do.

The earlier will had been thoroughly destroyed and was now in pieces and Martha felt confident even the scraps would go through the office shredder. Her mind was in turmoil and she had to think fast – if the police had seen her will, she was petrified they'd suspect her of ending the lives of all those mentioned in it – all those beneficiaries who had come before her in the order of inheritance. The police may not have been very successful in discovering who was responsible for the murders, but even they would be able to work out that she had an obvious motive. And she couldn't have let that happen – hence the angry shredding of her copy of the will before anyone else could see it. As for Malcolm – if ever it came up, she'd just deny its existence – it would only be his word against hers after all – and she was such a meek and mild lady, no-one would suspect her of lying.

So, she moved quickly before Wilma returned and as she travelled home on the bus, she realised she was seething and that all she felt after killing all those people, was pleasure – pure, unadulterated pleasure. She'd murdered them all and was proud of it. Even Peter, whose guilt had made him take the whisky and pills to his room and end it all. She'd whispered in his ear about how guilty he should feel – Maggie hadn't deserved what he'd done to her. His use of her as a servant to carry out his errands was the reason she'd been in the bank when it was being robbed. He was a weak man and she 'guilt-tripped' him very successfully. She wasn't in the least sorry she'd pushed him over the edge. In fact, she'd even provided the whisky and pills to move things along. It was the job of the home help to help her employer after all.

Yes, she'd 'd caused all those deaths, both directly and indirectly and all for what? For absolutely nothing, she'd just learned. Her stop was coming up and as she got up, she was smiling. She realised she'd really enjoyed ending the lives of those people for whom she'd worked for so many years – and worked hard for the pittance they'd given her. They had all looked down their noses at her – the woman from the rough end of town whom they liked to patronise. Oh, she knew how they saw her! Not once did they ever ask her to sit down and join them in a drink, never once did they invite her to join them in their stupid, pathetic game of Cluedo. They'd only ever treated her as a servant and enjoyed the times they could patronise her – even forcing old clothes on her that had belonged to someone not yet cold in his grave. Yes, they really had been something – those nouveau-riche middle class fools, who'd never understood what real charity and kindness was all about.

As she stepped onto the pavement, her thoughts were, 'And I've been out of pocket paying those men to rob the bank and shoot Maggie. But that cost was worth it and it allowed me to use my imagination and come up with 'a cunning plan.' She knew those two idiots she'd paid would keep their mouths shut – after all she had plenty on them. No price had been s too high to pay for that kind of satisfaction.'

Sitting in her own kitchen, the thoughts crowded into her head and she found she was still shaking with anger. She'd done it all for nothing! Although at least she still had her many valuable acquisitions. She crossed to her secret hiding place under the cooker and put her new trinkets safely inside. She had quite a haul now – a lot of money if she wasn't mistaken. She'd have to travel into the city soon to pass everything to her 'fence', who'd been successful in the past at finding good buyers for her. Yes, she had quite a lot in her bank account now.

She switched on the kettle – a nice cup of tea was what she deserved. But the bitterness she felt for Liz was like a bad taste in her mouth and spoiled the taste of the drink. What a vile, dishonest woman she'd turned out to be. And what a waste of effort it had all been! She had only her trinkets to show for it. Mind you, they were some trinkets!

As she sipped the bitter tea, she indulged in some self-praise - after all, she'd been pretty clever and shrewd the way she'd managed all the deaths – and no-one was any the wiser. The little trick of using the Cluedo cards was inspirational and she held her head with pride at her cleverness. It had added mystery to the murders and obviously confused the police – after all they'd made no arrests to date. She'd been questioned of course after every death, but then so had everyone else. They were obviously out of their league when dealing with this timid, little woman. Mind you, she'd always made sure it was a challenge for them - always taking care she wasn't anywhere near where and when the murders happened – oh yes, she'd been pretty clever.

Two days later, she again visited Bill's house as usual. She met Jonathan at work in the garden there, "Morning Jonathan, I've just come to see if he still wants my services now that there's only him in the house. How are you – still smarting from the disappointment of the will? I know I am!" It was a sore point with the young man and she knew it!

He decided to ignore her and answered, "It's bitter this morning, isn't it? I haven't seen the gentleman yet although I've rung the doorbell a few times." He went on digging the beds to aeriate the soil for the coming Spring. It was easy to see his disappointment and it made her smile – to see someone as miserable as she was. Sharing misery with someone else seemed to make it easier to bear.

"There's no point in my trying to see him then, if he's not answering the door. It's probably because he doesn't want to see anyone just yet," and she turned around and walked back down the path. She saw the big black car sitting across the road and she knew exactly who was inside.

"Good morning Inspector – Sergeant. Chilly today, isn't it?" She called out and nodded to the two men. Head high and straight backed, she didn't pause but continued to keep walking. She wouldn't have looked so smug however had she heard the conversation the men were having.

"Shouldn't we be taking her down to the station Inspector, now we've been closely monitoring her movements for some time – we're pretty sure she's been involved with everything that's gone on. She's obviously deranged if not just plain evil and she's cunning – so cunning." The police sergeant was eager to wipe the smug look from Martha's face.

"Everything we know to date Sergeant is circumstantial – we have no actual evidence. The CPS would throw it out as soon as it hit their desk – we'll have to keep right on digging until we have unequivocal evidence. You're right of course, she is a cunning and manipulative woman, who needs to be caught before she does more damage." He reached inside his jacket and produced a wallet which he opened and held out to the sergeant.

"Why, that's one of those game cards. Why have you got it Sir?" he looked at it closely, "Reverend Green, I don't think I've seen that one yet."

"It's the final character in the game – and still to be used, but it's up to us to make sure Martha doesn't use him." He smiled down at the card before returning it to his wallet. "We've still got some digging to do, but should we be unsuccessful in finding the evidence we need, this chap will take care of the home help. I've made a pledge to myself that she's not going to get away with the crimes she's committed."

"And how exactly are you going to do that, Sir? You said yourself the evidence we have is circumstantial – we need so much more." The sergeant was beginning to think his boss was imagining the power of the Reverend Green card.

Out of the blue, the inspector suddenly said, "You haven't forgotten that I retire next month, have you? I've given forty years dedicated service – and after next month, I'll be free to act differently – to do what needs doing and not just what society allows. I plan to take the bull by the horns and in this case, make sure justice is served. If we don't have Martha banged to rights by the time I leave, I'll seek help from the Reverent gentleman here and between us, we'll do the necessary. To put it bluntly, I'll end her life myself - and having done so I'll leave the Cluedo character as my calling card. Her death will be put down as yet another serial killing by whoever is obsessed by the game of Cluedo." He was obviously enjoying telling the sergeant of his intentions and had been planning to take him into his confidence for some time now.

He went on, "The other cards were deliberately used to mirror the victims' own characters, so I think a gentle, sensitive member of the clergy is about right for the timid unobtrusive Martha. She never pushed herself forward and rarely spoke unless she was asked a question - and yet, she somehow always managed to know everything that was going on."

For a moment or two, the sergeant didn't know what to say. Had he heard right? Morrison must be mad. "You can't do that Sir – I couldn't let you do that – not now you've confided in me. It's my duty to report your intentions, you know that." He paused again and added, " Why have you told me this now – my God, I wish you hadn't?"

"We work so closely together Sergeant and I had to tell someone – I needed to know how you would feel if she was to avoid arrest and get off scot free with all the cruel murders – and I think I know that now– you agree there's no question as to her guilt. You know she did it, don't you? "He didn't wait for an answer – he didn't need one.

"You should be aware though that if I have to carry out my plan and end her life, I intend to leave it up to your conscience, whether to report me or not. Only time will show what you decide but you should be aware I intend to deny this conversation ever took place – and as for the act itself, I think you know me well enough to know I'll leave absolutely no clues. You should remember a detective of forty years' service knows only too well how to conceal evidence. "He laughed at the sergeant's expression and said, "You'll never catch me Gov, Honest you won't!"

He asked one more question, "Tell me Sergeant – do you think it's right that someone like Martha is allowed to get away with such heinous crimes – crimes of which we both know she's guilty? Well Sergeant, answer that one."

"Oh, she's guilty all right but I agree it's all circumstantial evidence so far and without better leads and a few lucky breaks, it would probably be impossible to prove in a court of law. That is of course as things stand right now!"

The young sergeant, who still had his whole career before him and knew blotting his copy book at this stage would have catastrophic consequences for his future, nonetheless said with conviction, "As far as I'm concerned Sir, we've never had this conversation. In the meantime, will you promise that for the next month, we'll try our very best to get the necessary substantive evidence to charge her with the murders? And if you honour that promise, you can rely on my silence.

"You have my word Sergeant, now let's get started." And he started the engine but not before he'd patted Reverend Green's card nestling in his wallet. "But I have this chap ready, waiting and willing to be used - just in case we fail to find the evidence. In the meantime, let's allow her to enjoy her moment of triumph – she thinks she's in the clear, but we know different, don't we? She'll be very surprised too to learn that we know about the stolen jewellery and the Fence in the city. Sometimes justice let's guilty people slip through its fingers and that's why I have a contingency plan. We'll get her one way or the other Sergeant and if it turns out to be the other, we'll know we've done our very best first. Out of interest sergeant, did you notice the box that was sticking out of her shopping bag?"

"I'm afraid I didn't Sir. Why do you ask – is it important?"

"Not yet, but it may become important. It was a brand new, still in its cellophane wrapper, game of Cluedo. One wonders what she plans to do with that – another reason to watch her every move."

Whilst this conversation was taking place, Martha was already on the train to the city, her bag bulging with lovely trinkets, courtesy of her recent employers. She smiled at her reflection in the train window – it was the smile of someone in total control, someone who feels secure in the knowledge that the police suspect her of nothing whatsoever. You and I know she's wrong however – don't we – and that's for us to know and for her to find out? And she will – eventually - one way or the other.

She Didn't Let A Trivial Thing Like Death Stop Her

Her face was crushed against the hard concrete and although she tried to move her hands, she found she couldn't. She stopped trying to move then and just lay there on the cold ground, feeling the warm blood ooze from the wound in her head. She could feel it slowly trickling down her forehead, but strangely enough, she wasn't in pain. She was numb and feared she must be dying. Could a person die feeling no pain – yes, she was sure they could. The heavy sleet bit into her cheeks like small stones – they were coming down as fast as bullets from a gun and she worried that her new coat would be ruined – it was new after all. Despite what had just happened, she found the time to worry about her coat – how on earth was that? Why did she wear that coat tonight, it wasn't even water proof - she should have worn a different one, more in keeping with the weather man's predictions? She found it amazing that she was thinking of the most trivial things, especially at a time like this.

She'd already blanked out a couple of times, but had seen the man quite clearly as he leaned over her and pressed against her. He didn't seem in a hurry and must have been feeling quite confident, as when he'd finished his attack, he almost strolled away casually from her dead body.

Her friends in the pub had told her not to leave when she did, "Wait for us and we can all go home together – you know you're safe with us." They laughed as they spoke but it was the drink talking and one of them said, "It's not safe to go out alone at this time of night – someone might ravish you." More laughter as someone else shouted, "Oh, yes please." Amongst the raucous laughter, she managed to escape out of the door.

In the street she was thinking, 'God, it's really coming down! Better hurry!' And she pulled her collar up around her neck and started to walk as quickly as she could. She shouldn't have worn such high heels, they didn't help on the slippery pavement and for a moment, she contemplated taking them off. She could move so much more quickly in her bare feet. 'No, I can't do that – it's too cold.' And so, she hobbled on.

The street was very quiet. It was just a bit too early for the pubs to be emptying out yet. She'd only left her friends early because of a growing migraine – or she'd have been with them still, arguing about whose turn it was to buy the next round. The heels of her shoes tapped loudly in the quiet of the night and then, something made her turn around to look back into the darkness. Yes, there was a man there, but he seemed to be hurrying to get out of the heavy rain as well and showed no interest in her. She turned into the avenue across from the park. She lived at the far end of it and it wouldn't take her long to reach home. Now, she could hear the man's footsteps, keeping time with her own and she glanced back nervously. It was odd how being alone with just one other person brought on a feeling of paranoia. 'For Goodness Sake,' she told herself, 'It's just a man going home after a night out. He's not interested in you.'

But she'd begun to feel nervous and moved faster, the clickety-click of her shoes beating quick time on the pavement. 'Why weren't there any other people around – the avenue was so quiet tonight? She wished now that she'd done what her friends had suggested and waited for them, but 'Oh no, my head hurts! Anyway, I know best!' Her home was only five minutes away and she'd soon be there. She glanced over her shoulder again to see where he was – she supposed he must live in the avenue as well although she was sure she didn't recognise him. Now, there was no sign of him. 'Thank God, he'd gone!' She felt better and even began to walk slower, despite the rain which was fast becoming little bits of ice.

He hadn't gone away however, but had somehow slipped past her and was coming towards her now. He must have turned back at the park and moved very fast to get past her! 'Now, why did he do that?' she wondered. They would soon pass each other and she would keep her eyes lowered so he wouldn't see the fear in her eyes. 'I'm being silly! He's probably quite harmless,' she told herself, but as they met, she realised she'd been right to worry about him. He reached out and grabbed her, twisting her arms around her back before head-butting her hard on the forehead. She lost her balance and staggered against a hedge just as he put his hands around her neck. He was tall and he was strong, whereas she was quite small – too small to fight him off. She did try however, but couldn't manage it.

She tried to speak, to ask him to stop but no sound would come and he ripped off her long scarf and wound it tightly around her neck. He squeezed and squeezed, pulling it as tightly as he could. His eyes were bulging and his face was red. That was when she almost blanked out and slumped against him, but as she did, she grabbed the side of his head and tugged at his hair. In this position, she was staring directly into his eyes and she could see her own face reflected there. She was sure his face was burning into her own retina and would stay with her forever.Now, she could feel herself slipping down his front and when her body hit the ground, she heard his laughter. It wasn't an exaggerated, macabre laugh, just one that proved he was enjoying himself. For good measure and to make sure he'd finished her off, he pulled a heavy, metal torch from his coat pocket and cracked it hard against her head. That was when the blood came – the warm blood she felt running down her face - it contrasted with the cold hardness of the ground. Just for a second, she came to and saw him turn to walk away, but she'd already seen his face, when he'd had his hands around her throat. She'd definitely know him again she was sure – but she never got the chance and it was at that moment she died. A blackness filled her mind and she knew nothing more.

Her poor, crumpled body lay in the puddles, her long wet hair sticking to her face and the rain on the pavement slowly mixing with her blood. At least she knew no more and felt no pain or fear, but she did feel anger and her dying wish had been for revenge. It was strange that in the throes of death, she could think of such a thing as revenge – but she did! She could also hear her friends saying, "Don't go on your own – it's not safe out there." 'What rot,' she'd thought, 'I know these streets like the back of my hand.' But that knowledge hadn't helped, had it? On the point of death, she took with her a clear impression of his staring eyes as he squeezed and squeezed and a last thought struck her, 'I'll get even with you, see if I don't.'In her fingers, she held a few of his hairs from when she'd grabbed his head and her fingers closed automatically around them. Even at that moment, she knew she had to keep them safe – they might be useful.

Her body wasn't found until the next morning when the milk man made his deliveries. He could do nothing to help her, although he did try. She just had to lie there, knowing she'd lost her life and she watched as the police car and ambulance arrived together. She was dead and yet aware of everything that was going on around her. First, the police cordoned off the pavement and erected a temporary tent over her body. They worked around her with respect and care and even when she was enclosed in a long, black body bag, they did it gently. She watched them take away the tent and saw several policemen crawling up and down the road – into the road and up the nearest garden path. They even began knocking on the nearest doors in the hope someone had seen something. As she continued to stand there, she watched how busy everyone was and wished they'd been there the night before. 'He wouldn't have been so smart then,' she thought grimly. Slowly, she began to realise how surprising it was that she could watch and hear everything that was going on – but she could. She was there and yet she wasn't there – no-one seemed to be able to see her.

'My God, I'm a ghost, that's why they can't see me. I should have realised when I was able to sit beside my own body throughout the whole night. It was as if there were two of me – one alive and one dead. As the ambulance drove off with her inside, she suddenly saw him. He was standing behind a small crowd of onlookers and she heard him speak to another man, "What's happened here then?" The hypocrite looked genuinely concerned. When the man told him about the girl's death, she saw him shake his head in sympathy. He almost looked like a normal human being – but she knew better.

'What a hypocritical bastard." She thought and moved over to stand right in front of him. Of course, she was invisible to him, although he did try to swat away a non-existent fly that was obviously bothering him. His action made her wonder, 'Did she have even the tiniest power to make her presence felt? It would be great if she had - but she was just a fly to him! He walked off into the park and began to disappear into the distance. 'What did she do now? Did she follow him to see where he was going, or did she stay with the police who were still investigating the area? Decisions! Decisions!' She started to follow her murderer, decision made! She could probably do more good by seeing where he was going.

It was strange, but she knew exactly what she had to do. She may be dead, but she could still follow him and find out who he was, where he lived and worked etc. She was new to this spiritual existence so she didn't yet know her capabilities – if there were any. With the passage of time, she might find she had some powers. Either way, she knew what she had to do and that was to make sure he was caught and made to pay for what he'd done. That was her goal now and she would do whatever she could to make it happen. She found she suddenly had a steel-like determination that she'd never had when she was alive.

She followed him across the park and saw him disappear into a high building. 'His place of work, no doubt.' She passed through the large glass window on the ground floor, something she found easy now she was a ghost. She joined him in the lift and they both got out on the third floor. She was slowly becoming used to being around people, unseen and undetected.

"Good Morning Mr Roberts." A young receptionist called out and he smiled in reply.

Now, she knew not only where he worked but what his name was. She caught sight of herself in a large, guilt mirror and was astonished to see how normal she looked. She wore the same clothes she'd worn last night and her long, blond hair was curly and shiny again. She looked quite different from the drowned rat she'd been the night before and for a moment, she even questioned if she could really be dead – she looked so well and healthy, but she knew she was the only one who could see her reflection in the mirror. If she was dead, why was she still here, able to move around the place at will – she sensed she had a special mission and that was to help catch her murderer. Her hatred of the man's face as he strangled her had somehow worked a miracle and bestowed on her an ability to see what was happening after her own death. 'Well,' she thought, 'Ours is not to wonder why, ours is but to do or die!' And she'd certainly done the latter!

"Arabella." She heard her name being called and looked around in surprise. 'Could someone see her after all?' But it was the receptionist's name as well and not because she'd suddenly become visible. A random thought came into her mind, making her more determined to follow the man, 'Isabella Wright aged 24 – Rest in Peace.' It upset her to think she'd never reach 25 and she had him to thank for that.

She was already learning some ghostly skills and found that, by thinking of another place, she could manifest her spiritual self there. Now, she found herself standing in the detective's office – the detective who was handling her own case. He was discussing the murder with two other men and all agreed it had been a motiveless crime. A killing for killing's sake and nothing more. It was the worst kind of murder from their point of view as, with no motive, it was much harder to detect the killer.

"Nothing was taken from her it seemed – but the attack was horrendous. A spur of the moment killing – he was in the right place at the right time and the streets were quiet and dark with the heavy rain keeping people indoors."

One of the others added, "I reckon she was an easy target, walking alone. No-one even heard her cry out, but we're still checking on that – maybe someone will have heard something and only realise later."

Arabella spoke to herself, 'But I didn't call out – he didn't give me the chance, so there was nothing for people to hear. It was all over so quickly and when he produced that heavy torch, I knew my last moment had come.' She would have loved to be able to speak but of course, she couldn't. This is going to be frustrating, she thought, but I certainly won't give up trying.

She listened for a short time but learned nothing more. They were waiting for the forensic report they said, and for the post-mortem results and that was something she didn't want to see! She hoped they wouldn't forget the handful of his hair she'd managed to pull out, but of course they wouldn't do that – they just had to find the man it had belonged to.

She waited patiently in his building until he got up, put on his jacket and said goodnight to everyone there. He stopped at the receptionist's desk and appeared to flirt with her, but she was very young and kept her head down. Funny, but he seemed such an ordinary person – not someone who'd brutally murdered an innocent, young girl the night before. She knew she had a duty now to watch him closely – he could be a serial killer – she might not be the only victim. She couldn't let him kill again! 'Oh my God, had he killed before and how many times?' As she followed him home, she knew he was totally oblivious to her keeping so close. It was as though she was wearing a cloak of invisibility, which of course she was in a way.

He lived two streets away from the avenue where he'd killed her. She knew the place well and wondered how long he'd lived there – just two streets away from her own home. She'd probably passed him more than once without giving him a second glance. He suddenly turned into a small terraced house in a narrow street and she followed him inside the house. It was small and a bit cramped but decorated in a modern style with bright colours and some elegant furniture. She watched him as he opened his post and loosened his tie before throwing himself onto the sofa. Everything he did was so normal, totally unlike the actions of someone who'd killed a total stranger less than 24 hours before. How could he be so laid back? Why wasn't he reliving it in his mind? But then, maybe he was and it just didn't affect his conscience at all.

She supposed he was about 30 years of age, tall with dark hair – someone so ordinary, you could easily miss him in a crowd. That of course was his perfect protection – his everyday normality – a really ordinary bloke. She followed him later that night as he made his way to the pub that had been her local as well – the local she'd frequented with her friends. 'My God, it was her pub, yet she could have sworn she'd never noticed him there, but then why should she have done? She wondered if he'd been there on the night and followed her outside, having heard her girlfriends telling her not to go. 'It wasn't safe out there on her own.'

Isabella Wright again spent the evening in the pub and waited for him to decide it was time to go home. She'd watched him chatting with a couple of men and laughing as though he hadn't a care in the world. But he did stiffen and look uncomfortable when the pub door opened and two men came in to question people – especially any who'd been there the night before as well. Not for the first time, she wished she could make herself heard but all she could do was hover around whilst the detectives went from one person to another.

"And you Sir, did you happen to be here last night as well?" the younger man asked him.

"Why yes Officer, I was here last night. I usually pop in for a pint and a chat but never stay long. What's this all about anyway?"

The detective explained there'd been a murder not far from the pub, "A woman was attacked and left for dead and we're trying to find someone who might have seen her leaving the pub last night."

"How terrible – poor young girl!" He looked genuinely sorry for her and tutted loudly, shaking his head in disbelief.

"I didn't say it was a young girl Sir – I just said a woman. How did you know the victim was young?" The young policeman was pretty sharp. Alan Roberts told himself off – he'd have to be more careful in future if the police were going to be around here questioning people.

"Well, of course I didn't know – I just assumed, I suppose. Why on earth was she walking alone on such a dreadful night?" He actually looked concerned. "God, he's a good actor,' Arabella thought.

"Why shouldn't she have walked home in the rain? Are you suggesting she was wrong to do that?" Arabella was impressed with the young policeman.

"Now look here Officer, I meant no such thing. I'm just voicing an opinion, that's all. Are you quite finished with me now – it's my time for going home."

The detective wrote his name and address in a notebook 'Alan Roberts'. Isabella wasn't likely to forget that name in a hurry. Of course, she followed him home but he did nothing out of the ordinary. Well, he wouldn't, would he – with all the policemen nosing around?

She continued to follow him for a few days and nights, but he behaved impeccably. She went back to the police building and to the office where she'd first heard the detectives talking. She sat on one of the desks whilst her case was discussed and heard something to her advantage. They were looking at the forensic report which confirmed how she'd died – something, she already knew of course – but then they spoke about the hair that had been between her fingers.   According to the forensics, she'd apparently pulled out quite a bit of his hair – roots and all. Amazing! And now, she realised if only she could make them aware of Alan Roberts, they could tie him up with her murder and all from his DNA. She felt frustrated and useless but couldn't tell them anything. She consoled herself however, 'I think I'm making progress but I've a long way still to go.'

She had started to experiment – first with tiny objects and then slightly bigger ones - and after a while, she found she could move small, light things. 'What an achievement!'

She found that Alan Roberts actually led a very boring life. He went to an office every day and did the same tasks; he also flirted regularly with the girls in the office, especially the young receptionist. What he didn't know was that they all laughed at him behind his back. Arabella knew though! He wasn't a handsome man – just an ordinary one – and the girls weren't all that interested. That didn't stop him however, and each night at the pub, he offered to buy a drink for different young women. Of course, some of them accepted – why shouldn't they? It was better than having to buy their own. None of them ever left the pub with him and after her murder, they took to walking home in pairs or groups. They'd learned a lesson, it seemed – at her expense.

On this particular night, he finished his drink quickly and followed two girls out into the street. They were giggling and joking about how many drinks they'd had from the 'weird bloke' that night. He knew they were talking about him and he hated them. He thought, 'If only they'd part and go their separate ways, then I could teach at least one of them a lesson. Then, a miracle happened! He'd kept quite a distance behind as they walked along, giggling and screaming with laughter. They were quite drunk. 'What a pair of useless tarts they are'. He could help however, by ridding the world of one of them.'

They stopped at the corner and hugged each other good night, promising to meet up the next day. 'I'll see about that.' He smiled to himself cynically and followed the girl who went in the direction of the park. 'How ironic,' he murmured, 'the same direction as the floozy of the other night!'

'Floozy indeed! I'm no floozy, you creep!' And Isabella stuck right by his side whilst he carefully kept a safe distance between himself and the girl. He walked faster and closed in behind her – his trainers making no sound. Now, Isabella was scared – she knew what he was up to. 'What can I do? If only I could speak and warn her. She darted around him and even through him but he was intent on catching up with the girl and he waved her away like a fly. 'Can I really be mistaken for a fly?' she felt insulted. He was only a few feet away now and he could even hear the unsuspecting girl humming a tune. Isabella knew she had to do something – but what? She could think of nothing!

He grabbed the girl by the shoulders and held onto her. She didn't know what was happening. She tried to turn around to face him, but his strong grip was too much. She started to struggle but he held her by the neck - she could actually hear him laughing. She thought frantically and managed to blurt out, "Let me go please, I'll not tell anyone about you. I'm late home and my mother will be looking for me." It was a lot of words to find in such a situation, but she was desperate and naively hoped if she pleaded, he might let her go.

Her words only served to make him mad and he reached into his pocket for that handy, metal torch – the one he always carried with him – just in case. He raised it high above his head and brought it down on hers with a mighty force. Blood spurted over his hand, but he seemed to enjoy that. He was much taller and stronger and he felt her body slump against him. Good he thought, she was probably unconscious now. She wasn't though but she thought if she pretended to be, he might let her go, thinking her already dead. The empty streets and darkness added to the horror of what was happening. He stood there admiring his work but suddenly she screamed – not particularly loudly but enough to make him realise his job wasn't yet done – well, not satisfactorily done. He cursed at her and said, "All the couch potatoes are watching their tellies just now – no-one will hear you. You're as good as dead." And he raised his foot to kick her – one swift and hard kick to the head should do it.

But before he did, Arabella used the power she'd only just learned she had and whistled very loudly – it was shrill and piercing and distracted him for a moment. He thought someone must be coming – and that would never do. The girl also reacted to the loud whistle, which Arabella repeated again and again. She stared straight into the girl's eyes, desperately trying to get a message across. 'Run! Run!' She tried to say, but knew she wasn't capable of speech.

The girl was capable of reaching into her coat pocket and bringing out a small black object. She hadn't had the chance to do it before and her poor, blood-covered fingers were almost too weak to press its trigger, but Arabella put her hand over the girl's and squeezed as hard as a ghost could. She liked to think she could make a difference.

The girl's mother had insisted she carry it with her when she went to meet her friends, but she'd never thought she'd have to use it. In fact, she even forgot she had it. Well, she was wrong – she did have to use it! it slipped through her sweating, bloody fingers and fell to the ground, making a clattering noise. She reached out to pick it up and he saw what it was. The bitch had a taser. Now, it was his turn to be scared and he backed away, turned on his heels and ran into the dark park. There were no lights at all there, so he could disappear completely.

Suddenly, brightness flooded down the garden path and a light came on in the hallway of the nearest house. A man came to the door, shouting "What's all this commotion then? Get away from here or I'll ring the police."

He saw the young girl lying in the street and rushed down the path. She looked dreadful, but managed the words, "Please help me. He's gone now." No explanation was needed – she'd been attacked and left for dead. He rang 999.

Arabella left her then, knowing she was safe and rushed after Alan Roberts, but he'd disappeared amongst the trees and she decided not to follow him any longer – she'd helped the girl and that was all that mattered. She was still alive!" Arabella slowed down and made her way towards his house – she'd hang about there until he left for work the next day. At least, she'd helped to avoid a disaster. 'Funny,' she thought, 'I could never whistle before – well not well anyway – but I'm jolly good at it now.'

Two days later, newspapers and TV programs were full of, not only the girl's attack, but also of another attack on a separate girl – but this one hadn't lived to tell the tale. She had been attacked on the far side of the park and found very close to her home – at least her body had been found. She'd had no-one to help her, unlike her friend. Arabella realised she'd been found on the opposite side to where he'd attacked the 'taser' girl. These two must be the friends who'd left the pub together the previous night. Had he really struck twice on the same night? The newspaper reports said the dead girl had been going home after a night out with a friend, but it was too soon for any further details. The article went on to say it was the second attack carried out on the one night and that the first girl was presently in Intensive Care in hospital.

Arabella was thinking frantically 'My God, when he ran across the park, he must have come upon the second girl, and angry at having failed the first time, he'd done his worst and murdered her. He'd attacked another young, innocent girl – someone he'd picked at random and not because he had any grudge against her. The man was a fiend and was clearly a serial killer. Arabella 'thought' herself to where the dead girl had been found and could immediately sense all around the frightening atmosphere. The air reeked of murder and she could picture the girl lying there with him standing over her. Her poor young body lying on the ground, vulnerable and easy prey to an animal like Alan Roberts. She felt sad that whilst she'd been saving one girl, she'd left things wide open for him to attack the other. There was not one iota of doubt in her mind that the murder had been committed by the same man – plain, ordinary Alan Roberts that no-one would look at twice.

She went to the hospital to find the girl, who was being protected by a policeman, but he was stationed outside in the corridor. 'Maybe there was something she could learn from the girl. Anything at all would help and the more she learned, the better equipped she'd be to help the police. 'My powers are getting stronger very slowly, but they are getting stronger – maybe one day, I'll be able to tell the police who they should be looking for.' She could only hope!

The girl, who was called Judith, was fast asleep when she arrived in the hospital room. Arabella had all the time in the world, so she waited patiently for her to wake up and in due course, she did. 'How can I communicate with her? God, this is frustrating – to know so much, yet be unable to share it.' Judith was stirring from unconsciousness but wasn't yet really back in the room - it was a sort of limbo and for a moment, she thought she was back in the street being attacked. She was struggling and kicking at the blanket, trying to get away from him. Arabella tried to connect with the girl's muddled brain and she whistled – her only skill – and saw the girl's eyes widen with fear. She stopped struggling but was still confused. Arabella bent down and whispered in her ear, "Was it the man from the pub, the one who kept buying you drinks – was he the one who attacked you?' My God, she could whisper – she'd not tried it before, but it seemed to work.

The girl looked puzzled. She couldn't see anyone in the room and yet, she heard the whispered words. "I don't know," she whispered back, "I never saw his face." And then she said quite clearly, "I feel I'd met him before but it's no good, I don't think I could identify him." Arabella was disappointed but what could she do? Judith was confused, wounded and scared and certainly not up to any pressure – even from an invisible whisperer.

In the meantime, the Public Enemy Number One decided to keep a low profile for a while – but my, he had enjoyed himself the previous night. The rush of power it gave him at that moment when he squeezed the life out of the victim, was worth any risk. So, he'd failed with the first one, but he'd almost succeeded. He'd not managed to kill her, but he'd come pretty close and could still feel the pleasure of the attack. Next time, he'd be quicker – at least she'd not seen his face, so he felt pretty safe. He swore and murmured, 'The bitch has made it necessary for me to stay away from my regular pub – but I'm sure I'll be able to go back after a while, when the police have cleared off. I like to choose my victims from there – but it's not compulsory that I do – it might be safer to go elsewhere – safer in the long run.

He settled back on the sofa to relive the 'near murder' and wondered how many more killings he'd be able to do. 'As many as I want,' he reassured himself. He'd settled quite well in this area after he'd requested a transfer from his previous job in Sheffield.   Luckily, his company was big enough to have different offices around the country. His job and his current little house suited him very well – and it was far enough away from those nasty murders that had taken place in the Sheffield area. He thought he'd mix with a better class of people here – and killing them would be even better. Anyway, he'd already come close to being detected a couple of times when he'd been questioned by the police. 'As I thought, a superior class here – and they're all just waiting for me. And it's better to be hanged for a classy sheep, than for a dowdy lamb.' He smiled at his little joke and reached for a book from the pile on the sideboard. He'd read for a little, then he'd think about what to do next.

He soon dropped off however and found himself dreaming about his late mother. 'God, how he'd hated her! She was a real bitch and no mistake!' In the dream however, everything was surreal and she was sitting in the garden at home and pouring tea from a chintz teapot. "Come along Alan – tea's ready," and she cut him a generous slice of cake, which she laid on a pretty pink plate. He could see himself sitting there amongst the roses with a loving mother plying him with delicious food. In his sleep, he began to sweat. Something was wrong – he'd never done that with his mother – she'd always treated him like a stranger – no, not a stranger – more like an enemy. He'd hated his mother and could never do anything right in her eyes. She was the reason he'd always felt inferior – she'd always made him feel less than adequate. Oh yes, she had a lot to answer for.'

He remembered how she used to ridicule his attempts at homework and wouldn't come to the school on parents' night. She didn't even allow him to dress like the other kids – his clothes were usually tatty and more in fashion many years before – some of them were even torn and they always came from the charity shops. A couple of times, he'd tried to bring a friend home, but she'd always meet him at the door and send the friend away. She liked to embarrass him – and she was good at it. She used to blame him for her husband deserting her – she told him his father had said he'd never wanted a child and certainly not one like Alan.

"You're ugly and thick. I can't imagine where you've come from – certainly not from my side of the family." And she'd push him away and carry on with checking her Bingo cards. She really was a hateful woman. She treated him this way just once too often. It was on his eighteenth birthday and as was usual, he'd expected nothing, which was exactly what he got.

"It's time you found yourself another job, now you've lost the one you had – you're too useless to hold down even the simplest job.You've been fed and clothed at my expense all these years and I've had to deny myself things I wanted – and all because of you! It's time I was able to sit back and let you take the strain." As usual, she was sitting at the kitchen table with a glass of Gin in one hand and a cigarette in the other. Alan knew she'd never deprived herself of anything – deprived him, yes – but never herself.

He stood behind her and imagined what it would be like to put his hands around that scrawny neck and squeeze – very hard. Then he found himself doing it. She'd gasped and then choked. The cigarette fell to the floor and she spilled her drink on the tablecloth – it spread out slowly, into a dark circle. He could still see that circle even now. 'God, it felt good to see her lying there sprawled across the table. Her face had gone red, with blotches of blue from the lack of oxygen. He wouldn't have to listen to her ridiculing him any more – she was gone out of his life – and how he'd enjoyed doing it. The pleasure was immense.

He went upstairs and brought down a thick blanket. She was so thin, he could easily lift her and lay her on the floor, where he wrapped her up tightly. He bound the blanket with a thick plastic rope he'd had in his tool shed and tied it with very secure knots. 'They won't come loose in a hurry!' he told himself and stood back to admire his work. He was tempted to take a photo of the bundle, but realised that would be silly. He must leave no evidence of what had happened.

Calmly, he crossed to the stove and put the kettle on to boil. 'He needed a nice cup of tea, and something to eat – he was feeling rather peckish. He hadn't eaten for some time.' Replenished and content, he waited until it was dark and carried the bundle to a wheelbarrow in the back yard. He walked slowly and he hoped, innocently, towards a wooded area – not quite a forest – but with plenty of trees. He'd placed a shovel under the body in the barrow and when he arrived in the middle of the wood, he dug as deep a hole as he could. He dumped her body into the dark earth, with no qualms whatsoever. She was just another piece of rubbish to be got rid of. He carefully covered the earth and scattered around some rocks and broken pieces of branches. It looked quite natural and he was pleased with his excellent work. She wouldn't be found easily, he felt sure of that. If anyone asked about her, he'd tell them, 'the old drunk has gone off to join her husband.'

"What and left you to cope on your own?" some sympathisers asked.

"I'm almost nineteen, you know. I can manage." And that was that. She hadn't been a popular woman and she didn't get on with her neighbours, so no-one was really bothered.

That night, all these memories filled his dreams, all muddled with strange confusing images, but just before he awoke, he was back amongst the roses, drinking tea with his 'gentle mother.' That was how he would choose to remember his childhood and there was no-one to say different.

Arabella was watching him twisting and turning in his sleep. 'That must be some dream,' she thought. She didn't know he was actually a creation of his upbringing and that he'd turned out the way he had mainly because of an uncaring and cruel mother. She just knew he was a monster who found pleasure in doing evil things. She'd found some papers in his home and she learned that he'd come from Sheffield – only about six months before. Maybe she'd haunt the local library and see if she could discover anything about his time in Sheffield. She'd go at night when it was closed to the public – better that, than people seeing things move through the air, after all she'd have to move things about and would scare the living daylights out of the other book borrowers. She would need to use the microfiche to check back dated Sheffield newspapers and to do it, she'd have to practice some more moving small objects around. She'd recently learned she could push tiny things about with her finger, so she could probably press the buttons on the microfiche – well, she'd give it a damned good try anyway.

Even a ghost can't be in two places at once, so she had to leave Roberts to his own devices whilst she tried to dig up some dirt on him. He would probably keep a low profile for a while now since he'd so recently gorged himself on killing. It could turn out of course that he hadn't done anything wrong in Sheffield, but a leopard doesn't change his spots – she was sure she'd find something. Anyway, it would be interesting to look.

That afternoon, she didn't follow him as she had somewhere important to go. She attended her own funeral and stood at the graveside with a few others. Three of the mourners were her mother, father and young brother, who were all in tears. It broke her heart to see them so upset, especially young Billy, whom she used to babysit. She'd loved each one of them and had shared a happy family life. Not only had that man taken her life but he'd devastated her family as well. Billy was crying hard, he was only fifteen and he'd always looked up to his big sister. Her father put his arm around the boy, which seemed to embarrass him and he shook off the man's arm.

"I'm all right Dad. You just look after Mum," and he rubbed his swollen eyes with his coat sleeve.

"Damn you Alan Roberts – I'm going to make sure they catch you – see if I don't!" She turned to leave the funeral, watching her dear mother and father trying to comfort each other and swore in a way no well brought-up lady ever should. She thought about the girl in the Intensive Care ward and wondered how she was. With the thought, she suddenly found herself at the hospital where there seemed an unusual atmosphere about the place. There were a couple of nurses rushing to and fro and a policeman still standing outside the room. He turned however and went away, as though his job there was done. Arabella followed the nurses and heard their conversation,

"Poor young thing – it was just too much for her. He'd obviously done more damage than we originally thought. Her wounds were just too severe and her poor heart gave up."

The other nurse spoke then, "Do you know, I feel really upset? She was far too young to die – and to die in such a way. What kind of bastard could do something like this? I know what he needs doing to him – but of course, that won't happen. He'll just go away for a few years and then be allowed out again to wander freely amongst the unsuspecting public."

The two girls were obviously angry and upset – they were probably similar ages to the girl. Arabella felt her legs almost give way – 'Can that happen to a ghost? she wondered.

It obviously could and she sat down on one of the chairs in the corridor. She'd never get talking to the girl now – no more information would be forthcoming. She went into the room and saw the girl lying there, her face ashen grey, almost white. She'd been a pretty girl and so very young. Short blond curls and a slight build – she'd never have been able to fight him off. Arabella herself remembered clearly how strong he'd been.

Cautiously, she looked around the room and then out into the corridor. If she was here, where was the girl's ghost? After all, they'd both suffered the same fate as each other. Judith's friend's ghost hadn't materialised either, despite Arabella looking for her. There was no sign of another spirit in the hospital, no-one was wandering around looking lost and confused.

Where could the dead girl's ghost be? She leaned over the girl's body and whispered, "Where are you? If I'm here, you should be too.' She waited patiently, but nothing happened, except the nurses came back into the room to prepare the girl for the mortuary. Even after they'd gone, she waited in the empty room, but no ghost appeared. Was she unique? She couldn't understand it. Why was she allowed to be here? Why had she been able to stand outside herself and watch everything that happened?

She'd seen him as he was actually killing her and then afterwards, when he'd done the deed, she saw him walk away nonchalantly. It was as though he'd just had an enjoyable experience. Well, she couldn't explain it – but she was still here and able to do something about the deaths – if only she could. The one difference she could think of, between the girls' murders and her own, was that she'd stared intently into his eyes as he strangled her. She'd never forget those eyes, or that face – maybe she was allowed to stay on the earth because she'd taken his image into her own eyes at the point of her death. He was with her to stay – until she avenged herself. Tenuous reasoning perhaps, but she had seen her own image reflected in his cold blue eyes and that seemed to give her strength, even after her death? Who could explain it, certainly not her?

It was dark and all the library lights were out. Everything was quiet and the building looked empty. She passed through the wall and looked around, trying to assess where everything was. There was a separate room for computers and a couple of microfiches. This was what she was looking for. She took her time and examined the contents on the shelves. It took some time, but eventually she found the films for the microfiche which luckily, were filed in alphabetical order. She found what she was looking for 'The Daily Standard's Last Twenty Years.' There were 3 films but it would be worth the effort. She just knew it would. She spent all night in the library and between the Internet and the microfiche, she found the information she'd been looking for.

By checking through the past 10 years, rather than the intended 20, she found several interesting facts. With some gaps in time, there had been several murders of young girls in Sheffield, but then she also checked unsolved murders and of course, they were fewer in number. There had been 7 unsolved murders of young girls – murders which spread over 5 years. She could find no helpful details however, as being unsolved crimes, there was little for the papers to print. She checked all their ages and found they were between 20 and 25, with only 2 engaged to be married. She made a mental note of their names – it was a pity she couldn't yet hold a pen, or she could have written them down.   But she wouldn't forget them – she believed the information would be important one day.

At work next day, she found him flirting with the girls in the office as usual. They were probably safer than the girls in the wider community as they were a bit close to home for him to hurt. He wouldn't want to give the police any excuse to question him – again. She was amazed to hear him telling one of the girls that he'd joined a choir in town. He didn't seem like someone who would join a choir, but 'it takes all sorts' she decided.

"Why don't you come along too? I'm really looking forward to it – there's about 20 people in the group and they all seem good singers. They put on concerts for charity – and I'm told they do very well financially. What do you think - it's a good cause as well?" he was coming across as too desperate and the girl just shrugged her shoulders, said 'No thanks' and walked away. Inside, he was furious – the bitches were all the same. And women just didn't like him it seemed but that wouldn't stop him from trying. 'Thank God,' Arabella thought, 'it's safer for them that way.'

After work that day, she followed him to his choir. It was in an old church which wasn't used for services any longer and he was right – there were a lot of people there. The hall was full of noise and laughter and they were all chatting to each other like old friends. They'd been a choir for some time now, but were always looking for new voices. And here he was! In his usual casual manner, he walked into the middle of one group and said, "Hi, I'm Alan Roberts and I'm hoping to join your choir." Initially taken aback, they welcomed him and asked if he was a Tenor – apparently, they were very short of Tenors.

"I am most certainly a Tenor," he replied, but then he'd have answered positively, no matter what they'd needed. Arabella thought, 'I bet he's not what they need, but we'll soon see. He won't be able to fool this lot.'

One woman asked him, "By any chance are you also interested in amateur dramatics - several of us are part of a local Amdram group and we're always on the lookout for 'would-be actors'?" She was an attractive brunette and he immediately warmed to her. She might be easy pickings in the future. His flirtatious nature took over and the woman began to blush – he was almost too keen.

"Why yes, that would be wonderful and I might make some friends there. I've only lived here for 6 months and I'm still finding my way around the place." Sometimes, he liked to play for sympathy to get what he wanted – and it had worked in the past.

"Oh, we're a pretty friendly bunch – do join us. After choir practice, I'll tell you all about it." Arabella couldn't help thinking, 'Like a lamb to the slaughter, but not if I can help it.'

An hour later he'd met the choir master and listened to some familiar songs. He'd already made sure he was one of the gangs and was going to use them as a stepping stone to meet others.

Arabella stayed with him, amazed at how pleasant he could be when he wasn't murdering young girls.

He left just after the woman called Ruth. He knew not to leave with her, as people would notice they'd formed a sudden friendship – too sudden - and that might hinder any future plans he might have. They'd agreed to meet the following night by the river in the park. She was going to take him to the Amdram meeting, where the small company was putting on a comedy and they needed someone to play a policeman. He joked," I say! I say! I say – Evenin' all!" And she saw it again, more evidence of the man's friendly and affable nature – all a front of course, but he seemed just the sort they'd like in their group. He was careful over the next couple of weeks, attending both the choir and the Amdram, making a niche for himself and trying hard to make people like him. He helped with the play, not only learning his own lines, but patiently listening to the others at rehearsals. He even helped build the sets and scout around second hand shops, looking for props and costumes. In fact, he became invaluable and knew the others in the company thought that too. As for Ruth, he treated her just as he did others, not singling her out for special attention – she was his friend, that was all.

Excitement was rising in the group and after a few weeks, the first night of the play was only one week away – there was a rehearsal every night and the whole cast had to attend. His part was not a particularly important one, but it was vital to the humour in the play. He never pushed himself to the front – always modestly standing back and allowing others to take centre stage. He even held the director's script for him, like a proper toady. He knew how to worm his way into people's lives and Arabella saw yet another side to his character. 'The man was a chameleon and no mistake!'

The audience were seated, waiting for the curtain to rise. When it did, they all played their parts with distinction – especially Alan Roberts. At the end of the week, it was the last performance and a big party was thrown in the hall. It apparently was a tradition for the actors and actresses to exchange gifts after the last performance – apparently something left over from Victorian times. Roberts chose a pendant with an amber gem to give to Ruth and she returned the favour with a handsome cigarette case. As far as everyone was concerned, smoking was his only fault – he'd tried but couldn't stop.

It was midnight and the lights in the hall dimmed. Everyone said their goodnights and blew theatrical kisses into the air. Again, Alan Roberts made sure he didn't leave at the same time as Ruth. Arabella sensed something was brewing and she feared for the woman's life, but she kept beside him as he made his way from the church hall. He didn't make his way home though, but went in a totally different direction. He'd visited Ruth's home a couple of times, just for a coffee or a sherry but he never stayed long. He didn't want her telling others 'he was her 'special friend.'

In the meantime, Ruth was walking along the river bank - and foolishly, she was alone. Arabella thought, 'Why doesn't she get a bus or a taxi – why was she making it so easy for him?' Before leaving the hall, he'd secreted a prop under his coat – it was a cricket bat – a good, solid one that could do a lot of damage. Arabella walked closely behind the woman. She wasn't sure where he was at the moment, but she knew he'd soon appear. She whistled – her best party trick so far – but maybe Ruth was a bit deaf as she didn't seem to react at all. 'Odd thing for a singer to be a bit deaf!' Then she saw him at the end of the tow-path. He was hiding behind a tree, well away from the direction in which Ruth was walking. As she passed the tree, he stepped onto the path just behind her, and making sure no-one was around, he lifted the bat above his head and came down heavily on the back of her skull. 'Oh God, Arabella was going to witness another murder and she could do nothing to stop it.' The woman fell forward and lay motionless on the ground. He bent down to look into her face, but her eyes were closed. This was a moment of immense pleasure and something he'd been looking forward to for several weeks now. He breathed deeply and enjoyed the moment of triumph. He knew he was a perfectionist and prided himself on a job well done. His adrenalin was sky high.

"There you are, my lovely – you've been on stage for the last time – and you have me to thank for that." Her head was in a pool of oozing blood and he squinted to see her more clearly in the darkness. 'My Heavens, she looked just like his mother – that was why he'd singled her out all those weeks ago. Why hadn't he seen the resemblance before?   She was gasping for air and lifted one hand as if she thought he would help her. Instead, he reached down and snatched the amber pendant from her throat, stuffing it into his pocket. The chain left a line of small cuts on her throat and that pleased him even more.

"That's too good for you Mother – best let me look after it for you." Arabella was frantically whistling, hoping someone would hear her and help, but of course they didn't. It was well after midnight and most of them were probably tucked up in their beds. 'Why isn't my whistling distracting him this time?'

He rolled her down the slight bank and she slipped quietly into the cold river. 'Oh yes, a fitting end to a budding actress – now you'll live in people's minds forever. In fact, he'd probably done her a favour. "Oh, I enjoyed that so much – it really is the best feeling in the world." He was speaking to himself, "I wish that damned whistling would stop – it's driving me crazy." He watched as her body slipped under the surface of the river – her heavy tweed coat soaking up the water and she slowly disappeared. He turned, and with his usual nonchalance, walked casually away, back the way he'd come. He was tired now – it had been an exciting but exhausting day, what with work, the play, the party and then this – the culminating moment. He knew he'd sleep well that night. He walked away and did a little skip out of sheer enjoyment. 'Monster is too good a word for him,' Arabella thought and whistled all the harder. She could see him shake his head to rid himself of the irritating noise. The whistling failed to bring anyone!

Two days later, it was front page news and the Amdram group were horrified by Ruth's sudden death. They all met up in the hall to discuss it – and of course, Alan Roberts made sure he was one of them. It would have been suspicious if he hadn't come, and he was after all, every bit as shocked and upset as the others.

"Poor dear Ruth, was it murder – do we know yet, if it was murder? I can't believe she just fell into the river – but who would want to hurt her? She was such a good woman and always so kind." He spoke loudly amidst murmurs of agreement and kept his head bowed in respect but no-one answered his questions because there was no answer.

Arabella made sure she was at the point in the river where Ruth's body had been spotted and she mingled with the police there, her invisibility being very useful for over-hearing conversations. Her body had already been taken from the river and driven away to the police mortuary where the Forensic specialist would be waiting. The sight of the attractive brunette being dragged from the water must have upset the on-lookers. The police were doing a finger-tip search and eventually came upon a dark stain on the tow-path where the woman had been struck down. It was obviously dried blood. Her body had been found several yards downstream from where she'd gone into the water, but several police were covering the whole area. The dark stain on the ground stirred up a lot of interest andanother man in plastic overalls came forward and started to work on the ground.

As Alan Roberts was still at work, Arabella went back to his house and stood in the middle of the sitting room. She thought it odd, how tidy everything was. He was obsessed with tidiness and everything was exactly where it should be. 'A sign pf paranoid fussiness she was sure!She took the opportunity to search the house– to search it thoroughly. She didn't know what she was looking for but believed there must be something to tell of his life before coming there. She looked through the drawers, shelves and cupboards and then began to search more unlikely places. Eventually, she was rewarded and found a small book under his pillow. 'Ah, he obviously wants to keep this away from prying eyes – and yet close to himself for safety,' She thanked God she could now move small objects at will although she still couldn't manage to lift things, but moving them was now quite easy – she just pushed them with her mind as well as her fingers - and turning pages was a doddle.

Old habits dying hard, she settled down on the sofa, book in hand. She'd have loved to have a cup of tea as well, something she always did when she was starting a new book. Alas, those happy days were over – ghosts don't drink tea! She'd found an old diary – strange to keep it under your pillow – it even smelt old and was quite tatty – really well fingered. His name and address were proudly written on the fly-sheet in his most fastidious handwriting – and the first months were pretty non-descript. What she did notice right away was the way he'd written at the bottom of each page – 'I HATE MY MOTHER.' Straight to the point and no mistake. Arabella moved on through the Spring and then the Summer months, until she reached the end of October. Above his usual reference about disliking his mother, he'd written 'Still no Birthday present – the old bitch has never bought me one, but I thought maybe for my 18th birthday – but no, not her!'

She read on and found over the next two days, a lurid description of how he'd murdered his mother. He was pretty graphic and described how he'd felt as he strangled the life out of her – sheer and utter pleasure. He went on about how he wrapped her in a blanket and tied it up with rope: he told of how he'd moved the body in a wheelbarrow at the dead of night and buried it in a deep hole in the woods. It was worse than a horror story – it had really happened and he gloated over his actions. Not one word of remorse. 'My very first murder!' he'd written proudly and added that he'd found he enjoyed the sensation so much, that he vowed he would do it again. And the mad man was as good as his word.

After her disappearance, he wrote he'd behaved quietly for the next few months, accepting the neighbours' commiserations and sympathy. She wasn't missed as no-one had really liked her – she'd been as unfriendly to them as she'd been obnoxious to him. All of this, he described in detail in the diary.

One of the neighbours asked, "How could she just up and leave you Alan – your own mother. What'll you do now?"

"Oh. I'll get by. I start a new job next week so I'll have an income. Don't you worry about me – oh, and by the way, thank you for this cottage pie, I'll enjoy that for my supper." Feeling sorry for him, the neighbours were proving more generous than ever before.

It was all in the diary, which he continued until the next year. The insertions returned to boring news for a while and he stopped writing how much he hated his mother. He didn't have to do that now – she couldn't bother him anymore.

'I knew it! I knew he wasn't just your usual kind of murderer when he killed me. It was the look in his eyes that told me. No-one could get so much pleasure from doing such a motiveless thing.' Arabella felt vindicated – she knew she'd seen evil in those eyes. Now she knew a lot more about him and how long ago it had all started. He was a menace to society and had to be stopped. But How! She did something then that she'd never done before and she cried out to no-one in particular, 'Is there anybody there who can help me? Is there anybody who can teach me to lift objects and carry them around? Of course, there was no reply, but she tried again and shouted out the same request. She didn't know why she was doing it – but she felt there must be someone in the spiritual world who could hear her – she couldn't be alone.

A cold wind blew through the room, the curtains fluttered and Arabella knew she wasn't alone. An elderly woman suddenly appeared before her. She was very pale and had long white hair. She wore spectacles and looked more like a school teacher than a ghost – although she could probably have passed for a witch as well. But ghost she was – and not just any old ghost: "I am a Tutor and a very busy woman." You have called me from one of my seminars where my students are waiting for me. Now, what do you want, young lady – and can you make it quick? By the way, I don't re-call seeing you at any of my Seminars and yet you're new to the haunting business, if I'm not mistaken.'

How lovely it was to have someone to talk to and hopefully to hear her as well. "I want to attend one of your seminars Madam, but I'm sort of earth-bound until I can help catch my killer. I was murdered, you see and because I was staring into his eyes when he strangled me, I can't move on to other things until I've had my revenge.' Arabella knew how stupid it sounded, but here she was – a ghost talking to a Tutor ghost – and asking for advice. How crazy was that – and yet it was happening!

'Oh, that would do it right enough. If both pairs of eyes were staring into each at the moment of death, the ghost of the deceased would be earthbound until the murderer was paid back in full.' She seemed much more interested in Arabella's plight now and actually settled on the sofa beside her. The two of them spent the next hour chatting and the old ghost finally told the young one the secret she needed to know.

'You're perfectly capable now to move and carry objects, so you must get on with it and then you'll be able to join my seminars and finally learn how to be a normal ghost and scare people in the usual way. That's my job, you see, teaching new ghosts how to haunt and make the world of the living aware of their presence. As soon as you've completed your task, come and see me and I'll start your lessons right away. Now, remember what I told you, to have physical powers to move things around, you must stare directly at the object and use your mind to move it – not just your hands – it's the only way to do it. I must go now and get back to my waiting students – time and tide wait for no man nor ghost, you know.'

And she was gone – as quickly as she'd arrived. Arabella crossed to his bed again where the diary had been hidden and she flicked through the pages again. Tentatively she touched a vase on the bedside table and wound her fingers tightly around it – it was quite heavy. She knew she'd have to get a good grab if she was to move it. It didn't budge at first but she concentrated more and focussed on it – the way the Tutor had told her. 'My God, I can do it!' And the vase rose from the table and seemed to float in the air. As luck would have it, she suddenly heard his key in the lock and realised how much time had passed. She placed the vase back on the table – he mustn't suspect anything was out of place. She'd take the diary to the police next day, that would be time enough.

She saw him come into the sitting room and then saw the young receptionist from his work come in behind him. 'Heavens above, what am I going to do? She doesn't know the danger she's in. And she's only a child really – maybe 18 or 19. She'll be putty in his hands.'

She watched him as he opened a bottle of wine and filled two glasses. She told him she didn't drink much and he laughed and said he didn't either. The girl, whose name was Jane, sipped the wine slowly and Arabella could see she didn't find the taste very pleasant.

His conversation was easy and relaxed. He told her he just wanted to get to know her a bit better, "I've always liked you, ever since I began working at the firm, but I wasn't sure if you liked me."

"Of course, I like you Alan, but you're one of the managers and I'm just the receptionist – I don't think our positions really match." She was a nice young girl – too nice for someone like him.

"Now, you're being silly Jane – things aren't like that anymore – everyone's equal." He got up and crossed to a small bureau. From the drawer, he took out a small, flat box which he held out to her. "This is for you – I got it the other day and thought how lovely you'd look wearing it."

When she opened the box, she gasped at the lovely pendant. It held a large amber gem that she draped over the back of her hand. "Oh Alan, I can't possibly accept this – it's far too valuable and I don't think I have anything good enough to wear with it." She put it back in the box and held it out to him.

He pushed it back towards her and said, "You must keep it Jane – I chose it for you – and if you need new clothes, then perhaps I can help with that too." He was such a smoothie, Arabella thought she was going to be sick. She had to do something, the girl's life might be hanging in the balance, so she began whistling – a loud, piercing whistle that could have woken the dead. Jane reacted and held her hands over her ears – in fact, Alan Roberts did the same.

"I'm sorry my dear, I don't know where that's coming from. I've heard it before but I can never find the source." He looked disturbed and angry. His decorum was affected.

Jane stood up and said she must be going – she was expected at home. He tried to persuade her to stay, but the whistling was so annoying, even he had to leave the house. Jane deliberately left the box with the pendant on the coffee table – she knew it would be wrong to accept such a gift from him. Arabella was delighted at how annoying her whistling had been. What she didn't know however, was that the girl was safe whilst in his house – he'd never risk killing someone there – too difficult to get rid of the body. However, she realised it was too close a call and she mustn't wait until the next day to take the diary to the police. Whilst he was out of the house, she took it from under the pillow and left. She could whisk her way to wherever she wanted and do it quickly, so no on-lookers had the chance to spot the ghostly diary flying through the air.

She was in luck! Both of the main detectives were closeted in a room together, discussing the woman who'd recently been found in the river.

"Why do these women walk along the river path at midnight? It beggars belief, it really does." One of them shook his head.

However, the other one responded, "In all fairness, a woman should be able to do just that, don't you think? She should be able to walk about in her own town regardless of the hour – any blame has to be aimed at the attacker, not the victim."

"Come on now! In a perfect world that might be the case, but everyone knows there's scum out there, just waiting for unsuspecting and naïve women or men to come along. A pitch-black night, no street lighting and a location where people usually walk in the morning – not late at night. I'm sorry Bill, but I feel they're asking for trouble."

"Well, it's an argument that's been going on for a long time – and probably for time to come. Certainly at least until we rid the streets of all undesirables – and that's not going to be any time soon."

Arabella had listened to this with interest, realising how naïve she'd been to insist on walking home alone that night – if she'd listened to her wiser friends, she might still be alive. But that was another argument!

The two detectives were about to leave their office when a sudden need to check the desk drawers took hold of Bill. "I just have to get a new notebook – my old one's full. In the drawer, the first thing he saw was an alien, brown book and he swore saying, "What the Hell? Where has this come from? I'm sure it wasn't there 5 minutes ago. It's a diary – and looking at the dates, quite an old one."

She'd managed it. She'd brought the evidence to their attention. The two men changed their plan and sat down to read the diary contents. "My God, this makes interesting reading, doesn't it?" And it certainly did. They couldn't have had a better reason to initiate the start of another investigation and to contact the police force in the area near the address written on the fly sheet of the diary.

Arabella was amazed at how quickly the men worked and one of them even travelled to Sheffield to help the local police. He made himself known at their station and, with several men as back-up, he set out to search the woods where they hoped they would find a body. Of course, they took sniffer dogs with them who proved invaluable in the search. It took intense searching for three days and just as they were about to stop for the day, one of the dogs began to dig at the earth between two trees. Th dog was excited and the men knew they'd found what they were looking for. It wasn't a very nice find and some of the men turned away to be sick, but Bill was pleased at the outcome of the search -he hadn't wasted anyone's time and the search had been worthwhile. The forensic chaps were sent for and the skeleton – as that's all it was now – was taken away. There were still scraps of blanket and nylon rope in the soil and sticking to the bones – a truly ugly find.

It was all there, just as the diary had described and Bill wondered not for the first time, why the killer had been such an idiot to write it all down and then to hang onto the evidence. It was almost as though he'd wanted to be caught one day. But he couldn't fathom the reason the killer had done such a stupid thing. What he didn't know was how much the murderer enjoyed reading and re-reading the graphic details of the murder. If he had known, he would have been even more disgusted by the killer's twisted mind.

Before returning to his own area, Bill and a local policeman visited the actual address in the diary and found a young family living there. They only rented the property and had always paid rent to the same landlord. Yes, they could give details, "He's called Alan Roberts and these are his bank details. We always pay regularly by Direct Debit." They were obviously concerned that the police had called and feared they might be in trouble.

Bill told them not to worry – it wasn't them who were in trouble, but he would have to speak to the landlord. He went home then to continue with the current investigation, but he planned to work in parallel with the police force who'd just helped him. It was now a combined operation, but the murdered woman had been found in their area of jurisdiction, so they'd have a continued interest in the case.

Meanwhile, Arabella had kept a close eye on Alan Roberts. He had continued as a member with the local choir and Amdram group -it was an easy way to meet new people, all well away from where he worked and lived. A sensible precaution, considering he had already chosen his next victim. She was a school teacher and older than his usual victims, but she was pleasant looking and rather withdrawn, so she was easy to impress – and he set out to do just that. She sang in the choir and her name was Mary. She had a lovely singing voice which he told her left him feeling enraptured and he made a point of focussing his attention on her, rather than the other Sopranos.Of course, she was flattered – but she wasn't stupid, so when he asked if he could take her out one night after choir practice, she said 'No, but thank you'.

However, after another couple of invitations, she caved in and agreed to go for a drink with him. He took her to his favourite pub, the one Arabella knew best. After all, she'd spent her last night on earth there, so she should remember it. She sat beside the couple, promising herself she wouldn't let anything happen to the timid woman. After two drinks, he said he'd walk her home and Arabella followed. She lived quite a way from the pub, but he said he didn't mind. The expression on his face was full of care and concern – he was obviously a thoroughly nice chap, it seemed to her.

"Why don't we sit on this bench, you must be tired. You've already been working all day, haven't you?" He knew the age of the children she taught and added, "Seven-year olds must be very demanding. What do you do in your spare time?"

"Oh, I read a lot and of course, there's always homework to grade. My days are quite full usually and of course I love singing in the choir." She was proving to be the kind of woman he enjoyed killing, although stupid, young girls were more to his taste. Not many people would miss Mary - only her pupils and the school would soon find a replacement to teach her class. He could feel the adrenalin begin to rise in his body at the thought of ending her life. However, just as he was helping her from the bench, he heard it. He hadn't heard it for some time now, but it was just as shrill as ever. They both heard the whistling at the same time and she jumped up quickly,

"What on earth is that?" She asked and he pretended he couldn't hear it. He put his arm around her shoulders as though to protect her but she shrugged him off. He became more aggressive now and tried to pin her down by clasping her hands behind her back. He was suddenly being very rough and she was feeling scared and frantic to get away.

He loved to see the fear in her eyes and knew this one was going to be pleasant because of her resistance. He liked that – she would probably try to fight him off now - but it was okay as the road was very quiet, it being so late. In fact, the spot they'd stopped at really suited his purposes, not being on a bus route where they could be seen by any passengers.

She somehow freed herself and moved away. "I'd like you to leave me now please. I'd prefer to go the rest of the way on my own." And she started to walk away fast.

"Oh, I couldn't possibly let you do that, I'll have to see you all the way home. It's not safe for a woman to be out on her own this late at night." He was still being his usual smarmy self, despite having just desperately held on to her arms – now he tried to put his arm around her shoulders again, but she knew he'd grab her hands as he'd done before. This time, she ran from him, shouting over her shoulder, "Leave me alone - don't come near me or I'll scream."

"But, no-one will hear you above all this whistling. You're just being silly now." He was fast working up to the point when her death was imminent. He felt his adrenalin rise even more and his hands were curled into fists. "God, he would enjoy this one – she was such a prim and proper excuse for a human being.'

Arabella grabbed a broken part of a tree which was lying in the road. 'Thank God, she was able to lift things now. Raising it above her head, she brought it down with a heavy thud on the back of his head. The woman just stared at the branch flying through the air and whacking the man on the head. 'How on earth did that happen?' She didn't wait to find out, but ran away as fast as she could. She left him bending over as though trying to keep his balance and flew like the wind to reach her own road. She didn't look back once to see where he'd gone, but almost fell indoors, locking the door behind her. She promised herself she'd visit the police next day – he needed reporting and she was the one who'd do it.

Satisfied, Arabella followed him home. 'A job well done!' she thought grimly. When he turned the corner into his street, she was right behind him. Both of them were surprised to see a police car sitting right outside his house. In his usual confident manner, he tapped on the car window and asked, "Can I help you officer?" Butter wouldn't have melted in his mouth.

The two detectives who'd always been on the case, emerged from the car and one said, "Good Evening Sir, we have a few questions for you. May we come in, it would be better to talk inside." All three, plus a ghost, went inside. She was on a high, knowing what was coming. Firstly, they established who he was and that he'd once lived in a specific house, for which he was still the landlord.

A simple enough question, but Alan Roberts hesitated before replying. Hearing that address was the last thing he'd expected. He couldn't deny it as it could be easily proved.

"Before I answer, can you tell me why you believe I lived there?" His arrogance was fast crumbling and he sat down on a chair.

"We've traced your background through your current bank account, with helpful advice from the place you work. (No mention of the diary yet, Arabella noticed.) But that's all we're going to tell you – we're here to ask you questions." Bill knew from instinct that they'd got the culprit who'd buried the woman in the woods. Arabella had the pleasure of watching the man she hated more than anyone else in the world, being take away 'to answer questions at the station.' She followed them, needing to see him squirm as they fired questions at him. It was her right after all!

He was banged to rights but not once, did he admit anything. He told them he didn't know what they were talking about and that when he'd left the old address, his mother had been hale and hearty. They'd fallen out, that was all and hadn't been in contact with each other for several years. Arabella had to admit he told a good lie – but it was easily proved that he was lying. Some neighbours still lived in the old area and had been able to confirm his mother had disappeared long before he'd actually left the house. In fact, his trail was easy to follow, probably because of his arrogance. After all, he was superior to the law and couldn't ever be caught, so perhaps he hadn't concealed his trail as well as he could have done.

'You're for it now Mr Roberts!' Arabella gloated – she couldn't help it. Then she heard the magic words:

'Alan Roberts, you are under arrest in connection with the murder of Mrs Amelia Roberts, your mother. You do not have to say anything but it may harm your defence if you do not mention when questioned something you later rely on in court. Anything you do say may be given as evidence.'

The words were magic to Arabella's ears as she heard him say, "I want a lawyer!" And Bill, the detective complied with his request.

Now he was safely inside and the streets were safe from his menace – for the present anyway – now it was her turn to act again. She'd manipulated things so far, but she had more to do to make him pay for the women's lives he'd taken so cruelly. She hung about the detectives' office, listening and learning until one afternoon, a young policewoman came in with some documents in her hand.

"The forensic report on the grave findings have arrived and I think you'll find them most interesting. They were able to find skin scrapings on both the pieces of rope and the torn blanket the woman was wrapped in. The DNA report states there is no doubt that they once were handled by your man. You must feel really vindicated. So, I suppose the case can progress now." And when she'd dropped the welcome bombshell, she left them alone in the room, but not before she'd added that a second forensic report – carried out on a mere whim of the doctor – had shown the hairs the murdered woman Arabella Wright had pulled from her murderer's head were conclusively those of the same Alan Roberts. 'Thank God she'd found enough energy to rip the hairs from his head.'

Bill said, "My God, Pete – we've got our monster. To treat his own mother in such a way. Is bad enough, but to murder young girls whom he'd never even met, puts him in an entirely different level of killer. If he'd hated the mother so much, why didn't he just walk away from the problem. It would have been so easy, but he obviously saw his only option as being murder."

The other chap, Pete said, "It's almost as though they think they're never going to get caught, as though they're immune to it all. Or is there a part of them that almost wants to be caught. You know, the theory of 'five minutes of fame' being worth anything – even if it's bad fame. As for the young girl left for dead in the avenue, I take my hat off to her - her brave action of grabbing her attacker's hair– even as she was dying – has handed Roberts to us on a plate. A brave girl! Well, we can move the case along now to the next stage. We mustn't forget to thank the forensic doctor on his invaluable whim as well."

Arabella felt as though she'd been mentioned in despatches and was proud of how she'd managed to help the police. Strange words popped into her mind unexpectedly and she realised she'd watched too many gangster movies. 'You don't want to mess with me Punk, you must have been feeling lucky!'

Next day, she went somewhere she'd not been for a long time. She went home. She knew both her parents would be at work and her brother Billy, would be at school – not that they could have seen her anyway. There was something there she needed however and an empty house was essential, as she might have to make a little noise. She went to the room that had once been hers and had to smile when she found her computer had been moved into Billy's room. So much for my grieving brother, she thought, it obviously didn't affect his desire for a free computer. But then she'd always loved him dearly and could grudge him nothing!

She settled down at the desk in his room and knew she was about to write the most important letter of her life. It wouldn't be quick as there were so many details to relay - but if she didn't finish it today, she'd come back the next day. At least Alan Roberts was in jail and couldn't hurt anyone else just now. She almost started to write, 'To Whom it May Concern' and realised how silly that sounded. She knew exactly to whom it should be addressed and that was the police. She counted on her fingers how many murders she knew about but of course that didn't include the ones in Sheffield. 'My, God, he really was a serial killer and no mistake and there would have been even more, if she hadn't intervened with the woman from the choir.'

Luckily Billy hadn't changed the password on her computer. That would have been a disaster. She was so pleased she'd found the power to move objects – now she could tap the keyboard and produce the information she couldn't speak of. She'd even checked on the detectives' e-mail address, so she could send it direct from here - then delete the whole thing of course.

She began the letter: -

'To the Police

You don't know who I am and even if you did, you wouldn't believe it, but I know some things of which you should be aware. I am the victim of the murder of 17th April, when a young girl was left for dead – more accurately, I am the spirit of that girl. *I swear my killer was Alan Roberts* whom you now have in custody. He followed me home from the pub that night, attacked me and strangled me to death. A little while later he attacked two girls on the same night – one later died in hospital and the other where he'd done the deed. A while later, he struck a woman across the head, ripped a necklace from her neck which left small scars. Then he dragged her body to the river, where he let if float away. You'll find the necklace in a small box in a drawer at his house – you may find DNA evidence on it from when it cut into her neck. He also attacked a woman from the choir he attends, but I scared him off before he could kill her. There are people in the choir who can confirm he befriended the first woman from the choir and the Amdram Group. *I swear all of the above is true.*

You are already aware that he killed his own mother ten years ago – I left his diary in your office drawer – the diary where he describes her murder in great detail. After her death, he moved to live in Sheffield where there were several unsolved murders of young girls during the time he lived there. I found evidence of this in the library archives and on the Internet. I don't know the murdered girls' names, but I'm sure this is something you can discover. *Again, I swear this is true.*

I realise all of this is weird and uncanny, but I know the above because, since the night he left me for dead, I have made it my business to follow him everywhere and try my very best to get in his way. By the way, there is a very young girl, a receptionist, who works at his firm and he has his eye on her – perhaps a word of warning from you will keep her safe in the future.

I don't know how helpful this letter will be to you, but it is sent with the best intentions. You may not believe in spirits and ghosts, but I can't help that – I am the spirit of Arabella Wright, the girl he murdered and I can't escape from this earth until Alan Roberts gets his just deserts. I'm hoping this is something you can do.

Please stop this man – he mustn't be allowed to wander the streets ever again.

Sworn as the truth as though I am in a Court of Law.

Arabella Wright '

She stared at the keyboard and her fingers hovered in the air. She knew she would send it, but wanted to enjoy this moment – the moment that meant his reign of terror was finally over. She pressed 'Send' and it was gone – finding its way to the detectives at the police station. 'Boy, were they in for a surprise!' She felt instinctively that she'd avenged all those innocent women he'd murdered.

The 'Delete' button pressed, she left her brother's room, hoping he would never know she'd been there. Scaring Billy wasn't part of her plan.   She would have liked to pull his leg about how quickly her computer had been moved into his room – but that wasn't to be.

She moved quickly now to visit the detectives' room. What she found there could only be described as 'Uproar.' There were several policemen standing around a desk in the main room. Both the detectives she knew were there too. She'd never been in this room before and was shocked to see her own photo amongst several others – all in a line on the wall. 'My God, that used to be me before he got hold of me.' She thought sadly.

The policemen were pouring over several print-outs of her e-mail – they all had one each. The talk was about ghosts and spirits – and a couple of them were laughing at the thought.

"It won't stand up in court," one man said.

Another answered, "But does that matter? The information is invaluable and paints a clear picture of Robert's crimes – our job is to follow up everything the e-mail tell us – and in court, we only have to present the evidence we discover – she's given us all the facts. The e-mail address is less important but we can investigate that later – for now, we've got a lot of work to be done but she's made it easy for us. What do you think Bill?"

"I think we should lose no time in questioning him again. When he hears how much we know, he might even own up – sometimes serial killers are actually proud of what they've done. And there's only one way to find out. Ready Joe?" And his partner stood up and followed him eagerly out of the room.

Arabella moved quicker than they did and was standing in Alan Roberts' cell, looking down at his sleeping figure. 'Ah, the sleep of the innocent – and I don't think! I think I'll wake him with a little surprise.' And she let out the shrillest whistle she could manage - she even scared herself. He fell off the bunk and ended on the floor.

A loud voice from the corridor outside the cell shouted, "Less noise in there Roberts or I'll give you something that'll make you whistle louder." The guard shook his keys and then saw Ben and Joe coming around the corner.

"Bring him downstairs, will you? Interview room 4 is ready for him." Ben told the guard.

'Yes, they're going to start right away! I'm going to enjoy this.' And Arabella quickly flew downstairs towards Interview room 4. She settled down to wait.

He wouldn't answer the questions and kept asking for his lawyer, who soon appeared and sat down beside his client. Roberts continued to say nothing – and the solicitor repeated after each question. "No Comment." The prisoner knew this was an acceptable answer – he too, watched detective stories on TV. Ben pointed out to him that there was no doubt now that he had killed his mother – DNA had confirmed it. But Robert's lawyer just kept repeating "No Comment."

And he added, it'll go on being 'No Comment' until I speak with my client in private. Is that clear?" And of course, he was quite right. It was Roberts' prerogative.

Arabella had a long wait ahead. Questioning would take a long time, but she didn't mind. Time was of no importance to her. Between continuous interrogation of the prisoner and the tracing of the people mentioned in Arabella's e-mail, several long weeks passed. Alan Roberts began to look haggard, the stress was getting to him. He had lost some of his arrogance and knew from the questioning that they were finding information that confirmed the things he'd done. He was quite gaunt now and his eyes were dull and he stared straight ahead, only acknowledging the guard when he brought food.

Arabella hadn't planned to whisper in his ears, but impatience with his silence forced her to change her mind. 'Why don't you just give up and tell them what they want to know? Your silence won't stop the truth coming out at your court case and there's so much evidence stacking up against you, you should just confess now. You never know, it might lessen your sentence!' He couldn't see her and thought the words he was hearing were actually his own thoughts. She goaded him and suggested he would feel better when he'd owned up to everything. She tried hard but it didn't work.

The first day of his court case arrived and she made sure she hovered around the jury. There were lots of spectators in the gallery, after all it was a high-profile case – so many murders throughout the years and mostly of young, innocent women that he probably hadn't even know. The side area for the Press was full. There was a special seat for the artist, whose job it was to make a likeness of the prisoner. The jury was half men and half women – and they were all sitting expectantly in their places. There was a lot of noise and murmurings, but it all subsided when everyone was told to stand for the Judge. The Prosecution and Defence Barristers, along with their supporting lawyers and clerks, stood with the others and waited for the Judge to speak.

The trial slowly progressed. There were very few witnesses, especially for the Defence as most of those involved with him were long dead. A couple of character witnesses from his office were called and although they said nothing to hurt his case, they weren't exactly high in their praise either. A couple of neighbours who still lived beside his old house were called to take the stand, but all they said was that he'd never got on with his mother and how they'd always been fighting. One day, she just disappeared and they never saw her again. They said it hadn't seemed to bother her son, who actually seemed glad to see the back of her. Alan Roberts listened to all the evidence with a blank expression on his sallow face, only occasionally glancing at the jury. His pathetic demeanour was obviously for their benefit - but they all sat very still, paying close attention to the witnesses.

The young receptionist Jane, was called by the Crown and Arabella immediately felt sorry for her – she looked so afraid. She didn't hold back however and told the court how he'd hung about her desk, flirting with her. He'd even asked her out and because she felt embarrassed always turning him down, she went with him for a drink. That was when he coaxed her into his home and made her a present of a pendant - a large pendant with an amber gem as a decoration. She said she'd given it back, saying she couldn't accept it. The Prosecution then produced the actual piece of jewellery which had been found in the suspect's home – and on which the forensics team had found small pieces of skin and blood. Skin and blood from the poor woman's neck – the one who'd been taken from the river – proof that he'd taken it from her before smashing her head with a cricket bat. The young girl looked sick at this news and actually began to cry. She'd helped however and was dismissed from the stand.

Mary from the choir was called next and she told in detail how he'd tried to attack her, how he'd bad-mouthed her and how she'd managed to run away. She went on to say how loud, shrill whistling had suddenly filled the air and even he was shocked by the noise. She couldn't explain what it was, but it had saved her life. Arabella preened with pride at the woman's declaration.

Several medical and forensic specialists were called one by one, as well as the detectives who'd followed the clues in the case – they'd visited the pub for instance, the choir and the Amdram group. The ghostly e-mail was never mentioned – either by the police or by the Prosecution Barrister. There was no way it could be presented as evidence and would probably have harmed the validity of the evidence against Roberts. The mention of a ghost as a witness would make the police a laughing stock. The diary which had suddenly appeared at the police station was however offered as evidence and served as a self-confessed admission of the prisoner's guilt. It was reported as having been found at his home, safely guarded by him throughout the years.

The evidence over the next few days built up against him, but still Alan Roberts said nothing. Eventually, the case reached the point where the two Barristers did their summing up – one for the Prosecution and one for the Defence. They both spoke eloquently but the Barrister for the Defence had a much harder task than that of his colleague. In fact, it was hard to plead for his client because the case was so overwhelming against him. Mental Instability was about the best he could come up with – there was nothing else. However, Roberts was entitled to speak for himself and for a while, he donned his arrogant head and tried to brand the dead women as tarts and tramps, something that didn't help his case with the jury– he made it clear he considered the women who'd died – at whoever's hand – were easy women with no sense of pride. He told them he was certainly not the sort of man who would have chosen to befriends such women. At this, Arabella became furious and wished so hard she could speak, but she told herself she'd done her duty – she'd damned him by providing the police with so much evidence. It didn't matter, she told herself, she'd done her damage and got her revenge. Of course, when asked how he pleaded, he told the court he was 'Not Guilty' of any of the murders, a claim it seemed hardly anyone in the court room could believe. It was his right however to say it.

When the summing up was over, the Judge directed the jury to leave and go to a specially prepared room, until they reached a majority verdict. Of course, Arabella joined them there – if anyone was entitled to be there, it was certainly her.

"Well, this isn't going to take us long, is it?" A tall man said. He had a very bald head that shone in the harsh sunlight streaming in the window. "We've had all the evidence we need. The man is a fiend and a murderer – at least that's how I see him." he seemed to have appointed himself as the leader of the jury. Several voices reacted to what he said, by murmuring their agreement. One man however said he wasn't too sure – and he wondered if Roberts was being held up as a scapegoat for some of the murders. "And if he did do any of the murders, he must surely be able to claim diminished responsibility – no-one in his right mind could possibly do what he's accused of.For example, can we accept that he murdered the two young girls – the ones who were both attacked on the same night? What proof have we of that? Also, the murder of the first girl he was supposed to follow home from the pub – what evidence was there to say he was responsible for that? None, I think!"

"You're just being ridiculous," a woman joined in the discussion, "There's no doubt he killed his mother, we've all seen the diary and the woman who was found in the river, well. the forensic specialist confirmed his DNA was proved from the pendant, the one he'd ripped from her neck as he strangled her. Then he had the audacity to offer the same pendant to the young receptionist.He was definitely involved in her murder. I would say the Laws of Probability are enough to point the finger at him for all the murders." She looked around at the other jurors and again, several of them murmured their agreement. Then she remembered about the hair and added that to her list – the DNA from the hair, proved his guilt.

"Am I the only one who feels there's not sufficient evidence to prove his guilt for all the murders?" The man was sweating now and knew he was probably flogging a dead horse – and that the others believed the man was guilty. However, he still added,

"You do realise we're talking about the rest of this man's life. Now, there's no such thing as a death penalty and if he's found guilty, he'll be in prison for the rest of his life."

"Tell that to the girls he murdered, why don't you?" the woman said sarcastically. Arabella decided she liked her. "Trust a woman to see sense!'

"Is it too soon to take a vote? We've only been in here for hour?" The bald man intervened. "Tell you what, let's take an interim vote, just to see how things stand. We'll ask for some teas – may as well get something out of this – and then we'll discuss more before taking the final vote." And that's what they did! Arabella was impatient as the way ahead seemed clear to her, but she knew, 'Due justice must be allowed to run its course.' She had to be patient and philosophical!

After tea and a further discussion about the case, the final vote was taken. This time, the results were a !00% in agreement. It had taken 2 hours to get to this point, but the court clerk was summoned and told the jury was ready to come back into court. The man who'd argued in defence of Alan Roberts knew he had no leg to stand on – the others were right and he now agreed with them. The verdict was now supported by all jurors.

Back in the court room, the judge was still absent but the prisoner had been brought up from below. Arabella noticed he'd changed his shirt, probably because the one he'd been wearing was soaked with the sweat of guilt. At least, she hoped so. The reporters were on the edge of their seats, poised to run from the court once the verdict was known, as this would be front page news. The jurors were brought back to their seats. Only one of them looked at the prisoner in the dock and that was the chairman, the man with the bald head – all the others kept their eyes lowered which was apparently a sign to the 'knowing' in the court that they'd found against the prisoner.

The Judge appeared and everyone got to their feet, "Well, members of the jury, have you reached an agreed verdict – and if so, who will speak for you?"

The chairman stood to his full height and looked at the Judge, "We are agreed, my Lord and I will speak on behalf of my colleagues."

"The court clerk will read out to you, one by one, each accusation that has been considered by this Court of Law and you should give your findings in each case." The bald man nodded his head.

One by one, the individual charges were read out and the chairman was asked for the verdict – and one by one, he spoke for the whole jury and said" We find the prisoner guilty." This was the verdict given to each charge and Arabella's excitement knew no bounds. As this process was taking place, she took the opportunity to look around the court and to her amazement, she saw dotted amongst the spectators, ghostly faces she hadn't seen there before. She knew who they were however, especially the one older woman who must have been Robert's mother – the others were obviously all the women he'd murdered through the years. 'My God, if anyone has the right to witness this moment of glory, it's them.' And she felt privileged to be one of them. Of course, no-one but a fellow-ghost could see them but they had every right to be there amongst the living.

As each charge of murder was read out by the court clerk, the jury spokesman replied in a strong voice. Including the charge against him of killing his own mother, there were a further 12 charges of murder and each victim was named individually. It seemed to go on for ever. There was no mistake, he was a serial killer. As the charges were read out, there was a hush in the court, although on hearing their own name read out, each ghost reacted in a similar way. No-one saw or heard them, but Arabella did – and she saw the great sadness on their young faces, some raising their hand to cover their mouth. When her own murder charge was read out, she did the same – a sadness came over her – a sadness for her life cut short by that man in the dock. A man she'd never hurt in any way and who'd killed her for no reason. She moved across the room to get closer to him. She had to be able to stare straight into his eyes when the Judge passed the sentence. This was the only way to get closure for herself and she mustn't miss the opportunity. She remembered the tutor ghost's words – 'Stare right into his eyes and your vindication will come.'

The Judge, looking his most serious asked, "Members of the jury, are you all agreed on each verdict?" and the jurors answered in one voice, "We are, my Lord."The Judge sat back in his chair and looked directly at Alan Roberts, who didn't move a muscle. His face was unchanged by what he'd heard.

"You Alan Roberts have been found guilty by a Jury of just and wise men and women – your peers. I agree wholeheartedly with their findings and know there could be no different verdicts. I must commend both barristers, who fought a good case against each other, although your Defence has my every sympathy for having to fight a case on behalf of such an unworthy client. I totally concur with the Jury and would like it put on record, that I have noted the excellent work of the Police Department in collating evidence against you – in particular the detectives on the case and the work of their Forensic Department. 'I should have been commended as well – they couldn't have done it without me.' But, she'd had her own reward now!

The Judge went on, "To sum up, you have been found guilty of the most heinous, cruel and vicious crimes I have ever encountered and I sentence you to a lifetime in prison, with no expectation of a reduced sentence for good behaviour. You are a menace to Society and you must not be allowed to walk again amongst the decent and innocent people of this country.

That is the judgement of this Court."

As he said the last words, Arabella hovered in front of the prisoner and whistled softly. He looked up and knew that sound – it was the sound that had plagued him for a long time now. She whispered as loudly as she could, 'Yes, look into my eyes. Do you see yourself reflected there - just as I once saw myself reflected in yours, on the night you strangled me to death? Now, you'll carry my image for ever and it will plague you 'till you die, just as your image has haunted me since my death. You'll see me when you're awake and you'll see me when you're asleep – you won't be able to escape me.' And for good measure, she whistled just once more, so he'd know it was she who'd helped bring him to this place.

As she moved back, the Judge instructed the police guards to 'take the prisoner down', before leaving the Court having fulfilled his duties. As he stood to leave, he turned to the Jury and thanked them for their help, patience and wisdom over the past few weeks and in particular for the inevitable verdict.He then returned to his chambers whilst the reporters moved in one body, rushing to get their reports on the front pages.

Alan Roberts said nothing at all, just followed the prison guards. The court slowly emptied and Arabella was left alone with the other ghosts. They didn't say much to each other– what could they say? The situation was completely surreal but they were all glad it was over, as was Arabella herself. One by one, they all disappeared – they'd seen what they'd come for.

However, Arabella couldn't deny herself the pleasure of actually visiting him in prison. He was in isolation as the other prisoners would have hurt him when they found out why he was inside. They would find out in the end – they always did – and although the death penalty was abolished, they'd find ways of plaguing him for what he'd done. It seemed his peers had the right to judge him as well.

When Arabella visited him, she was delighted to see the dark, dank and lonely cell he had been given. Even her spiritual life must be better than this existence. She began to visit him regularly, just to annoy him of course and she always ended each visit with a shrill whistling that would have wakened the dead. She toyed with the idea of stopping her visits as she could now search for the Tutor ghost who ran the seminars – and she would be able to join her fellow spirits. However, something held her back and she knew she hadn't finished with him yet. Okay, the Law couldn't take his life, something he'd never hesitated in doing, but she could always try to make his life just that bit more unbearable.

So, she continued to go to his cell and liked the way he'd become thinner and thinner – and more haggard every day. She turned up one day and found his cell empty. She soon found out where he was by visiting the admin office in the prison. Alan Roberts had been moved from the prison as he seemed to be getting worse every day and regularly losing control. Apparently, his mental health was suffering and the prison Psychologist had brought in a private Psychologist from outside, for both of them to examine him. They confirmed unanimously that he should be moved to a special hospital prison for the criminally insane. And that's where her murderer was now. He was believed to be a danger, not just to other people, but to himself as well, and so he ended up in a padded cell.

At the hospital, she whistled to let him know she was there. She knew he suffered just that little bit more when he sensed her presence.

"Why don't you leave me alone? I bet you're one of the bitches I'm accused of killing – well, you can't do much to hurt me now, so why do you keep coming?"'My God, he was actually speaking to her?'

She whispered in his ear, 'I come so you don't forget your victims – victims who aren't able to come themselves, but who are pleased that I can. I helped the police collect evidence against you and I gave them the diary you kept under your pillow. I also told them where to find the pendant you tore from the woman's neck. I like to think I was instrumental in your arrest. In fact, I know I was.' She'd waited a long time to tell him that but now he could converse with her, there was nothing to hold her back.

He stood up from his narrow bed and crossed to the other wall where he began to systematically bang his head against the padded surface. Bang! Bang! There was no sound from the padded walls, so no-one came to see if he was all right. 'Ah, the happy sound of silence which no guard could hear.'

'That's right, you demented fiend, you just keep on doing that – punishing yourself is the best medicine for what ails you. You may not admit to feelings of guilt – but that's exactly what you're feeling right now.'

She left him then as she had to find her Tutor ghost friend, who'd promised to help her. One backward glance saw him continuously bang his head hard, which unfortunately didn't hurt him half as much as she'd have liked. But, it was still further progress in his eventual destruction.

'Ah, Revenge is a dish, best served cold – and I've served it in great freezing dollops! The moral is, 'Don't mess with a ghost who just won't die!' And her earth-bound spirit was at last free!

Only a Little Wooden Man –
Or Was He?

He was <u>not</u> the most attractive ventriloquist's dummy, with his curly black hair and ears that stuck out on each side. His eyes were bright blue and protruded from a face with exaggerated rosy cheeks - and his nose was bulbous. He had a large mouth with thick lips and a tongue that really was very large. His name was Mortimer – Morty for short – and he was really rather old – considerably more than a hundred years. Of course, he didn't look that old – he'd been 'done over' throughout the years with fresh paint. This then, was Mortimer.

He lived with his master, Tom Reynolds, who'd looked after him for many years and who often showed him off at parties where he was would perform in front of an audience. He didn't mind that, as he enjoyed the adoration of children, but sometimes he had to entertain adult audiences, which wasn't nearly so easy as there was always a smart-ass in the audience, ready to hackle. His master Tom however, preferred adults, as he was paid better by them.

"Dear me Morty – you're going to need some repairs before I take you to another show. Your clothes are getting tatty and your cheeks need another coat of paint- they've got to be rosy."

Of course, Morty said nothing but was quite pleased to hear he was going to get some new clothes. He'd actually been inherited by Tom about 50 years before, at which time he'd already had several previous owners. He really was a venerable 'old' gentleman but actually looked like a World War 2 spiv – the black-market type. He'd long been able to understand more than Tom knew, and the old man had held many one-sided conversations with his dummy, who always agreed with him.

Tom lived with his family – he and Morty had a room of their own and were quite happy there. Tom was the Grandfather and had his daughter to thank for 'taking him in' when his wife suddenly passed away. His daughter Molly was married to Fred and their two teenage children also lived in the house. Tom fitted in well and paid what he could in rent, but he wasn't a wealthy man – just a proud one, who liked to do his bit. This was the reason he continued to take Morty along to the occasional show or party – it gave him a little money to pay for his keep.

"Hi Pops, supper won't be long," Molly was a handsome woman about 40 years old, and she worked in an Estate Agent's office in town. She enjoyed her work, as dis her husband Fred , who worked in the local factory and between them, they could just manage to support the family, which included two teenage children. Tom always referred to Morty as though he was human and therefore, so did the family. They wouldn't have hurt the old man's feelings for a fortune but enjoyed the odd joke now and again.

"How's Morty these days Grandpa, I haven't seen him for a while?" Young Freddie had just arrived home from school and as usual had dropped his haversack in the middle of the floor. He was 16 and a typical teenager, who knew someone would come along and pick up the bag.

"Morty's fine Freddie, in fact he's due for an outing next week – at the church bazaar. I was going to ask you if you could come up with any new jokes or funny stories that I can add to his repertoire – he has a lot, but hasn't added many new ones for some time now. Morty's repertoire is very important, you know – I want to keep him quick and snappy!"

"I'll have a look on the Interest if you like Grandpa and see what I can find. I like to think Morty has something of me inside him, you know," he said with crossed fingers, knowing that would please the old man. He went into the kitchen and re-emerged carrying a large peanut butter sandwich. "Would you like one Grandpa?"

"Not just now lad, maybe later." Tom went on reading his newspaper. The next day Morty was to be fitted for a new suit and Tom took him in a large canvas bag to the cheapest and best tailor he knew. The small shop was called simply 'Samuel Golder The Tailor' and the man was a genuine Jewish tradesman, skilled in his craft.

"Ah Tom, have you brought our mutual friend for his second fitting – I have it in the back here – and the material I've used is of the very best quality – only the best for young Morty here. It's been in stock for a while but I've never been able to use it before as there wasn't enough material for a full suit. For Mortimer's dimensions however, there was plenty. Come, come – through to the back and I'll show you."

Samuel led the way through a heavy curtain and ushered Old Tom into a small dark room at the back of the shop. Spread on the big table in the middle of the room was a suit of clothes. It was a two-tone mustard colour with a checked pattern. It was very theatrical and just right for a stage performer such as Morty.

The two old men dressed Morty in his new clothes and Tom's first thought was Morty looked even more life-like than before. He looked just like a 'Flash Harry', but in Tom's eyes, he looked more like a country gent. Samuel added a spotted bow tie over a small white shirt and stood back to admire his handiwork.

"Because it is for a very special customer, such as Morty, I have sewn a good luck charm into the lining of the jacket. It is the custom of the Jewish people to do such things and you are my old friend Tom, so I wish you both the best." Samuel was perfectly serious and Tom brought out his wallet.

Now, how much do Morty and I owe you? I am very pleased with his new suit – he couldn't look smarter." Samuel put his own hand over Tom's, "It was a pleasure I assure you, and I want no money for doing it. I owe you Tom, more than I could ever say. I remember how kind and considerate you were when my dear wife was dying and I needed a friend. I couldn't have got through it without you – and Morty of course."

The two old friends shared a pot of tea together before parting, shaking hands solemnly and promising neither would leave it so long to meet up next time. Morty was safely packed in the haversack and was now dressed to kill, as they say.

"Well, let's have a look at him Pops." Tom's son-in-law Fred called out when he arrived home. "Let's have a look at the handsome chap then."

Tom took Morty out of the haversack and sat him on his knee. Molly came in from the kitchen to have a look as well.

"Well Pops, he's one good-looking dummy. The new suit is lovely. Was it very expensive?" She asked, feeling the lapel of the jacket between her fingers.

"It cost me naught a penny, 'Luv – Old Samuel was insistent about that – for 'Old Time's Sake', he said. "Now, I'm the tatty one. If we're to perform together, I'll have to rummage through my clothes – I can't let Morty down!"

His daughter laughed, "You don't look bad to me Old 'Un – I think you look handsome but not as handsome as Mortimer of course," and she went back into the kitchen to finish off her baking.

It was only one day until the performance at the church hall and Tom had been practising the new jokes young Freddie had found for him.He was sitting in his own room with Morty on his knee. "Now then Old Chap, what have you been up to lately? Tell the ladies and gentlemen. For instance, I heard you were seen at the Bookies – have you been gambling again? You know you promised to stop that."

"Whoever says they saw me there must be short-sighted – it must have been someone who looked like me." Morty challenged Tom.

"There's not too many who look like you Matey." Tom responded.

"What, not many suave, well-dressed gentlemen, do you mean?" And the dummy preened and brushed a lock of his hair from his forehead. The gesture usually brought a laugh from the audience.

The two continued for some time with their usual banter and told each other a couple of jokes,

Tom said, " Knock Knock." Morty of course replied, "Who's there?

Tom, "Broken pencil who?."Morty, "Oh never mind, it's pointless now."

Tom, "Knock Knock," Morty, "Who's there?"

Tom, " Lettuce."Morty, "Lettuce in – it's cold out here."

These jokes always encouraged groans from the audience and who could blame them? But the jokes that followed were better and the audience really loved how badly Tom spoke for the dummy – 'A Gottle of Geer.' was a phrase he liked to use, as it made the audience laugh at his incompetence.

The night of the performance arrived and after the dreadful 'Knock Knock' jokes, Tom told a few funny stories and Morty always ruined them, by giving the punch-line before he should have.

It was an entertaining half- an-hour and everyone decided the old codger was harmless and quite unskilled - but they knew he lapped up their applause, so they clapped and shouted out in loud appreciation. That was, except for the group of lads at the back of the hall, who cat-whistled and blew raspberries all the way through the act. The rest of the audience were annoyed with them and the hall caretaker eventually made them leave – in fact, he threw them out into the street. The people clapped louder as they disappeared outside. For good measure, Tom and Morty told more dreadful 'Knock' jokes, which the audience lapped up. "We did well tonight Matey – did you hear how people laughed?" He packed Morty safely in his haversack and left the hall before the show had ended. He was an old man and he wanted to get home quickly. He started to walk along the street and shifted his bag to the other hand - he couldn't manage it on his shoulders. "My God Morty, I swear you're getting heavier." He told the bag.

He lived about fifteen minutes from the church hall. He always thought the walk did him good, but this night was really dark and rainy. He passed a group of young men standing on the corner and thought he recognised them – they were the lads who'd been put out of the hall for cat-calling. He averted his gaze as he felt it could be a tricky situation and walked on. Three of the boys started to walk behind him and soon caught up with him. Tom knew he was in danger.

They ran around and stopped in front of him, saying "Get out of the way Grandpa – you and that bag are taking up the whole pavement." Tom stood to one side to allow them to pass, but they stayed right in front of him and one of them tried to grab his bag.

"Let's have it Grandpa – the little man must be worth a few bob." The others laughed.

"Now then lads," Tom said, "Let me past, will you? I'm tired and I need to get home." Now. he really felt worried and quickened his pace.

The tallest of the three snatched the bag and threw it against the wall, "And we want the money you earned tonight for that pitiful performance. Come on, hand it over!" One of the others was reaching for the haversack again. Old Tom was really scared now and knew he was no match for the gang.

"It's only a few shillings boys – that's all. I only get a pension you know, and a few shillings means more to me than it does to you." Tom was shaking and he was worried about what they might do to Morty, so he reached into his pocket, thinking it would be safer to give them his night's earnings.

The boy who had the haversack began to unzip it, whilst the others were waiting for the old man to empty his pockets. It didn't unfold quite the way they anticipated though. The haversack suddenly flew across the pavement right out of the boy's hands.

"What the Hell?" the boy said, "That bag just jumped on its own – maybe there's a wild animal inside."

It wasn't an animal though. The zip came completely undone and two feet emerged – followed by a little man in a mustard, checked suit. He stood bolt upright and straightened his back. In his hand, he held a knife, which he flourished to and fro in the air. He looked menacing and ready to take on the boys.

"Come on then boys, or are you too chicken to take me on?" Morty stood tall, stretching to his full 3 feet. His knife was shining in the street lamp and Old Tom suddenly passed out, falling to the pavement. The little wooden man and his knife were having an effect on the gang of boys. Two of them had already run off and the third backed away from the dummy. "I must be seeing things!" he managed to blurt out, but Morty challenged him, "Come on and see if you can take me – you're not seeing things – you're just chicken." And he jabbed the knife in the air before pointing it straight at the boy. The boy took to his heels and disappeared after his mates. He forgot all about the old man lying on the pavement and about his money. He ran away fast, thinking 'Who's ever going to believe this? A dummy with a knife!"

A stranger was walking along the opposite pavement when he spotted the old man lying on the ground. There was no-one else around – not even a short man in a checked suit. Morty had quickly concealed himself back in the bag, knife safely intact in his pocket. The man ran to the telephone box on the corner and dialled 999. Soon, the ambulance arrived to take Tom - and his bag - to the hospital but no-one called the police as there seemed no actual crime had been committed – the old man had just collapsed.

Coming around in the Emergency Unit, he realised he was safe and asked the nurse, "Have they gone now? I'm safe now, am I? The nurse soothed him and reassured him.

"There were three of them, you know and they wanted my money." The nurse spoke with the Sister who called the police, and when they arrived, she explained the patient might be concussed and may be muddled about what had happened. The police spoke with him but when he told them his ventriloquist's dummy had chased the attackers off, they put it down to the concussion, telling him, if he remembered anything else, he was to call in at the police station. Tom knew they didn't believe him, but he knew what he'd seen. Then again, had he been imagining things – how could Morty have climbed out of the bag and strutted around the street? He was a dummy for Heaven's Sake! 'Maybe I was concussed – but I hadn't fallen over when I saw him.' Now, he was really confused!

He was kept in hospital overnight, but he did get out of bed at one point, to look in the haversack. 'Yes, Morty was there – quite secure and lying in his usual heap. 'Had his eyes deceived him then? Had he seen what he'd wanted to see – a Good Samaritan who would save him? But if that were so, why had the three boys run off in fear? He climbed back into bed, more confused than ever.

Molly and Fred came to pick him up next day and when they got home, they made him go straight to bed and brought him a tray of tea and scones. "Now, you stay there Pops, you've had a nasty scare, but you're okay now."

She had placed Morty on his usual chair opposite Tom's bed and before dropping off, the old man said, "I know what I saw Morty – I don't care what others will say – you saved me and I'm grateful." Of course, the dummy didn't move a muscle, but just sat there motionless, although his wide eyes seemed to be protruding even more

Next day, Tom felt much better and was alone in the house when his granddaughter, Margaret, came home unexpectedly from school. She was 13 years old and usually bright and bubbly, but not today. She threw her satchel onto the floor and plonked herself on the sofa.

"I've been sent home from school because I was feeling sick," she said grumpily and her ashen face showed up her red eyes – she'd been crying.

"I'm sorry my darlin', can I get you anything – an aspirin perhaps?" He wasn't very good when someone was ill but she looked so dejected, he felt he should do something.

"No thanks Grandpa, the teacher gave me one. I 've got a bad stomach ache – I think I'll go and lie down for a while." But instead of doing that, she burst into tears and covered her face with the sofa cushion.

"Honey-bunch, tell your old Gramps what's really wrong. You never know, maybe I can help." For five minutes, she didn't talk and he used the silence to fetch both of them a cup of tea.

"And I've remembered biscuits too!" He sat beside her on the sofa this time. "Now come on my pet, spill the beans or I'll think it's something I've done wrong."

She hesitated for a few moments and sipped her tea, "It's two girls at school – they don't like me. I've tried to ignore them but they keep saying mean things and I'm such a baby, I start to cry. I don't know what I've done to make them hate me so much – or I'd apologise, but I can't do that if I don't know what I've done." Tom held out the plate of biscuits. 'If only Molly were here – he could pass on the problem to her.' But there was only him.

"Well Margaret, I'm not going to tell you not to mind them – they've obviously upset you. What kind of things do they say? Only tell me if you want to." Inside, he was actually furious as he'd always believed bullying was the worst thing anyone could do to another person.

"Oh, you don't want to hear that! They just call me names and they hide my books. When it's gym time they snigger at me when I'm changing. They whisper about me and other girls laugh – I don't know what they're saying." She began to cry again and asked, "Can I stay off school tomorrow Grandpa – I don't want to go and face them."

Tom knew there was more to come and he waited patiently until she said, "They call me Fatso and make noises like a chimpanzee when I'm around – and worst of all, they say I smell and they tell people I'm dirty."

There! It was out now. No wonder she was so upset. Why do these kind of kids exist – they're positively evil? His first thought was to go straight to the school and confront the girls – but he knew if he suggested that, she wouldn't like it. So, he let her cry it out first and then he explained that girls like the bullies were usually jealous of their victim and that they only disliked someone who was more clever and pretty than they were.

"They actually want to be you, my love! Not just like you – but actually be you. What I should tell you is to ignore them, to go on being nice and friendly - even offer to help them – maybe with homework or such things. You should never copy them though – being cruel and mean is easy for some people. You should go on being your nice self and that will affect their behaviour - they'll realise there's no point in picking on you cause you just don't care!" He told her what he knew he should tell her, but deep down, he wanted to confront the bullies.

Margaret seemed better after the chat and their tea and she said, "I think I'll really go and lie down for a while Grandpa – I feel better now and I know what you say is right. It's just so hard, you know!" And she went off with a tear-stained face and the last biscuit.

Now he was on his own, he turned to Morty, "What'll I do Morty? Do you think I should go to the school and speak with the teacher? If I say anything to the girls themselves, that'll give them more ammunition to pick on her – getting her Grandpa to defend her - and I don't want to make matters worse." She was so young and those young girls' tongues were probably vicious

He looked at Morty, "Well, young man, what should I do? Do I tell her mum and dad, do I go to the school and look for the girls or do I keep quiet and just go on being her confidant? Don't stare at me with those big eyes, I know you heard our conversation and you're bound to have an opinion." He lifted the dummy from the chair and sat him on his knee. "There you are, now you can talk to me." And he began to move Morty's head and turned him around so they were face to face.

Morty decided to speak, "Well Old Chap, I think you should get someone to confront the girls – you shouldn't do it yourself however – that wouldn't help Margaret." Morty's words were wise and Tom knew it, but who could he ask to speak to the bullies?" Tom pondered the problem and reached for his pipe and tobacco – that always helped him to reason things out.

As he puffed away, Morty spoke again, "You promised your daughter you'd given up that nasty habit. You know she'll smell it when she gets home – but in the meantime, I suppose I'll have to keep your secret."

He knew he could rely on his old mate and puffed at his pipe contentedly. After a few minutes, he stopped smoking and put the pipe away. He laid back against the chair and closed his eyes – a little nap, that's what he needed. He wasn't sure if Morty really had spoken to him, or if he'd imagined the dummy's advice.

When the old man began to snore, Morty climbed down from his knee and went to the back door. It was the only door handle he could reach – the front door was too high. He stepped outside onto the doorstep. People didn't know he could walk and talk – and he wanted to keep it that way. Even Old Tom didn't know what he was capable of – the old man thought he knew, but of course he didn't. Having to rescue him the other night could have blown his cover but he hoped not. However, the old man was becoming more aware of his dummy's capabilities but hopefully, it was still the little wooden man's secret.

Outside the school gates, Morty waited patiently, tapping his foot on the ground. He did attract some curious glances – his height in particular, although his rosy cheeks and large ears always raised a few eyebrows. He saw two sniggering girls coming towards him and knew instinctively it was them. They were following a little blond girl across the playground and pulling her pigtails. She was much smaller than they were and was already in tears. Oh yes, it was definitely them!

Casually he walked towards them and the little blond girl seized the chance to run away. He was exactly the same height as the girl, but that's where the similarity ended. He looked the part of a gangster-type-spiv in his natty suit and gent's hat. The hat belonged to Fred.

The girls thought he looked like a little Mafia thug and laughingly told each other, he was 'carrying a piece' in his inside pocket. Men who looked like that always did – they'd seen it at the cinema. Then they made their first mistake – they started to laugh at him. "Gosh, you're scary," one of them said and the other added, "So scary, I'm going to laugh some more."

Morty pulled himself up to his tallest three feet and asked if they knew Margaret.

"Yeah and what's it to you? Of course, we know Fatso – the snivelling little twerp - but she's not at school today or we'd be following her home.   But as she's not here, we'll follow you instead." Both girls folded their arms across their chest and looked defiantly at the 'spiv'.

"I've come to tell you both something – something I hope you hear loud and clear. I may look rather strange to you but that's nothing compared to how you look to me. You're a pair of ugly brats who'll just go on getting uglier the older you get. But if you don't stop picking on Margaret, I might decide not to let you get any older – you see, I'm your worst nightmare and I plan to visit you in your sleep. You can see I'm not ordinary but special, and   I have inhuman skills to punish people like you."

Their expressions changed and although they tried to laugh, they couldn't. They realised he meant what he said and they knew it was time to leave. He might only be the same height as them, but he looked quite evil. One of the girls pulled her friend's jumper – it was time to go – and now. Morty began to follow them out of the playground and along the street.

"You won't forget me and if you don't start being nice to Margaret, I'll visit both of you every night for the rest of your lives. And you should know, I'm crazy – not silly crazy, but crazy like a murderer. I eat little bullies like you for breakfast. Have I made myself clear – do you understand? Just so I know you understand, tell me what you're going to do and say to Margaret tomorrow." His rosy red cheeks no longer looked friendly – but threatening.

One girl spoke up, "We're going to say hello to her and ask if she'd like to join our game at play-time." Her friend was nodding vehemently.

'Who was this horrible little man? Why did they find him so scary? He could only have been their height! Ut, it didn't really matter who he was, as they believed he'd visit them at night.

They didn't care about Margaret, she was just a dumb freak – but although he was a freak as well, he was a scarier one.

He left them then and turned back the way he'd come. Like all bullies, they shouted after him once he was a safe distance away. He turned again in their direction and that did it – they ran off screaming. He called after them, "Don't forget me now girls – remember I'm your worst nightmare. And I'll be checking with my friend Margaret, to see if you're being nice to her."

He went back to the house, where Old Tom was still dozing in the armchair. He didn't even move when Morty slipped back onto his knee and slumped forward into a dummy pose. 'A good job done and I enjoyed it – if it helps Tom and Margaret, so much the better.'

A couple of days later, Tom asked his granddaughter if things were any better with the girls at school, 'How are things Margaret – have they done anything else to upset you?"

"Oh Grandad, have you done something about what I told you? Both the girls are treating me so nicely – in fact, they seem to want to be my friends. Betty even gave me half her lunch today – and Dotty did the same, but I couldn't eat any more. I'm sure you've done something – you have, haven't you?" She was a completely different girl. When she'd gone, he looked at Morty with a questioning look, "Don't sit there as though butter wouldn't melt in your mouth – have you had anything to do with Margaret's bullies?" But Morty just stared back – his blue eyes vacant as ever, and didn't move a muscle.

"Come on old chap, talk to me – I know you can, or must you be on my knee to make it happen?" He could have sworn Morty blinked one eye – but he couldn't be sure.

He lifted the dummy onto his knee and turned his head towards his own, "We've known each other for a long time now, but it's only recently that I've become aware you're not what you seem. Has something happened to change you? There, you've done it again – you winked at me, I know you did."

Morty spoke without moving his lips, but it was the same voice that Tom used to speak for him. It sounded like he was having a conversation with himself. "I'm always here if you need me, but especially for as long as I need you." The old man wondered if he'd taken to talking to himself in his old age.

He had a dream that night, a dream of how he could change his act with Morty – change it into something quite different, but much better. It was something he'd never tried before, but he knew people were getting tired of his 'Knock-Knock' jokes. Next morning, he got out of bed eagerly and went downstairs where Molly was preparing everyone's breakfast. He put Morty on his usual chair behind the kitchen door.

" What's next on the agenda Pops? Have you any shows pending?" She liked to encourage his hobby and she knew he really did love Morty. She plonked his ham and eggs on the table.

"Thank you dearie, and yes, I have two performances due – one at the church hall and one at a private function. I think it's someone's birthday and her family want to do something a bit different. I suppose Morty and I will have to accept we're something different." He was enjoying his breakfast, "As long as they pay me, I won't complain. Actually, I wouldn't mind your opinion about something I'm thinking of trying – I think it might amuse people. I might need young Freddie's help though – I don't know whether you'd be happy about that."

"Well Pops – what will he have to do? You know he thinks the world of you and would help if he could– but he's quite shy and I wouldn't want people to laugh at him." Tom agreed with her – he'd never let anyone laugh at Freddie – laugh with him maybe - quite a different thing.

Tom explained his idea. He'd seen it being done a few years back and he'd thought it fascinating then. Morty and he would sit on stage or at the front of the room in the usual way and Freddie would move amongst the audience, asking certain members to volunteer keepsakes or something personal to them. He would hold the item in his hand and ask Morty what he had and also did he know anything about the owner. The trick of course was the words Freddie would use – they would tell Tom and therefore, Morty what he held and what sort of a person it belonged to. It would mean both Freddie and himself would have to learn the 'secret' words needed.

"If he was interested Molly, I'd give him half what they pay me. It would be a good way for him to earn some extra pocket money. What do you think?" Tom was obviously very excited.

"We'll have to ask Freddie – it's really up to him. I don't have a problem with it myself. Have a word with him when he comes home today." And she reached for her coat, she'd have to hurry or she'd be late for work. "Bye Pops – see you later."

"Well Morty, what do you think? Do you think we could pull it off? It gives a ventriloquist's performance a new twist, don't you think? I know I'm an old codger to be starting something new – but why not? It keeps me young – and it might make enough money to buy you another new suit."

Freddie was very keen on the idea and even went to the library to see if he could find some books on the subject. Needless to say, there weren't many, but there was one with good suggestions about the questions and the tricks to learn them.

"Grandad, we'll have to make the room atmospheric – sort of creepy. That'll get people's imaginations working." Freddie may have been only sixteen – nearly seventeen - but he was a bright lad and liked to think Grandpa needed him.

"Great idea son, we'll do that – dimmed lights and a couple of candles should do the trick. I think the audience will like that and of course, it'll still be Morty who talks to them about their trinkets, not me. It'll make him seem even more alive and the candlelight will help."

And so, the old man and his grandson started to rehearse their 'patter.' They studied the library books and between them, soon knew the kind of performance they wanted to give. They discussed the key words which Freddie would use as he held the man or woman's trinket in his hand. There were many such words and they all had specific meanings. The words lovely, beautiful, old, shiny, young woman, mature lady, gentleman – all gave the signals to Tom and so to Morty, who then told the audience about the trinket and its owner.

"It's going to be fun Grandpa and don't forget your promise that I get half your wages."

"All right Boy – keep your hair on, I won't forget. Anyway, you won't let me forget." Despite the age difference, the two got on famously together – they even had the same sense of humour

Margaret wanted to be part of the act as well, but Tom explained she was too young – it was illegal."I'm not that much younger than Freddie – and I'm smarter than he is." She said petulantly. But the next moment, she'd forgotten all about it. She was a much happier these days.

The evening had arrived for the new-style performance and Freddie, Tom and Morty nervously arrived early at the hall. They made sure the main lights were dimmed and the stage set with a comfortable chair for the ventriloquist and his dummy. Large candles were placed safely around the room and it all worked well to create an atmospheric ambiance – just a little threatening, even eerie. As the audience arrived in ones and twos, they gasped in surprise at the unexpected setting and some immediately looked worried as they feared what was coming next. Tom, with Morty on his lap, was already seated and young Freddie was at the side of the stage, waiting to do his part.

As it was a special occasion, Molly, Fred and Margaret had come along. In fact, they wouldn't have missed it for the world – Molly's words because she was very proud of her 'old dad.' The family had seats near the front and Margaret especially was waiting with bated breath - and a bag of boiled sweets.

The audience finally settled and gentle classical music filled the hall, all due to Freddie's ability to be in two places at once. Tom spoke and introduced Morty and himself, before turning to Freddie who was now standing in the midst of the audience.

"This young man will move amongst you and any of you who would like to take part should give him a personal trinket, a book or a treasured piece of material such as a scarf – in fact, anything." He produced from his pocket a black mask and continued, "I will then ask someone from amongst you to tie this securely around my eyes, so that I can see nothing. But, not too tight!" he joked before holding up the mask for everyone to see and asking for a volunteer to come and help. A man came forward, looking rather ill at ease, but he was determined to examine the solidity of the mask. When he was satisfied, he placed it around the ventriloquist's eyes and left the stage.

Everything was now set to begin and Freddie introduced himself. He asked if anyone would like to start the ball rolling and give him some personal keepsake. The first was a woman who handed over a ruby ring and whispered it had belonged to her mother.

"I have here a lovely object which has a red addition. It belongs to Mary now. What am I holding?" And so it went on. Freddie had used the key words which told Tom it was a ring that had once belonged to another owner.

Tom hesitated and played to the audience, "Could the lady tell me her name- I need to hear her voice." His voice boomed from Morty's mouth and the dummy joined his hands together and closed his eyes as though to concentrate. The woman said, "I am Mary!"

Tom thought for a few moments before Morty spoke again. He said in the dummy's voice, "It's small and round and has a touch of red about it but it used to belong to someone before it came to Mary. Am I just a little right?" Morty's mouth moved in line with Tom's words. Then he shouted, "It's a ring – a gold ring with a red gem, a ruby I think and it once belonged to Mary's mother."

The audience burst out in loud applause as Mary nodded her head and Morty bowed his head in appreciation. Tom sat there in his mask and said nohing. Freddie moved on amongst the people and a young woman gave him a letter in an envelope. Freddie asked if he could read the letter and the woman nodded.

"Yes…yes Morty. " Freddie said, " It's easy to understand this and to appreciate what's being said. A young woman has given me this object and she's carried it about with her for a long time. Tell me if you can, what I'm holding." He spoke directly to the dummy, completely ignoring Tom.

"Smell it for me and tell me if it smells of roses." Morty hesitated and then waited for an answer.

Freddie did as he was bid and said, "Well yes, amazingly it does. In fact, it smells of strong perfume – but I don't know what kind. It could be roses of course."

"Don't try to help me," the dummy said, "I can do it by myself. Tell me one more thing however, 'Is it heavy or light?

On being told it wasn't heavy, Morty seemed to have an 'Eureka' moment and folded his arms across his chest. "It's paper, I know that much and it has writing on it – writing in a man's hand. It's a letter, isn't it?" And the audience applauded loudly, The dummy really was amazing – or the old man was.

Suddenly, the old man sat up and the dummy almost slipped from his knee. Tom grabbed Morty tightly and spoke more words through his friend.

"That letter was written some time ago – several years in fact – and contains a message for the young woman in the audience. May I have her name please, as I like to know to whom I'm talking."

The woman spoke up, "I'm called Mavis and yes, it is a letter written some time ago. " That was all she said, but the sadness in her voice was obvious. Morty stared at her, his protruding eyes drilling into hers and then he leaned forward to make sure she could hear him.

"You once loved the writer – no, strike that – you still love the writer." The words sounded strange coming from a little, wooden man but they were said with real feeling and sympathy. 'But how could a dummy show emotion?' Even Freddie wondered that. The audience were spell-bound and a pin could have dropped without making a sound. The silence lasted for some moments and then Morty almost slipped from Tom's knee - it was as though he intended to stand up, but of course he couldn't. Tom pulled him backwards and Morty told the girl to go away and trace the man who'd written the letter.

"He's a decent bloke and he really loved you. In fact, like yourself, he still does. If you want to be happy, then do as I say. He's waiting for you to contact him – it's not too late."

Tom was amazed at Morty's words as he certainly hadn't put them in his mouth. It seemed the wooden chap on his knee was growing more adventurous every day.

The woman grabbed the letter from Freddie and ran from the hall. She was crying but seemed determined.

Freddie looked confused and for a moment, wasn't sure what was going on. Despite his mask, the ventriloquist looked exhausted and Freddie waited for him to speak. The boy hadn't expected things to get so serious, he'd thought it was going to be fun and light hearted. He moved on, and in an attempt to bring the performance back to where it should be, he asked if anyone else had something to test Morty. A man gave him a wrist watch, a very elaborate and expensive wrist watch, which Freddie thought was probably a Rolex. He held it in his hand for a moment or so, he was very impressed at its value.

"Morty, I've been given something that belongs to a gentleman. I think you would like to own this, but I'm afraid it's his. Perhaps you've seen one like it!" Freddie was dropping clues all over the place for Tom, who already knew the object was a watch. The old man already knew it was an expensive item and searched his brain for makes of watches and of course the first one to come to mind, was a Rolex.

Morty began to laugh and held up both hands in disbelief – at least that's what it looked like. "I'm afraid that's as close as you're likely to get to a 'Rolex' watch young man." He said to Freddie. "Yes, ladies and gentlemen, I feel strongly the gentleman has allowed Freddie the privilege of holding something worth a great deal of money."

The audience applauded enthusiastically and Morty took another bow. Tom was sitting quietly and suddenly held up his hand to silence the audience. He jiggled Morty on his knee and the dummy suddenly held up his hand before saying, "Sir, I have a question for you. Did the watch cost you a great deal of money?"

The man was returning the watch to his wrist, and answered proudly, "I know it cost a lot of money – my wife gave it to me as an anniversary gift and I gave her a necklace that cost exactly the same amount of money. We'd agreed what to spend before-hand." He looked at his wife sitting in the next seat, "She is a very generous woman and I could do nothing less than honour our agreement."

Morty continued, "I think perhaps you may have lost out on the deal Sir – your Rolex watch is a fake and can be bought for a just a few pounds, if you know where to go."

The dummy had dropped a bombshell. The audience held their breath and the man looked at his wife questioningly. She said nothing, but rose from her seat and walked out of the hall.

Morty concluded the contretemps he'd caused, by saying, "I'd love to be a fly on the wall when they get home tonight – wouldn't you?" Of course, the audience laughed again – it was proving to be an exciting night, full of human drama, well worth the entrance fee.

Freddie said they had time for one more object. The act was tiring and the performers needed a rest, so he asked if there was anyone else who'd like to test them one more time. There was a long pause until a woman stood up and handed a silk scarf to Freddie. The boy seemed confused and looked embarrassed for a moment. It was Molly his mother, and she didn't speak as Tom would have recognised her voice. She smiled at her son and nodded that he was to get on with it. She also whispered to him, "Tell him it was a gift from an elderly gentleman - Grandpa himself gave it to me."

"Sir, I have here an object that was given to the person as a gift. You've probably seen a similar one before – but I'm not sure." The message was hidden in his words and Tom immediately realised it was a lady's headscarf. Molly was enjoying herself and was eager to see how her father handled the situation. Freddie had waved the silk scarf in the air as he held it aloft but what he didn't know was its perfume – applied liberally by Molly before she left the house – wafted from the front row to the spot where Tom and Morty sat.

Morty said, "It's a lady's headscarf and it's made of silk. Is that correct? If you like, I can even tell you the colour, and he did! The audience were beside themselves with amazement and began to applaud but the dummy again held up his hand – what was he going to say this time, what further drama was coming?

"I have a message for the owner of the object – and it's important she listens to me. She is planning to visit a pub on her way home tonight – with her husband and daughter. She mustn't do that – I say again, she mustn't do that. If she does, her family will be in danger."

Freddie looked at his mother and returned the scarf – he didn't know what to say, so he said nothing. The performance was over and the hall began to empty, but the audience's applause was heartfelt and Tom and Freddie took their bow – as did Morty - again. They were much later leaving the hall than the other people and returned home to a well-lit house, so someone was already at home. They'd discussed how the evening had gone on their way and Freddie couldn't understand why his Grandpa had told Molly to go straight home and not visit the pub.

"Do you know son, I honestly don't know why Morty said what he did. It was the

strangest experience – I seemed to lose control and wasn't sure what I was saying. In fact, I think a lot of it actually came from Morty himself – my voice perhaps, but his words."

Freddie was carrying the bag with the dummy inside and looked dubious, "Now you're just being silly, you know he can't talk. If you tell people that, they'll say you've gone mad." He was laughing at his Grandpa but Tom wasn't laughing. He knew how stupid it sounded, but he also knew it was true.

Indoors, Molly and Fred were sitting by the fire. Molly had a stunned expression on her face and Fred was knocking back G&Ts as though they'd gone out of fashion.

"Pops, am I glad to see you? How did you know what was going to happen?" She stood up and put her arms around Tom's neck. "You probably saved our lives."

Tom was confused and sat down on his chair, reaching for his pipe and baccy. "What's all this about? I know, I know Molly – but after the night I've had, I need a smoke." he said, as his daughter grimaced at the smelly pipe.

But she said, "You enjoy your pipe Dad -you deserve it! A bus ran into the front of the pub – the pub we were going to, until you told us not to. How on earth did you know what was going to happen?" Molly was still shocked and Fred was just beginning to feel merry after his 'near death experience.'

"The Number 9 bus lost control and smashed into the pub at full speed. Apparently, the driver had a heart attack and just passed out. We'd probably have been sitting in our usual place by the door and we'd have felt the full force of the collision." She was so upset, Fred gave her one of his G&Ts.

"You're joking Ma – you must be. We haven't heard anything about a bus crashing into a pub.' Freddie switched on the TV and looked for a local news channel. And there it was! Some people had been seriously hurt and two were dead.

Old Tom and Freddie looked at one another, then Tom said, "I don't know how I knew what was going to happen, but the words just kept coming out of my mouth – or out of Morty's to be accurate." And he crossed the room, took the dummy from his bag and settled his friend on his usual chair.

"There you go, my man, you get comfortable now – you certainly deserve it. You're a very clever chap." Molly stared at him and looked at Freddie, who twirled his finger to his ear meaning, "Grandpa's gone mad."

"Oh no I'm not boy – I'm perfectly sane. This chap here is more special than you think. He didn't used to be – he was only a wooden dummy but in recent months, he's undergone some changes and I believe he has a mind of his own now." Molly was looking at her father sympathetically.

No-one spoke. They didn't want to upset the old man. Anyhow, what could they say? Next day, the house was in an uproar. The morning newspaper had been delivered and even the milkman mentioned the headlines:

'Local hero saves lives in tragedy. But for an amateur performance at the local church hall, more people would have died when a bus driver had a heart attack and ploughed his bus into a busy pub.'

The report went on with the details of the accident and named Tom and his grandson as the heroes. It said how remarkable the ventriloquist act had been and encouraged people to find out where the next performance was being held – and make sure they were there. Apparently, it was not something to be missed.

In the middle of breakfast, the shrill sound of the telephone made everyone jump. And that was the start of it! Calls came regularly and frequently. Newspapers wanted to speak with Tom and Freddie in a face-to-face interview. The question on everyone's lips was 'How could they have known a bus would crash into a building and kill people?' There was no answer and some readers couldn't believe it - but many did – after all there were enough witnesses in the church hall who'd heard the prediction. Theatres and their agents contacted Tom asking if he'd like to perform there and Tom was so taken aback, he couldn't believe it. He had a conversation with Morty as he was the only one who really knew what was going on.

He asked the dummy outright, "How did you know Morty? I know it was you speaking although the audience thought it was me – don't ignore me, we're alone here so you can talk. I won't tell anyone you've suddenly developed special powers, honest I won't, but you're beginning to scare me."

Morty said nothing but just sat there on his own chair, his expression the same as always. He had indeed developed an ability to think and imagine, something for which he had no explanation. On occasion, he could not only talk, but he could walk as well – as the bully girls had discovered. It was his secret however and he didn't even want to share it with Tom, his oldest friend. It was all too ridiculous and people would begin to treat him like a freak, which he would most certainly be – a small wooden man with no vocal chords nor muscle and bone – and yet he could walk and talk. He'd only recently discovered that he could see into people's minds, read their thoughts and predict their future. 'My world is changing and I have to change with it, but I'm safe as long as I keep it my secret. If people learned what I can really do, they'd treat me like a monster!'

He looked at Tom and wondered if he could risk a few words. Well, it was Tom after all – he could trust Tom, he was sure. He blinked his blue, glass eyes and sat bolt upright in his chair.

"As long as you swear to secrecy, I can tell you." Morty's own voice sounded just like Tom's, in fact, it was exactly like Tom's.

"You have my word, I won't tell a soul. But now they're inviting us to perform in their theatres, I need to know what you're capable of. We've been friends a long time Morty and you know you can trust me."

Morty explained about his new senses and how he really didn't know how it had happened, but he was willing to go on working with the act and playing the part of a complete dummy. "As long as you understand I'm not dumb Tom." The two friends nodded their heads in agreement – they felt like kindred spirits and conspirators.

They were performing in the next town which was much bigger and busier than the church hall. It was a proper theatre and they had a dressing room all to themselves. Important or what? Tom and Freddie even had to wear makeup because of the bright lights. At least that was something Morty didn't have to do, as his makeup was permanent. Their act was due half way through the show, not the 'Top of the Bill' of course, but still an act the audience were excited about. They heard the other acts coming and going and then there was an intermission.   They were due on after the break and they waited patiently in the wings.

The heavy curtain went up to find an elderly man sitting in the middle of the stage with his dummy perched on his knee. Young Freddie stood by his side, waiting to go down and mix with the audience. The stage was mainly dark but with subdued lighting at each side. Tom sat in an ancient armchair with a high back – a good theatre prop – and it looked as though the audience were sharing a sitting room. The stage looked eerie and a spotlight shone on Morty's face, making his cheeks seem more rosier than ever. It was a good setting and just what the performance needed. The audience sat stiff-backed, waiting nervously.

Object after object was given to Freddie and object after object was recognised by Morty. Tom of course wore a blindfold as usual and couldn't see what Freddie was holding. What the audience – and even Freddie – didn't know was that it was the wooden dummy himself who could clearly see what Freddie was holding up.

The first few personal objects were straightforward and Morty described them in detail, much to the owners' amazement. A diary, a wallet, a pearl necklace and such things were the usual and Morty made sure his skill didn't come across as too easy – he would hesitate every so often for realism. The incredible skills of the performers were certainly appreciated by the audience.

Tom added to the suspense by asking for a glass of water in the middle of the performance – and asking the audience if they would forgive him if he removed his blindfold for a few moments. "I need to breathe." It all added to the theatrics and built up the tension. While he was doing it, he allowed Morty to slip to the floor where he lay in a crumpled heap.

Now, there was a young woman – a very pretty young woman, Freddie noticed. She was dressed in a heavy coat that looked too big for her and she looked harassed with a flushed complexion. She handed Freddie a bangle which she'd just taken off and whispered to him, "My boyfriend gave me this some months ago and now he's disappeared. I wonder if the ventriloquist could tell me where he's gone." She sounded quite desperate and her eyes had filled with tears.

Freddie asked Morty what he held in his hands. He used the secret code words and although Tom couldn't see the bangle, Morty could. He could also see how distressed she seemed. Tom began to ask some questions, but suddenly Morty cut him short and started to speak.

Firstly, he asked the young woman her name and was told it was Judith. "Sit down Judith, you look exhausted." The little wooden man looked as concerned as an immobile piece of carved wood could look.

"Judith, I want you to listen to what I have to say. Your problem should really be discussed in private but as you've already chosen this public place, then so must I. You've recently been through quite an ordeal, haven't you – something you knew was coming but not exactly when? Is that right?" Even Tom was fidgeting in his chair, unsure of what Morty was up to. Freddie just looked awkward. 'What was going to happen – what was Grandpa up to?' He looked confused, standing there, holding Judith's bangle.

"You've left something outside, haven't you? Something very precious but something you don't want? Is it fair to say that?" Morty asked.

Judith nodded her head and great tears rolled down her cheeks. Everyone in the audience was staring at her.

"You remember where you left it, don't you? If you were to go back there now, it would still be there. Before you decide what to do, I want to tell you something. What you've abandoned under that tree in the park, could become the best friend you'll ever have. I want you to go back and check it's all right – only you know exactly where it is."

She stood up but made no move to leave the theatre, "I can't! I really can't! It's better off without me – I'm no use, you see. I've never been much use."

"Nonsense!" The wooden dummy sounded quite severe, "You will be of great use to your son or daughter. What is it, by the way?"

The entire audience were on the edge of their seats and those furthest away were craning their necks to see the woman's face.

"It's a girl! A very little girl!" was all she could manage and she held out her hand as though asking for help.

Morty went on, "Go quickly – back to the park before the night gets any colder. Take the baby to the hospital by the park and tell them what's happened to you – they'll help. You won't be punished – but if you were to leave the baby abandoned there, the police wouldn't be happy. It's all out in the open now, so you must do the right thing."

And she did! She took her bangle from Freddie, pulled her coat collar up around her face and walked slowly out of the theatre. She had an unusual gait and walked unsteadily, probably because she'd had no medical attention since giving birth. She must have felt she'd been to Hell and back! Why she'd chosen to come into the theatre was a mystery, but thank God she did, or that baby could have died – in fact, still might.

Tom pulled off his blindfold to the spontaneous applause breaking out all around him.

"You're a bloody hero," a man shouted from the audience and several others echoed his words. Tom didn't know what to say, so he said nothing. Another member of the audience, who turned out to be a nurse, followed the young woman to the park. The baby girl was still lying there, wrapped in a blanket and the nurse was pleased to hear her crying. She took the woman and the baby to the hospital and as Morty had said, they treated them well. After all, they weren't there to judge!

Back in the theatre, the stage manager tried to get the show back on track – but it just wasn't possible and the rest of the performers had to accept they wouldn't be 'going on' that night. It had all been too traumatic and the audience wanted to leave, to tell others what they'd just witnessed. The man was a positive hero and of course, the newspapers would soon get to hear of the story.

Next day, Tom and Freddie were forced to hide at home, as several reporters were camped outside the door. It was a good story and they weren't going to miss out on it. Tom and Freddie talked non-stop, going over what had happened. Freddie kept asking, "How could you have known about the baby Grandpa?" And of course, Tom didn't know what to tell him – it was all Morty's doing. If he said that however, the new act would be finished for good or he'd be committed to an asylum. One or the other!

Freddie let to go meet his friends, who were all eager to hear about the night before. He had to push his way through the reporters and avoided their questions about his Grandfather. Tom and Morty were left alone together in the sitting room, and to Tom's surprise, Morty jumped off his chair and stood in the middle of the room. He may only have been a metre high but he looked quite imposing nonetheless, standing there in his gentleman's suit. His wooden face still shone in the sunlight and his fixed smile seemed genuine enough.

"Well Tom, you knew I could talk, but you've never actually seen me walk. Are you suitably impressed?" The dummy enjoyed the expression on Tom's face.

He was speechless – his ventriloquist's dummy never ceased to amaze him. He just sat there and waited for Morty to say more.

"I've decided to make you a very rich man, Tom – you and your family, that is. I know I've become a walking, talking miracle and I don't know how it's happened – but it has – and you'll have to accept it."

"A rich man, you say and how do you propose to make that happen?" Despite his astonishment, Tom was intrigued.

"Surely you can see this miracle standing before you. Our act is already becoming known nationally and if we continue performing, we'll be wanted by many more theatres. The sky will be the limit – as you've already witnessed, I can see everything quite clearly. I could talk to the people without your help, you know – but I must admit your voice is my voice, so I do need you. We can go on reading peoples' minds - a masked ventriloquist and a little, wooden man. That is the amazing part of the act but we must keep the secret between you and me – and no-one else." It was a long speech, but it made sense.

"Is that how you knew about the girl's baby last night – did you read her mind? Can you really do that?"

"Got it in one – she was so distraught by what she'd just done, it was the only thing on her mind, so it was easy. She could think of nothing else, you see and I think she came into the theatre because she had nowhere else to go. That's all – but it was good for us."

As he puffed at his pipe, Tom asked, "How long have you known about your new ability? I'm sure not that long ago, you couldn't have done such a thing. Is that right?"

"That's exactly right – I don't know exactly when it changed, but it meant I could get around by myself and talk when I wanted – the only thing that hasn't changed is my appearance. I'm a ventriloquist's dummy and I look like it, so people still look at me twice, or even three times. I should tell you now, I was the one who found the two bullies at the school – and I gave them what for, I can tell you. You were too upset at the time and didn't know what to do about it, so I stepped in."

"Well, it certainly worked, I've not heard her mention them since. Thank you for doing that. So, where do we go from here, Morty?"

"Well, as I said before, our act could become very special and sought-after, and we could make a lot of money. That wouldn't only benefit you, but also your family. But remember, no-one else can ever know what I'm capable of – the miracle must remain our secret. People already point at me in the street and I don't want it to get worse. They'd call me a circus freak and my life would be miserable. Remember what happened to the Elephant Man when he became well known – his life wasn't worth living. You can see that, can't you Tom?

"Of course, but it's not going to be easy keeping the secret, especially from Freddie. He wants to leave school now and become my full-time assistant, so if his parents allow it, he'll be around a lot of the time."

"Not a problem – Freddie's an important part of our act, so he must stay. But now you must speak with those reporters and tell them you're going to be putting on more shows where you intend to astonish the audiences even more. And I'll make sure you do just that!"

And that was how Tom and his dummy hit the big time. The papers printed the story and gave all the credit to the old man and not to the wooden one. It suited everyone! Freddie was allowed to leave school and he and his Grandpa practised secret words even more. The new arrangements put very little pressure on Tom, who had to do nothing more than sit on the stage wearing a blindfold.

Molly was unsure about the whole thing however and worried it would put too great a strain on her father. After all, he wasn't getting any younger. She tackled him one evening. "Pops, how can you read some peoples' minds and not others? How did you teach yourself to do it – you certainly couldn't do it before, so what changed? I'm only asking because I'm worried about you."

And who could blame her? She couldn't complain however as the household had never been so well off and everyone was benefitting from Tom and Freddie's performances. In fact, the act was becoming so popular, Molly offered to give up her job and become the pair's personal agent. It was now a real family affair and Margaret even helped design the adverts, posters and programmes. The only problem was there was much more travel needed now, as theatres far and wide had started to contact Tom. He didn't really care for travel but it was the name of the game and he knew how much everyone else was enjoying it. He also knew he was making the family's future safe – his way of paying them back for taking him in when he lost Molly's mum.

The words 'Partners in Crime' seemed appropriate or the old man and his dummy, but Tom was still curious as to how Morty had gained his exceptional skills. He'd even begun to have an opinion on most issues, even politics and he and Tom had regular discussions on 'who was right and who was wrong.' Inevitably, Morty won!

"You mark my words," Tom was on his soapbox as he loved political arguments and Morty was always prepared to be his sparring partner, "The next Election is a foregone conclusion," he would say to irritate the old man."

"Never overlook the slow horse coming up on the inside Tom – it's happened before and if I were you, I'd put my cross against the least expected candidate – that is if you don't want to waste your vote." Needless to say, Morty didn't have a vote of his own but that didn't stop him from having an opinion about Tom's. Yes, for a while, they continued as good companions.

"Did I hear you talking to yourself again Grandpa? They'll be taking you away to the Loony Bin before long." Margaret had arrived home from school.

"I'll have you know I was talking to my good friend Morty here, so less of your cheek." But she'd already disappeared into the kitchen for an after-school snack – she'd always suspected Grandpa was a bit mad.

The next performance for the trio was an important one. It was to be at a private function, paid for by the couple hosting the big party. The evening was to be primarily a Casino, with gambling tables set up in the vast drawing room. There was to be an intermission and that was when Tom and his partners were to perform. The money was good, and they looked forward to something different. They travelled by train and booked into a hotel – Tom of course shared his room with Morty and they had a good chat well into the early hours of the morning.

'You'd better be good at this function Morty- we'll be surrounded by important people, worth a lot of money." Tom reached for his pipe and lit up.

"You just look after yourself old man – leave the rest to the real star of the show!" Morty thought again how sad it was that he didn't eat or drink as he watched Tom tuck into a large sandwich. Ah well. that was the cross he had to bear. "By the way, I think it's time I had another new suit – after all I'm the reason you've got so much money nowadays. I think I should always look as smart as possible."

"We can afford to get you a suit made by one of the best tailors in town Morty. When we get back home, I'll start the ball rolling." Tom knew he couldn't really grudge him a new suit.

"Oh no Tom, we should go back to the Jewish tailor Samuel, who made this suit. I like it and he probably needs the business." Morty felt quite magnanimous – and rich!

"Your call Morty – it'll save me money, so why should I argue?" and he finished off his tankard of beer, much to Morty's jealousy. He thought for a while and added, "You know, I think my special skills only began when Samuel made me this suit – so we certainly mustn't change tailors."

That evening, with Freddie in toe, they set off for the big house on the edge of town. Of course, they always travelled by taxi nowadays and when it drove up to the front door, they were astonished by how large the house was. In fact, it was really a mansion - no wonder the people could pay so much money. Freddie carried Morty in his holdall and rang the doorbell. To his amazement, a butler answered his call – at least he looked like a butler. He showed Freddie inside and waited for Tom to arrive behind him.

They were shown into a room where they could prepare themselves for the performance. Freddie excused himself and said he was going to have a shower, so Tom and Morty were left on their own.

"We've never done a Casino private party before – how different do you think it'll be?" Tom had placed Morty in an armchair and was busy re-tying the dummy's shoelaces. Morty jumped down and said, "I can do that myself Tom – I'm perfectly capable, you know."

"I don't doubt it, but you'd better not let Freddie see you bouncing around the room like that. As for the party tonight, I don't know how it'll go, but my instructions are that we mill around the big room where everyone will be, and at the intermission, we settle in a spot that's been set up with candles and curtains – it'll be made to look a bit scary, I've been told. Everyone will have to stop what they're doing and watch our performance. Pretty simple, eh?"

Morty was back on the chair when Freddie returned and so, was silent from then on, whilst Tom and his grandson went over their act - again. The code words were well known to both of them by now and of course, Freddie was still none the wiser about Morty's exceptional skills.

As promised, the drawing room was laid out as a casino with glittering lights, plush furniture and several small tables. Some tables had roulette wheels set up and some others had plush green tablecloths for cards. At the side was a bar, with drinks of all sorts ready for the thirsty crowd and a long table covered in buffet snacks. There were a couple of waiters as well, who floated around the room offering trays of drinks. The setting was wonderful and very authentic, with a slightly smoky haze in the room that added to the atmosphere. Tom and Freddie moved about but Morty had to stay perched on a chair much to his annoyance. He was curious and would have liked to join the others. The two chaps had one drink – as they couldn't risk having more – and they helped themselves to some savouries. They were enjoying themselves and they even placed a bet at one of the roulette tables – and lost!

At a signal from the host, they crossed to Morty and Tom settled down, lifting the dummy onto his knee. It was almost time and Freddie was feeling pretty nervous. People were all around the room and he even recognised some of the celebrities there. Tom of course was oblivious to this as he was already fiddling with his blindfold. The host -Mr Carmichael – introduced the evening's performers, who were 'brought to you at great expense.'

Freddie took his cue and moved nearer to the seated ladies and standing gentlemen, all of whom had a full glass in their hands. Freddie gave his usual speech and explained he would need some personal objects from the audience and then, how a blind-folded Tom would tell them things he couldn't possibly have known. They would be flabbergasted and amazed at his knowledge – he was blind and only the dummy would talk!

"This is Morty, Ladies and Gentlemen – proper name Mortimer. Your questions will be answered by him and he will provide details about your objects. Now, who amongst you would like to be first to test young Morty?" Tom's blindfold was firmly in place and Morty's legs dangled from his lap.

Everything went well. A few ladies and a couple of men gave objects to Freddie who described them to Tom, using the agreed words. There was a lot of laughter and innuendo and people seemed to warm to the little wooden chap in the mustard checked suit. He could be a cheeky chappie when he wanted to be. One man even shouted out, "Who's your tailor Morty – I'd like a suit like that, but with longer trousers!" Morty responded, "I'm afraid you couldn't afford my tailor." Everyone enjoyed the witty banter that went to and fro – the dummy being able to give as good as he got.

It was the usual type of objects and Morty managed to amaze the guests. Some tried to trick him and swopped their bits and pieces for different things but sharp-eyed Morty saw what they were up to and stayed in control of the show. When it was over, the performers were invited to stay for the rest of the evening and perhaps place a bet or two. They were wildly applauded by everyone and they felt they'd given good value for their money.

Freddie and Tom mingled with the guests, but Morty had to remain propped on a chair at the side of the room. His eyes followed them around though and he felt envious of the fun they were obviously having. In the second half of the evening, many people set off home but those left behind, mostly settled down to play poker. Tom and Freddie kept well out of it – the stakes were too high – but some of the men were obsessed with winning more and more. Mr Carmichael the host, was one of those and he was making some large bets, rarely winning, but clearly enjoying the excitement of the game. He was at a table of six men and all of them were very serious players, equally determined to win. Tom and Freddie were mesmerised at the enormity of the bets being placed and hung around to see what would happen. Mr Carmichael was pretty drunk and getting even more so by the minute, but still he kept right on placing bets. He seemed to see one particular man at the table as his rival. Tom and Freddie moved closer to the table and listened to the conversation. There seemed to be a lot of 'I'll raise you' and 'I'll cover that', and one by one, the other four men withdrew saying they'd 'folded' and the betting was 'too rich' for them. Only Mr Carmichael (Bob) and Pete his opponent, were still in the game, neither willing to give in.

Pete put down another pile of notes and when he ran out of money, he began to place I.O.Yous to keep up with Bob Carmichael's bets. It was beginning to be ridiculous and the two men were sweating, whilst the other players actually pushed their chairs away from the table, murmuring someone should stop them.

"Okay Bill, tell you what. I'll throw in my car and you know it's a good one!" Pete was becoming desperate.

"That's damned generous Pete, I'll take that bet and I'll put up this house and everything in it!" His eyes were glassy and his hands were shaking, but he was sure he was going to win.

"Darling, you're being silly. This has gone on long enough and remember this roof also covers your children's heads – and mine." His wife was becoming frantic and many of the guests were whispering loudly to each other. " They're both mad!"

"Darling, remind me if you will, who owns this house? I think you'll find it's me!" and he called to the waiter to bring him another drink.

Suddenly and in a room of whispers and sighs, a strong male voice spoke out, "Don't do it! You'll regret it if you do!" And everyone looked towards the voice – it seemed to be coming from the ventriloquist's dummy himself, but everyone knew that wasn't possible.   To try to conceal wat was happening, Tom crossed the room towards Morty, but before he reached him, Bill asked who had spoken.

Morty spoke again, "Don't place that bet, I tell you. You must allow your opponent to see your cards – stop betting now or you'll lose your house and everything you own! If you don't do as I say, you'll be a sorry man for the rest of your life!"

All the guests were quiet and wondered how the old man knew what was going to happen. Not for one moment, did they believe the words came from the dummy – they must have come from the ventriloquist.

Bill threw up his hands in despair! It was all too much for him and he knew really that he was behaving like a fool. He looked at Pete, "Okay, I'll see you now and if your hands better than mine, then you've won the game so far."

Pete slowly placed his cards on the table and everyone strained to see them. Bill threw his hand of cards down, saying, "All I needed was one more good card. Out of interest Pete, can I see what the next card would have been? I know I'm a glutton for punishment but that's just the way I am."

Pete flicked the next card from the pack and it was a Deuce, which was far lower than Bill needed to win. Pete gathered up his winnings and left the room, knowing he wasn't very popular at the moment.

Mrs Carmichael walked over to Tom and Morty. Tears were streaming down her face and she reached out and kissed Tom on his cheek. "Thank you so much! You've saved my life and that of my children. But for you, we would have been homeless. How did you know however – how did you know how low the card would be?"

Tom said nothing, just smiled and looked at Morty, who as usual was sitting there, silent and still. He gathered up the dummy and beckoned Freddie to join him. The night was over and there was a taxi waiting to take them home. 'Home.' God it sounded good.

The hostess followed them to the door to say goodnight and asked if she could call on them in a couple of days, to say thank them properly.

"Of course, Madam, you're most welcome." And the two men with Morty, climbed into the taxi and left behind what had turned out to be a very strange evening.

When the whole household had gone to bed for the night and after Tom had been given a thorough questioning by Freddie, a flustered Grandpa stuttered a few words that made no sense - he had no answer to give and was unable to explain how he'd thrown his voice to Morty – all the way across the room. He told Freddie, "I managed it and that's all you need to know."

In the quiet of their shared room, Tom questioned Morty. "Well young man, what exactly went on tonight? You could have knocked me down with a feather when I heard you talk and I was no-where near you. You could have blown it then, you know!"

Morty was relaxing on Tom's bed and looked almost like a real, but very short man, His feet were crossed and his hands were behind his back. He smiled, "I had no option Tom – I had to stop the stupid man from losing his home. He was placing everything on the turn of one card – and I could see what that card was. He'd have lost everything, the stupid berk!"

"How on earth could you see the next card in the deck? That's impossible!" Tom was getting ready for bed and hoped Morty would soon remove himself from that bed.

"Not impossible Old Chap – I've told you about all the extra skills I've developed recently – and seeing through things is just one of them."   The dummy was becoming more and more conceited with each passing day.

"You're going to have to learn to curb your skills young man – I admit you've become amazing but don't get too big for your boots or what you dread most will happen – people will learn the little wooden man can walk and talk, as well as do the most amazing tricks. You'll never get peace then – you'll become that circus freak you hate to think about."

Morty didn't answer the old man, just climbed off the bed and onto his own bedroom chair – he was finished talking – he'd done rather a lot that particular day.

Two days later, a very swanky car drove up outside the house and Mrs Carmichael climbed out. Molly opened the door and invited her inside, although she wasn't sure who she was. She was a charming lady however and settled on the sofa in the front room, opposite Tom.

"Tea? Coffee?" Molly asked and then scuttled off into the kitchen to allow them to talk. She was curious of course, but she knew the lady's name and as her father's agent, she was aware she'd booked the recent private party, 'What's amiss?' she as thinking.

"I've just come to say thank you again for your intervention at last night's 'Do'. If it hadn't been for you, I might have been searching for digs as we speak."

Tom made some disparaging sounds and mumbled she was welcome. He was very aware he was being thanked for something Morty had done – he was taking the credit for his dummy's quick thinking. But that was how it had to be!

"Please call me Beatrice – Mrs Carmichael sounds so formal – and you're Tom, I know. Actually, I've not only come to say thank you but to tell you I believe you've even saved my marriage – not just the roof over my head. You see, my husband was fast going to wrack and ruin – he was drinking morning and night and his gambling was going to bankrupt us. You see the picture I'm painting?"

Tom just nodded, before she went on, "I was at my wit's end and knew something had to be done but I didn't know what. Then, you came along and gave him such a scare that he's like a different man today. He swears he'll never have another drink and he won't be gambling any more – his shock was so huge when he realised he'd almost lost our home and all it contained. And all on the turn of one card – even he was dismayed by his own stupidity – and how close he came to punishing his family."

"Ma'am, I'm sorry for all you've been through but I'm pleased there's a light at the end of the tunnel. It's going to be rough for a time, I'm afraid, giving up both vices at the same time won't be easy - but with you beside him, I'm sure he'll succeed."

"Thank you, Tom, – and I have something here for you. You really deserve it – and if you refuse it, I'll be greatly offended.

She handed him a slip of paper and drained her coffee cup before she rose.

Tom's eyes grew round in disbelief, he was lost for words, "I can't accept this Beatrice – it's far too much." He looked down at the cheque for £10,000 and swallowed hard. He'd never seen so much money!

"Now Tom, remember what I said, if you refuse the cheque, I'll be offended – and you wouldn't want that, would you?" She bent down and for the second time, kissed his withered cheek, then left the house and disappeared into her swanky car.

Tom just sat there! My God, what on earth would happen next – and all these strange things happened because of Morty. 'I must go and tell him!' Then he realised he was treating the dummy as a real person and wondered if that was wise.

In his bedroom, Morty was again stretched out on Tom's bed. "You've got to stop moving about so much or someone's going to catch you – and then you'll have to come clean." Tom felt annoyed with Morty now, he was fast becoming too big for his boots and enjoyed showing off. Anyway, Tom didn't like him lying on his bed.

"That's a nice sum of money you've got there, although I think it really belongs to me." He was studying his finger nails in an affected way, but he really meant every word.

"And what would you do with a cheque? You don't even have a bank account." Tom was losing his patience.

"I bet I could get one though although I admit having no Passport or Birth Certificate might make it a bit problematic. No, I think it's best in your safe hands, but now you're rolling in it, when am I to have my new suit? I know exactly the material I want – a tweed mixture of heather colours."

"That's a bit over the top Morty, you don't want to look ridiculous." Tom was teasing him as Morty already looked quite ridiculous in his mustard check. To Morty however, he was a toff and should get anything he wanted.

"A pity I'm not taller," he said. "If I could just be as tall as you and Freddie, I'd be quite happy." He flicked an imaginary fleck from his sleeve as he'd seen another toff do at the party.

"My God, you're a dandy Morty – a veritable dandy and I think you're also developing a chip on your shoulder. You're developing human feelings and emotions, I'm afraid." He was laughing at the little man, but Morty was deadly serious and pushed the imaginary 'chip' from his shoulder. Tom realised his vanity was making him easy to tease.

"When can we go and see our friend, the tailor – the Jewish one mind you, I'll have no-one else, but Samuel." And so, after depositing the cheque in the bank, Tom took him back to see his Jewish tailor.

"Tom – how good to see you and your little friend. Now, which one of you do I have to measure? So, it's Morty again – two new suits in a few months – business must be good."

Samuel was delighted to see his old friend and told him to take a seat while he went to the back to fill the kettle. He was a typical Jewish man and spoke in the usual, lilting voice of his people.

A cup of tea and much reminiscing later, Samuel reached for his tape measure, "At least I don't have to measure my customer again – I still have his measurements from last time. Now what is it you say, a heather style tweed material – now that's unusual and I'll have to dig deep into my stock to see what I have. Nothing but the best for young Morty!" And he disappeared behind the curtain.

Tom was worried about Morty – he could be unpredictable when he wanted – and he was becoming cheekier and almost too confident of late. Samuel soon returned with a brown coloured bolt of cloth. "This is a good tweed Tom, do you think Morty would like this? I can make up a smart suit with this and he'll receive lots of admiring glances."

Pretending to examine the cloth, Tom looked at Morty and clearly saw his mouth say, 'No'. "It's a lovely piece of cloth Samuel, but I know Morty wanted something with a bit of blue – sort of heather-like. Have you got something like that?" Samuel went back behind the curtain and sounds of heavy bolts of cloth being moved were heard.

Tom put his finger to his lips to remind Morty he mustn't talk. The dummy just smirked. Samuel returned and this time, he had just the kind of cloth Morty wanted.

"That's the one Samuel – that's what Morty wants." Tom was relieved as he was becoming less sure of what Morty would do if he wasn't satisfied.

"Leave everything to me Tom and it'll be ready for Morty in a week. By the way, I'm moving premises – just down the road to those purpose-built shops – built especially for good quality businesses like mine. It'll be lighter than this one and not so damp." He made to take the cloth into the back, when Tom felt a sudden impulse to grab his friend's arm. Morty was signalling to him.

"Morty has something to tell you Samuel. I know that sounds odd but sometimes he does that. Of course, I'll be throwing my voice, but he wants to tell you himself." Now Tom really was worried.

He lifted Morty onto his knee and moved the dummy's head around so it was looking at Samuel. The dummy began to talk, "You should stay in this shop Mr Tailor and not go to those new ones down the road. If you do, you'll regret it almost immediately."

"Why Tom – Morty – what do you mean?" It's a great opportunity for me and I'd be a fool to miss it." Samuel was bemused and wondered what his old friend was trying to tell him.

Tom spoke again, through Morty, "Something bad is going to happen around those shops and if you're there, you'll suffer with everyone else.

Samuel looked straight at Tom, "Tom, my friend, why are you saying this? I really want to move my premises. Now, you're making me question my decision. Are you just pulling my leg – is it your little joke perhaps?" Samuel sat down behind his counter, looking perplexed.

Tom put Morty back into his bag and looked at the friend he'd known for more years than he cared to remember. "Samuel, I know you probably think Morty and I are mad – but we're truly not. He wanted you to hear the message from his own lips and I've seen him do such things before. He and I have a 'kindred-spirit' relationship now and I know when he wants to give advice. To be absolutely honest, he's usually right so perhaps you should take note of his warning. The decision is yours however and I'll leave you with Morty's message to do with what you will."

He took his bag and his dummy and left Samuel's premises, saying he'd come back in a week's time – either to this shop or failing that, to the new shop down the road.

That night, Molly had prepared a lovely dinner to celebrate Tom's large windfall from Mrs Carmichael. The whole family were sitting around the table and Tom raised his wine glass to toast the generous lady, then he went to his room to fetch Morty. He should be at the special 'do' as well!

"It's only fair that he joins the celebrations – after all it was really he who gave the warning on the night." Everyone laughed and held up their glasses to toast Morty – but their toast sounded insincere, after all they knew Tom was the true hero. The dummy's forehead seemed to have extra deep lines and the old man knew he was angry. In fact, Morty was seething! His mind was working overtime, 'What right did they have to laugh? He was the hero in the house and because of his quick thinking, they now had a generous amount of money to spend. They were telling Tom what a wonderful man he was and ignoring the little wooden hero sitting in their midst. He slumped forward and Freddie laughed and said, "Who did that? Who pushed Morty?" Morty remained with his head on the table, 'He didn't want to be here amongst these ignorant people. But they were just like everyone else and thought of him as nothing more than a lump of dead wood. They were the sort of people who'd probably call him freak and weird, if they knew of what he was capable. The world could do without such people and he'd have to teach them a lesson!

Tom quickly removed him back to the bedroom and placed him on the chair – Morty however, had other ideas and threw himself onto the bed. 'He was too important now to sit on the hard chair.' Tom told him he must behave better or people would suspect his secret. Hoping he'd made his point, he left an angry Morty to think.

A few days passed and Molly was working flat-out arranging theatre performances, one after the other. She made a very competent secretary and kept Tom aware of what was happening. One day, she happened to say," Pops, have you ever thought of getting a new dummy – Morty's getting rather old now and perhaps a bright, new one would engage the audience more – you know, a more modern dummy perhaps. What do you think?

Tom looked at Freddie who was relaxing in front of the telly and the young man grimaced at such a suggestion. "You'd better not let Morty hear you say that Mum."

"Don't be silly Freddie, Morty can't hear what I say, he's made of wood." She laughed at such a thought but of course, Freddie was right, 'A good thing Morty hadn't heard Molly's words.' Morty may not have heard the woman's words, but he knew exactly what she was thinking.

'Change dummy indeed! Where on earth would Tom find a dummy like me? Nowhere – that's where!' He tackled Tom later that day, "What's that stupid woman been saying now? Does she really believe your performances would be better with a different dummy?

"Calm down Morty – she didn't mean it," and in an attempt to change the subject, he produced that morning's newspaper. "Look at page two and you'll see something amazing."

The bold headline read:

' NEW SHOPS BURN DOWN WITH ALL STOCK INSIDE

A fault in the electric system sparked off a fire in one of the stock rooms. Only one man was hurt whilst trying to tackle the blaze, which quickly spread from one shop to another.

He is now recovering from smoke-inhalation in hospital and should be discharged next week.

It's not known how the faulty electricity occurred as work had only recently finished on the premises, but the stock in several shops was completely destroyed.'

"You told old Samuel not to move to one of those shops – let's hope he listened to you. We'll be going there in a couple of days, so well find out." Tom had been astounded when he'd read about the line of new shops going up in flames, and again found himself amazed by Morty's strange skills. The little wooden man was growing weirder and more prophetic every day, but he certainly had his uses. Tom could cope with the weirdness, but the dummy's increasing bad temper was harder to take.

Samuel's tailor shop was still where it had always been when Tom arrived outside. All the stock was still around the shop and it was obvious that Samuel had thought twice about moving to the new shop.

"Tom, my you're a sight for sore eyes! Welcome! Welcome my friend! You've never been more welcome! I've been waiting to ask how you knew the new shops would go on fire. One that burned to the ground would have been mine – and I would have lost everything. By everything, I don't mean just bolts of cloth but all the equipment I've had for years – things I'd be lost without." He didn't pause for an answer, before going through the curtain to the back – of course he was going to get a fresh pot of tea.

They all sat there together – Tom and Samuel on chairs and Morty, out of his bag and on top of the counter. Tom said, "Samuel, I honestly don't know how I knew to warn you, but something told me it would be a bad idea for you to move." From the corner of his eye, he saw Morty move slightly - luckily Samuel saw nothing. He knew Morty wasn't pleased that, yet again, Tom was being given credit that right-fully belonged to him. To cover the silence, Tom asked, "Is this young man's suit ready Samuel?"

" Indeed, it is and I'm very proud of it!" He reached beneath the counter and patted Morty's head as he did so, "Now then Master Morty, wait 'till you see what I've got for you." And he produced an immaculate suit of clothes in a beautiful, heather material, which shone in the sunlight in shades of mauve, green and even pink. It was an amazing suit of clothes.

"Eh Morty Lad – he's done you proud and no mistake!" Tom was very pleased.

"And I've sewn the same lucky charm into the lining – my Jewish way of taking care of him – I won't tell you what it is, as that would spoil the luck. Just be assured it will keep him from harm – in fact, it will bring him only good things – it's an ancient Jewish charm, often used by my people throughout many generations. I always sew it into my own clothes." Samuel was really convinced his Jewish charm would bring good luck – and Tom was happy to go along with it.

The old friends parted and yet again, the tailor refused to take any money for his service, telling Tom he wouldn't be standing where he was – nor would his business – but for his timely warning. Tom had plenty money these days and could easily afford to pay, but he couldn't very well force the money on his friend. As an old Jewish gentleman, Samuel's pride was more important than any money.

Dressed in his new heather-coloured suit, Morty gave a perfect performance at the next show, which was in a town where they'd never played before. It was a good audience who immediately became involved in the act. There was a lot of laughing and gasps of astonishment when the dummy voiced their secrets. It was a successful act and as long as people kept coming up with different objects – all of which Morty could see quite clearly – there was no limit to the entertainment. The best thing however was the little stories he told about some of the things – things the old man couldn't possibly have known, but Morty did. He was becoming increasingly confident and came up with jokes and funny stories about the objects – and sometimes about the people themselves.

After the show and in the privacy of their bedroom, Tom tentatively raised the subject of Morty's increasing 'adlibbing'. "You should remember people think I am the one saying the things and sometimes, you say things that might offend. That's not supposed to be part of the act."

The dummy stretched to his full height and faced the old man. "Just who do you think you're talking to? The act would be nothing without me and my amazing ability. I'm who the public really come to see – not you, and that half-witted boy, Freddie." The dummy was certainly on his high horse.

"How dare you call Freddie a half-wit? He's a bright lad and he's always been nice to you. A year ago, you were my ventriloquist's dummy and now you're trying to take over the act. What's made you change so much Morty – I don't understand you anymore. We always got on so well, but that's not been the case for some time now. Is there anything you want to tell me?"

There was no doubt – Morty was angry. He flicked an imaginary fleck of dust from his jacket and Tom knew something bad was coming. He always did that just before he let rip about something or other – he even did it during the act when he was being insulting to people. It seemed he was becoming a 'Jekyll and Hide character, with Hide emerging more and more.

"You know Tom – you're becoming as critical as my previous owner and in the end, he and I couldn't even speak to each other. In fact, at the very end, I even had to get rid of him - I wouldn't want to have to do something like that to you, now would I?"

The little man's face began to change and the two lines around his mouth definitely became deeper. It gave him a sinister look and in his natty suit, he really looked like an American gangster - going in for the kill. His brow was more furrowed than Tom had seen it before and suddenly his rosy red cheeks didn't look rosy anymore – they just looked angry.

"And don't even think about shutting me up by putting me in the bag – I'm tougher than you think and I just won't let you do it. I know how to defend myself and would be quite happy to hurt you, if it was necessary! I used to think you were my friend but I was quite wrong."

Tom stood up and told the dummy he was leaving. He would be sleeping on the sofa in the living room from then on. All Morty did then, was to remove his smart jacket and lie down on the bed – his bed now, if he chose. He'd like a night without the old man's snoring anyway!

Tom was scared, very scared in fact – the dummy was beyond his control and he knew it. Luckily, the rest of the house had already gone to bed and he had the living room to himself.Otherwise, he'd have found it difficult to explain the sofa! It was creepy now – at the beginning it was amusing and Morty's skills really did make the act – but now he had completely changed and had become sinister. He was angry all the time and always ready to pick a fight with anyone and everyone. Even with the audiences, he was always ready to argue the toss with someone. 'What on earth am I going to do?' Tom wondered. 'I can't really tell anyone about him and how human he's becoming – not only human, but a bad-tempered and angry human. Who would believe me anyhow?"

Lying on the sofa, in the still grey early hours of the morning, he knew it was time he did something. There was no doubt that

Morty was becoming unbearable and very unstable. But what could he do? A year ago, the dummy had just been a dummy. but something drastic had changed him in the last few months. Tom realised he was becoming scared of Morty and of what he might do next. He could walk and talk - and worse, he could think and plan. He feared for his family as he now knew Morty didn't like them at all. Then a new thought suddenly struck him – a new and incredible thought. The only changes to Morty in the past year were his two new suits made by Jewish Samuel. But suits couldn't affect him, could they? Of course not, but now he'd had the thought, he decided to go and visit his old friend and ask for his advice.

"Well, the only thing I did to Morty's suits was to sew a lucky charm inside the lining, other than that, I did nothing. A lucky charm couldn't have affected a dummy – that could never happen. Why are you so worried about him? When all's said and done, he is only a ventriloquist's dummy – and you've had him for many years, so why should you think he's changed so much? And how can a man made of wood change at all?"

Tom couldn't tell him the truth. He'd only said that Morty was becoming more difficult to handle of late and the act was not as streamlined as it had once been. He couldn't very well tell Samuel that Morty walked, talked, had bouts of temper and frequently talked out of turn. He'd also developed a need to criticise everyone – he'd become cruel and imagined bad in everyone, when there was none. No, he couldn't tell the tailor the real reason the dummy was harder to handle these days. Samuel didn't think it was the lucky charms and he must accept that and anyway, the tailor had only done it to show his gratitude. Nothing sinister in that!

He went straight home then and took out the first suit Samuel had made. When he tore the lining, he found the lucky charm – and that's all it was – a lucky charm. He spoke with another Jewish friend and discovered it was the Jewish 'Hand of Hasma' – known for representing the relationship between God and man. Maybe it should only be worn by Jews and Morty certainly wasn't that. Tom told himself he was being silly – the little brass 'Hand of Hasma' he held couldn't have affected Morty.

In his haste, he forgot to return the suit to the wardrobe and left the charm on the bedside table. Careless or what! Morty had been lying on the bed and if he'd been human, Tom would have thought he was asleep, but his permanently-open eyes told a different story. He sat up and looked at Tom with distaste in his eyes. "You've ripped my suit? Why have you done that? You know I love my suits. And you've removed the little charm Samuel gave, to keep me safe. Why are you turning against me? I won't stand for it – I'm finished being your dummy – I'm a man in my own right and I won't work with you any longer. You're just an amateur, not a star like me."

The dummy was fuming. Tom had never seen him like this before. He knew now that he had to dismantle his friend, but Morty was able to read his thoughts and said, "Don't you come near me, you stupid old fool. I'm far too strong now. In fact, I'm going to tell you something – something you should know. I'm going to tell you this so you'll realise you have to go on looking after me. I may be far more capable than anyone knows, but I still need someone to put a roof over my head and get me what I want, when I want it. I don't like my dependency on people – but I'm stuck with it."''

He was sitting on the edge of the bed now, swinging his short legs over the side. "The master I had before you, was just like you and after I'd been with him for a while, he began to resent my increasing skills- just as you're doing now. The changes happen every 50 years or so and then, I become stronger and more capable. This has been happening over the past year and although I knew the changes were due, I didn't think it was actually time yet. My old master became more and more suspicious – again just like you – and he started to deny me what I wanted. He was an old codger just like you, so it wasn't too hard to deal with him. I just placed a pillow over his face one night and I lay on top until he stopped breathing. It was so easy, I could hardly believe it. In fact, it was really actually funny and made me laugh." As he was talking, he was fingering the little lucky charm and he suddenly threw it at Tom, "And tell that lazy cow of a daughter you have, to sew this back into my suit. It's a load of rubbish of course – stupid little trinket - that's all it is, but why take the chance? A little bit of luck won't hurt me!"

Tom took the jacket to Molly and asked her to sew it for him. She asked, "But how did it get so badly torn Pops – it couldn't have been Morty," she said laughing." But she fetched her sewing basket and did as she was asked. Her husband Fred had just returned from work and he was hungry. "Supper's nearly ready Fred – just give me a minute to sew this for Pops."

When Tom went back to his room, Morty wasn't there. 'Now where could he be? He rarely went out on his own, in case people laughed at him, so, where was he?

However, the dummy had returned when Tom came back – but he seemed to be avoiding Tom's eyes. 'Now, what had he been up to?' Tom had decided he couldn't sleep in his own bedroom anymore – Morty had made him aware of what might happen, and now he couldn't get the vision of the dummy on top of a pillow pressing down and down until the man could breathe no more.

Molly had objected at first, "Pops you can't sleep on the sofa every night – not when you've got your own bed. Your back, you say – the mattress is too firm and you can't get comfortable." She thought it didn't ring true but he was an old man and he should be allowed to be eccentric on occasion.

Morty looked up when he entered his room to get a book. "Well now Tom, have I scared you? A little man like me who couldn't hurt a fly – or could I?" and he laughed a villain's theatrical laugh. Tom coughed to cover the dummy laughter, as he knew Margaret and Freddie were home and would hear it.

That night around the table, the family had just eaten a very tasty supper. "Pops, it's your favourite pudding, you've got to have some." But Tom was adamant and pushed his plate away. "Not tonight Molly – I think I've eaten too much already – a pudding would be just too much. Keep it for me and I'll have it tomorrow."

After the meal, they all settled down to a game of Five Card Trumps – a favourite of theirs and one at which the youngsters were especially good. They laughed and teased each other and enjoyed a very good evening. Fred went to fetch another beer from the fridge and when he came back he'd thought of another joke- not a good joke – more of a groan joke, but it didn't matter. It was a happy atmosphere and everyone felt relaxed and at ease

– they had enough money now, thanks to Pop's new act, and they could have pretty much anything they wanted.

"Would you look at the time everybody – it's almost midnight. Where have the hours gone? I suppose none of you will say no to a mug of hot chocolate?" Molly already knew the answer to that and went into the kitchen. It had become a habit of theirs lately.

"Mum, I don't want hot chocolate – I've got a bit of a stomach ache – maybe I ate too much pudding!" Everyone was surprised at that, as Margaret rarely refused anything sweet.

That night, the weather was atrocious. The heavy rain battered against the windows and the sound of tree branches breaking from the trunks, could be heard amongst the heavy thunder and lightning. The wind was wild and a couple of slates from the roof had come loose – the noises could be heard all through the house. The weather was obviously disturbing the sleepers and the toilet chain could be heard regularly - everyone was obviously having difficulty settling down. The sounds of the storm reached their peak about four in the morning and eventually Tom managed to fall asleep, just as the first light of appeared.

The first thing he did when he awoke was fill the kettle – nothing like a cup of tea after such a wild night like. He also boiled a few eggs and filled the toaster with bread. 'I think I'll take them a cup of tea in bed today – after all, it's Sunday and no-one has to get up early. He bustled about in the kitchen and covered a tray with cups, saucers and a teapot.

He gently tapped on Molly and Fred's bedroom door and waited for a response, but none was forthcoming, so he knocked louder. 'They must be deeply asleep.' he thought. Still, no sound from inside the room, so he gently turned the door handle and opened the door. The curtains were still closed and the room was dark, but he could see the two people asleep under the covers. He put the tray down on the bedside table, thinking the sound would wake them up – but it didn't. 'My God, they are deeply asleep!' He coughed loudly and touched Molly's shoulder. There was no response and for the first time, he began to feel worried. He spoke louder then and shook his daughter – she didn't move and suddenly he knew. He dashed around to the other side of the bed and went through the same motions with Fred. He got the same response – that is, none!

His dear daughter and lovely son-in-law were dead. They'd obviously died in the night, but how? They'd both been perfectly healthy the day before – and yet here they were, dead and cold in their bed. Tom's first thought was to telephone for an ambulance, although he could tell from the stiffness of their bodies, that it was too late for a paramedic to help. He still dialled 999 however as he didn't know what else to do.

His next thought was to try and keep the two youngsters out of the room. They mustn't see their parents like this. 'What could he tell them? How could he keep them from going into their parents' bedroom?' He knew he probably couldn't, but he'd try anyway.

Across the landing the two doors of the kids' rooms were still firmly closed. They'd heard nothing it seemed – even his attempts to waken their parents hadn't disturbed them. He knocked and went into Freddie's room – it was Deja-vu and the young man was lying in a crumpled heap, as though he'd been in pain – e was screwed up in the foetal position. He too, was cold to the touch – as was young Margaret, when he eventually went into her room. Tom couldn't understand how he was managing to keep his feet - he couldn't feel his legs. The shock of finding everyone like that had started him shaking uncontrollably – an old man's thing, he knew, but unpleasant nonetheless. His head was swimming and his balance was off, but he knew there was something he had to do before he rang the police. Now, what was it? He'd remember in a moment!

He went into his own bedroom then and found Morty already sitting on his chair, his arms defiantly folded across his chest. He was obviously waiting for Tom. "Isn't it a lovely day, old man – one we can enjoy, I'm sure? You look a little agitated – is there perhaps something wrong?" There was an unmistakable sneer on his wooden face.

"It's you, isn't it? I can't think how you did it, but I know you did." He was crying, the tears running down his cheeks and he crossed the floor towards the dummy. With both hands he grabbed Morty's neck but with one blow from the little man's hand, he was knocked to the floor – in fact, the force of the ferocious blow landed him right across the room. The dummy really was strong and Tom knew he was no match for him.

"I've sent for the police as well and I'm going to tell them all about you when they arrive. Your little secret won't be a secret anymore and you'll be carted off as the evil swine you are." He'd only kept the dummy's secret because he'd been asked to and because the all-seeing, all-knowing little upstart had made the act more outstanding than it had been before.

Morty stood up, "Are you really the moron you seem old man – do you really think anyone's going to believe you? Are you going to tell them this little wooden puppet can walk and talk and read people's minds? Look at me, I don't have lungs to breathe, I don't eat or drink and I certainly don't have a heart. I can feel nothing! You're on a losing wicket I'm afraid – although I'm looking forward to the expression on the policeman's face when you blame me for murdering those stupid morons of yours. It was poison, you know, an easily traceable one. The Forensic people will soon identify it. And just to seal your fate, they'll also find traces of it in the pudding in the kitchen – the one you turned down last night – the favourite pudding you usually love – but not last night and not because you'd already eaten too much, as you claimed, but because of the poison you'd put there. You can deny it all you want, but I'm afraid, you'll be blamed for all those deaths, and people will say, 'He murdered his whole family, would you believe? What an evil man, they'll say!' And your name will go down in history – as a multi murderer. You'll be famous Tom but not for your ventriloquist skills, but for your cruelty. It' a pity they no longer hang people!" He plucked an imaginary piece of fluff from his sleeve as he spoke – making it clear how little he cared at what he'd done.

He climbed back onto his chair, his speech over, and Tom spoke to the dummy for the last time, "You really are evil, aren't you – in fact, you're a son of a bitch and no mistake." He heard loud banging at the front door and knew I was both the paramedics and the police.

Tom tried – oh, how he tried, but the detective and two constables just looked at him as if he was mad – and he knew he couldn't blame them. His family's bodies were taken out of the house one by one, whilst the police kept him in the kitchen until it they'd gone. The only sympathy the police had for the man was because of his age, but their gut instincts were that he had done the deed. They pretended to listen to him but he rabbited on about a wooden dummy who killed all the people, and how he wasn't a wooden dummy at all, but a vicious killer.

He even took them into his bedroom and showed them an odd-looking character sitting on a chair. He was dressed smartly but he was what he looked like – a toy of some sort or a prop for a show. The detective picked him up and held him out to Tom, "Is this the one? Is this who murdered your family? I admit he has a mean look, but he couldn't be the killer – he's not real." The detective wasn't smiling – he realised the old man was probably just clutching at straws – but if he wasn't mad, surely, he could have come up with a better story than this?

Morty was hanging from the detective's hand – completely still and limp. Tom could see Morty's staring, blue eyes and knew the dummy was goading him. He was enjoying the whole things and Tom knew it.

The old man spluttered, "He's the one Officer – don't be fooled – he can walk and talk and even murder if he wants to. He's as alive as you and me." He reached out to the dummy, dangling from the policeman's hand and said, "Come on Morty, tell them what you did - tell them about the pudding you poisoned – you'll have to admit it in the end."

Stony silence, whilst Morty sat there, a frozen look on his wooden face. He was obviously what he looked like, a little man made of wood and with a badly painted face.

"We're going to take you with us now Sir – we're going to the station where you'll be questioned further. He read Tom his rights and the old man said nothing, but continued to stare at Morty, hoping he would make a mistake and move in front of the police. Morty's glazed eyes stared straight ahead. Tom tried again to make the police see he wasn't mad, adding, "That little swine there is guilty as sin and you mustn't let him get away with it." As he spoke, Tom suddenly remembered what it was he had to do before the police arrived, but it was too late now – the blue arsenic bottle he'd left in the cupboard under the sink might never be found.

As they left the house, the detective turned to one of the constables, "Go into the kitchen and see if you can find any residue of last night's pudding and bring it to the station. I don't want to risk it's disappearing before we can analyse it." And they all left – the house was eerily silent, except for the family's voices lingering in what had once been a happy home. Now there was nothing.

Sitting in the back of the police car, Tom envisaged what Morty would be doing right then – the dummy was clever and no mistake. In his mind's eye, he could see Morty jump from his chair and go into the sitting room. He had one last thing to do before the police came back – as he knew they would. There would be a lot of searching around he knew, so he'd have to be quick and then get back onto his chair – sitting exactly in the same position as they'd last seen him. He found a sheet of paper and a pen and in block capitals, scribbled down a few words. He put the note in his jacket pocket and went back to the bedroom. That was that! He'd secured his future and Tom would never be coming back! 'The dummy' had seen to that.' He smiled at his own cleverness – he knew he was definitely not dumb, but cruel and evil, well that was an altogether different question.

The note nestled in his pocket for the police to find. They'd probably decide the little chap should go someplace safe – now he had no master. He was just a toy with no-one to look after him. Pleased with himself, he remembered the words he'd written in the note:

'To Whom This May Concern

This is Morty – he's a fine and decent chap. Please make sure nothing bad happens to him and that he's delivered to Mr Samuel Golder, the Jewish tailor in town. He will take him in and care for him. This is what I, as his master, wants to have done.

Tom Reynolds.

As Tom was taken from the police car into the station, he could see the words quite clearly, after all he'd written them himself, at Morty's insistence of course. 'Ah well,' he thought, 'the future belongs to the little wooden man now -I wonder what he'll do with it.'

Morty thought he would enjoy having a new master and he knew he would soon lick him into shape, 'After all, if he doesn't do as I say, I'll just have to sort him out the same way as I did Tom – and his numerous predecessors! I've survived more times than I care to remember – but it's all in the past now, all in the past! And he fingered the 'Hand of Hasma' in anticipation of his new Jewish master. The question remained however, 'Who was the guilty party – was it Morty or Tom? Unfortunately, there was no-one left to answer the question!!

You Don't Remember Me, do You?

"How many things can go wrong with this wedding? First the cake I wanted is going to be too tall to go in the door, so I've had to lose a tier; then the band has double-booked themselves so I have no band to date; and of course, my chief bridesmaid has been in a car crash and has a broken arm and leg." Charlie plonked herself down on her mother's sofa and her eyes filled with tears. Her speech was long but unfortunately, very true.

"Oh Mum, it's much harder than I thought it would be – so much to do in such a short time. I know I told Phil that I could manage everything but I'm beginning to think I'm not as smart as I thought I was."

Her mother laughed at her daughter's woeful expression, "Oh I don't know dear, I've always thought you pretty smart – these are things that can go wrong for anybody. Dry those tears, nothing's so bad – and we're fixing everything, aren't we?" She handed Charlie a glass of wine and sat down opposite her, "This'll help my girl, now pull yourself together – nothing's beyond you. Daddy always used to say that about you and what did he make you say every morning at breakfast?" And they mouthed the same words together, "I can, I can, I know I can."

"You're right Mum, I'm just being silly." And she stood up, emptied her glass and said, "Come on into the kitchen, I'm going to make you the best omelette you've ever had." Her tears were over and she felt more like her old self again.

Her fiancé Phil, was still at sea and would be for another two months. He'd been away for four months already, which is why she'd said she would make all the wedding arrangements. He was an officer in the Navy and still had several years to serve, but he loved what he did and enjoyed Navy life. As a couple, they were ideally suited to each other and had been engaged for just over a year, so a wedding was the logical next step.

Charlie was a children's teacher and had been lucky enough to land a job in the local town school, where she taught the junior classes. In fact, it had all fallen into place straight after university, the vacant post coming up at just the right time. It was her home town, so she was surrounded by friends and family – she didn't have much to complain about. She'd met Phil in his final year at Uni – he'd been a year ahead of her in his studies and they'd been an item for almost three years now. Everything was looking rosy and she knew she had no right to be such a 'saddo'! And her omelettes really were special.

"Please Miss, may I be excused – I need a wee?" The little boy's voice broke into her thoughts and she said, "What, another wee Johnnie, how much have you been drinking?" The rest of the class laughed and poor Johnnie's cheeks turned red with embarrassment. He didn't like his ablutions to be discussed so openly.

"Go on then, off you go." And the boy slipped quietly from the room. It was just another day at school – one amongst many – and Charlie finished off the afternoon with a story about the Snowman and the Snow Dog. Every pair of eyes watched her closely and they even mouthed some of the words - they knew the story so well, having heard it more than once or twice. She had soon learned children liked repetition - but not too much, of course. Only certain stories could stand repetition, but she knew this was one of them.

Leaving the playground later, she stopped off at the post office nearest the school where Mrs Jones the store-keeper, had agreed to hold any letters for her, especially ones that looked like returning RSVP's. The post mistress was a wizard at knowing what the envelopes contained – it was as though she had X-ray Vision.

"Four today Charlie, that must be nearly all of them now. Is that right?" The grey-haired woman looked over her spectacles in a short-sighted way – 'short-sighted, but able to miss nothing that happened in the town.' kind of way.

"Thank you, Mrs Jones, let's hope they're all acceptances this time - I've had a few 'can't make its' so far. "She smiled at the elderly woman, "But at least I know you'll be there, don't I?" The woman nodded her head as though making a solemn promise.

"I wouldn't miss it for the world, my dear – I love a good wedding." She looked thoughtful for a moment and then added, "Mind you, I like a good funeral as well." And on that cheerful note, Charlie left the shop. She knew it wouldn't be wise to get Mrs Jones started on her likes and dislikes, or she'd never get home that day.

Back at the school where she'd left her car, she happened to glance at the windows across the playground. It was dusk now and she could see a light had been left on in one of the classrooms. It might be the cleaner of course, but she thought she'd better check.

"Have you finished with the classroom at the end of the corridor Maisie? If you have, I think you might have left the lights on – but I'll switch them off now, if you like." She passed by the cleaner and headed to the end of the corridor. She knew the building so well, after all she'd been a pupil here herself many years ago. Although it was quite dark, the light from the classroom shone through the small window above the door. 'Was that someone sitting there on the ground? It looked like a little girl leaning back against the wall. The child

seemed to be crying. Charlie approached the small figure quietly, careful not to scare her.

"Why my dear, what on earth is wrong and what are you doing here at this time? May I ask your name, I don't recognise you I'm afraid." The little girl kept her head lowered, her long brown hair concealing her features - and her hands clasped tightly around her knees. Charlie thought she was dressed rather strangely with long skirts and a grey pinafore that completely covered her frail body – heavy boots adorned her small feet and stuck out from under her skirts. Charlie's immediate thought was that she looked more like a child from Victorian times and not one of today's pupils. 'And what was she doing in the school at this time? Maybe she was Maisie's child and had come along with her mum to clean the school.'

"Is your mum Maisie? Come along and I'll take you to her." She reached down to take the child's hand, but the girl pulled away from her, still keeping her face hidden behind the abundant hair. Charlie went on, "I'll just switch off the light in the classroom and then we'll go and find your mum." She went into the room and checked there was no-one else there before switching off the light. Now, the corridor really was dark and as she closed the door, she reached down to take the child's hand. There was nothing there! She looked closer to where the girl had been sitting but there was no girl! Where could she have gone? Charlie searched around but could see no-one.'

She could do nothing but suddenly she felt a chilly air moving along the corridor towards her and something told her it was time she gave up and went home. She walked quickly, telling herself she was being silly— so the girl had gone to find her mother and was probably with her already. She reached the main door, where she'd last seen Maisie, but the cleaner too had disappeared. Well, it was late and if she'd finished her work, she'd probably left the school and taken her daughter with her.

Driving home, Charlie couldn't help thinking about the girl and about her old-fashioned clothes, but she was soon home and knew her mother would have a tasty supper waiting for her. "Four more R.S.V.P.'s Mum – I've not opened them yet. Sorry - I know I'm a bit late, but the strangest thing happened on my way home." And she told her mother about the weeping girl in the school.

"It is a very old school Charlie – perhaps it has its own little ghosts from years gone by." That was something Charlie preferred not to think about but her mother still went on, "You know that building was put up as the town school in the mid-eighteenth century - so long ago - and was known then as the 'Penny School'. If parents couldn't afford a penny a day, the teacher wouldn't teach their child – and it was a penny for each child too and not just for a family of children, so schooling was only available to folk with money. But wasn't that the way of the world in those days? One wonders how much things have really changed." And Mrs Collins looked pensive for a few minutes.

"Ah yes, but the really well-off people employed governesses and tutors for their children – and if the others had a penny, they were okay. Anyway, what's this got to do with the girl I saw today? You're changing the subject, aren't you?"

"I am not Charlie – but I'm thinking of the really poor families, who could have had bright children – but without that penny, they never had the benefit of education." Mrs Collins was a bit of a philosopher on the quiet.

Charlie could smell the nice supper her mother had prepared, so she ended the conversation and ran upstairs to get changed. If she encouraged her mother, she'd go on at length about the inequalities in life and the school teacher's day had already been a long one and she was hungry.

"Oh yes Mum, that was incredibly tasty, thank you." She opened the RSVP letters at last, "Oh no, two more can't make it to the wedding – that's the numbers down to fifty." Charlie reached for her wedding planner and crossed off two more names.

"But the other two say they plan to come, don't they?" Mrs Collin could always see the glass half full, never half empty and she always made it her business to take away her daughter's everincreasing lines of worry. "You won't forget to collect the voile and sugared almonds tomorrow, so we can start making the guests' favours for the table. Now that's a chore you'll enjoy doing."

Charlie promised she wouldn't forget and then asked, "Mum, if the school opened so long ago, do you think my three-times great grandparents might have attended it in the nineteenth century? Do you think our family would have had the daily penny, or would they have been too poor to pay for education?" Suddenly, she was back in school, in the dark corridor staring down at the crying girl. "She could have been my great great great grandma – that is if she'd been lucky enough to have a penny each day. My, that's a lot of greats!" The hardships suffered by children in the past suddenly seemed very real.

"I really can't imagine dear. I know your great great great grandfather was a farm labourer so they weren't well off – but he may have been in advance of his times and recognised the need to educate girls as well as boys. I'm afraid we'll never know that. You should make enquiries at the school – there must be old records kept there and you know your three-times great grandma's name was Bell, Jennifer Bell. When she grew up and married, her name became MacDonald – yes, if I remember correctly he was called James MacDonald, not really a local name. If the school's records don't go back far enough, you could always check at the town library. And by the way, don't forget the ancestors who came after them, after all our family have always lived hereabouts and there'll be other names you'll recognise – but Bell and MacDonald are a good start. Obviously, I can help you with my parents' and grand parents' details – but I know very little nothing before them."

She wanted to encourage Charlie's interest in the family as it might stop her worrying so much about the wedding and about the things she couldn't change. It would be good therapy for her at this time.

"I'll do that Mum, yes I think I'll do that. In fact, I can't think why I've not done it before. I've got names to start with, so I'll see what I can find out, in fact I'll start tomorrow."

And she made her way up to bed, but not before she noticed that nosey woman across the street was watching this house again. She was standing boldly in the window, staring directly into the Collins' windows. She couldn't have known how clearly her silhouette showed by the light behind her. She was new to the area apparently and didn't know anyone yet – maybe she'd make a point of bumping into her in the street and introducing herself. Yes, that would be the neighbourly thing to do, but then her mum was probably on the case already!

Next day, she had no class after two o'clock, so she went to see the school secretary, who doubled as the librarian as well. Margaret was a woman in her sixties and had worked at the school for many years – so she knew most of what went on there. The secretary had considered retiring, but she liked both being busy and truly believed the school still needed her experience and knowledge – or it would fall apart. She'd never married, devoting herself to her work instead – and looked every inch the fragile spinster, with her white hair in a tight bun on top of her head and her brogue shoes so highly polished, she could see her face in them.

Today, she was double-checking the children's vaccine records – they might not like injections but Margaret knew what was good for them – and she lined them up for the school nurse with absolutely no sympathy whatsoever.

"Hello Miss Collins, what can I do for you today? Shouldn't you be teaching 3A just now – oh no, that class has been cancelled, hasn't it?" She ticked off some more names and waited for Charlie to speak although the young teacher's question surprised her.

"Margaret, how far back do the school records go? Particularly, the names and details of the pupils?"

"Well now, there's a question I didn't expect." She went on ticking off more names. "Why on earth do you want to know that, may I ask?"

Charlie explained she was trying to find out if her great great great grand parents had been pupils at the school. "It would have been when it was still called a penny school I think – you know when children had to pay to come to school."

"Oh, I know all about penny schools – and yes, this school started off as one of them, but you're asking to go back at least a hundred years – and probably more – a very long time indeed." Suddenly she was interested and stopped checking the children's names. To be honest I think you should start with your own record and work back through your parents – I should think they all attended this school. Your family's always been local, haven't they?" Margaret crossed the office and switched on the kettle. *That's a good sign – she's going to help me. She'd never stop to make coffee otherwise.'* Charlie knew a cup of coffee meant Margaret was interested and she waited patiently for the older woman to speak.

"I can give you access to the school's archives, it's true – but I'm afraid I don't have time to check the records for you – you'll have to do it yourself. Is that okay?" She fetched two cups from the cupboard and spooned coffee granules into both. "I don't actually know how far back our records go – but there's always the town library where many of the area's records are held. You can always go there as well."

And over coffee, the two women discussed how old the school was and how few local families there were left nowadays – very few families could boast their ancestors went all the way back to penny schools.

"I wish you luck, my dear – come with me and I'll show you where we keep the old records and you can pop in there when you have any spare time between lessons. She showed Charlie up the stairs to a small room in the attic where the walls were covered in folders, books and boxes. "Quite a challenge, isn't it?" she smiled at Charlie and left her alone in the room.

"By the way Margaret, just before you go, have you ever heard of a young girl being seen in the school corridors after dark – a young girl who seemed to be crying but who wouldn't speak? I'm embarrassed to ask because I suppose I mean a ghost, unlikely though that is." She waited expectantly.

"Well now, that's the second unexpected question you've asked my dear – I've never seen the child myself, but others have throughout the years. Her name was apparently Rachel Mercer and she was once a pupil at the school – but that's all I know about her, except that she never does anyone harm and is usually trying to tell them something – something that'll help them. At least, that's how the story goes. I'm not at all surprised to hear you've seen Rachel – she's probably trying to make you feel better – I bet you've been worrying about your wedding, is that right? She seems to appear to people who are suffering from mental stress - she'll just be trying to cheer you up - or indeed, there's something she wants to warn you about. Give a thought to the number of children who've passed through this school – it's not surprising that they might pop back from time to time just to see what's going on. There would have been many child deaths throughout the years as well – many of them didn't have much food and yet, they had to go to work after school – and I'm talking about hard, manual work. They were expected to contribute to the home you know, no matter how young they were." And with that, she closed the door behind her and left Charlie alone in the room. Charlie was thinking how well Margaret would get on with her mother – they were a pair of philosophers! At first, she kept looking nervously over her shoulder – but curiosity soon took over and she started looking through the folders.

She worked for what seemed like a short time and so carried away with her work, she was surprised to look up and see it had become dark. She glanced at her watch and saw it was six o'clock. The school would have been closed long ago and even the cleaner would have gone home by this time. She was alone in the dark building *'or am I? she wondered.'*

She had made some progress however and the cobwebs clinging to her clothes proved it. It actually looked as if there were sufficient records in the school archives so she probably wouldn't have to go to the town library. There was so much to go through however and she realised it was going to take a long time – but to find actual details about her ancestors would make it all worthwhile. She left some of the folders piled neatly in separate blocks, so she could pick up where she'd left off, but that wouldn't be for a couple of days now, as her timetable was full until then. *'Maybe I'll be able to come back at the weekend, after all Margaret said the room was hers as long as she needed it. Yes, she was sure she'd be able to come back then.'*

As she stepped down the narrow staircase, she found the eerie silence disturbing and then as if from nowhere, she heard sobs and sniffling floating upwards from the corridor below. Now the hairs on the back of her neck stood on end and she stopped moving completely, she listened intently to the sound. Of course, her first thought was that it was the same little girl she'd heard before and despite logic telling her not to be silly, she now found she'd accepted the possibility. *'Could she bring herself to go to the bottom of the stairs? Of course, she could, in fact she had to if she wanted to get home that night.'*

One creaking stair after another brought her down to the corridor and she wasn't surprised to see the little girl in the strange clothes sitting exactly where she'd been before. Again, her long brown hair hung around her face and Charlie couldn't discern her features.

"Little girl, is there something I can do for you? My name's Charlie and I'd like to be your friend." She held her breath in anticipation and saw the girl raise her head for a moment as if listening to her words. Charlie could only have been about ten yards from the girl, but she knew she mustn't move closer until she was invited to do so. "Can you tell me why you're crying? Maybe I can help." She tried again but the girl suddenly stood up and walked away in the opposite direction. Charlie made to follow her but before she made any progress, the figure slowly disappeared into the darkness and the school teacher was left on her own again. She switched on the light but could see no-one. All she could do was to leave the building and go home to the warm comfort of her supper. The child had gone – just like before. *"I'm going to chat with my mother about this and with Margaret too – I can't keep it to myself.* And she was gone quickly, locking the door firmly behind her.

She found she was shaking as she crossed the playground towards her car. *'Thank God for the security light that shone all the way across the playground, was her one thought.'*

"Mum, I saw her again – I saw her tonight – and she disappeared as suddenly as she had before. She seems so real and then, she disappears as if in a puff of smoke." She kicked off her shoes and sniffed the appetising smell from the kitchen. "What do you think Mum?"

Mrs Collins had been waiting for her daughter to come home before dishing up and she stared at her daughter before pursing her lips, "I don't know what to think daughter – I know you're not going mad so I want to believe you, but you must admit it doesn't seem likely that a child dressed in Victorian clothes is still appearing in the school." She made Charlie sit down at the table and patted her shoulders. "Let's talk about it after supper, shall we – you've not eaten since lunchtime and you must be ravenous."

Next day Charlie had one class after the other and didn't get a chance to check through any more records. Feeling pretty tired – some juniors were especially naughty that day, she was glad to be going straight home after work. When she drove into her road, she was astounded to see a fire engine drawing away from her gateway.

"Mum, Mum, where are you? Are you all right?" She rushed into the kitchen and was hit by the smell of burning, although there were no apparent flames. Her mother wasn't in the house and she rushed back outside, where she spotted her mother standing on the doorstep of the house across the road. She was talking to the woman who'd just moved there. The distraught girl ran quickly across and grabbed her mother's shoulders, "Mum, are you okay? What on earth happened?" She didn't know why, but she could feel the tears coming into her eyes. *'What if something had happened and her mother was hurt? And why was she across the road talking to that stranger?'*

For the first time, she looked at the stranger and was surprised to see she was actually younger than she'd thought. She was holding onto her mother's hand – holding it in both of her own. Charlie thought she looked a bit over-familiar with her mother.

They both looked at the fretting newcomer, and her mother spoke reassuringly, "Oh Charlie dear, it's all right – I'm not hurt – and Liz here has just made me a cup of sweet tea – for the shock, you know." Charlie reached out and took her mother's hand away from the stranger, "Let's go home now Mum and I can take care of you. Thank you for caring for her – Liz, is it? My name's Charlie and I live with my mother – but then, you probably know that already." She wasn't sure why she felt aggressive towards the stranger, after all she'd just helped her mother, but there was something about her that seemed rather odd and Charlie couldn't figure it out.

Liz spoke for the first time, "I'm afraid you're in for a disappointment Charlie. There's been a fire at the back of your house and the rubbish in the bin helped fuel it. It quickly took hold and was blazing away when I spotted it from here." *What a weird thing to happen – it's never happened before. And why had she taken such a quick dislike to the woman, it didn't make sense.*

Back at home, she settled her mother in an armchair and lit the fire. She had to make it cosy for Mum an she fetched a brandy and stood over the older woman until she'd finished the lot, then she re-filled the glass one more time.

Mrs Collins laughed and said, "Now dear, are you trying to make me drunk – cause that's what will happen if I have any more brandy. Sit down beside me, I'm afraid I have something to tell you – something you're not going to like. You see, the fire started when I was out shopping and it was Liz who rang for the fire brigade. I can't imagine how the fire started but I know now what was used to fuel it. You'll see when you go into the study that your wedding papers have been disturbed – in fact, they've been scattered all around the room. I have no idea who did it but someone must have broken in while I was at the shops." Jill Collins looked very upset but knew she had to tell the rest. She stood up and crossed to the sink where some burnt papers were still lying.

"One of the firemen brought these into the house when they'd put out the fire." She held out a couple of cards and Charlie took them hesitantly before looking up at her mother in disbelief. "My God Mum, what's this all about? Why would anyone do this? It's almost as though someone's targeting me personally?" The burnt paper crumpled in her fingers and fell into the sink in shreds. *'My God, it's all my R.S.V.P. answers – how am I going to sort out this lot? I won't know who's coming and who's not now and there's not much time before the wedding. I don't have enough time left to organise sending invites again and getting answers back. What kind of weirdo has done this?'*

Her mind was in turmoil and she just leaned forward onto the kitchen table and cried. Her mother gently touched her shoulders but said nothing. What words were there? It was an unbelievable situation.

Charlie suddenly looked up, "It's jinxed, isn't it? My wedding's jinxed – I told you it was – so many things have gone wrong already. What else can happen?"

Neither mother nor daughter said any more – they couldn't. The kitchen was quiet and all they could do now, was go to bed. Before the comfort of sleep, Charlie's last thought was 'someone out there must hate me' – and in that moment, she really believed it.

"How are you getting on with your quest?" Next day, Margaret popped her head around the door of the room where Charlie was surrounded by piles of records. It was two days after the 'burning' incident and Charlie was coming to terms with her personal disaster. She'd even got a new batch of invitations and found the original list of guests and their addresses. Of course, she had to write an explanatory note with each one, explaining why she was sending them again.

"Fine Margaret – I'm getting on really well – and I've got the Head's permission to come in on Saturday and work in the peace of a quiet school." She smiled at the school secretary who'd turned out to be a Godsend, in suggesting the best places to search. She'd even found a journal dating back to the mid-nineteenth century – it was a record the school had made of the day the famous Charles Dickens had actually visited the penny school. Charlie read how he'd spoken with many of the children, encouraging them to study hard and believe in themselves. He even told them his own story, how he'd had to work in a blacking factory at the age of twelve – but how he'd learned from his experiences and used them to create his famous novels. The school record explained in detail how interested he was in the welfare and education of children who didn't have much in life. In fact, he was instrumental in lobbying the government to make the lot of poor children better – he was working hard towards free education for all children. This wouldn't actually arrive until around 1870 – but at least it would come. And of course, he was right! Charlie had always loved Dicken's works but now she admired the author himself for his foresight and for his dedication to making the country a better place for children of poor families.

"Have you read this Margaret – it's truly amazing. What a wise man Charles Dickens must have been. In the school record about his visit, it says he gave every child an orange – can you imagine it, I bet most of them had never seen one before?" She handed the record to the secretary, who left the attic, clutching the important document in her hands.

'Jennifer Bell is an eleven-year-old girl who regularly arrives each morning and is always on time. She is clean and tidy but as with many others, her clothes are patched and obviously hand-me-downs. She appears to have a grasp of the basic '3 Rs' but she's especially interested in reading and has been allowed on occasion, to borrow a book to take home. This is exceptional and only allowed when the pupil can be trusted to take care of it.'

Well now, that's a grand write-up and no mistake! She'd found a copy of her three-times great grandma's school report for the year 1850. What a find! She found her hands were shaking as she held the yellowed paper. It was just a few words but it made her feel so close to the child-that-once-was. All the pupils of that year had a few words written about them, including one James MacDonald – her great great great grandad. They had obviously met as children and when they married, they must have already known each other for a number of years. *'I can picture them – the young girl looking just like the ghostly child in the corridor and a boy with tousled hair that badly needed cutting.*

*His clothes would be old and probably second-hand – just like
the girl's.'*

Further down the list, she found James' report which made
picturing him even easier.

'James MacDonald is twelve years of age and in his short time
at this school has managed to learn **some** of the basics of the '3
Rs'. (And the word some was heavily under-lined) It is doubtful
he'll ever aspire to anything academic in life but he appears to be
practical and good with his hands. He often arrives late at school
but it never seems to bother him. He has a pleasant manner
however and makes friends easily.' He sounded just as she'd
pictured him and she felt as though she'd known him. And these
two were her great great great grandparents. *'Not many people
had the privilege of reading their ancestors' school reports – I
feel very proud.'*

Now, she was even more intrigued and wanted to know more.
*'Where had they lived? She knew they'd stayed local when they
married but what had they become and how **many** children did
they have?'* She decided to visit the town Registry Office where
all births, deaths and marriages would show up in the records.
But that would be for tomorrow!

The town records revealed Mrs Collins had been right. The
couple had married in 1850 and James had worked as a farm
labourer. They'd lived in a small cottage tied to the farm and
they'd had two children, one of whom had unfortunately died in
infancy. There were no records that mentioned the death of the
child, which was unusual for the times, but she did find the other
child, whose address was the same as Jennifer and James'
farming cottage – she was a girl called Melany MacDonald, born
in 1854 – there was no evidence of any other children who went
by the surname MacDonald. *Odd that they'd only had one live
child – families then tended to have several children, but then I
don't know their story, do I? Maybe the one child's death had
so affected them, they decided the risk was too much. Anyway,
I'll never know!*

Before leaving the Registry Office, she had time to look for
Melany's wedding date and found that she'd married in 1875
when she was twenty-one. She'd married one Thomas Millican
whose occupation was recorded as vicar. *Well I never! My great*

great grandad was a member of the clergy. This is getting more and more interesting the more I discover. Now I know the names to look for in the school records and hopefully I can find their actual reports – that way, I'll get to know them as well.

When she arrived home that night, she was delighted to find a letter had come from Phil - just what she needed to cheer her up. She'd decided not to tell him about the ' burning' incident.' Why worry him? He had enough to contend with in the middle of the ocean. Anyway, she was sorting it all out.

"Well, you've certainly perked up Charlie. Is there anything in the letter you can share with me?" Jill was delighted to see her daughter looking happy again.

"That's for me to know and you to find out." And she tucked the letter inside her bag – looking forward to reading it later. "How was your day Mum? Anything to report?"

Jill said she didn't think so and then added, "I invited Liz from across the street for coffee this morning and we had a good old chin-wag. She's very interesting you know – not much older than you – but with a much harder life than your own."

"For Goodness Sake Mum, don't start taking in waifs and strays again. You know you're a sucker for a tale of woe." She actually meant it as it had happened before, especially when dad was still alive.

"Oh, I'm not going to do that dear – once bitten, twice shy. No, it's just that she grew up in an orphanage and left there when she was sixteen. They found her a job in the naval college down the road where she worked in the canteen. It couldn't have been an easy life as the work was hard and the hours long. It's only now when she's approaching thirty that she's been able to move into the house across the way – it's her first proper home. She rents of course as she still doesn't earn much money."

"Oh Mum, you're starting again. That sounds very much like a sob story to me – the same kind of sob story that woman in the supermarket spun you – and you ended up by paying for all her groceries – and never seeing her again. You never did get that money back, did you?"

Jill Collins was a pushover and no mistake. But really, she was just a very kind woman who liked to trust people. Yes, she'd made a few mistakes in her life, but nothing too detrimental. Her husband had been the cautious one and had kept his eye on her, the philanthropist-cum-mug for sad stories. She hadn't been taken in by anyone for a while now – but that was probably thanks to Charlie who'd stepped in and taken her dad's place. She liked to look out for her mother and sometimes felt more like the mother than the daughter, but she loved the bones of the woman and knew she'd always be happy to care for her. She owed that much to dad.

"Come on Mum, we're going out for our supper tonight – my treat. But I'm just going upstairs to read my letter first and I might even share some of his news with you – I'll see. And I want to fill you in with some of the things I've discovered today, about our family." She disappeared clutching her handbag.

The meal in the local pub was excellent and they were just glancing over the dessert menu when Charlie felt someone standing behind her. She looked up and recognised Liz from the house across the way. "Why Jill – Charlie – I didn't expect to find you here. This is my usual haunt where I come to enjoy my solitary meals." Of course, Jill invited her to join them and even tried to persuade her to have a second dessert, "Just to keep us company!" she joked. Liz pulled up a chair and sat opposite them, "I won't have any more to eat, thank you but I will order some coffee. It won't be as nice as yours Jill – I'm sure of that."

Again, Charlie couldn't help resenting the arrival of the neighbour she hardly knew. In fact, she knew she really didn't warm to the woman at all and for a moment, she had a sudden flash of recognition. *Have I met know her before – I feel as though I have? And not from seeing her staring from behind her curtains - or from the day of the fire brigade, but before then, in fact quite some time before. She dismissed the thought and turned her attention back to the conversation.*

Liz was talking, "Have you heard about the vicar from the church in our street – the old church with the beautiful interior, all carved pillars and gold ornaments. Apparently, he was walking around the ancient graveyard practising his next sermon – something he did regularly – when he was attacked by someone. He was hit across the head by a heavy iron bar and wasn't found for several hours. By that time, he'd been lying on the frozen ground long enough to develop frost bite. You'll remember the heavy frost that covered the ground that night." She looked really sad about the elderly vicar.

"Oh my God, poor Reverend Johnson. Is he all right?" Jill had known the vicar for years and had been a member of his church since she was a girl. "He's quite an elderly man and quite frail – I do hope he's all right. He is, isn't he?"

"Well, apparently he's in Intensive Care in the town hospital so, we can only hope he'll recover. "Both Charlie and Jill were upset by the news and decided they didn't want dessert after all. Charlie especially was upset by the news – Reverend Johnson and his beautiful church were her choice revenue for her wedding. *Dear God, another jinx on the wedding – dear Reverend Johnson, the perfect vicar and good friend. Phil knew him too and liked him. Please let him recover from the attack – and not just because of my wedding but because he was such a loved person.*

Charlie never did get around to telling her mother about her findings about Jennifer Bell and James MacDonald - and their one-surviving daughter Melany MacDonald. But it would wait for another day – it wasn't exactly breaking news.

The friendly post mistress had promised again to hold her wedding mail until she'd finished work. She'd been shocked when Charlie told her of the fire – and of how someone had deliberately added her RSVPs to the fire. Mrs Jones was more than happy to help with the letters.

"What a wicked thing to do – and it was definitely a burglary, not just an accidental fire? The mind boggles at the wickedness of some people! By the way, talking about strange people, how well do you know that woman who lives near you, Elizabeth Miller? She's taken to coming in here for the occasional grocery and always quizzes me about you. But I tell her nothing as I'm not sure I like her. Why do you think she's so interested in you – I think it's very odd?" And she handed over the R.S.V.P.s that had started to arrive again.

Charlie told her she didn't know the woman well, although she thought she recognised her from sometime in the past. "I know nothing about her Mrs Jones but she's made friends with my mother, and you know what mum's like - she's a real sucker for hard luck stories."

Next day, she heard the news that the Reverend Johnson had died. That lovely man had also been the school vicar, so it was an even bigger blow to the community. Things were serious now as his death had apparently been murder and the culprit had to be caught or no-one in the town was safe. If he or she would kill a kindly old vicar, he or she would have no qualms about killing someone else. It was not surprising how such a thing affected a community, after all as everyone knew, anyone was fair game.

The police even visited the school, interviewing the staff and even some of the older children. The vicar's association with the school was known to most people but unfortunately no one there could help the police and so they had to continue to contact those known by the vicar. Following Charlie's own interview, she learned that news of his death had only been released to the media the day after he'd been found. *There's something wrong with that information and I can't think what it is. Come on Charlie – think! Something's bothering you but don't try to remember what it is just now – it'll come back to you in due course. And she left it like that!*

She got on with her work which lasted until late that afternoon, when a special extra lesson was held for those children, particularly interested in history. It was something she'd started for the older kids as she was especially interested in history herself. As the last pupils left the classroom, Charlie gathered up her bits and pieces and made her way up to the room in the attic. Maisie, the cleaner was still working and she called out to Charlie, "Hi Miss Collins, working late tonight? I'll be sure to lock up when I leave tonight – you have a key of your own, don't you?" And she got on with mopping up the muddy foot prints left by most of the children.

Charlie was eager to search through more of the records and she'd be starting with Melany MacDonald, her two-times great grandmother. *Had she married and taken on another name or had she died a spinster? Another trip to the registry office was needed, looking for a marriage in the late 1870s into the 80s and starring a bride named Melany MacDonald.*

Her visit to the registry office was successful and she found the girl had married one Simon Edwards in the early 1880s – which made her quite old for the fashion of the day as she must have been almost 30 years of age. But she now had the names of her ancestors – Melany and Thomas Edwards and she was now creeping towards the turn of the nineteenth century.

She was working quietly in the school attic two days later when she heard a strange sound coming through the floorboards. She knew she was going to get a visit from little Rachel – she could hear the familiar, faint sobbing coming from outside the room. She was surprised however when the door slowly creaked open and the little girl herself stepped into the room. This had never happened before and was a significant step forward for the little girl.

"Hello Rachel, I'm really pleased to see you – but you're still crying. Why? Is there something you want me to know – is that why you visit me? Tell me dear, you'll feel better if you do." Charlie waited, hoping the child would talk this time and in due course, her patience was rewarded.

It was faint but she could just make out the child's words, "Have you remembered yet?" That was all she heard before the girl's long hair swung over her face again.

"Remember? Remember what, Rachel? What are you trying to tell me? Am I in any danger -is that why you keep coming to see me? Is there something I should know?" Charlie felt afraid – very afraid and racked her brains but nothing came to mind.

Rachel swept her hair from her face, a child-like gesture that touched Charlie. She looked straight into the school teacher's eyes and said, "She told you before the police knew." And having said what she'd come for, she faded from the room and disappeared as if by magic. '*The only thing she'd had to do with the police had involved Reverend Johnson's murder – why was Rachel concerned about his murder? It had nothing to do with her. Charlie was confused and sat there going over everything in her mind.*

Suddenly, it dawned on her! She wasn't the one in danger – Rachel was trying to tell her something about the vicar. And yet, the child kept coming to her and implying she too, should be on the lookout for danger. '*I know what it's about – she's trying to make me remember that Liz told mum and me about the vicar's attack the night before the police released the news to the media or to the public. So, how could she have known about the attack?*

*Unless…………………….' And she stopped thinking then – it had
all become too confusing!'*

Suddenly feeling bitterly cold, she packed up her belongings
in a rush and left the school, being careful to lock the building
securely, as Maisie had reminded her.

"Mum, I'm home – sorry to be so late but wait 'till you hear
what's just happened." No answer and the kitchen light weren't
on, which was unusual. She heard voices coming from the sitting
room – and there sat her mother and Liz, chatting like old friends
over a bottle of wine – and there was very little wine left in the
bottle.

"Hello dear, I didn't hear you come in." Jill Collins was
looking rather glassy-eyed, full as she was of three large glasses.
It seemed that Liz had also brought an extra bottle with her. *'**Oh
God,' Liz thought**, 'I do hope this isn't an example of In Vino
Veritas.' She certainly hoped this woman hadn't loosened her
mother's tongue too much. Now she'd have to wait 'till
tomorrow to tell Mum about the little girl and the vicar's murder
– and possibly his murderer.'*

"Is that my wedding journal you've got there?" Charlie was
amazed to see her RSVPs spread across the coffee table, with
two of them still held in Liz's hand. "Mum, you know I don't
like anyone messing about with those." And she crossed the
room to gather up her invitations.

"We're not messing with them dear. I'm just showing Liz
how good – and quick – people have been in contacting you for
a second time – after the fire. Do sit down and join us, we're just
having a glass of wine - or two." Jill was obviously one sheet in
the wind already – Liz on the other hand, seemed in total control
of herself. She obviously hadn't drunk nearly as much as her
mother had.

No thank you Mum, I'm very tired – it's been a difficult day,
so if you don't mind I'm just going straight up and I'll speak with
you in the morning." She spotted a letter propped against the
clock on the mantlepiece, the place Mum always put Phil's
letters. She collected it on her way out of the room, glancing
back to see her mother refill her glass yet again. Liz had said
nothing which in itself, was rather unusual. However, she did
call out after Charlie, "It'll be nice for you to see your fiancé

again – it's been quite a time, hasn't it?" Charlie turned and came back into the room. *How did this stranger know the letter was from Phil – and how did she know he'd been at sea for a long time? She seemed to know things she shouldn't have. That would be mum again!*

"What makes you think my fiancé's coming home – he's not due for another two weeks?" Charlie felt on the defensive and wasn't sure why. Before Jill could admit to telling her friend, Liz spoke up, "Why, your mum told me." But as soon as she'd said the words, she quickly covered her mouth with her hand – an over-the-top and childish action, not genuine in the least.

"Jill spluttered, "My dear, I took it on myself to write to Phil because I was worried about you, what with all the things going wrong with the wedding plans. In fact, you've lost so much weight over the past few weeks you'll have to have your dress altered again. I just dropped him a note and asked if there was any chance he could come home a few days early – please forgive me, I was just worried about you." She looked as though she was about to cry, but it was probably the wine speaking. Charlie told her there was nothing to forgive – she knew she'd done it out of the goodness of her heart. But her mum spoiled it then, by adding, "In fact, it was Liz here who suggested I do it and you'll see, it's worked – he'll be home by Friday to help with the wedding."

Now Charlie was angry. *How dare that woman interfere with her life – she had absolutely no right. She'd only moved in across the street a couple of months ago – she doesn't know me at all. Wait a minute, my problems began only two months ago – that's a bit of a coincidence. Now I know I'm becoming paranoid – I must stop this.*

Still, looking on the bright side, she'd see Phil sooner than she'd thought she would.

She wasn't quite ready for bed, so she sorted out her short-hand version of her ancestors' details. Tomorrow, she planned to search for the school records of Melany MacDonald and Simon Edwards – her great great grandparents. She was curious to find out what kind of pupils they'd been and also to find out at the Registry Office if they'd had children of their own. And so it went on! *You're being a bit silly Charlie, they must have had*

*children or you wouldn't be doing what you're doing right now
– you wouldn't exist to do it – had they had no children, you for
one wouldn't be here to tell the tale!*

"Mum's where did you say?" The voice on the phone was
rather low and Charlie had difficulty hearing the words. "She was
arrested where? Why was she arrested - oh don't bother
explaining, I'll be right there?"

She spoke with the headmistress who agreed to take over her
class and she immediately headed off for the police station. At
the front desk, she asked the desk sergeant if she could see Mrs
Jill Collins, "I can't imagine why she's even here, she'll be so
scared as she's never been arrested in her life."

The sergeant explained Mrs Collins was being questioned
right then and she'd have to wait to see her, "I'm afraid your
mother's been arrested on a shop-lifting charge – and that's all I
can tell you just now." He showed her to a small waiting room
where she could wait and there, she spotted that damned woman,
Liz. She was sitting there, casually reading a magazine. "Hello
Charlie, I'm waiting for your mother as well. They won't tell me
anything and we've been here for two hours already. How did
you know she was here?"

"The police rang me at work and I came straight here." She
didn't like having to explain herself to the woman but as she still
didn't know what her mother was supposed to have stolen, she
felt forced to answer her. "Were you with my mother when she
was arrested, what shop were you in – and what is she being
accused of stealing?"

It transpired that they had been looking at some jewellery in
one of the better shops in town when suddenly the front door
clicked shut and the sales assistant asked them to take a seat,
"Everything will soon be sorted out," she told them. Next
minute, two constables banged on the door. As quick as a flash,
they asked to see inside Mrs Collins' large handbag and one
policeman lifted out a beautiful gold necklace

"Well Madam, what do you have to say about this little lot?"
he'd obviously made up his mind already and showed no
sympathy for the elderly woman. Liz was standing beside her
and even she was looking at her friend with surprise in her eyes.
She started to say, "Why Jill, what were you think……..?" She

stopped in time however, realising she was saying too much being just as accusing as the police.

"And now, I'm just waiting to see what they plan to do with your mother." Liz finished her story and waited for Charlie to speak.

Through gritted teeth, Charlie said defiantly, "My mother has never stolen anything in her life – in fact, she's known for giving things away to all and sundry and asking for nothing in return. I thought you might have spotted that in her."

After another hour, she was allowed to stand bail and take her mother home. Liz was waiting outside the police station and Charlie had no option but offer her a lift home – something she really didn't want to do. Jill Collins looked both haggard and tearful. She'd never had an experience like this in her entire life and found she couldn't actually remember what had happened in the shop. Her daughter soon had her settled by the fire and produced a fresh pot of tea and some sweet biscuits. She'd deliberately not invited Liz to join them and had left her in the darkness outside her own house.

Jill kept saying over and over again that she hadn't stolen anything, "Honestly Charlie dear, I'm not a thief – I wouldn't steal, you know that – so how did the jewellery get into my bag? I saw it myself when the policeman found it. And yet, I have no recollection of putting it there. How could it have happened?"

"Drink your tea Mum and eat a couple of biscuits. When you're feeling more settled, we'll talk about it." To try and take her mind off the most recent disaster, she changed the subject and told her how well she was progressing with her investigations into their family history. She told her how she'd seen the crying child again and this time, she'd spoken to Charlie. "In fact, Mum, she told me I had to be careful and hinted there was someone out there who wished me harm. Can you imagine that? I don't believe I can think of any enemy I have. Can you?"

"Of course, not dear, everybody's always liked you and I'm sure no-one could ever mean you harm." But she was finding it difficult to think about anything else, other than the jewellery, so Charlie fetched a warm blanket and put it across he knees. 'Tomorrow was another day' and this one had been a particularly difficult one. Later, as she helped her mother upstairs to bed, she spotted Liz watching from her bedroom window, but there was nothing unusual about that – she was always watching the Collins' household.

Charlie asked for a couple of days of compassionate leave to look after her mother, who seemed to lapse into a period of depression and no longer liked the idea of leaving the house. At first, Charlie was there with her but she had to go to work or she'd be letting down the school. Jill reassured her, saying she'd be okay – and anyway she said, "I have Liz across the way – I'm sure she'd be willing to help me should I need anything."

Charlie bristled at the suggestion and reminded her mother she couldn't just go over the street, "Liz has to work just as I do Mum – you know that and I'm sure she can't just stay away from the naval canteen or she'll lose her job." Jill nodded her head, Charlie was right of course.

Charlie wanted to tell her mother about the strange realisation that Liz had somehow known about the vicar's murder before the police had made the news public knowledge, but she couldn't bring herself to share the bad news. Jill seemed to really like the newcomer and after what she'd just been through, she didn't wasn't to spoil her mother's new friendship. So, she waited and in the meantime, she visited the town Registry Office again to see what offspring her Millican ancestors had produced at the turn of the century.

As it turned out they'd produced five children – but two had died in infancy, leaving two live sons and one daughter. The terribly sad thing was however, that both boys had been killed whilst serving on the Somme in France and so Charlie had only one daughter to investigate – and amazingly, she had been named Charlotte. *'My God, my name is a family name – how wonderful!'* She knew she was following the maternal line of her family, but she fully intended to do her paternal line in due course.

The well-kept records showed that Charlotte Millican had married one Cuthbert Edwards in the year 1920 – and a search through the birth records produced a baby girl born two years later. Despite looking several years further on, there was no other Edwards child mentioned – but the couple had obviously liked the name Charlotte – and for that, Charlie was grateful.

Therefore, Charlotte Edwards was the next name she'd look for in the school records. *'I wonder what sort of a child she'll turn out to be and if there is a report available to describe her – there should be. With the family name of Charlotte, she'd be a good girl, I'm sure!'*

And there it was! The most recent records had become better kept and quite detailed in describing the pupils – in fact there were even some photographs attached to some of them. Now that will be interesting – if there was a photograph of Charlotte Edwards, then she'd be able to look into the eyes of her great grandmother. Now she was fast approaching her close relatives and at the Registry Office, she discovered that Charlotte had married a Peter Jenkins, whose school report made him out to be quite a naughty boy. *'Someone I'm sure I would have liked – they may be more work but they're also more interesting.'*

Suddenly the sobbing girl arrived unexpectedly. This time, she was actually waiting in the attic room and was sitting on the wooden floor, her back against the wall. She wasn't crying so hard and her hair was pulled back from her face – a very pretty face it turned out to be.

"Why Rachel, you're looking better than I've ever seen you look. It's always pleasant to see you." Charlie had lost her initial fear of the little ghost and was genuinely pleased to see her. After further searching, Charlie found a leaving school report in the name of Charlotte Millikan– and a report about a young boy called Peter Jenkins, who was of course to be Charlotte's future husband.She looked at the two reports on the children when they were about twelve, which seemed the usual age for an achievement report to be raised, but the it was also the age children had completed their education. For further education, people would be expected to pay for the privilege and not many people would be able to afford that and so, at the tender age of twelve, children would be expected to go out and find work.

The faces staring from the photo looked friendly enough and Charlie could see a similarity to the girl's own ancestor, Jennifer Bell, of whom there'd been a hand-drawn paper attached to her report. Most unusual in those days! The two faces were so similar, it could have been the same person – and not of two people born so many years apart. In fact, Charlotte's amazingly light blue coloured eyes were exactly the same as Jennifer's. Truth to tell, people had often remarked on her own exceptional blue eyes – calling them beautiful. Now, she felt even closer to the little faces in the photos.

My great grandma and grandpa! Mum will love to see these photos – I know she never had any so it'll be a great surprise. She told me how family photos were burned in a house fire when she was only five. Apparently, a German incendiary bomb had come down the chimney during the Second World War and wiped out their home. A common occurrence in the war Charlie thought.

She placed the photos safely in an envelope, planning to have copies made. Before they were safely inside the envelope, she noticed Rachel was very interested in them. The girl had stopped crying and was using her little, ghostly finger to trace around Charlotte's face – the same face as Jennifer's.

"Did you know that girl Rachel? Was she perhaps at the school the same time as you were? Her clothes look different – more from an earlier time – but I've discovered she was an excellent likeness to her own relative, Jennifer Bell. Does she remind you of Jennifer, is that what it is?" Charlie was really interested and noticed the little ghost smiled for the first time and it was like the sun coming from behind the clouds.

She spoke for the first time and her voice was low but clear, "Jennifer……:…. it's Jennifer Bell. She was my best friend – but then I went and died, didn't I?" Her words made Charlie shiver, even more so when she realised the girl was speaking about her own 3 times Great Grandmother from the mid 1850s – best friend of the little ghost. *My God, Rachel had been haunting the school since the last century.*

She turned to the child and asked gently, "Rachel, did you happen to die someplace in the school grounds – is that why your spirit is earth bound here at the school?" She saw the tears gather again in Rachel's pretty blue eyes. "Are you able to tell me how you died? Did you fall from a window perhaps or did you come to grief in the playground, maybe banging your head? Or did you eat some meat that had gone off or something like that and your stomach couldn't cope with it?" *The girl must have died on the premises – but how? Maybe she was constitutionally weak and had just happened to die at the school? For her ghost to linger here for so many years, she must have died unexpectedly and perhaps violently. And perhaps there was something left behind that she believed she had to finish - that could be it – some unfinished business. But what?*

"Yes Miss – I came to school one day and I felt poorly. I'd only been here a few hours when something in my stomach burst and I retched and retched – and there was sick all around me. It was no good and I died with Jennifer Bell by my side and holding my hand. Jennifer knew what had poisoned me and burst my stomach. She asked me if I'd eaten something recently – something unusual." Now she'd begun to speak, she couldn't stop and went on, "She asked me if I'd eaten the orange Mr Dickens had given us children – and I had to tell her the truth because I had eaten it – but it had looked quite different than when Mr Dickens gave one to all the children. It had been bright and shiny at first, a beautiful bright orange colour – but I hid mine under the floorboards as I wanted to still have it when all the others had eaten theirs. It didn't taste nice though and it had turned grey and blue and smelt musty. Despite what all the other children told me, my orange didn't taste nice but I still ate it because it was a gift from that nice man."

Now, she was crying bitterly again and great tears were running down her ghostly cheeks. Charlie tried to put her arms around her – but of course, she couldn't. Between sobs, the child added, "I've always wanted to say thank you to Jennifer – she'd stayed by me and held my hand until I passed into this world. I didn't want to go Miss, but I didn't have the strength to stay. And that's why I've come to you – I know she's your great great great grandmother and I hope she'll know I've tried to help you. I was trying to help that night you first saw me but our connection wasn't strong enough – I had to get to know you more. Not everyone can see me, you know

Charlie asked, "Have you really visited me to warn me? Is something bad going to happen to me?"

"You have an enemy who is close to you and you must watch out for her." Rachel's voice seemed stronger than before and she was eager to talk.

"Can you tell me the name of who is trying to hurt me – is it a man or a woman? If I know that, perhaps I'll be able to avoid them. "Now, she was beginning to feel pretty panicky.

"I don't know her name – but she lives close to your home." *Immediately Charlie saw Liz's face in her mind's eye and realised how she'd been around every time something bad had happened. And then, she imagined the Reverend Johnson's sweet, wrinkled face and she knew she should speak with the police as soon as she could.*

"Rachel, I've got to go now but you've helped me more than you'll ever know. I know now who my enemy is! I'll be back however and you must come and visit me when I do." As if on cue, the little ghost disappeared, leaving Charlie alone in the eerily attic room. She gathered up some records to take home to search and thought how lucky she'd been that her mother had suggested she investigate her family line – or she'd never have met Rachel and learned about a potential enemy. *But why? Why did Liz want to hurt someone she didn't know and I'm quite sure I don't know the woman. Could she be from my past and I've forgotten her? I'll have to find out – and soon!*

She drove home, hoping her Mother was feeling better – and that she'd kept away from Liz that day. But her hopes were dashed as when she drew up in front of the house as she saw there were no lights at any of the windows. *Perhaps Mum was upstairs, asleep in bed and was quite safe – but something told her it wasn't likely. Where was Jill Collins?*

She turned her key in the lock calling out, "Mum, it's me. Where are you? It's Charlie Mum." Looking around, she noticed Liz's house across the way was also in darkness – most likely an ominous sign.an ominous sign. *I mustn't panic – was this mum's bingo night? Ah, that was a Wednesday, wasn't it and today was Wednesday? And she'd still be there at this time with 'her eyes down and running three books at once' – as the regulars were used to doing – and Mum was certainly a regular bingo enthusiast. Knowing her mother's soft heart, she'd probably invited the 'hard-done-by' from across the street to join her.*

She reached over and filled the kettle. She'd sit down with a nice cup of tea – and then, she'd ring the police. She knew she should have contacted them before, but to accuse a neighbour of murder, especially a vicar's murder, wasn't something she felt comfortable with. But tonight, was the night and she'd feel better when she'd shared her suspicions with the authorities.

"You'd best come down to the station if you can and we can take down your statement formally. Can you come now?" The detective sounded eager to speak with her – they hadn't got far with the attack on the vicar, so any help from the public was invaluable. She left the washing up in the sink and went back outside into the cold night, first scribbling a note to her mother, explaining she'd be back later – there was something she had to do. The detective was waiting for her and took her into a private room, accompanied by a young sergeant who was obviously there just to take notes. Both men listened to her story about her strange neighbour Liz Dawson and how she'd known about the vicar's murder before anyone else had.

"You see Detective, she couldn't have known about it – no-one did at the time." She rambled on for a while and knew she was beginning to sound desperate - they weren't taking her seriously.

"Ma'am, thank you for bringing this to our attention but I'm going to stop you there." He looked slightly embarrassed and went on to explain that they'd already interviewed the lady in question and checked her alibi for the evening the vicar was attacked. Apparently, she had a full-proof alibi given by two of her work colleagues. He said he couldn't explain how she'd known about the vicar's attack but she had suggested she was an amateur psychic and often sensed when such trauma took place. *'What a load of baloney, Charlie thought.'*

"Of course, we don't take much notice of such things – it's all a bit airy-fairy. The only reason her interview was followed up by checking her alibi, was because she'd actually met with the vicar on the day of his death – she apparently knew him quite well and was receiving counselling from him – counselling for the problems she experiences from having psychic powers – at least, that's what she told us. She says she doesn't look upon her powers as a blessing – more of a curse. And when all's said and done, I'm afraid I only have your word that she told you the news on the day you claim. You may have got that wrong."

Charlie interrupted him, "But she told me when my mother was there - I wasn't alone." She'll confirm when that was." She felt foolish and certainly didn't believe Liz's story about her psychic powers – she wasn't under stress. And, she'd never heard her mother mention the woman's special powers or indeed, there'd been no mention of her receiving counselling from the vicar. A load of claptrap, Charlie was sure. *She'd have told Jill Collins abut such a special skill – but she never had!*

She left the police station feeling very let down. She'd tried to do her duty but no-one had taken her seriously. And yet, she was convinced her neighbour was telling lies and that she was a danger to innocent people. *But why does she hate me so much – what can I ever have done to make her try to ruin my life. A sudden thought came into her mind, 'Is she responsible for all the bad things that have happened around my wedding plans? In fact, they all started not long after she moved to across the street -the band's double booking, the disaster with the wedding cake, her bridesmaid being involved in a car crash and worst of all, the lovely vicar whom she wanted to conduct her marriage ceremony. Maybe worst of all was her fear of the sudden friendship between her and Jill Collins. Oh God, was Mum in danger?*

The house was still in darkness although there were now lights at the window across the street – but there was no sign of a watching figure this time. As she locked the car, she noticed a strange vehicle sitting at the end of her drive. A tall man climbed out and walked towards her. She knew him – she was so glad to see him and couldn't believe he was actually standing in front of her. He was still in uniform and looked so handsome, she couldn't stop the tears. She wasn't sure if they were happy tears at seeing him – or if they were sad tears because of everything that had happened lately? It didn't matter and she rushed into his arms.

"Why Charlie, I hope you're glad to see me." Even his deep voice made her feel safer. *It would be all right now – everything would work out.* "When I arrived, I thought at least your mother would have been here – ready with the kettle as she always is." He sounded amused but quickly realised there was something wrong. "What's wrong darling – is it your mother? Where is she?"

Charlie explained that she hoped mum was still at her bingo – although it seemed rather late for that now. They went indoors together and it was he who had to fill the kettle this time. Hours later they were still waiting for Jill to come home. Charlie couldn't keep still and Phil said, "Sit down woman or you'll wear the pile from the carpet." It wasn't the home-coming he'd expected.

She reached for her coat and although it was after midnight, she said, "I'm going across the street – her lights are still on. Perhaps she knows where Mum is – she seems to know everything else." He offered to go with her but she said she didn't want that – his presence might unnerve the woman – she was very unpredictable.

Knocking on the door, she had to wait a while for an answer, but soon she heard the door being unbolted and Liz stood there in her dressing gown. "Oh, hello Charlie – I was just on my way to bed. Is there something wrong?"

"Is my mother with you? She hasn't come home yet from her bingo and I'm worried." Charlie explained in a rush.

Liz's eyes opened wide in surprise and she gripped her dressing gown tighter around her neck, "Why no Charlie, I haven't seen her at all today – I do hope she's all right." Charlie tried to listen for any noises coming from inside the house, but she could hear nothing – everything was deathly silent. Something told her Liz's concern wasn't genuine, there was no real sympathy in her voice, in fact she was almost sneering. All Charlie could do was say thank you and turn away from the door. As she walked back home, she heard Liz's voice calling, "Let me know if there's anything I can do – you only have to say the word." And she quickly closed the door.

Say the word – I don't think I'd ever ask for your help lady. I don't think I could trust you as far as I could throw you. But she didn't voice the words – what was the point after all? Everything had started going wrong from the moment she'd moved into the street – and this was just another thing. At least, she had Phil here now.

When she got indoors, he would brook no argument and rang the police right away. He was told however there was nothing they could do about Jill's disappearance – at least, not yet. She was an adult and, in her sixties, so they couldn't assume something bad had happened to her – they'd have to wait 48 hours before treating it as a missing person. The man on the phone was sympathetic but said he could do nothing – just yet.

Jill Collins never came home that night although both Charlie and Phil sat up 'till dawn in case she appeared. Early next morning, the shrill sound of the doorbell woke them from their uneasy napping in the sitting room. They just couldn't bring themselves to go upstairs to bed whilst Jill was out there in the cold. Phil jumped up first and went to answer the door. He hoped it would be the police saying they'd changed their minds about waiting 48 hours – but no, it was a just a woman, who'd come to ask if Jill had come home. He didn't recognise her.

As she stood there, he had a strange feeling that maybe he did know her. For a moment, she looked familiar – from his past. But no, that couldn't be, his path could never have crossed with hers in the past – he'd have remembered. Or could it? Charlie appeared behind him but when she saw who it was, she backed away, whispering that she didn't want to speak to the woman. Of course, Liz heard her but Charlie didn't care. - she was too worried about her missing mother.

Liz was staring intently at Phil, "You don't recognise me, do you Phillip? We've met before you know– I work in the Officers' Mess at the naval depot and I've actually served you a few times there."

Always polite, he said, "I do apologise for not remembering you but I've only used that Mess a few times – I'm more often away at sea. How do you know my name by the way?" She explained she'd heard someone using it last time he'd eaten at the Mess and she hadn't forgotten. He began to back away from the door as he didn't know what to say next. She somehow made him feel uneasy as stretched out her hand and touched his arm, "Do tell Charlie I'm here for her. I'm worried about Jill too – she's been my friend since I moved here two or three months ago and we've become good friends." He thanked her and promised to tell Charlie but he had to quickly close the door as she didn't seem inclined to go step away.

He and Charlie visited all the places they could think of, the places where Jill might have gone – but they had no luck. Charlie had to tell the school she wouldn't be back at work until the next day – she knew she'd have to go back then as they'd been short-staffed for a while. They started searching again and didn't go home until late that night. They even went to the bingo parlour but the woman caller there said Jill hadn't been since the previous week. "Odd, I thought because she loved her bingo and was usually quite lucky."

Charlie was astounded by the news - Mum miss her bingo? That wasn't normal behaviour at all.

"Try not to worry too much darling, we'll go straight to the police in the morning. They'll find her I'm sure – perhaps she's fallen over somewhere and banged her head. She might be concussed and forgotten who she was. We'll go on searching ourselves of course – between us, we'll find her." However, Charlie didn't look too convinced.

Now, the police were acting on a missing person's report and immediately became a hive of activity. They explained how they would begin searching for the missing woman whose description and photo would be sent across the county. They insisted the couple go home and wait there in case she tried to contact them – and of course there was a chance that she'd return home with a perfectly satisfactory explanation for her disappearance. It was a reasonable possibility so they did as they were asked.

As they settled down to wait at home, it was a good thing they didn't know what was occurring not very far away.

"Eat that, your old witch, it's all you're going to get from me." Liz had taken a bowl of soup down to the woman in the cellar – and the woman wasn't in the least grateful. *Typical she thought. People are so ungrateful. She knew she'd have to get even nastier to the old woman!*

Jill looked scared and confused "Why are you keeping me here Liz – I thought we were friends. We are friends, weren't we?"

Liz sneered at her and her expression wasn't in the least friendly, "Don't be stupid old woman, I was never your friend. I just needed to get to know that snob of a daughter of yours and the easiest way was through you. School teacher indeed, anyone could do her job – I bet she's not even a good teacher."

Jill said again, "Why are you doing this – I only came here for a cup of coffee and a natter." Liz went back upstairs and left the woman alone with only a weak gas lamp for light, a tatty mattress with a blanket and a bucket in the corner to 'use however she wanted.'

She called over her shoulder, "And remember to eat that soup – there'll be nothing else until you do."

She had lured the older woman into her house whilst Charlie was still at school and on the pretext of showing her an antique in the cellar, she'd drugged her coffee and left her down there, feeling drowsy from the drugged coffee and unsure of what was going on. She searched around the cellar but it was quite dark and there was nothing she could use to bang on the trap door – even a broom wouldn't be long enough for her to reach it. She was still confused from the trauma of her recent arrest by the police and coupled with being drugged and locked in the cellar by someone she thought of as a friend, she was feeling as low as possible. She lay down on the old mattress, unable to stand any longer. She felt utterly exhausted and pulled the blanket around her shaking shoulders. But she must drink that soup before Liz came back or she'd be very angry and who knew what she'd do then?

Meanwhile Liz was making herself an omelette when she spotted Phil and Charlie driving up in the car. They both looked crestfallen and obviously upset by being unable to find Jill. She smiled to herself, enjoying the sight of the 'two lovers' looking so miserable. *That's a sight pleasing to the eye. Let's hope they're both feeling as bad as each other!'*

Not remembering me is typical – well perhaps they'll remember me after this.

The doorbell rang shrilly and the sound made her drop one of the eggs. A uniformed policeman stood there, notebook in hand. He was just a young bobby and she knew how to deal with him. She forced tears into her eyes and let them fall down her cheeks. 'She'd *always been a good actress and now she had to make herself look like a woman whose best friend had just gone missing.'*

"I'm so sorry about Jill, Officer – she was my best friend, you know – but I haven't seen her since yesterday morning when she called here. She had a quick coffee and then went off shopping." She knew he believed her from the way he reached over and touched her shoulder. Policemen didn't usually do that. "Don't upset yourself so Ma'am, we'll find your friend for you." And he went off to question the rest of the people in the street. She watched him go and thought how young and naïve he was. Thank God!

Across the way, Phil was listening to Charlie's list of disasters of all the things that had gone wrong with the wedding plans. "And everything's happened since that woman over there moved in. You say you might know her from before Phil?" She asked, curiously.

"I don't remember her – but she seems to know me. She even knew my name. She says she works in the officers' Mess at the depot but I don't recall having seen her." He obviously wanted to disassociate himself from the woman Charlie disliked so much.

Charlie's thoughts were in turmoil. 'She thought, how could she know him so well, even knowing his name and yet he claims not to know her at all? It didn't seem logical. Then she realised was being paranoid. Phil was the love of her life and would never hurt her – or her mother. Probably yet another trick to cause trouble – despite how 'friendly' she always acted towards her, Charlie knew all was not right with that particular neighbour.'

"Can you find out anything about her – perhaps visit the mess and talk to her colleagues there? Just to get a feel for her background – how she's regarded by them and where she worked before. Anything in fact to give us a clearer picture of her. I can't explain it Phil, I just feel there's something strange about her and he's had a connection to everything's that's been happening to me."

He did as she asked and went to the naval depot where he learned very little about the woman. He learned she'd worked there for a few years only and usually kept herself to herself. She was a quiet fellow-worker and never caused any trouble. She'd recently moved house and had a few days off work to organise things. One young girl mentioned that she'd attended the local university for a while but had given up her studies as she had no income and needed that to continue with her studies – and that was when she came to work in the Mess.

"And that's all I could find about her, I'm afraid." He was as disappointed with the results of his visit as she was.

"We'll have to cancel the wedding, Phil. You know that, don't you? We can' possibly celebrate such a thing while Mum is missing." Charlie knew she had to be realistic in this - the strangest of circumstances.

He looked upset but knew she was right, "But there's so much to cancel darling and you've worked so hard to arrange everything. I understand we can't marry right now– but why don't we just delay it for two weeks – two weeks exactly, when I'm sure this'll all be over." It sounded so reasonable that she agreed. They sat in front of the TV's blank screen, both holding a glass of wine they couldn't bring themselves to drink. Charlie felt it might choke her!

'Was that a rat in the corner? Something was definitely moving over there.' Jill was so scared she was frozen to the spot. Also she knew she had to use that terrible bucket – what could she do – her bladder was full and she felt in real pain. It was the most humiliating thing she'd ever had to do – but there was no option. So, she used the bucket and was left feeling like an animal. No, worse than an animal, they didn't know any better.

The trap door overhead was suddenly thrown back and Liz's face glared down into the gloom below. "Keep away from the bottom of the stairs old woman or I'll just tread on you." She climbed down, closing the trap door behind her. Safer to keep it closed - you never knew who was looking through the window!

"We're going to have a little chat Jill and I'm going to keep you here until you do what I want. I'll come straight out with it – I hate your daughter. I attended the same university as she did and I was there for two years before I was forced to jack it in – unlike her who had all the financial support she needed. I was an orphan you see and didn't have anyone to help with my living costs, so I was forced to leave my studies early and find a job.

Of course, your daughter went on and completed her studies whilst she had you and her doting father to support her. When I moved to live across from you, she didn't even recognise me - or she pretended she didn't. Either way, she chose to ignore me!"

Later, I was told by the woman at the post office that Charlie was getting married to Philip MacDonald - the boy I fell in love with at university and whom I've gone on loving ever since. Needless to say, he only had eyes for your daughter although I tried again and again to catch his eye. We went on a couple of dates, but when she arrived on the scene, I was yesterday's news." She was leaning against the wall to make this long speech as she didn't want to sit on the floor or on the dirty steps. She moved about the cellar nervously telling her story but was obviously relishing being able to say it at last. The surprise and horror on Jill's face pleased her captor, who didn't conceal the strength of her hatred for Charlie – and the depth of her adoration of the young, naval officer.

Jill managed to speak at last, "Have you been responsible for all the things that have gone wrong with the wedding? Did you run down the bridesmaid and break her bones? And the vicar – the poor, poor vicar – did you hurt him because he was the only one Charlie wanted to marry her? How many things have you done? I bet it was you who double-booked the band – it was, wasn't it? " Now she was beginning to see the picture – Charlie had been right after all, her wedding was jinxed, jinxed by an old university colleague. She realised too she'd been the supplier of much of the information, given over several coffee mornings when the two women had had a good, old natter. *My God, she'd been responsible for telling Charlie's arch-enemy of her daughter's most intimate desires and plans'.*

Liz stood up and snatched the blanket from the floor, "Let's see how you get on without this, shall we? Maybe the cold and damp will persuade you to see sense, and to prove I'm not completely inhuman!" And she placed a packet of sandwiches and a bottle of water on the bottom step. "These are for you, old woman – eat them slowly cause it's all you're going to get for the foreseeable future."

She told Jill she wanted to make things clear and explained she wanted Charlie and Phil to split up. "He's mine you see and only mine! All the things I tried to destroy the perfect wedding, failed – no matter how cruel I was, nothing seemed to work and so I decided to make friends with you and learn all about the wedding plans. You're going to be my nuclear deterrent you see, you're going to break up your daughter's romance with MY man - and if you do, I might decide to let you live. If you don't, well you know what'll happen – and don't think I won't do it, I assure you I will if it proves to be necessary." She stopped speaking and turned to climb the stairs, not saying another word. She'd left Jill with a surprise bombshell and that was enough for now.

She felt weak with hunger and swallowed her pride, so she grabbed the sandwiches and water and demolished them in a few seconds. That felt a little better. Now, she understood what had been happening over the past few months – it was about a woman scorned and ignored by an innocent young woman who was lucky enough to be loved by a handsome young man. How ridiculous and yet, how sad! What was that old saying about a woman scorned? She couldn't remember but knew it wasn't good.

Jill knew she had to get out of the cellar as Charlie was in great danger – and so was she, for that matter. A new thought suddenly struck her and she remembered being told about the little ghost at the school who'd told Charlie she was in danger. The little ghost must have been talking about Liz! That must have been what the ghost had meant!

For a little while, she even tried screaming as loudly as she could but her voice soon gave out and she had to stop, especially when Liz put her head through the trapdoor and shouted, "If you don't shut up, I'll take away your mattress as well and see how you like that."

It was enough of a threat to silence Jill, who knew the walls were thick and probably no-one could hear her anyway. All the houses in the street had been built a long time ago, they were solid with no fabrication or light materials. That night passed badly for Jill who slept in fits and starts. She couldn't have felt more miserable – and cold.

Next day, Charlie set off for school good and early. She was spied on getting into her car by the fluttering curtains across the street. 'Excellent – *she's going to work. That means I'm free to visit Philip today. She'd bring him one of the Mess's cooked dishes, that's what she'd do. She could finish work at 2 o'clock and Charlie wouldn't be home for a while after that. She'd be quite safe and maybe he'd remember her, now that she'd jogged his memory.'*

At 2.30 exactly, she stood on his doorstep holding a warm casserole and dressed casually but nicely. She felt attractive and hoped he would think so too. He opened the door and looked taken-aback when he saw who it was. He was well aware that Charlie didn't like her and wouldn't like to know she was visiting him. What could he say? She was doing a kind thing and the casserole did smell lovely, so he thanked her profusely and made to take it out of her hands. She wouldn't let go however, saying it was too hot and he'd burn his hands. She was wearing a pair of oven gloves and pushed past him towards the kitchen.

"There you are Philip, I made it especially for you although you can keep some for Charlie if you like." Of course, she didn't mean it, but she wasn't stupid!

"Any news of Jill yet?" She asked innocently and on being told there wasn't, she added, "Where on earth can she be? I must say she doesn't seem like the sort of person who would just go off without telling anyone." Phil agreed she wasn't and made to put the casserole in the oven.

"Oh, you don't have to do that, you should eat it now – it's still nice and hot. If you cook it any more, it'll dry out." She went to the cupboards where she knew the plates were kept – and placed two of them on the kitchen table. "I hope you don't mind if I join you – I've had no lunch yet – been too busy making this for you."

He hesitated. He didn't want her to join him but what option did he have? So, they both sat together at the table and shared a bottle from the wine rack. She was behaving as though she was the hostess.

It didn't feel right at all to Phil, but Liz was quite comfortable and between mouthfuls, asked if he remembered her now. Embarrassed, he said he didn't but immediately felt he was being rude again – she was only trying to do the decent thing after all. "I tend not to notice people around me when I'm eating – sorry but I'm a bit of a pig I'm afraid." He thought it might lessen the blow if he blamed his own failings rather than her invisibility in the Mess.

She hesitated before saying, "We didn't just meet at the mess – we'd met before then." She explained she'd attended the same university as he had but it had been a long time ago, so he might have forgotten. She said she remembered him well and that she remembered Charlie too. "You and she were an item then, weren't you?"

Now, he was surprised, "Really? I don't recall meeting you at university." He felt he was being pushed into a corner now – she was relentless! "Mind you. I was a pretty arrogant chap then – I remember being told by one of the professors that I was only interested in myself." Another attempt to blame himself for not recognising her. He really was an officer and a gentleman!

"You seemed pretty interested in Charlie though. I remember you both well, but I left university without completing my degree and I never saw you again."

They'd finished their meal and for whatever reason, he knew their conversation was taking an odd turn. It seemed too personal and he stood up and began clearing away the plates. He told her he had to go out – he had some business to discuss with his superior at the depot. He even reached for his jacket, so she could do nothing else but grab her coat and leave the house, deliberately leaving her casserole dish behind. 'Let him explain that to the wonderful Charlie – hopefully, it'll get him into trouble. What a bad boy, eating with the enemy!"

Of course, he didn't have to speak with his boss and he went for a walk in the park instead. The whole incident with Liz Dawson had been awkward and embarrassing – almost surreal. Charlie was right, the woman was quite odd. And no matter how hard he tried, he still couldn't remember her from before.

That day, after the last lesson, Charlie climbed the stairs to the school attic. She had almost reached the present day with her search – she was now looking for the reports of her grandma and of course her mother. She'd be able to see her own if she liked – but was that a good idea? *'Yes, it should be easy from now on and I can probably do it quite quickly. It was strange but I feel quite nostalgic now – I don't want my searches to come to an end. Will I see little Rachel again – I do hope so!'*

The day light was almost gone and she switched on the lights in the attic. She looked for Rachel but there was no sign, so she began to go through the folders of reports. Now, they were no longer musty and covered with dust – they were easier to read and the paper was still quite crisp. Then she found Grandma Jane's report. She'd been born to Charlotte Jenkins and Cuthbert Edwards. Her name was Jane Edwards and Charlie remembered her although she'd died many years ago. She'd been a lovely lady, kind and generous and with the most beautiful head of abundant, white hair.

She read Jane's report – written just before she went on to her secondary school. Children were luckier by this time and were being offered a secondary education, unlike their predecessors, who'd been expected to find work as young as the age of twelve.

Jane's report said: ' Jane Edwards is a clever girl and has excelled in English language - she is also an avid reader. She has a good ear for the French language and has cooking skills that many grown-ups would envy. She enjoys keeping fit and has found a natural ability in arithmetic. She should do well with her Secondary studies.'

Clever Little Jane. I hope I take after her. Jane Edwards had married David Paget , her grandpa whom she remembered well – but neither had lived a long life, so she hadn't known them as well as she'd have liked. Now, she'd arrived at her mother Jill's report and there it was, Jill Paget, who'd married one William Collins, her father.

Now for Jill – she'd really looked forward to this report so she could pull Mum's leg about its contents – that is once she'd come home again. Her eyes filled with tears as she thought of her mum and wondered where on earth she was.

Jill Paget's report said,

'Jill Paget is a lively and cheerful girl, always neat and tidy. She arrives punctually for her lessons and is very good at art. Academically she is also in the top classes. She is about to move to her secondary school to continue her studies and should do well in that environment. On occasion, she can be rather stubborn and even wilful but this is probably because of her strong will and natural intelligence. A good all-rounder.'

I must take a photocopy of that, so I can pull her leg – at the right time of course. Actually, the young Jill had the kind of angelic expression that usually meant the opposite. Not many daughters get the opportunity to read their own mother's school report and, in a way, it felt like an invasion of privacy. – but I'm still enjoying learning what mum had been like as a child. Ah, there's my own report but I'm not interested in that– I remember it clearly and some things are best left undisturbed!

As she was tidying away the reports, she heard a voice singing an odd little tune. She had no doubt it was Rachel but for some reason, she was being shy and not making an appearance that day.

"Rachel, are you here? Do you have something to tell me? She turned around and searched every corner. The tuneful voice was still ringing in her ears,

'Lizzie Dawson took an axe and gave her mother forty whacks
When she saw what she had done, she gave her father forty-one.'

The sweet, little voice continued to sing and the words sent a chill up and down Charlie's spine. *Was it a warning? Of course, it was! Rachel is telling me mum's in imminent danger and I have to move quickly. The song was about Lizzie Borden who murdered her parents – and not about Liz Dawson, her mother's alleged friend. But Charlie knew exactly who the song was about!*

"What are you trying to tell me Rachel? I know it's about Mum – can't you just tell me where she is – or maybe you don't you know?" The little ghost obviously took umbrage at her knowledge being questioned and the young voice grew even louder. Before, she'd said she didn't know Charlie's enemy's name – but for whatever reason, she felt she could tell now. Charlie had become her friend after all and she obviously trusted her. She knew she should rush home now and hoped Phil would have some news for her. *Perhaps the police had found Jill!*

Relaxing after supper and disappointed there was no news, Charlie tentatively asked, "Phil, please will you do me a favour?

I know you think I'm besotted with the woman across the street – but I swear I'm not – it's just that my every sense tells me she's involved with everything that's gone wrong with our wedding – even with the fatal attack on Reverend Johnson."   Something told her not to mention the little ghosts' song as he might think she'd gone mad.

"What I need you to do is to wear your full-dress uniform and use your officer status to find and talk to the two women who provided her with an alibi for the night the vicar was killed. If your officer status doesn't work on them and they stick to their original story – you must offer them a reward for telling the truth. A decent award mind you – don't be too stingy – but also stress they'd be doing the right thing and correcting misinformation. You might even add the police had asked you to help them – only a little white lie. " She paused and took a deep breath, "Will you do that for me? I also feel she's got something to do with Mum's disappearance – but nothing I can prove."

"Actually darling, you don't have to make such a song and dance about asking me because I'm beginning to think you might be right not to trust her." And he told her in detail of his lunch hour with the woman – and of the strange story she told him about knowing him at university.

"She just turned up on the doorstep clutching a hot casserole dish and invited herself inside. It was embarrassing – I didn't know how to get rid of her. To be honest, I actually think she was coming on to me, implying she'd always liked me and blaming you for taking my attention away from her. I know it all sounds crazy and although I still don't remember her claim that we'd met in the Mess, I began to have vague recollections of seeing her all those years ago." He looked quite disturbed as his words sounded weak even to him.   The woman had really unnerved him.

It was as though she read his thoughts, "Well, I'm not that kind of person my darling – I know how creepy she can be. Will you do what I ask then – it must be tomorrow however as we're running out of time to find mum safely? I feel it in my bones." That sounded better than admitting it had really been Rachels' little song.

Next day Phil, looking tall and handsome in his smart uniform, set out to intimidate two strangers and find the truth about the alibi they'd provided for Liz Dawson. He first made sure she wasn't on duty that afternoon before he strode into the building. He found the young women hovering over a dish washer in the big kitchen and laughing over some gossip. He could hear 'She didn't, did she?' How did you discover that?' And lots of sniggering and laughing.

He marched boldly into the kitchen and both girls jumped at the sight. And no wonder, he looked imposing and very much in authority. The older girl asked if she could help him, to which he said she could. "I'm asking questions on behalf of the local police, (*Well, it wasn't exactly a lie – he was trying to help the police)* and I was specifically looking for the two people who'd been with Ms Liz Dawson on the night the local vicar was attacked in the graveyard. Could that be you two perhaps?" He waited patiently whilst they looked nervously into each other's eyes.

"Well young ladies, speak up, I don't have time to waste here." He removed his officer's hat and held it under his arm. Somehow, the gesture made him seem even more in authority.

The younger one said, "That's us, but we've already been interviewed by the police. Liz was with us that night, having a drink in the pub. We can't tell you anything different." Her body language told Phil she was being economical with the truth. The lie was so obvious, the way she was fiddling with her overall buttons.

"The police suspect you may have got the night in question wrong. I'd like you to think again and confirm you got it right. I should warn you however that they already doubt the accuracy of your statement and need you to make a new verbal statement to me. Do be aware though that if you wilfully told them an untruth, you'll be charged with obstructing them in their duty and distorting evidence in a murder case."

Silence! Phil said nothing else but waited for one of them to crack. The younger of the two cracked first, "We don't want anything like that." She looked questioningly at her friend, who nodded her head – it was all the agreement she needed and she blurted out, "What'll happen to us if we change our statement now – will we be charged with anything?"

The naval officer told them he'd make sure the police understood they'd been confused. "Which night was she really with you?" The flood gates opened and both started to talk at the same time, "Liz wasn't with us on any night that week but she gave us a tenner each to say she was. Please don't tell our boss here or we'll lose our jobs."

Hat back on head, he nodded his agreement and said again he'd explain things to the police. "Thank you for your time ladies. You've been very helpful. *They noticed the change in his tone and that now they were ladies and not women or girls. Telling the truth obviously raised their status as far as he was concerned.*

He went straight home, collected Charlie and told her they had to see the police. En route, he told her she'd been right in her hunch about the woman and that the two girls had come up trumps. "She wasn't with them on the night the vicar was attacked – put that together with the fact she knew about the attack before she should have done – and I think the police will be willing to dig deeper and interview her again."

Whilst they were talking at the station, Liz was visiting Jill in the cellar. "Well, have you decided to instruct your daughter that she mustn't marry Philip MacDonald - you must tell her it was her father's dying wish that she stays with you. Anyway, it's me he really loves, not her – he told me so only yesterday. I hope you're not going to be difficult now or I'll have to think of something to change your mind." She was carrying a thick rope and Jill knew what she was going to do.

"Please Liz – please let me go. If you do, I promise you that I'll say nothing about where I've been for – how many days has it been - I've lost count I'm afraid?" Jill looked haggard and very tired. Her hair was straggly and hung loose about her face, her clothes were crumpled and dirty and she smelt. In fact, she was embarrassed as even she could smell herself.

Liz walked over to the bucket which was about half full and kicked it viciously against the wall. The urine ran across the floor and the cellar smelt even worse. In fact, it possibly wasn't only urine -Jill was only human after all! She pulled her legs beneath her and saw the wetness slowly soak into the mattress.

"Do you think I'm going to fall for that lie? You'll blab the moment you're free. Well, it's not going to happen – I've still not got your promise that you'll stop Charlie from marrying Philip."

"Liz, Charlie won't listen to me. She can be very stubborn – she's always been like that.   Why not forget about the two of them – you're worth more than both of them put together." Jill was desperate and tried reverse psychology on her captor. It didn't work however and Liz started up the stairs, turning at the top, "You do realise it would be easier if I just killed you now and buried your body in this very cellar. No-one would ever find you and the police have already interviewed and cleared me. I'm pure as the driven snow, as far as they're concerned. I'll think about this overnight but just in case, don't forget to say your prayers as you might be meeting your Maker sooner than you think." She laughed as she closed the trapdoor and Jill realised the woman was completely mad. To think she could persuade her daughter to send away the man she loved, just because she asked her, proved she was unhinged. Also, how would killing her and burying her down here help the situation – logic says it wouldn't – but Liz Dawson was not being logical.

Jill lay down on the wet mattress, feeling disgusted and very scared of what was to come. She thought this could be her last night on earth -and she would die starving hungry, as well.

At eleven o'clock that night, Liz's doorbell rang unexpectedly. Liz had already changed for bed and wondered who on earth could be calling at this late hour. She did notice her neighbours across the street were still awake – she saw them clearly silhouetted in the light from the sitting room window. She put her hand on the lock and called out, "Who is it? It's late to be calling on a decent woman."

A heavier hand knocked the door this time and a man's deep voice called out, "Open the door Miss Dawson, it's the police. We have a few more questions for you."

"Oh, do go away, it's too late. You can question me in the morning." And she turned away to go upstairs. The door was knocked even harder this time and the same voice told her if she didn't open the door, they'd break it down. *How melodramatic! Were they mad? She knew she had to let them in and so, she unlocked the door.*

"Come in officers, no need for violence." She pulled her dressing gown around her shoulders and stood back to let them enter. Her mind was working overtime, *'Have they come for me? No, that can't be, I've done nothing wrong. She felt confused – but told herself not to be silly – she was an innocent woman, wasn't she? She decided, 'I must offer them a cup of tea. Yes, that's what I'll do'.*

"Would you care for a drink officers? I have some brandy or would you prefer some tea perhaps?" *'The men's expressions were serious and their eyes unblinking – no, she wouldn't offer them her expensive brandy. Tea was all they deserved.'*

And so, they spoke with her about the night the vicar was attacked. They told her how her two friends had withdrawn their statement, taking away her alibi. They explained she had to come down to the station with them – there were further questions they wanted to ask. *Her mind was suddenly racing. She knew there was something she had to hide from them – but what was it? She was standing directly over the trap door and noticed she'd forgotten to return the rugs she used to conceal the opening. She moved her foot to straighten it out. What'll I do now? What if Jill Collins made a noise and they heard it? She knew they'd probably blame her for the old witch in the cellar. Although that wasn't her fault – it was that stuck-up bitch Charlie's fault!*

A loud clattering noise filled the kitchen and the two men jumped at the noise. Bang, bang – the sound was getting louder. They removed her bodily from the crumpled rug and made her sit at the table. One of the men opened the trapdoor and the smell of urine, faeces and dampness wafted upwards to greet them. From the light of a torch one of the policemen had, they saw the haggard face of a grey-haired woman staring up at them – and they knew at once that they'd found Jill Collins.

Gently, the younger of the policemen went down into the cellar and found the woman exhausted by her efforts of throwing the bucket around the room. It was all she'd had to make some noise. She threw herself against the officer and asked if it was going to be all right. "It's going to be all right, isn't it?" Her body was shaking and she looked terrified.

"It's going to be all right now Ma'am. It is Mrs Jill Collins, isn't it?" She could only nod. Slowly and one step at a time, he helped her up the stairs. The bright kitchen light forced her to cover her eyes and she was temporarily blinded for a few moments. The other policeman had already telephoned for an ambulance and whilst they waited for the medics to arrive, Liz smiled at Jill in a friendly way, "Why Jill, I didn't know you were here – would you like cup of coffee? " *'She had suddenly turned into a softly spoken and frail woman who seemed genuinely pleased to see her friend. She knew she had to appear friendly towards her neighbour – after all, what did she have to hide?'*

The policemen couldn't believe their ears and Jill just sat there, her head fallen forwards onto her chest. *Was the ordeal really over she thought? She believed it was - and she could hear Liz talking as though nothing out of the ordinary had happened. The woman really was deranged.*

The loud sirens screamed in the quiet suburban street and as the paramedics rushed up the garden path, Charlie and Phil also arrived from across the street. Charlie attempted to take her mother in her arms but was warned not to touch the woman, until the hospital had given her the once over.

"Hello Charlie – and Philip – how nice to see you both. Are we having a party?" Liz was smiling at the newcomers, obviously delighted to see them both. Charlie was furious at her words and couldn't believe how callous the woman was being – she leapt across the threshold to grab a handful of the woman's hair but was stopped by the young policeman. He said, "It's all right Miss, just leave her to us. We'll take care of her."

The worst night of their lives was over at last. Jill was alive but far from well – though hopefully she'd get better. The couple followed the ambulance to the hospital and waited whilst Jill was being settled but the doctor told them to go home, "There's no point in your waiting here – there's nothing you can do tonight and you know she's in safe hands. Come and see her tomorrow – she'll be more compos mentis by then."

Exhausted after the strangest day ever, they did as they were told. Meanwhile, the police had taken Liz Dawson to the station,

where for a while, there was nothing could be done with her –
she wasn't even sure who she really was. The police surgeon was
called to check on her and gradually, her senses seemed to return
and she became aware of what had happened. Or had she? Only
the psychiatrist would be able to tell. Was the woman mad and
not to be held responsible for her actions – or was she just plain
evil. It would take time to answer that!

Next day and after visiting Jill in hospital, Charlie went on to
school and forced herself to take her classes as normal. She
considered asking the Head if she could have some special
annual leave, but the school was so under-staffed at the moment,
she knew it wouldn't be fair on the other teachers, let alone the
pupils.

Later at home, she relaxed with Phil, safe in the knowledge
that mum was going to be all right – she was safe in the hospital
and being well looked after. The couple were sharing a bottle of
wine and found they couldn't stop talking about everything that
had happened. The room was cosy and the heat from the open
fire along with the effects of wine, made them both sleepy.

"You know Charlie, I can't get over how accurate your hunch
was about Liz Dawson. What made you so suspicious of her?
You still don't remember her either, do you?" Phil was genuinely
puzzled, "I've never believed in the paranormal or second sight
– call it what you will – but I can't explain how you had a sixth
sense about that woman."

"Ah, but I had help – you mustn't forget that. Granted, I
didn't take to her when I met her but my little friend Rachel
confirmed what I was already feeling. She told me I had an
enemy – an enemy who lived close by and who was planning
only bad things for me." She smiled at his expression but went
on to explain about the Victorian child who'd helped her. She
knew it was a tall story – and that he'd have difficulty accepting
it, but it was the truth and she couldn't change that. "She is my
little friend Phil, please don't laugh – one day, maybe you'll get
the chance to meet her – all you have to do, is believe!"

She suddenly remembered her school report which she'd
decided to bring home after all and changing the subject would
help get their minds off Liz Dawson. Spreading it across the

coffee table, she began to read aloud, telling him she was going to give him a laugh. God only knows, they both needed a laugh.

"This is my own school report, written when I was about eleven. She read aloud,

'Charlotte Collins is an eleven-year-old, who regularly arrives each morning and is always on time. She is clean and tidy and seems to have a good grasp of the '3 Rs' but is especially interested in reading and has been allowed on occasion, to borrow books to take home. This is exceptional and only allowed where the pupil is highly thought of and can be trusted to take care of them.'

As she read the w she'd seen them quite recently and yet, she hadn't seen her own copy for several years. *Why did the words seem so familiar? She'd definitely seen them not long ago.* Jumping up from the coffee table, she emptied her briefcase, finding copies of the older reports she'd been finding over the weeks. She knew what she was looking for and went straight to one of the oldest files. It was the school report of Jennifer Bell, written so long ago about a child from the last century.

Without explaining what she was doing, she held both reports in either hand. Her own report was almost word-for-word the same as that of Jennifer Bell's, written a hundred years before. It was uncanny – both girls had been good at the same things and were described as neat, tidy, punctual and in love with books. *My God, I've never felt so close to my ancestors as I do now. I could have been Jennifer and she could have been me. History repeating itself has always seemed a nothing phrase - but not now – I am her and she is me. I feel it in my bones!*

She showed the reports to Phil and on this occasion, he couldn't deny they were uncannily alike. "Maybe now you'll believe in my little ghost Rachel – after all, there's many a thing on this earth……….. etc. etc. etc." She misquoted but didn't care. She'd just experienced a miracle. "And something else Phil ,"she went on, " Charlotte was the name of two of my great grandmothers and when I marry you, I'll be Mrs Charlotte MacDonald – Macdonald was the surname of my great great great grandfather. I don't believe that's just coincidence – it's meant to be."

He admitted it was uncanny – but added it wasn't impossible. Charlie laughed and said, "Oh Ye of little faith. Perhaps I'll convert you once you've met my friend Rachel." Phil looked uncomfortable. He regarded Charlie's words, not as a promise, but more of a threat – did he want to meet the little ghost? He thought not!

"That reminds me, the hospital rang and asked if we could collect mum after the doctor's rounds tomorrow. I'll feel better once she's home again where I can keep an eye on her. I don't want to stop her making friends, but I think I'll have to vet everyone she meets in future."

Arriving back in the street, Jill was a little nervous `and stared across at Liz Dawson's house with apprehension. "It's all right Mum, she's in police custody and can never harm you again." Charlie settled her on the sofa and wrapped a blanket around her knees.

The invalid accepted a mug of hot chocolate from Phil. She stared into his eyes for a few minutes and then said, "You know Phil, I never agreed to do what she wanted. I would never try to come between you and Charlie - but that's what the evil woman wanted. She said if I agreed to do it, she'd set me free, but she wouldn't have, would she? I made up my mind immediately and I'd have let her kill me as she threatened, rather than agree to her order. You believe that, don't you Phil? And you Charlie, you know how stubborn I can be, especially if I'm being told to hurt those I love most."

Realising how low her mother was feeling, Charlie fetched her briefcase from the hall and rifled through the school reports again. She pulled out one of the most recent ones and held it out, "Read that Mum- you don't have to tell us how stubborn you can be."

"I think you'll find that interesting Jill – in fact I'm sure you will." Phil couldn't hide his smile.

Jill read her own school report aloud,

'Jill Paget is a lively and cheerful girl, always neat and tidy. She arrives punctually for her lessons and is very good at art. Academically she is also in the top classes. She is about to move to her secondary school to continue her studies and should do well in that environment. On occasion she can be rather stubborn and even wilful, but this is probably because of her strong will and natural intelligence. A good all-rounder.'

Even she had to laugh. "Isn't that just what I've been saying? Although I can agree with natural intelligence part, but stubborn and wilful I'm not so sure about." Charlie had been right; the report did cheer up her mother and it was just the right time to 'pull her leg.' She was clearly on the mend, despite her terrible experience.

The wedding was right back on track and the day dawned sunny and bright. Charlie's bridesmaid had arrived to do her friend's hair, something she managed quite well, considering she still walked on crutches. Jill was rushing around like a demented chicken, doing and then re-doing everything. She looked so well now and was dressed in a lovely, lilac suit with a pretty little fascinator hat on her beautifully coiffured hair. (That clever bridesmaid again!)

"Calm down Mum, you'll give yourself a heart attack. Everything's fine and going according to plan." Charlie looked really lovely in her cream coloured dress of satin and pearl beads sewn all over the bodice. It had been altered by a seamstress and now fitted her perfectly. She looked tall and elegant and wore a set of large pearls that had belonged to her grandmother (Jane). Her bouquet was made up of pink roses and white freesia and smelled heavenly. Her bridesmaid and flower girls were in powder blue and the two little flower girls in pink, couldn't stop admiring themselves in the mirror. They were the neighbour's children – but *not that neighbour.'*

Even the church had managed to contact Reverend Johnson's nephew – also a vicar – and asked if he would conduct the marriage ceremony. He was delighted, especially when he heard Charlie had been broken-hearted when his uncle couldn't do it. In fact, he even looked like Charlie's favourite vicar. When she walked down the aisle and saw Phil waiting there, dressed in full naval uniform and with his fellow officer also in uniform, her heart swelled fit to burst.

The ceremony went without a hitch and Mr and Mrs MacDonald walked out of the old church to the rich sound of church bells. There were daffodils in flower all over the graveyard and after pausing for photographs, the bride took the groom's hand and led him to a particular grave at the back of the church. There, she placed her bouquet with its trailing, silk ribbons against the tombstone of the Reverend Johnson. It seemed the fitting thing to do – as he should have been there with them. Out of the corner of her eye, she saw her mother approach, her lilac dress billowing in the gentle breeze. She removed her buttonhole flower and placed it reverently alongside her daughter's flowers.

"It's the right thing to do – he was such a gentleman and he would have been here, but for that awful woman." Jill had tears in her eyes but they were happy tears. She couldn't feel anything but happy on this wonderful day, especially as they'd all had to climb mountains to reach it.

Charlie put her arm around her mum's shoulders, "Let's not even think of her today, Mum. She's gone out of our lives forever and we're going to the wedding breakfast now to drink lots and lots of lovely champagne. Come on." And Jill took her daughter and new son's arms and clung onto them tightly, as the bridal car arrived to take them to the wedding breakfast at the hotel. (And the wedding cake did fit through the door after all)

Changing into her going-away clothes, Charlie surreptitiously grabbed a piece of fruit from the large bowl on the table. Phil remarked, "You glutton Mrs MacDonald, you're never still hungry after that feast." Charlie just smiled and put the piece of fruit in her bag.

Everyone came to the hotel door to wave them off and soon the couple were smothered in confetti, although no-one actually had the nerve to hang a 'Just Married' sign on the car's bumper. As they sped off, Charlie said she had one stop to make before they got to the airport – and very soon, she asked him to stop the car – right in front of the school.

"But darling, it's Saturday, none of the kids will be there. She smiled and replied, "Oh I think there'll be one there at least. She took his hand and led him to the front door where she used the key she'd borrowed from Margaret, the school secretary. "This way!" she told him mysteriously.

Along the corridor and up the stairs, they arrived in the attic. The day was nearing its end and the light was lowly disappearing, so she switched on the small light on the desk. "Now we must wait Phil – we must just wait for her. She will come – I know she will, especially with it being my wedding day. She won't want to miss that." They sat in silence – she, eager to see Rachel – he, not so much. Then they heard a soft giggle rather than the usual sobbing and suddenly she appeared silhouetted against the window. Phil saw a small, Victorian girl dressed in rather tatty clothes but with the most glorious head of hair he'd ever seen. She was quite dainty, almost frail – but today, she had a happy smile on her face.

Charlie spoke, "You knew I'd come, didn't you – and I'd bring my new husband to meet you? I'm going on my honeymoon now but I had to see you before I left. You know, you probably saved my life – and certainly my mother's life." Phil was speechless and just stared at the apparition. Rachel giggled again – she was used to people throughout the last century looking awkward around her. Although pleased to see her friend – she was sad to hear Charlie was going away.

"I'm coming back dear. I'll only be away for two weeks and then I'll be teaching the children again and when I get back, I promise to come and see you first thing – after all not everyone is lucky to have a ghost as a friend. In the meantime," and she paused for a moment before lifting her bag onto the desk. The atmosphere in the room was tense with expectation. *What had Charlie brought for her friend? What did one usually give a ghost?* She went on, "I have something for you." Like any child, Rachel peeped into the bag and gasped when Charlie lifted out the biggest, brightest orange anyone had ever seen.

"An orange!" Phil couldn't hide the disappointment in his voice. "I thought it was going to be something wonderful." Rachel's eyes however had grown large and round as she stared at the wondrous fruit. It was the same as what that nice Mr Dickens had given her a long time ago – the one she'd hidden under the floorboards and then ate it when it was rotten – a very foolish thing to do. But here was another gift of an orange, she was being given the chance to do the right thing this time – to eat the orange and eat it soon, before it went off. *Once bitten, twice shy, she thought. 'And I won't be hiding this one under the floor boards.'*

"Off you go little friend – and I'll see you soon." Rachel snatched the orange from off the desk before Charlie changed her mind. Holding it fiercely in her hands, she skipped out of the room and into the corridor. The newly-weds watched her go, staring into the darkness, although all Phil could really see was an orange floating in the air and weaving from side to side until it disappeared altogether.

"Why an orange Charlie? Why was she so pleased about something so simple? he asked incredulously.

Charlie just smiled, "Ah, there hangs a tail – a tail I'll tell you when we're airborne. You've read a few of Charles Dickens' novels, haven't you? Well I've going to tell you a story you've never heard before and it's to do with him......................................."

Murder Even More Foul

The year was 1915 and the world was on the brink of great changes. This story however, takes place in a rural backwater, where things hadn't changed much over the centuries. The locals still believed that witches and warlocks could be hiding behind every tree – so they kept well away from the woods in the darkness of night.

It was late and the heavy clouds were scudding across the rainy moon and bumping into each other as they went. It had rained heavily that day and the ground was completely saturated. Bad things could happen on such a night and they were just about to do so. A crackle of thunder, followed by lightning shook the very roots of the trees. Sleeping children awakened from their scary dreams as they were trying to get away from the evil monsters, who all looked very hungry. That's the sort of night it was!

Two young men, Bill and Joe, were walking home from the village pub, both the worse of wear from the numerous pints they'd downed in just a few hours. Joe was a gardener at the big house and Bill worked there as a footman and both liked to argue about who had the better job.

"A night for murder," Joe said, "Aye, it's a night for murder and no mistake." And he splashed his steel-capped boots into every muddy puddle he could find. It was fun, but the more sober Bill told him to stop. Then he added, "Aye, you're right there – it's a miserable night."

Joe laughed, "I bet there's some poor soul not a million miles away, taking a last breath and staring right into the eyes of his killer."

"Cor Joe, you really have a way with words, don't you?" His friend had scared him and he quickly changed the conversation, "Soon be home though and I bet Ma's got a good fire burning in the grate."

"Aye, and bowls of good hot broth on the table, do you think?" Bill had been living as a lodger with Joe's widowed mother for a couple of years now and blessed the day she agreed to take him in. He'd come straight from the orphanage, grateful to live with a family at last. Joe's mother was a kindly woman who enjoyed both the young men's company and support when she needed it. She also worked as a cleaner at the same big house as the lads.

Off to one side of the road, both young men noticed a glow coming from behind some trees and realised it was either a fire or a strong gas lamp. What on earth was it on a night like this one?

"Shall we nip into the woods to see what it is? Someone may need help." Bill didn't wait for Joe's response but started off in the direction of the light. Joe had no option but to follow him. As they came closer, they could hear the sound of a spade striking the ground. They both saw the man at the same time. He was wearing a heavy oilcloth coat and a black sou'wester - pulled down over his face. The young men watched from behind a large oak tree and saw him begin to drag a large, black sack towards the edge of the hole he'd dug.

They backed away slowly, glad the ground was so wet, as they made no sounds. Quietly, Bill whispered, "Joe, run back to the pub and get the landlord to ring for the police – that man's up to no good." Joe hesitated at first – he was petrified – but then he did as Bill said.

It was half an hour later when the police finally showed up, with Joe as a passenger. He was having difficulty in remembering the exact spot where he'd left Bill. It wasn't easy – the darkness makes the trees all look alike. The car splashed through a very deep puddle – almost a lake really - and Joe suddenly shouted 'Stop, it's here. I'm sure it's here!'

Joe led the two policemen into the woods, searching for the light that had long disappeared. There was no light, so they had to pick their way over trampled ground that was covered with forest debris brought down by the recent bad weather.

"There's nothing here. It's impossible in this weather anyway. I'm afraid we'll have to put it off until daylight, when we can come back with more support." The police were adamant nothing could be done that night.

"But, what about Bill? He stayed here to keep an eye on what was going on. He should still be here – he said he would wait until I fetched you." Joe was panicking even more, worried about his friend.

The second policeman said, "We'll drive you home and I bet when you get there, you'll find your friend's already there." He put his arm around the young man's shaking shoulders and led him back through the trees. Joe had no option but to go along.

At the cottage, there was indeed a light glowing in the window as it usually did. Mrs Mellors always left it there until the two young men were home.

"Go inside and check if your friend's home yet, will you? We'll wait here until you come back." Joe went into the cottage and the police could hear voices – but it sounded like a man's and a woman's but not two men. Joe came out of the door, his mother standing behind him. "Bill's still not home – I told you he said he'd wait in the woods until I came back. I told you that, didn't I?"

"Go back inside with your mother and we'll return to the spot you took us to. We'll look around again and call out for him. He's probably still on his way home now – it's easy to get lost in the dark woods.

At daybreak next morning a small police car drew up outside the cottage. The police had telephoned earlier to check if Bill had turned up. He hadn't! Joe's mother was sitting at the kitchen table, her head in her hands. She'd obviously been crying and one constable filled the kettle.

"A cup of sweet tea Ma'am – it'll do you the world of good. I've yet to find a better cure for shock – except of course, brandy." His colleague sat down beside her and asked if she had any idea where Bill could have stayed last night.

She shook her head and said, "No, there's no-one I can think of, but then he wasn't my son, you know, he was my lodger – and a good friend of Joe's." Joe stood behind her, his hands on her shoulders. "I can still hear him clearly, telling me to go and fetch the police and he'd wait until I came back. And that was the last time I saw him." Joes had been crying too.

On being asked how long he'd known Bill, he replied, "I've known him for some years now. We first met at the Scouts and became friends from then on. He lived at the Orphanage and sometimes came home for tea with me. My Mum's known him from that time too."

"And you stopped there because you saw a light in the woods, then you saw a man digging and trying to dump a black sack into a hole he'd just made. Is that right?" The constable watched for Joe's reaction.

"That's exactly what happened and although we'd had a few pints, we weren't drunk." Joe persisted.

"The landlord said both of you had drunk quite heavily throughout the whole evening and when you left, you were very merry – very merry indeed, he said. Could that and the horrific weather have muddled you? Or did you and Bill have an argument and he went off in anger?

"No way, that didn't happen. We stayed together when we went into the woods – I can still see Bill as clear as crystal, promising he'd stay there until I came back."

The two policemen looked at each other and one shrugged his shoulders before saying, "In that case Sir, I'm afraid we'll have to ask you to accompany us to the station in town, so we can question you further. You're not being arrested, you understand, you're just being asked to help us with our enquiries." Mrs Mellors reached for her son's hand, "Oh Joe, what does that mean? Where is Bill?" Joe just patted her hand and stood up. "I've got to go with these gents Ma – that's all and I'll be back."

As they passed the spot in the woods, Joe saw several men working amongst the trees. Some carried long poles which they used to clear the ground of leaves and broken branches. A couple even carried spades, obviously intending to do some digging.

"They're working in the right areas, aren't they?" the constable asked.

"Exactly right." Joe replied sadly. "Do you think you're going to find Bill's body in there? What they will find is the buried black sack the man buried -but not Bill, unless the same man hurt him. The two policemen just looked at each other again.

Joe sat in a drab, plain room, feeling very much alone. He knew what the big mirror on the wall was all about – he'd seen it on the television enough times. He wasn't offered the use of a Duty Solicitor just yet as he wasn't under arrest, but should that happen, he decided he would ask for one.

Two plain-clothed detectives came into the room, one carrying a clipboard and the other, a notebook. They asked the same questions as the others had, but pressed further in case Joe had remembered anything new. Joe remembered nothing new. It seemed his friend had just disappeared from the face of the earth. It was like a nightmare – a very scary nightmare. He suddenly felt he needed his Ma, but knew that was childish, so said nothing.

After about an hour and a repetition of the same questions, there was a knock at the door and a uniformed policeman came in and asked if he could speak with his colleagues – outside the room. Once again, Joe found himself alone. His throat was dry, but he was too nervous to ask for water. He was very conscious of the wall mirror and the watchful eyes behind it. The detectives came back and asked him to stand up. One of them formally arrested him, using the same words Joe had heard many times in his favourite TV 'Who Dunnits.'

He was taken to a police cell and told he would be further questioned soon and then, he would be provided by a Duty Solicitor. He hesitated and then asked, "Have you found Bill yet? Is he okay?"

The jailer with the keys said, "Oh we've found your friend all right – don't you worry about that and we've found him exactly where you said he was – in a deep hole in the middle of some woods." The man had probably spoken out of turn, but he hated the prisoners who always acted so innocently, when usually they turned out to be guilty. He banged the heavy door behind him and went off down the corridor whistling. Joe had been given a t-shirt and some jogging pants to wear while they collected all the clothes he'd been wearing. They were apparently to be checked for clues and for any of Bill's bloodstains. He looked down at the strange clothes he was wearing and this time, started to cry. He couldn't help it – he was scared, lonely and broken hearted at the loss of his friend. One minute they'd been walking home through the rain, their bellies full of good ale and suddenly they were involved in a drama that neither understood. He wished, in a way, they'd never spotted the light in the woods, but just gone on tramping through the mud to Ma's welcome fire and hot soup.

Luckily, he fell asleep quickly, stretched along the hard bunk. He hadn't got much sleep the night before because his mind had been in such turmoil.

At the big house – The Grange – Mrs Mellors had just arrived to start her daily cleaning. She went into the kitchen to say good morning to the cook, who'd always been a friend.

"Hello Martha, the kettles just boiled." The warming smell of coffee filled Martha's nostrils and she accepted a mug of the nectar gratefully. "Now get that inside you before you start your jobs. Now I look at you, you don't look too great – are you feeling ill?" The rosy cheeked woman genuinely cared about people and Martha was one of her favourites.

"I'm all right Cook, but this coffee's making me feel better." She didn't know how to tell Cook all that had happened in the last few hours. She didn't mince her words however, "My Bill is no more I'm afraid and Joe's being held by the police for his murder." There, it was out! Cook sat beside her and reached for her well-worn hand – a hand well used to hard work.

They sat in companionable silence for a few minutes and then Cook told her to take a deep breath and tell her again what had happened. Her mind was racing ahead - she knew she'd have to tell the butler after all he'd be missing one footman and one assistant gardener. At the moment however, she knew Martha needed her full attention.

As the two women sat there, both feeling better because of the other and Martha explained what had happened. The kitchen door swung open and the butler came in. Mr Stewart was a commanding figure, very straight- backed and with an obvious air of someone in control. Very much as a butler should be.

"Why are you two sitting here chatting when you should both be about your duties?" he asked abruptly.

Cook was first to reply, "Now then Mr Stewart, Mrs Mellors here has had some bad news, so you'll have to be kind to her." Cook was the only one in the household who could get away with talking to him like that – and she knew it.

"Oh dear, has our precious cleaning lady broken another finger nail?" He was known for his sarcasm and didn't believe for one moment, that either of them had anything to be upset about.

"Nothing so trivial Mr Stewart, her son Joe has just been arrested for murder – and murder of his best friend, Bill." She gave him a minute for the news to sink in and for him to realise he was two men down for household duties.

"What on earth are you saying, woman – I saw both of them leaving here yesterday after work. They were walking and laughing together as usual." He sat at the table suddenly lost for words and with a confused look on his haughty face.

"Be that as it may, one of them is dead now and one is being held by the police." Cook offered him a fresh cup of coffee - he looked as though he needed it. He was actually taking the news worse then she'd thought he would and his face had turned quite ash-grey in colour.

He gulped down the hot coffee, scalded his throat as he did so. "I'll have to go an tell the Master what's happened – he should know." And he disappeared from the kitchen, offering no sympathy to Mrs Mellors, who stood up, saying she had to get on with her work. "Do you think Mavis the maid could be spared today to give me a hand? I have to admit I'm not feeling as strong as I usually do." She looked hopefully at Cook.

"Normally, I'd certainly allow it, but I'm afraid there's been a bit of a dilemma with her as well. She's only up and run off without telling anyone where she was going. I don't know how I'm going to manage without her – but manage I must – or the house will be in an uproar. I was just on the point of going into town when you arrived – I have to go to the agency where you can rent help. I've never had to do it before, but it's my only option as I need a maid."

"Don't you worry about me Cook, I'll manage and you've got enough problems of your own. But why would Mavis leave without a word – she always seemed so happy here?" Cook shrugged her ample shoulders and reached for her coat. Mrs Mellors found herself alone in the kitchen.

As things turned out, the maid's sudden disappearance actually helped her. As the maid wasn't there to strip the beds of their sheets, Mrs Mellors couldn't wash them in the usual way – and so the family had to sleep in their bed sheets for longer than usual. She started washing the kitchen floor. 'Best to keep busy – it took her mind off Joe and Bill for a little while anyhow.

The big house was in turmoil. Even the incredibly competent butler couldn't magic staff out of thin air – and he too, had to travel to the town agency to try and find both a replacement footman and someone to help the gardener. There would be a lot of training needed over the next few days.

Finishing her work, Mrs Mellors returned to her empty cottage. Sometimes she complained at how noisy they could be, but now she'd have given anything to hear their voices. Not for one moment did she believe the rubbish that Joe had killed Bill – she knew better than that. There was a knock at the door, '*Now who on earth could that be- it was quite late and most of her neighbours would be having supper after a long day's work?*'

She opened the door and almost fell backwards into the room. The Mistress stood there, looking as grand as she always did. She was a tall, elegant lady in her forties and she'd never been known before to come to a servant's cottage.

"May I come in Mrs Mellors?" she asked politely and stepped over the threshold into a world she'd never seen before. The cottage was small and rather cramped, but it was clean and tidy.

"Would it sound terribly rude if I asked you to put the kettle on Mrs Mellors? I feel rather parched." And suddenly, it seemed natural for the lady from the big house to visit her cleaning lady's home. Her request for a cup of tea made it all seem so normal. She'd heard about Joe and Bill from the butler – and also about Mavis the maid. The sudden staff shortages were significant, but Cook and Mr Stewart were both endeavouring to rectify the situation. Lady Roberts however was more concerned about how her cleaner was feeling and if there was anything she could do to help.

"Joe has a lawyer, doesn't he?" she asked and was told he had, but that was all Mrs Mellors knew. "I just don't believe Joe would ever hurt Bill, your Ladyship. The two lads were good friends."

Lady Roberts nodded her agreement, "two nice young men and always such good friends. As for little Mavis, I can't imagine what drove her to run away – she'd always seemed so happy at the house. Had she perhaps ever mentioned anything to you?"

"No Ma'am, she never did. I can't understand it. "Mrs Mellors couldn't really think of anything other than Joe's dilemma, so Lady Roberts stood up and thanked her for the tea.

"Remember I'm always there if you need me. I know we're short of staff, but I'm sure we'll manage. Now, you must take whatever time you need to help Joe – your job will be there when you decide to come back." She left as suddenly as she'd arrived.

The policemen arrived at the big house by appointment. They wanted to speak to all the staff as well as to the family. Mr Stewart took them into the drawing room where Lord and Lady Roberts were waiting.

"If it's okay with you my Lord, we'll see the staff at their place of work. We find it's easier to talk to them that way. Before we do however, we'd appreciate words with you both."

"Would you like me to ring for coffee or tea officers? We've just started a new maid who isn't sure of her duties yet, but I'm sure the butler, Mr Stewart would fetch it or us. After all, the circumstances are most unusual. "Lady Roberts pulled the cord and Stewart arrived immediately, as though he'd been waiting outside the door.

"Stewart, I know it's not strictly your job, but after what's happened recently, I'm sure you'd be happy to fetch some tea and coffee." The butler nodded his head and disappeared. Lady Roberts turned again to the policemen. Her husband had said nothing yet, but was watching the newcomers with curiosity.

"What can you tell us about the man who was murdered – William Jones, he was called? He was your footman I believe. For example, how long have you known him and how long has he worked for you? Very importantly, do you know anything about his relationship with Joseph Mellors?" One of the policemen asked, pen and notebook poised in hand.

Lord Roberts took over the conversation. "He had been with us for about 3 years and before that, he'd come from the Town Orphanage. He was acceptable at his duties, although Stewart could probably tell you more about that – he trained the young man. Young Bill lodged with Mrs Mellors, Joe's mother. She is our cleaning lady and comes in each day. Is that all correct, my dear?" He turned to his wife.

She agreed absolutely and added that she couldn't believe Joe Mellors was responsible for Bill's death, as they'd always been such good friends.

"Thank you for that M'Lady – and you M'Lord - but I assure you we wouldn't have arrested Mellors without reasonable cause." Stewart arrived at that moment with a silver tray, obviously prepared by cook as she'd added some freshly baked biscuits as well.

"Just leave it there Stewart, I'll pour." Lady Roberts indicated the table in the middle of the room. "Just before you go, perhaps you could answer some of these gentlemen's questions." She looked at the policemen, "It might be easier to talk to Stewart here – he's quite comfortable with us."

The same questions about the two young men were asked and Stewart thought for a few moments before answering. "Well Sir, I knew both the men well – perhaps I knew Bill a little better than Joe, because he worked directly under me. Joe worked with the gardener." He explained he'd known them both for about three or four years and that they appeared to have formed some kind of friendship. He paused at that point and coughed before adding, "I must admit I've noticed recently they seemed to be arguing more than before, but I have no idea what the problem was. Perhaps Joe confided more in his boss, the gardener."

"Really Stewart, I didn't know that. I thought they were still great friends." Her Ladyship looked at her husband, "Did you know they'd been falling out?" Lord Roberts said he hadn't known, but then added "Why should I know if the servants fall out with each other?"

"What about the maid Mr Stewart – the one who seems to have run away? What did you know about her? Do you find it odd that she's disappeared at the same time as the two men have been involved in a crime?" It was a planted question, but one that might elicit Stewart's true feelings on the matter in hand.

The butler seemed hesitant before replying and after a moment's silence, he said "Would it be possible to have a word with the police in private, my Lord?" And he looked directly at the Master.

"I'm sure that wouldn't be a problem Stewart – it's what the gentlemen first suggested after all, although what you can't say in front of us, I can't imagine!" He was obviously quite annoyed but knew he had no option but to agree to the butler's request.

"If you'll follow me Gentlemen, I'll take you to the butler's pantry and after we've spoken, I'll introduce you to Cook who will certainly have something to say on the subject. She always does!" Lord and Lady Roberts were left alone then, both wondering what Stewart wanted to tell the police.

In the corridor, they passed a young girl in a maid's uniform that was obviously too big for her. She could only have been about fifteen and Stewart explained she was the new maid, taken on to replace the missing Mavis and that she'd never have known Bill and Joe.

"What age was Mavis?" one policeman asked and Stewart replied, "I'm not sure, but I think she was about sixteen – Cook will be able to tell you." A butler didn't bother himself with such trivial things as servant's ages. The three men settled in the small room – comfortable, but not spacious and one immediately reached for his notebook.

The first question rather surprised Stewart, "How well did you know Joe Mellors? I understand you must have known the footman well, but what about his friend – after all he must have spent most of his time on the land?"

"I didn't know Joe very well at all. Sometimes, he came to the kitchen door to speak with William, but other than that, our paths rarely crossed. The main gardener's your man. "He hesitated for a moment and then all in a rush said, "What might interest you is that I heard the two lads arguing more than once about Mavis, the maid – the one who's disappeared. I think she may have been stringing both of them along, even leading them on. Mind you, I only ever heard snatches of their conversations – but I believe Mavis was a bit of a girl, if you know what I mean."

"Well now, that is interesting and no mistake." The notebook was filling up fast.

"Now you'll understand why I didn't want to tell you in front of the Master and Mistress – they'd have been very shocked." There, Stewart had done his duty and he had nothing more to tell them.

"Thank you, Mr Stewart, you've been most helpful. Would you be good enough to take us along and introduce us to your cook? She probably worked quite closely with the maid, so no doubt she'll corroborate your opinion of the girl – and of the two lads of course."

Cook was elbow deep in a great bowl of flour when Stewart brought the police into her kitchen. Asked for her opinion of Mavis and the two young lads, she put her floury hands on her ample hips and said, "All three of them are – or were in young Bill's case – good-natured and helpful. Any mother would have been proud of them, that I can tell you for nothing."

Rather deviously, the younger policeman said, "That's not necessarily the picture we're receiving from other people. It's been suggested that Mavis was a bit of a girl."

"Absolute balderdash, she was a lovely and quite timid young woman. She'd worked here for about three years, since she was a child and I've never heard anyone have a bad word to say about her." She was flustered and quite angry at the policeman's suggestion and stared at him with accusation in her eyes. "And as for the lads – William the footman and Joe the gardener – both fine young men, or my name's not Nellie Glover." She plonked herself down on a chair and unexpectedly asked if they'd like a cup of tea.

Taken aback at her change of mood, they just nodded and said they would like that very much although it would be their second of the night. The atmosphere in the kitchen settled down and Cook turned to fill the kettle. She'd made her point and felt better for it, although she kept tutting later, when she remembered their words.

Tea and freshly baked cake over, the men asked if she would take them to Mavis's room. It turned out to be small and plain and was next door to the kitchen. Without knowing where the missing girl was, it seemed very sad and quite desolate. There was one plain chest of drawers and a cupboard in the corner. A simple bed looked as if it had not been slept in recently and the girl's little nightshirt was still folded under the pillow.

Cook went over to the cupboard and opened the door, "Look, her one dress for going to church is still there – why on earth would she run away without taking that? She didn't earn enough to have more than one dress, so she'd surely have taken it with her when she left. And look here," she pointed at the side of the bed, "those are her best shoes – she was wearing her work pair the last time I saw her." Cook was crying now but used her apron to hide her tears.

"You're fond of the girl, aren't you? She was more than just the maid, wasn't she?" One policeman was obviously the softer of the two and he made a point of speaking of the girl in the present tense although he already had his doubts about that.

"I liked the lass an' no mistake, but to run off without even saying goodbye, probably means she wasn't as nice as I'd thought." But the men knew she didn't mean it. "Would you tell us exactly when you last saw her and if she said anything unexpected or out of character? Was she afraid of anything or disappointed about someone?"

Cook shook her head silently, "No, Mavis was just as usual – bright and cheerful and looking forward to her next baking lesson with me."

"Well in that case, could you take us to where we might find the gardener? We'd like to have a word with him about his assistant. Thank you for giving us your time – we appreciate it."

At the cottage, Martha Mellors heard she was to be allowed to visit her son and when she was taken to the cell at the back of the police station, she was shocked at how much weight he'd lost in such a short time. "Eh Lad, you're nothing' but skin and bone. Are they feeding you at all?" Her poor boy's normal ruddy complexion was sallow now and she feared for his health.

"Oh Ma. Don't be silly, I'm all right – although I really miss your cooking." He smiled ruefully and she thought how young he looked. He was young of course, both he and Bill had been the same age – both just about to turn twenty. Their whole lives had been ahead of them until that dark, rainy night just over a week ago.

"What do you think happened on that night Joe? It couldn't have been more than an hour from when you left Bill watching the man until you arrived back with the police. In that time, Bill was murdered and buried in the ground. It seems almost impossible, except that's what must have happened."

"But it did happen Ma, Bill was safe and alive when he sent me back to fetch the police. If I close my eyes, I can still see him standing by the tree and watching the man digging the hole. At least, I think it was a man but with his big coat and sou'wester, he was well hidden." He dropped his head into his hands, "Even I can see why the police think I did it but I didn't Ma. He was my friend and I'd never have hurt him. You believe me, don't you?"

"'Course I do, Son. You might be many things, but a liar's not one of them." Cook had told her the police had asked if he was sweet on Mavis the maid – and also if Bill was as well and she asked him outright.

"No Ma – Mavis is a nice girl but we didn't hanker after her. She's very young for her age and really immature – in fact, she behaves like a child. No, definitely not Ma – and I can speak for Bill as well." Joe dropped his head again, shocked that he was being questioned about the maid's disappearance as well. "What am I going to do Ma – I have no money for a really good lawyer and I feel sure the police are desperate to prove I'm a murderer.

"Ah well, that's something I've come to tell you about. Lady Roberts from the big house came to visit me in my cottage the other evening. I could have died with shock when I opened the door and found her standing there. I was surprised that she even knew where I lived – but there you are, she did. You're not alone Son, she told me if there was anything you need, I was to tell her and she and the master would help. I'm going to tell her you need a lawyer, so leave it with me and I'll go and see her first thing tomorrow."

When he heard this, Joe reached out to his mother and she took him in her arms and held him tight. "I'll be back soon – just give me time." And she called for the guard to let her out.

"Joe! Joe! It's me, wake up. I need to talk to you." Joe heard the familiar voice and opened his eyes wide. *It couldn't be – yet he knew that voice well.* He pulled the thin blanket tighter around his shoulders. *If he ignored it, perhaps it would go away. Just don't move, he told himself – pretend to be asleep.*

Yet he heard it again," Joe! Wake up! You know it's me and that I won't hurt you." Bill must have been close by, his words were very clear. Joe turned onto his back and looked up. It was

Bill, still in his work clothes – the clothes he was wearing the last time he'd seen his friend. He tried to speak but had no voice, so he just stared at the apparition

Bill smiled ruefully and sat down on the edge of the bunk, "I'm allowed to come to see you because there's unfinished business between us. No-one is more aware than I am, that you didn't hurt me." It was amazing – he looked just like the old Bill, except for a misty cloud all around him, "Even I don't know who cracked my head open with a shovel – but I know it was a man. You saw him that night too, but he was completely wrapped up in clothes too big for him. You didn't recognise him either, did you?"

Joe's voice was stronger now, "I didn't see who he was – he made sure of that with the sou'wester covering' his face. But how did he see you? When I left, you were hiding behind a tree – did you move and show yourself?"

"I must have done – perhaps I made a noise or something, because suddenly he stopped digging and looked towards the tree where I was hiding. He took a step forward and called out *'Who's there – come out. I know you're there.'* And he moved towards me, the shovel held above his head. I turned to run away but he was too quick for me and the next thing I knew was a heavy blow across the back of my head – and then nothing. I think I didn't die right away because I felt myself being dragged along the ground – towards the hole he'd just dug."

Bill's ghostly figure stopped talking for a while, obviously reliving the horrific memory of that night. Joe reached out his hand towards his friend, but finding nothing solid there, he let it fall again.

"Bill, I'm so sorry for what you went through. I can't imagine anything more terrible. The darkness and the storm were scary enough without what you were put through. Can you remember anything else? Was he tall or short? Did you recognise his voice perhaps?" Joe was desperate – he was after all facing the hangman's   noose.

"No my friend, afraid I didn't." He was quite tall – taller than me at least – the only thing I did see was, as he raised the shovel to strike again, I stared straight into his eyes. I only saw his eyes – not his face – but I believe my last thought was about those eyes – there was something odd about them, but I can't tell you what it was. It was almost as though I'd seen them before – something familiar, you understand."   The ghost-like figure stood up and said," My time is up, I'm afraid and I have to go now – but I'm told I can visit you again if I remember anything else that might help you. I promise I'll wrack my brain and try to remember something – something that'll prove you had nothing to do with my death. All I remember is that, just before he struck me for a second time, he accidentally tripped over the black sack he'd been originally going to bury. After that, I'm afraid everything went dark and 'Your's Truly' was no more. Who are you going to drink with now Friend?"   And unbelievingly, the ghost who'd been so recently alive, tried to smile at his old friend, but couldn't quite manage it – and disappeared instead.

Joe found he was shivering but didn't know if it was from cold or fear – either way, it made him wrap himself tighter in the useless blanket and he lay there unmoving until daybreak. Thankfully, he fell asleep just as the sky was becoming light and woke up to the clanging of his cell door, as a policeman came in carrying a mug of tea and a bowl of thin porridge.

Later that morning, Lord and Lady Roberts were taking coffee in the drawing room, "Yes, my dear, of course we'll find a lawyer for young Joe. I'm sure he doesn't deserve what he's going through. I'll speak with our own lawyer and ask for his recommendation – he'll know someone more suited to this type of case. Had you ever heard or noticed any bad blood between William and Joe? I must say I never had, but then I probably wouldn't have noticed it."

"Personally no, but Stewart has mentioned once or twice that he had to have words with William, as he'd failed in his duties now and again and always blamed it on Joe's interference. Stewart is a very astute man and I'm sure he'd never have mentioned it if it hadn't happened."

At that moment, the butler himself came into the room. He was the only servant in the house who didn't have to knock on the door. His status was above that. "My Lord, My Lady, there is a person at the front door asking if he can see you. He says he's only after some information about the missing maid, Mavis and he's from the Orphanage she came from."

Lady Roberts asked, "Did Mavis and William come from the same Orphanage then – I never knew that – but I suppose I should have remembered. The housekeeper we had then, made all those arrangements, so I was never involved."

Her husband said that shouldn't have made any difference – lots of orphanage children were found work locally and, "They weren't the same age, were they, so they must have been there at different times. Show him in Stewart, we'll see him."

It turned out that the little maid's own mother had recently approached the Orphanage, asking to see her daughter. The administrator had promised her nothing, but said he would see what he could do.

It's not our policy to force any child from the Orphanage to meet with a parent, especially one who turns up so long after the child was left with us. Should the child however want to see the relative, then we're more than happy to arrange it."

The man from the Orphanage obviously didn't know about the maid's disappearance and looked shocked when he did. "Would it be possible for her to come and see her daughter's room? I realise this sounds a weird request but I think it might help her to accept the child is missing. Perhaps seeing the empty room and abandoned bits and pieces might help her." He looked awkward but went on, "Would you be kind enough to allow this?

The couple looked at each other and Lady Roberts said, "It doesn't seem a lot to allow Husband, I think we should. In any case, the child might reappear any day now, having learned the world out there isn't always a good place – especially for a young girl. Do you agree?" And the administrator went away to arrange things.

Meanwhile, Mrs Mellors had been introduced to her son's lawyer. He'd come to the house to see Lord Roberts and Mrs Mellors was sent for – she was cleaning the upstairs bedroom when he called and she hurried to the sitting room. The man was very tall and thin and had a slight stoop. He was probably younger than his appearance suggested and he'd been left alone in the sitting room to await Mrs Mellors.

"Good Afternoon Sir, I'm Martha Mellors. Are you the gentleman who's going to help my son?" She was wringing her hands anxiously and hesitated when he invited her to sit down. She wasn't used to sitting down in her superior's company, but he insisted.

"I sincerely hope I can help your son, Mrs Mellors – but before I go to see him, I'd appreciate your giving me your account as to what's happened. Obviously, I know the facts but would like to hear your own words about your son Joseph. Just start wherever you like and I'll just listen – after a while, I may have some questions for you. Will that be all right?"

"Oh yes Sir, that will be fine. I want to help as much as I can."

And the two of them sat there for at least an hour, talking about how Joe and Bill. It was strange but the smart lawyer and the elderly cleaning lady seemed to get together and spoke easily in the unusual surroundings.The butler didn't come in and offer tea, something he would normally do when there were visitors in the sitting room, but he really couldn't be expected to serve tea to the cleaning lady.

She said the two lads had always got on well together and she'd rarely heard them arguing – although boys being boys, they sometimes thought differently. They'd both set off early each morning – one to work in the garden and one to his footman duties. Sometimes, they'd come home separately as Bill was needed in the house longer, especially when there was a dinner party or some such thing. "They were both considering joining the army, you know – but that was for the future."

"As for my Joe killing Bill – never! He's a gentle chap, used to working on the land and caring for his plants and shrubs. I don't think there's a bad bone in his body Sir and he thought of Bill as his brother. She was crying by this time and apologised for her tears.

The lawyer went straight to see Joe then. They spoke for a long time and although Mr Tomkins quickly assessed his client as honest and probably trustworthy, the evidence against him was considerable – and he knew he had his work cut out if he was to save him from the hangman's noose.

As he left the cell, Joe reached out and touched his arm, "He was my mate Mr Tomkins – honest he was. I'd never hurt him – but I'd love to know who did. Bill died just because he was in the wrong place at the wrong time and there's a man out there who did it. Please save me Sir, so I can find him, even if the police can't." The lawyer just smiled and touched Joe's shoulder. He made no promises.

The new maid at the big house was settling in to her new duties. She was only fifteen and had never lived anywhere other than the orphanage. She had a smiley face and bouncy, brown hair. She wasn't exactly pretty but she was very presentable. She liked to watch Cook preparing food and hung about the kitchen whenever she had a spare moment – which wasn't very often.

"Roll that out for me, there's a good girl. It's for the crust of an apple pie - the Master's favourite. Are you comfortable in Mavis's old room and have you gathered all her possessions into the box I gave you? She'll probably come back one day and be looking for them. I know some people are saying she's dead, but I can't bring myself to think that. She's just a silly young girl who didn't know which side her bread was buttered."

Little Mary stared at her as she fingered the pastry, "Did she like bread and butter then, Mrs Glover? I like bread and especially butter – but there wasn't much butter at the Orphanage." Cook raised her eyes in disbelief, *God, the girl was young and very innocent. She certainly had her work cut out if she was to teach her anything.*

Stewart came into the kitchen and asked, "Is everything ship shape and Bristol fashion Mrs Glover? The master and mistress are dining at home this evening, so they'll be looking forward to your cooking." He stared at the new maid and said, "How are you Mary? Are you enjoying your time here – it's a grand house, isn't it?" Mary nodded her head shyly – she found she was in awe of the great man – the status of butler being so far above her own – and so, she kept her eyes lowered.

"Answer Mr Stewart Mary when he speaks to you." Cook knew the girl was feeling awkward but she knew too, she'd have to learn to speak up for herself, if she was to survive working in the house.

"I'm very happy here Sir, really I am – and Mrs Glover has been so kind to me, showing me my duties and chores." Mary tried to speak up.

"Good – and you don't have to call me 'Sir', just Mr Stewart. I am your superior but I hope to be your friend as well." And he disappeared, leaving Cook raising her eyebrows to the girl as though to say, 'Take a pinch of salt with that, my dear.'

At the orphanage, a timid looking woman was ringing the doorbell. She was neat and clean, but obviously living on the poverty line as her clothes were well worn and patched. She was taken along a corridor where Simon Walker, the administrator, was waiting for her.

"Am I going to be allowed to see my daughter, Sir?" The question was out before he had time to take a breath. He ignored the question and made two cups of tea from a small gas cooker – he felt she would need one with what he had to tell her.

"She'd been placed in a good position in one of our gentry's great houses – not too far from here actually. She was apparently happy there and good at her duties as maid, but for some obscure reason, she decided to run away. The police have been looking for her for quite some time now." He handed her the tea and went on, "I have however spoken with Lord and Lady Roberts, her employers and they've agreed that you should come to the house and see the room where she'd lived. Her personal possessions are still there – and you might find comfort in them. Of course, the family haven't given up the expectation that Mavis will return one day – and if so, they'd be more than happy to give her job back."

The woman was staring at her feet, but sipping the hot tea at the same time. She was obviously shocked by the news, something she'd not been expecting. She'd worked herself up to facing the daughter she'd never known and felt incredibly let down to hear it wasn't possible. "I would like that Sir – I would like to see her possessions. Can I really go to the big house?"

"I must take you there but that won't be a problem. Do you plan to stay in the area – at least for a few days? If so, we'll go to the house tomorrow – in the meantime, I'll send a note to tell them." Mavis's mother left the building and went to the cheap digs she'd found close by.

That night, she had the same dream, except this time it seemed even more real. She woke up sweating and breathing heavily. She'd heard her daughter's voice again, calling out to her in the dream. The words were clear, 'Mum, please help me. I realise you don't know me, but I'm Mavis – the name you gave me when you left me at the Orphanage."

The bed covers were damp with sweat and the dream seemed so real, she could almost feel her daughter's presence in the room, "Where are you daughter? I can hear you but I can't see you. " No reply, just the sound of a young girl crying softly – and then, nothing. Absolute silence! The dreams were the reason she'd come looking for her Mavis – she'd been having them for weeks now. She knew then she had to find the girl she'd abandoned so long ago – her daughter needed her, or she wouldn't be disturbing her in this way. She fell back onto the pillow and closed her eyes, but she didn't have to wait long before Simon Walker arrived to take her to the big house.

This time, he went to the back door where he knew the cook was expecting him – and also Mavis's mother. Mrs Glover opened the door and stood back to allow the couple inside. She looked exactly as a cook should – she wore a white apron that seemed too big for her and her white hair was tied in a bun on top of her head.

"Come in Sir, Miss, I've been expecting you," but she couldn't hide her surprise when she looked at the woman. For a moment, she thought the man had brought Mavis back, but then she saw the woman was older. Cook couldn't help saying, "My God, I'd have known you were Mavis's mother – you're her spittinc' image. But come in, come in and have a seat at the table. The mistress said I was to offer you some tea and scones." She looked at the man, "Will that be all right, Sir?"

"It would be most welcome Mrs Glover." And he smiled at the cook's obvious surprise.

"This is her room, but young Mary occupies it now – until Mavis comes back, you understand. This box here has all her personal bits and pieces." She was very careful to speak about Mavis's return – although the passage of time, was giving her doubts. "Bring the box back to the kitchen – it's warmer there and you can take as much time as you like."

The visitor was called Lizzie and she looked through the meagre possessions in the box. In a small scrap of muslin, she found a silver threepenny bit. It was an old one, but still very shiny. She held it up to the light and then closed her fingers around it. She looked at Simon Walker and Mrs Glover, "She hasn't run away. If she had, I know she would have taken this. I left it in the folds of her shawl when I left her on the Orphanage steps. She's obviously kept it all these years and wouldn't have parted with it. It was her contact with the past and a piece of who she was and where she'd come from." The tears were running down her cheeks as she realised what she was suggesting. If the maid hadn't run off, where was she – and was she still alive?

Before anyone else could say a word, the kitchen door opened and Mr Stewart came in. He stopped abruptly when he saw the strangers and did a double-take when his gaze fell on Lizzie. He too, obviously thought the maid had come back suddenly, but he soon pulled himself together.

"Have you arranged the afternoon tea tray for the Mistress yet?" He spoke rather abruptly and seemed embarrassed at the sight of the two strangers. He didn't know why they were there. Mrs Glover tried to introduce him to them, but he cut her short and asked the question about the tea tray again.

"I'll be back in ten minutes Cook – see that the tray's ready then." He quickly disappeared.

"I'm sorry my dear, he's not usually so rude – I think your resemblance to your daughter took him aback and he didn't know what to say. Personally, I think you should take the silver coin although the police have said we weren't to disturb her belongings. I'll tell you what – I'll make sure it stays safe in her box – and as soon as we're able, I'll let you have it. Having said that however, Mavis will probably come back and claim it herself. What do you say?"

Lizzie smiled and asked Cook if she knew of any cheap lodgings in the area. She wanted to stay for a while to find out more about her daughter's disappearance. Cook thought for a few moments and then suggested she speak with Mrs Mellors as she probably had spare rooms available. She didn't go on to elaborate that of her two lodgers, one was dead and one was awaiting trial. "In fact, if you want to hang on for a few minutes,

I'll send our Mary to fetch her." As good as her word, Mrs Mellors appeared almost immediately and agreed she had room in her home for Lizzie."But my Joe could be coming home any day, you know." She was determined to think positively.

Later, she was clearing up in Bill's room – she knew he would never be back again, but Joe's room, she kept as neat as a new pin.

She felt very sad as she tidied up Bill's bits and pieces, to make the room ready for the missing maid's mother. She sat on the edge of the bed and looked down at Bill's spare shoes – just where he'd left them. She reached out to touch them, when she suddenly became aware of someone else in the room.

"Are you here, Bill? She asked, "I think you are – and you want to tell me something, don't you?" She sat quite still and waited. Silence! "Come on Son, you know you can talk to me. I 'm sorry for what happened to you but Joe didn't do it, did he? And yet he's been charged with your murder." The curtains at the window fluttered – gently at first and then blew straight out into the room – almost horizontal to the floor.

She went on, "Did you know him, Bill? Was it someone you knew? Was it someone I might know?" The curtains started to move again. "You did know him, didn't you? Joe never saw his face but you did. You saw his face when he struck you with the spade."

The curtains were now blowing furiously in the window and Mrs Mellors knew she was onto something. Please don't go, Bill – not until you've given me some idea of who hurt you." A sudden knock on the door broke into the atmosphere and she reluctantly moved to answer the door.

Lizzie stood there with a small bag at her feet. "I hope this isn't an awkward time to arrive, but I've nowhere else to go." She looked so pitiful and alone, the older woman reached out her hand and brought her inside the cottage.

"Come in my dear – you're welcome. I've just been sorting out your room – you'll be comfortable there, I promise you." She seated her guest by the fireplace and went into the kitchen to put the kettle onto boil. Lizzie went to bed that night early – everything that had happened in the last couple of days, had exhausted her. Mrs Mellor's sat by the dwindling fire and made herself think of Bill, in the hope that she could make contact with him again. She had no luck however and actually fell asleep in the chair.

In the big house, little Mary was cleaning out the fire in the ground floor rooms. The hour was really early and dawn was just breaking. She brushed her forehead and left a black smear on her face. *Oh dear, I'll never get it right. I bet Mavis was a much better maid than I am. I wish I could always help Cook in the kitchen – I love doing that. These other chores are much harder.*

The door opened quietly and the butler came in. "Why, you're still here Mary – have you almost finished setting the fire?" He crossed the room and stood behind the kneeling girl.

"Yes Mr Stewart, I'm finished now but I still have the bedroom fireplaces to clear out and re-set." She stood up and bobbed a curtsey, although she'd been told she didn't have to.

"Why Mary, you don't have to curtsey to me – you know that." He smiled at her and raised his hand to tuck a stray curl behind her ear. "There now, that's better – we have to keep you tidy, don't we? Here, borrows my handkerchief to wipe that soot from your face." He held out a spotlessly clean handkerchief.

"Oh no Sir, I couldn't possibly use your nice handkerchief – Mrs Glover would kill me if I did. She smiled shyly and hurried from the room, carrying the heavy bucket. She always felt awkward talking to the butler although he'd never been anything but pleasant to her.

At the same time in her armchair in the cottage, Mrs Mellors was waking up. The grey light of dawn was coming in the window and she knew immediately, something was wrong. "It's you Bill, isn't it? I can feel your presence." She looked around, desperate to see where he was. And then, she saw him. He was sitting in the armchair he'd liked when he'd lived there.

She cleared her throat and asked, "Have you come to tell me something that'll help Joe? He needs all the help he can get, you know." She didn't move, in case she chased him away.

The ghostly figure said nothing - he just stared straight ahead. Outside in the greyness, heavy rain had started to fall and was smashing against the window. In a strange way, it was a comforting sound but that was because she was indoors and sheltered. Very quickly, the window began to steam up and the day outside was hidden from view. The figure of Bill suddenly stood up and crossed the room. He didn't speak – perhaps he couldn't, not to her anyway. He raised his arm, and using his first finger, began writing on the steamed-up glass.

Mrs Mellors could see the message quite clearly and read aloud, ' L.F.I.T.W.' She heard him speaking then, "Ma, tell the police these letters. They'll be able to work out what they mean." He was gone and the atmosphere became normal again. *Oh, why didn't he just tell me what the letters mean? Perhaps he's not allowed to do that, but why?*

Although still very early, she left the cottage with her new lodger still asleep and hurried towards the police station in town. It was a fair walk and she felt tired when she finally arrived there. She'd written down the letters on a piece of paper. She told the man on the desk why she'd come and he left his post, to return with a tired-looking constable. *He's probably been up all night – I hope he's awake enough to know the importance of the letters.*

Luckily, he was quite awake and took the paper into the back, first telling the desk clerk to fetch the lady a cup of hot tea. She was cold and very wet, but the drink calmed her and soon she removed her wet shawl and hung it over the back of the chair. She had to wait there a long time, before being taken into a small room and asked to explain the piece of paper.

The detective asked, "Are you really trying to tell us you saw these letters being written on a misty window and that that's all you know." He couldn't be blamed for doubting her story. "Was there anyone else in the room at the time?"

She told him she was alone, but had been talking to her dead friend Bill, who'd allegedly been murdered by her own son, Joe. She could see how sceptically he was looking at her, so she repeated, "Bill told me to tell you about the letters, but wouldn't – or couldn't – tell me what they mean. He seemed to think you would work it out – but alas, that's not true, is it?"

She left the piece of paper at the station and went on to her chores in the big house. The lawyer, Mr Tomkins, was waiting there for her and asked if she could spare him five minutes. With Cook's permission, she took him into the small scullery.

"Your son's been given a date for his trial and I have secured a barrister to defend him in court." He started to talk, but she interrupted him quickly, saying "Oh Sir, won't that cost a lot of money – money I don't have?" He reassured her by saying, "Your employers are prepared to meet the costs of his defence because they don't believe him to be guilty."

What could she say? Such generosity was more than she could bear. She'd known they'd said they would, but this was all too much! Such kindness was unbelievable!

"Of course, you'll be a character witness, although a loving mother doesn't always make a great witness – she's unlikely to say anything bad, is she? Anyway, we'll be calling more character witnesses, mainly from this house – but also from the town, so you must just be patient."

In the kitchen, Cook was working on some afternoon cakes for the master and mistress and the two guests they were expecting. Mr Stewart was having a cup of coffee at the table and reached over to break off a piece of marzipan. He loved marzipan. Cook playfully slapped his hand and said, "That's not for you."

He looked around the kitchen and asked where Mary, the maid was. "I like that girl – she's always so willing and friendly – not at all like Mavis who was always so snappy."

Cook looked at him accusingly, "Mavis was not snappy, I don't know what you're talking about. She was a nice girl – I mean is a 'nice' girl, who knew right from wrong. Mary is still very young and of course, she's afraid of you in your butler's uniform." Cook didn't believe in mincing her words and was one of the few in the household who would tell him straight what she was thinking.

He got up to leave, knowing there was no point in arguing with Cook when she was in a mood. The woman added, "On your travels through the house, when you come upon Mrs Mellors, would you tell her there's a pot of coffee on the stove?"

As the two women sat quietly, enjoying the coffee, their minds were on the same thing – what would happen to Joe and where was young Mavis.

"isn't it strange that both incidents happened at the same time. You'd almost think they were connected in some way – but that can't be, can it? They had so little to do with each other. Cook really missed Mavis and prayed she would turn up one day, safe and sound.

Mrs Mellors told her friend about the incident at the cottage when Bill appeared from nowhere. Unlike the police, Cook had no problem believing the story – after all there were many things 'twixt Heaven and Earth that we didn't understand.' She couldn't remember where she'd first heard that saying, but she believed it.

"Did he not talk to you then – just wrote the letters on the window?" Cook was really intrigued.

"He did talk but only to tell me to tell the police about his visit. He didn't explain what the letters meant. I think the police are baffled – I know I am. L.F.I.T.W. could mean so many things but I know it's meant to help find his murderer."

"I can't even make a guess I'm afraid. I have a thought though. There might be someone who could help – your new lodger, Lizzie." Mrs Mellors looked puzzled, how on earth could the missing maid's mother help decipher a message from beyond the grave? *Cook was getting old and might not be thinking straight, but then she was also a wise woman who didn't usually talk rubbish so, Martha told her to go on.*

"When she came to see her daughter's room and belongings, she sat with me right where you are now and told me she was a mystic – a medium – who could contact dead. Of course, I took it all with a pinch of salt, but only at first – after she'd told me of some of the things she'd done, I found it easier to believe." Cook paused and re-filled their cups. "Well, what do you think?"

"A few weeks ago, I would have said I didn't believe in such things, but not now and not ever again." She crossed her booted feet under the table and promised to speak with Lizzie as soon as she got home. For good measure, she also made the sign of the cross on her chest although she wasn't Catholic. *You could never be sure!*

"Sometimes, I can see into the future, but what I'm particularly good at is contacting those who've passed over – you know, crossed to the other side. Some people think it's just my foolishness, but I swear I can do it – sometimes it works, but not always." Lizzie was surprised that Mrs Mellors knew about her 'secret skill', but understood when Cook's name was mentioned.

"Cook suggests that we – all three of us – meet together one evening in the kitchen at the big house and have a séance. Would you be up for that? That way, we could ask Bill to tell us what happened that night in the woods – and what his message, L.F.I.T.W. means. We can then tell the police what we've found out."

Lizzie said she was willing to join the two ladies, but first had a question for Martha, "Since your lodger has been gone, has his spirit ever visited you? It sometimes happens you see, especially with those who've died suddenly. Has he ever come back to see you?"

Martha told her Bill had indeed visited her since passing over, "but why does it matter? Does it affect your special skills?"

Lizzie explained that unfortunately it did. She said that if a murdered victim still wandered the earth and hadn't yet reached his final resting place, it was much harder to contact him. She didn't know the reason this happened, but it did. "Having said that however we can still try."

Martha hesitated but knew she had to ask the obvious question, "Is that the reason you've never been able to contact your daughter – do you think she might be dead?"

"I know my daughter is still alive – she visits me in my dreams you know, but tells me nothing. It would break my heart to use my skill to contact her – if it worked, then I'd know for certain she was dead. Not knowing is better as it leaves me with hope."

The cleaning lady understood Lizzie and reached across to take her hand. Coincidently, Mavis chose that night to interrupt her mother's sleep. Lizzie could see her quite clearly standing at the end of her bed. "What is it daughter? Where are you? Wherever it is, I'll come and find you. You can trust me." The dream woke her up and the room was empty.

Joe's trial day arrived and the witnesses were told when they would be needed to give evidence. The prosecuting barrister knew he had a good case against Joe – everything pointed towards the young man, who repeatedly claimed Bill had been alive in the woods. But how could he prove it?

One by one, the defence barrister called his witnesses and they all said that Joe was a decent and honest man. Both his mother and Mrs Glover told the court of how the two friends had liked each other and even been fond of each other – like brothers really.

Unfortunately, Mr Stewart the butler, told the opposite. He said he'd often heard them quarrelling and more than once, it had been about the young maid Mavis, who'd worked at the house. He added that he'd told Cook about this on more than one occasion. Cook looked quite flustered by his words. The head gardener praised Joe's work and his character. He'd never heard him arguing with his friend Bill.

The trial took three days and it was late in the final day when the jury returned from their private room. The Judge told Joe to stand for the verdict and he asked the jury if everyone was in agreement with the verdict. The foreman stood up and waited. Joe was visibly shaking and his knuckles were white as he gripped the edge of the dock.

The Juror spoke loud and clear and condemned Joe by giving a guilty verdict. Fortunately for Joe, the judge never donned his black cap but explained the death sentence was not appropriate in the case, as the accused had been convicted on circumstantial evidence only. He said Joe would spend the rest of his life in prison and added that he agreed with the verdict given by the jury. Joseph Mellors was definitely guilty!

There were cries from one or two of the onlookers in the gallery, but they had no say in the matter and a tearful Joe was led from the dock down the steep stairs to the cell beneath the courtroom. There was nothing left to do and everyone left the court, some relieved, some content but most very unhappy with the verdict. Mr Tomkins waited outside to offer comfort to Mrs Mellors and reassured her they'd appeal the decision – but his words were unconvincing and she left him on the stairs of the courthouse.

Lord Roberts had sent his carriage to bring those from the big house back home. They'd either be happy or miserable and one look at Mrs Glover's face told him all.

"A travesty of justice, that's what it is!" and she kept repeating the phrase to anyone who would listen. She'd hear someone saying it as she'd left the court and she liked the sound of it.

"There, there Cook – don't take on so. You did your best to help the young man, but it wasn't enough to change the way the case was going." Mr Stewart made her sit down at the kitchen table and offered to make her some tea.

"Yes thank you Mr Stewart, I did do my best. Although I have to say your evidence didn't help young Joe one bit – saying he quarrelled with Bill so many times." She was feeling very huffy with the butler.

"I only told the truth, my dear and that's what I was sworn to do. He plonked the cup in front of her and left the kitchen, going to the drawing room to tell the master and mistress exactly how the case had gone. Lady Roberts was very sorry but her husband thought they'd done all they could to help Joe, "It doesn't seem right though, Joe just didn't seem that sort of chap. What I find most odd is the way the murder and the disappearance of the maid happened at exactly the same time. Coincidence or what?"

His wife was staring into the flames of the fire when she added, "Do you remember that other maid we had, long before Mavis – the one who just up and ran away as well? What was her name Stewart? I can't remember."

The butler told her she'd been called Mary – just like the one they had now. He added, "But she was a bit older if I remember correctly. And yet, she just up and ran away like Mavis. I'm beginning to feel these Orphanage girls might leave a lot to be desired." The butler looked rather tired with the whole business.

"I'd forgotten her name – imagine you remembering it – and the fact she'd also come from the orphanage. You have a good memory Stewart." Lady Roberts rose to go upstairs to change for dinner. "Mind you tell Cook we're not expecting anything but a light meal tonight, after what she's been through today." She dismissed the butler, but still looked thoughtful.

Two nights later, the three women met as agreed, in the kitchen of the big house. Cook hadn't told Stewart, as she thought he'd be less than impressed and she was sure he'd regard a séance as a frivolity. The month was late October and it was already dark when the three sat down at the table - a warm fire was burning brightly in the hearth. There was nothing left for

Cook to do, so she concentrated on the matter in hand. Three small snifters of brandy also helped strengthen backbones as well as minds and, at Lizzie's instructions, they all linked hands.

"I'll open the séance with a request for any spirit to contact us. If luck is on our side, we'll maybe summon up Bill, but do remember, because his spirit still roams the earth, he can only tell us certain things. When he passes further on, he'll be able to tell us more – but not just yet."

The room was silent and when a piece of coal fell from the fire, all three women jumped. The kitchen door was suddenly thrown open and a surprised Mary came in. She was rubbing the sleep from her eyes and yawning at the same time. She stopped in her tracks, staring at the group around the table. She didn't know what to say, so she said nothing. Cook broke the circle of hands and crossed the room towards her.

"Why Mary, I thought you'd already gone to bed. What are you doing wandering around at this hour?" Cook put her hand on the scared girl's arm – and it was her turn to be surprised at what she saw there.

"I only got up for a drink of water Cook. Something woke me up and I thought someone was in my room." She fetched herself a mug of water and drank thirstily. "I'm all right now Cook – but I really did think someone was in my room. It wasn't you, was it?" Mary looked even younger in her nightshirt and bare feet.

"Nay child, it weren't me. You've just been dreamin', that's all. Now, go back to bed – you've got to get up in a few hours." Cook sat back down at the table and reached for the other's hands again, "Mary won't say anything about us – she's a good girl."

Silence returned to the room and the women sat quietly for at least five minutes. Then Lizzie's head fell forward onto her chest and her breathing changed. When she spoke, she seemed to have a different voice, "I know someone's there. I can feel your presence. Who is it – what is your name and do you have a message for anyone here?" The heavy wooden table rocked suddenly and the legs banged against the floor.

Lizzie lifted her head again and her mouth fell open. Without seeming to use her mouth, the other two heard a strange voice. It said, "My name's Mary and I used to work here.

I was a maid and happy in my work, but a bad man stole me away and left me for dead. I know the mistress thought I'd run away, but I'd never have done that. This was my home - except for the bad man who used to come and visit me." Cook and the cleaning lady stared at each other, then Cook said, "I remember you Mary. It must have been about ten years ago when you disappeared - and although we looked everywhere, we never could find you. You are that Mary, aren't you?"

"It's me Cook – I recognise you. You were always good to me and I think I missed you most of all. I'd never have left you but the bad man in the black, shiny coat and sou'wester came to my room and dragged me out of the house."

Lizzie sat up suddenly and broke into the conversation, "Why have you come here? Do you want to tell us something?' Her voice was still gruff and quite unlike her usual tone.

Mary the maid spoke again, "I came to tell you I've met Bill – your Bill, who was murdered. He's here standing beside me – he wants you to know he misses his friends, especially Mrs Mellors and Cook. He keeps repeating that the man who killed him, had very strange eyes."

Mrs Mellors spoke at last, "Yes, he told me that before – but I've racked my brains and I don't know anyone like that. He said the man had strange eyes - odd eyes – so, you'd think he'd stand out in a crowd, wouldn't you? But for the life of me, I can't think of anyone.""

Mary's voice became weaker, "I only came tonight because you invited me. I've never been invited before, you see. But before I go, I want to tell you to watch out for that young girl who was just here – she could be in danger. I don't know more than that and I'm not allowed to tell you if I did – but keep your eye on her."

She was gone but another voice took over, a much deeper voice, "Ma Mellors, it's Bill and I wanted to tell you to keep on with what you're doing – gathering bits of evidence all the time – and one day, you'll have Joe back home. Don't forget L.F.I.T.W. and you'll learn what really happened that night."

From the midst of her trance, Lizzie asked him, "Is my daughter alive or dead? You can tell me the worst, I can take it.

I need to know." But Bill said he couldn't tell her that – not yet
- but he repeated L.F.I.T.W. and urged her to keep searching.

Next morning, the butler came uninvited into the drawing
room, "My Lady, were you aware that Cook held a séance in the
kitchen last night? I'm sure you couldn't have known or you'd
have forbidden her. Shall I fetch her so you can give her a
reprimand?"

Lady Roberts was quite taken aback by the butler's obvious
annoyance at Mrs Glover and she certainly didn't like being told
what she should do with her staff. She was the mistress and she
made the decisions!

"Why Stewart, you seem more upset than the occasion merits.
What's gotten into you?"

"Well my Lady, she invited Mrs Mellors and Mavis's mother
to come to the house and she asked neither your, nor my
permission. Surely, you agree that's wrong." Stewart was not
his usual calm self.

"I agree with nothing Stewart. What Mrs Glover does in her
own time – and after she's completed her chores - is her business
and not yours. In fact, this might be a good opportunity to tell
you the master and I have decided to offer the woman Lizzie, a
position in this household. She has come looking for a daughter
she abandoned long ago, possibly through no fault of her own. I
think she's been punished enough and she has nowhere else to
go. The master agrees with my decision, so perhaps you'll
acquaint Cook of my decision. Young Mary wants to train under
cook – she's very interested in food preparation and Cook thinks
she'll do very well. Now, I know that's a lot of information to
take in, but it's how things are going to be. Is all that quite
clear?" And she turned from the man and picked up her
embroidery again. The matter was closed and the butler made
his way rather sheepishly from the room.

In prison, Joe had been visited by Bill's ghost on two more
occasions. Until he settled into prison life, he was being kept in
a single cell, so conversations with a visiting ghost wasn't a
problem. Strangely enough, he wasn't scared of the apparition –
it looked exactly as Bill had looked in life. except for the grey
pallor

"Bill, why do you keep visiting me, yet tell me nothing about who murdered you? What you know could get me released from here and yet you say nothing. Surely you know who he was – did he speak at all?" Joe was more desperate than before, now he'd experienced prison life - and a prison life that stretched before him forever. "Think man, is there nothing you can tell me?" He sat on his bunk and held his head in his hands. *What was the point? Bill obviously hadn't recognised the killer and was continuing to visit him out of friendship.*

"Bill, do you know anything about the maid, Mavis? She disappeared at the same time

and could have been who we both saw being buried that night. I've thought about it over and over again but I never saw who was in that sack. It could have been her – she's still missing, you know."

Bill held up his hand and put his first finger to his lips. He obviously didn't want to discuss the missing maid – or perhaps he knew nothing about her whereabouts. Joe's thoughts were moving fast, *Surely the two incidents were related. Bill's not being helpful – but why?*

Meanwhile, Lizzie started work as a maid at the big house. She looked so like her daughter although her temperament was quite different. She was much quieter and on occasion, quite subdued. Mavis had been jolly and good natured – a good person to have around.

The weeks were passing and soon it would be Christmas. The police had been working on the cryptic message Bill was supposed to have sent them. Some of their solutions were amusing and some made no sense at all. In a room at the police station, a group had formed to play around with the message. No-one really believed it had come from beyond the grave and when all was said and done, the culprit Joe Mellors had already been found guilty of the crime. His mother however wouldn't let it lie and called at the station every week to enquire if they'd found more evidence. She just wouldn't give up!

'Like Flies inside the Wardrobe
Leave First Isolate the Wanderers
Land Fish in the Wet

Crazy suggestions were put forward and caused a lot of laughter in the room. Unfortunately, no progress was made that day and the stumped officers decided to break for a cup of tea.

One very young constable said shyly, "You realise the last three letters could be 'in the woods' – and that might be a real clue. Does it mean the real answer to the murder lies in the woods?"

"But we've spent a lot of time there already and we found the body very quickly, the earth hadn't had time to settle. There's can't be any evidence still there. We found the murderer and it couldn't have been clearer – even the judge and jury saw it that way." A more experienced policeman in the group lectured the youngster, who appeared to accept his words – but did he? He walked away thoughtfully, still wondering about the woods.

Lizzie was still convinced Mavis was alive - if dead, why had she not come through the other night when she had the chance? Mavis was still breaking into her dreams however and obviously wanted to tell her mother something. It all seemed so pointless. At the big house, she had started work and moved into young Mary's room. It wasn't very big but there was room for two beds. It felt odd at first, sleeping where Mavis had slept, but Mary was nice, so all was well.

Very early one morning just as dawn was breaking, Lizzie was already up and about, but Mary was allowed another hour in bed as her working day differed from the maid's. Her work in the kitchen sometimes went on into the evening and so she didn't have to begin quite so early. She stretched languorously under the woollen blanket and her feet touched the bottom bed rail. Suddenly she stiffened as she felt the blanket move – gently and slowly until her bare feet were exposed to the cold air. She lay quite still, her eyes bold and staring into the gloom, 'Was that a hand she felt cradling one of her feet? Surely not! She eased her knees upwards and again felt the comfort of the blanket. The invisible hands moved further up her legs, past her ankles and she knew she wasn't imagining it. She cried out and sat up in the bed. Through the greyness of dawn, she saw the figure of a man bending over her and she recognised the butler, Mr Stewart. He stood up straight and dropped his hands to his sides.

"I was looking for Lizzie – is she not here? I have to talk to her about her duties today." He spoke with authority, not embarrassed in the least. He stepped back from the bed and peered into the gloom. "Is that you Mary? I'm so sorry, I thought you were Lizzie." And he turned abruptly and left the room. Mary was left shaken and afraid – she'd been scared and didn't quite believe the butler. He wouldn't have touched her feet and legs in that way – it just didn't feel right. He'd have called out her name when he knocked on the door. It was odd, but she felt violated and she didn't know why. She got up then and dressed quickly before creeping along the corridor towards the safety of the kitchen. Cook was already preparing breakfast and as always, the reassuring smell of coffee filled the room and made her feel safe and secure.

"Why Mary, you're up and about early today. Since you're here, you can help with the porridge." She didn't actually look at the girl, or she'd have seen someone on the verge of tears. The household would shortly be demanding its breakfast and that was Cook's priority. The back door was suddenly thrown open and Martha Mellolrs almost fell over the doorstep.

"Cook, Cook – you'll never believe it but they're going to release Joe from prison. Willy Barbour has come forward and given himself up. Apparently, he's confessed to Bill's murder." She was out of breath, having run all the way from the cottage and she collapsed into a chair.

"Calm down Martha or you'll give yourself a heart attack." Both Cook and Mary gathered around the distressed woman and Mary fetched her a glass of water.

Cook made her take a few deep breaths before allowing her to speak again. "Now, tell us all about it, my dear – we're here for you." She sat down beside her and touched her shoulder sympathetically.

"You know Willy Barbour – that young lad who lives with his mother. He's definitely sixpence short of a shilling and that's no mistake. He just walked into the police station two nights ago and told them he'd hit Bill over the head with a shovel, then buried him in a deep hole in the woods. Apparently, after having quarrelled with Bill in the pub earlier that night, he followed the two lads along the road out of town. When he saw Joe turn back and run towards the town again, he stayed in the woods, watching Bill." She really was breathless by this time and held up her glass for some more water.

"But why did he attack Bill – even if they'd quarrelled earlier, that wasn't enough to make him murder the lad." She looked at Mary, "You agree, don't you Mary, no-one would murder over such a trivial thing? "

Mary didn't know how to answer and dropped her eyes, murmuring something about, "I suppose it depends what they'd quarrelled about."

"Eh Lass – surely nothing could have been that bad." Cook reached for the coffee pot which was now ready and poured them all a comforting drink.

Stewart arrived in the kitchen, expecting a breakfast tray for Lord and Lady Roberts to be ready. Young Mary was careful to avoid his eyes. He listened to the conversation and asked Mrs Mellors, "And the police have Willy Barbour in custody now?

She nodded and tried to look sorry for the lad, but couldn't hide the relief in her eyes. *She was going to get her son back – Joe would be coming home. She'd always known he hadn't hurt his friend and felt a fresh rush of hatred against the judge and jury who'd sentenced him to life.*

In a controlled manner, Stewart told Cook to prepare the breakfast tray but he did add, "I'm very pleased to hear your son will be coming back to you Mrs Mellors – and that he's been absolved of any guilt. I'm pleased to hear the real culprit of the heinous crime has been identified at last." He left the kitchen.

Half an hour later, Lord Roberts himself came down to the kitchen to express his delight, "My wife and I always knew young Joe was innocent. I'm only sorry the police weren't able to establish his innocence much earlier. My wife also sends her regards and asks that you come to see her when you've finished your duties in the house." He made the most unexpected gesture and sympathetically touched the cleaning lady's shoulder. He was a real gentleman and no mistake!

Young Willy Barbour was only eighteen years old and had never been schooled. He'd always lived with his mother in the town and helped out on a farm quite close to the big house. He may have been only eighteen, but he was tall and well built – in fact, he was very strong, but he was a simple soul who'd always been treated well by the community.

He was kept at the police station for questioning and his mother was invited to join him – for moral support. Of course, he didn't have a lawyer but the police found a duty one to support him. The lawyer's job was not an easy one as their private conversation had made little sense, except that Willy repeatedly told him he'd hit Bill with a shovel. "Bill fell down at my feet and I rolled him into a hole I'd dug – he wasn't the tough man he thought he was." Unfortunately, he smiled as he talked and looked rather pleased with himself. Not very advisable in the circumstances.

When questioned, his mother was forced to confirm he wasn't at home on the night of Bill's murder – he'd gone to the local pub as usual, where he only ever had one pint of cider. The landlord knew that was Willy's limit and would give him no more. Everyone protected Willy!

"He came home that night maybe a little later than normal. I remember it quite clearly as he was soaked to the skin. It was a dreadful night, proper stormy and thundery that even wild animals sheltered from." Willy's mother tried hard to defend her son, "He's a lovely lad and never been in trouble before. Will I be able to speak to him – I can get him to tell the truth, you know – sometimes, he exaggerates."

The police asked her, "When he got home that night, did he happen to tell you he'd had a fall-out with Bill? Maybe just a disagreement – and not an argument?"

She told them he had mentioned a fall-out with Bill. "Bill had been pulling his leg apparently about the work he did on the farm. It wasn't a very serious thing, but Willy doesn't always understand people's humour – and he gets angry if he thinks someone is making fun of him. I swear he wasn't angry that night, just a little upset. He's a good boy and very gentle with the animals on the farm – ask the farmer if you don't believe me."She went home to a quiet house that night and wondered what was going to happen next.

Mrs Mellors however was happily preparing Joe's room – although she hadn't moved anything since he'd last been there, she felt it needed it. Some flowers on the window sill gave the room a welcoming feel – and she put freshly laundered linen on his bed. As she looked around, she was happy with her efforts. Now she only had to wait until he was released. Bill hadn't visited her again since he'd given her the message for the police, but she often felt his presence in the house and was grateful for the comfort it gave her. She wondered afresh what the message L.F.I.T.W. meant – but it didn't matter so much now, or did it? She'd still like to know what the letters stood for and why Bill had been so sure they'd help.

In the kitchen, Cook and Mary were preparing some baking for visitors due the next day. Cook's usually rosy cheeks were white with flour and when she looked at Mary, the girl couldn't help laughing. Cook looked so funny.

"Are you laughin' at me, young woman? I'll have yer guts for garters, if ye are." She beamed at the youngster.

"Oh Cook, I'd never laugh at you, but you do look funny just now." Mary was rolling out marzipan for the main cake and couldn't resist breaking off a tiny piece to taste. "May I ask you a question Cook? It's actually something serious."

"Spill the beans child, I don't have all night. There's work to be done." But she wondered what was suddenly making the girl's expression seem so serious.

"It happened the other morning – very early in the morning. Lizzie had already gotten up but I was enjoying my extra hour in bed. I woke up when I felt someone caressing my feet and legs. I froze with fear but eventually took my head from under the blanket and saw it was Mr Stewart. He explained he was looking for Lizzie, but I'm not sure he was. Now I'm afraid to go to sleep Cook, in case he comes into my room again. I'm very afraid of him now but what can I do, he's the butler and very important? " Cook realised the innocent child was almost blaming herself for what had happened, instead of being angry with the middle-aged man, who should have known better.

"I'll tell you what ye'll do child. When Lizzie leaves the room, you'll get up and prop a chair against the door 'andle – that'll stop anyone comin' into your room. Tomorrow, I'll speak with Mike the head gardener and get him to fit a lock on the inside of your door. How's that? Will that make you feel safer?"

"Oh yes Cook, it will. Can you really do that for me? I know Mr Stewart probably meant me no harm, but it did scare me."

Cook bit back the words that she wasn't too sure he'd meant no harm – he'd hung around the young maids before.

At the police station, Willy Barbour was still being questioned and he was so adamant that he'd killed Bill, the police were finding it difficult to learn what had really happened on the night.   The matter was particularly serious as, if a Jury found him guilty, Willy would face hanging, simple-minded or not. The evidence wouldn't be superficial as he'd confessed to the murder. His simplicity alone wouldn't be sufficient excuse for what he'd done. They   took turns in questioning him but he treated it like a game and kept bragging about how Bill had hit the ground.

" 'E deserved it and I let 'im 'aver it," was a line he kept repeating and eventually, the police had no option but to charge him with murde There was little his mother could do to help – she told everyone who would listen, that Willy wasn't the whole shilling and that the police shouldn't listen to him, but it was all pointless. Willy was formally charged and consequently Joe Mellors was released from prison. He came to the big house, cap in hand, and asked to speak with the head gardener who was delighted to give him his job back. His room with his mother was waiting for him and he soon settled into a familiar way of life. One thing he could never give up on was finding out who really killed Bill. He refused to believe Willy Barbour capable of doing such a thing. Yes, he had the strength to do it, but his simple mind wouldn't have allowed it. There'd never been a mean bone in that boy's body. He had a good memory and could still see the man in the shiny black coat and the sou'wester – but what could he do?   He had the time and patience now to take things slowly and keep watching everyone around him. The police might have decided on the murderer but Joe certainly had not.

Young Mary felt much safer in her room now that a new lock had been fitted and she arrived bright eyed and bushy tailed every morning to work alongside Cook. Lizzie continued to share the bedroom with her and the two women got on well together. Lizzie often thought of her daughter and the more time passed, the more she couldn't understand why she just up and left such a nice house.

"Do you think we could try to contact that other young girl again, the one called Mary?" Lizzie was having her five-minute break from cleaning.

"Don't see why not, dearie. It'll give us something to do one quiet evening. Best tell Mrs Mellors though – she tells me Bill has taken to paying her a visit again. Not when Joe's around of course, but when she's on her own in the cottage. Bill says that Willy Barbour didn't kill him either - he said the boy's being more crazy than usual. The argument they had in the pub was something and nothing and not worth talking about." Cook was resting her aching legs on a low wooden stool she kept just for that purpose.

The two women discussed how strange it was that a maid had disappeared some years ago, long before Mavis did and Lizzie asked, "Cook, did Mavis ever tell you something was worrying her – here at the house? She couldn't have been happy all the time. Was there never anyone she disliked?"

"Well now that you ask, she wasn't fond of the butler, but that was because he ordered her about.It was his job you know, to keep the household running smoothly and sometimes, perhaps he spoke to Mavis a bit sharply. But you know how young girls are – sometimes up and sometimes down." She eased herself up and started a casserole for the evening meal. They both agreed Tuesday evening would be the best night for the séance and Lizzie returned to cleaning the silver.

Pending his trial, young Willy wanted to go home. He was fed up with the restrictions of the jail and he asked the police repeatedly when he could leave. "My Ma will be missin' me – I know I'm missin' 'er." But the police just turned a deaf ear and ignored his pleas – his trial wasn't far off now and he soon became known as Daft Willy. Joe asked for permission to visit him – he felt sorry for him and knew well he was innocent. *Maybe if I talk to him, I can persuade him to tell the truth. When Bill and I left the pub that night, he was still sitting, nursing his tankard of cider. So, what did he do then?*

"Willy, it's me, Joe! They said I could come to see you and here I am." The boy looked at him with a puzzled look but then realised it was Joe Mellors and told him to sit down.

"Sit on my bunk there! Bill'll make room for ye'." And he moved over to a corner of the room.

Joe felt very uneasy, "Is Bill here just now Willy? Does he often come to see you?"

"'e comes nearly every day but I'm fed up wi' 'im – 'e keeps telling' me off. 'E says I made up the story about hittin' 'mi wae' a shovel – and I tell 'im 'e's wrong – but 'e just keeps right on saying' it." Willy rubbed his nose on his sleeve. He looked very young – even younger than his eighteen years. He was snivelling now and Joe fished a hanky from his pocket.

"Here you are mate – use this and just keep it." Willy's expression was as if he'd just been given the crown jewels. "Really Joe – can I really keep it?" Joe was cautious and he certainly couldn't see Bill's ghost anywhere – but Willy could and that was what mattered.

"Have you told the police that Bill visits you? It might be a good idea if you tell them." If he could get Willy to do this, it might show the police how unstable the young man really was. Willy looked up suspiciously and folded Joe's hanky several times until it was quite small. He didn't answer. Joe suddenly thought of another tack and asked if he remembered what Bill had been wearing when he hit him with the shovel. He didn't know why, but the question suddenly came to him.

"'Course I do Joe, I remember it as though it were yesterday." He looked confused and asked, "T'weren't yesterday, were it?

"No, it wasn't yesterday Willy but do you remember what Bill was wearing just before you hit him?

"A big, black shiny coat an' a 'at pulled down over 'is face. 'E tried to muddle me, but I knew t'were 'im, right enough. I stood behind 'im in the pourin' rain an' then I saw all the blood. It splattered onto my 'and – an' I 'ad to rub it off." Willy rubbed his hand again as though the blood was still there.

There was no way, Bill was wearing the clothes Willy thought he had. It was the man Joe had seen digging the hole and dragging the black sack across the ground, that's who it was. Willy's mind must have mixed up what had happened and he thought he'd hit the man in the black coat, whereas it was the man who'd hit Bill. Willy must have downed his cider quickly and followed them from the pub. Why he did that wasn't clear, but it seemed that's what he'd done on the night.

He tried something else, "Did the man in the black coat speak to you Willy? What did he say?" Joe could feel his adrenalin rising.

"T'were Bill who spoke tae me – in that black coat – and 'e asked me why I'd killed the other man. He said if I told anyone about 'im, I'd go to prison an' I might even be 'anged by my neck 'till I wer' dead. I didn't want that to 'appen Joe, so I just crept out o' the woods an' kept my mouth shut – like Bill told me." So, the man in the black coat had warned Willy to keep his mouth shut – or else.

My God, what a muddle, Joe's head was full of 'what if's' but he was convinced he was getting somewhere with Willy's story. It had been really worth coming to see him. He left Willy then and went home to think about things. He'd have to sort them out in his own head first before he took the idea to the police. At home in the comfort of the cottage, he mulled things over and realised what a convoluted story it was turning out to be. The police would probably laugh at him at first – he'd learned they didn't like hunches and guesswork and anyway, they were most likely still suspicious that he still might be Bill's murderer.

Then an idea began to form in his mind and the more he thought about it, the more it made sense. He'd go to Lord Robert and see what he thought, that's what he'd do. In fact, he had the ideal opportunity the next afternoon, as his lordship had asked to see him at three o'clock. A very unusual invitation!

That night was the night of the séance and the atmosphere in the kitchen was just right. Cook had set out a few tit-bits and Martha and Lizzie were both there. After a snack and a fortifying mug of tea later, Lizzie adopted her Medium persona and told the others to join hands around the table. She did exactly the same as before and suddenly, the candles in the room flickered and two went completely out.

Cook almost jumped out of her skin when Lizzie's gruff voice said she had a message for Nellie Glover. "I'm Nellie Glover," she said in a faltering voice, "What is it you want – and who are you?" "I am Mary, the house's maid of years ago and my companion is Mavis. a younger maid but one who suffered the same fate as I did. She's here with me now and wants to speak to Lizzie, her mother." Lizzie didn't falter and remained in a trance – she was the Medium and not the listener. A much younger voice spoke then and her words shocked Cook, "It's Mavis dear Mrs Glover and I know my mother now works here as well."

She explained that she couldn't appear at the previous séance because her spirit hadn't passed over properly into the other world. "But now, Mary has brought me here so I can tell both of you not to grieve for me – nor for her. I am no longer of this Earth and my death came about exactly as Mary's did – some years before my own."

Cook stuttered, "Can you tell us what happened to you both? Neither of you ran away, did you – who was it who made you leave this place – and why?

"I'm not allowed to speak names – and in any case – I was never sure who actually did the deed. Being struck from behind, I couldn't see his face – but it was a man, I'm sure of that. He took me to a secret place in the woods – a place he promised where I would find something to my advantage - but he attacked me before I knew what was happening. We were both innocent girls and maybe not all that bright but we didn't deserve what he did to us."

"You most certainly didn't." Cook was angry now about the young lives cut so short. "Tell me though, are you happy where you are now?"

The older girl answered, "Both of us are happy Cook – you mustn't worry about that. We're in a far better place than we could ever have imagined. Young Mavis here wanted to come tonight to put your mind at ease – she knew you'd never stopped worrying about her. And she wanted her natural mother to know she would never now meet the daughter she gave away so long ago. She asks that you tell her mother everything that's been said here tonight as she has most likely missed a lot because of being in a trance." The two voices slowly faded away and everyone noticed at once that something had been written on the big, steamed-up kitchen window. The letters were quite clear and bold. The message said 'L.F.I.T.W. Still an. Enigma to all those in. the room.

Cook agreed she and Martha would break the news gently to the other woman and as soon as she'd said the last word, all the candles lit up brightly again and Lizzie sat bolt upright in her chair. It was all over and now they had to tell her the sad news. *But did she perhaps always known Mavis was gone – the dreams she'd had must have fuelled her thinking and she probably already knew the worst had happened.*

Cook fetched a bottle of sherry from a high cupboard – Lizzie would need this – and truth to tell, so did she. Pouring large glasses, the two women told Lizzie all that had happened whilst she was in a trance. She looked quite unwell and Cook quickly refilled her glass. *I must remember to order another bottle of sherry when placing my next order. Even in the midst of chaos and confusion, Cook always managed to be pragmatic.*

Lizzie took the news as best she could. Part of her had always suspected Mavis was dead, but she'd hoped it wasn't so. The three women sat and chatted for at least another hour and Martha was the first to rise – she had the furthest to go. She went back home to where Joe was waiting and told him all that had happened.

Next morning, standing outside the door to the big house's drawing room, Joe tried to pluck up the courage to knock. "Come in lad, there's something I want to talk to you about." Lord Roberts was sitting by a roaring fire. He told Joe there was a vacancy at the house for a footman and it was his if he wanted it. "After all, you've been through rather a lot lately, haven't you?"

This was the last thing he'd thought to hear and didn't know what to say. He liked working in the gardens and his boss was a kind man, but a place inside the house was something he'd never dreamed of. He hesitated, but only for a moment, before accepting the offer. "You'll be working directly under Mr Stewart the butler – who will treat you well and teach you all he knows. Will you tell the head gardener he'll have to find a replacement for you – I hope he won't have a problem with that."

In the kitchen, the butler was watching young Mary. Since she'd started working with the cook, she was looking even prettier than before. He knew he was weak where the young ladies were concerned and he'd gone to the kitchen for his morning coffee, although he usually had it in the butler's private pantry.

"Why Mary, your cheeks are more rosy than usual." But before she could answer, Cook butted in, "And what about my cheeks Mr Stewart – are they not rosy too?"

"Of course, they are Cook, but then they're always so." Cook wasn't sure whether it was a compliment or an insult, so she chose to ignore it. "Is the coffee to your liking Mr Stewart? Mary made it today."

"It's very nice Mary, thank you." He knew he sounded condescending but he couldn't help it.

"Are you all ready for Christmas? You'll like the house at Christmas Mary – everything is so bright and we've adopted the royal family's habit of bringing a tree inside and decorating it. Lady Roberts always insists she decorate it herself of course. Have you ever had a Christmas tree?"

"Oh no Sir, there never was one at the Orphanage. There wasn't any spare money for one." The girl was smiling at the thought of a bright Christmas Tree.

A hesitant knock on the door and Joe came in, "Mr Stewart, I was told to report to you to be fitted for my uniform. Is it all right now?" Joe wasn't really welcome as far as the butler was concerned – The healthy-looking young man with his brown curls and eyes to match, was too much competition. He told Joe to go away and come back in half an hour when he'd finished his coffee. It suited him to remind everyone he was their superior and he continued to sit in the kitchen, slowly sipping his drink.

As Joe turned to go, Cook asked if he'd like a coffee, "There's plenty left in the pot."

"No Cook, that won't be necessary, Joe has other chores to see to. Off you go lad– get on with it."

"Don't you like the lad Mr Stewart, you certainly act as if you don't." As usual, Cook was always ready to defend anyone who seemed to need her support.

The butler pushed back his chair and told her it was none of her business, "The footman answers to me Cook – not to you."

He smiled at young Mary as he left the room – he liked her so she could do no wrong in his eyes

Joe used the free time to return to speak with his Lordship, "Well Joe, what did you want to discuss?"

Joe then told him about his recent visit to see Willy Barbour in prison. Although feeling quite tongue- tied, he managed to explain quite well. Even Lord Roberts was aware that Willy wasn't the full shilling and easily accepted that the lad had somehow mixed up Bill and the man in the black coat.

"So, what you're suggesting is that Willy was definitely in the woods that night and he saw the stranger crack the footman's head with a shovel. When the stranger asked him why he'd done it, he immediately accepted it had been his crime - he must have done it, the man said so, didn't he? And so, the lad just ran away. The stranger must have dumped whatever was in the sack into the hole he'd already dug – and then he then dragged his own black sack to someplace deeper in the woods. Is that what you're trying to tell me – have I got it right?"

"That's it in a nutshell your Lordship. I haven't mentioned it to anyone else yet as I think the police will probably think me mad." Joe was really pleased the master had grasped everything so quickly – and he certainly wasn't laughing at the idea.

"So, the real culprit in the black coat and sou'wester is the murderer and that's who the police have to look for. Until now, they've not been looking for him, as they believing there was no such person. You were their first suspect and now it's Willy – but they should really be looking for the stranger. My God lad, you could very well be right but how do we convince the police – that's the dilemma. Willy's confession and insistence that he's the murderer made it so easy for them and why should they look further? But look further they will – I'm going to contact my lawyer for advice right now. In the meantime, will you say nothing about this to anyone else until I come back to you?"

When Joe went to have his footman's uniform fitted, he felt as if a weight had been lifted from his shoulders. It had been easier to talk to the master than he'd thought and now he no longer felt alone in his attempts to find Bill's real murderer.

"That night in the cottage, he asked his mother about Mary, the new maid. She smiled and said the maid had nothing to do with him. He knew she was just teasing him and asked no more questions. *I wonder if he's forming an attachment to the young maid – well, I suppose he could do a lot worse! She began again to think of those letters L.F.I.T.W. knowing what they meant could reveal the truth.*

A few nights later, Lord and Lady Roberts were attending a musical evening at a friend's house. Their coachman had gone back home to visit his elderly mother and so Lord Roberts drove the carriage himself. Robert the coachman had much news for his mother after all he'd recently been questioned by the police about a local murder and he knew she would enjoy the excitement. Funnily enough he too had been in the pub on the night it all started and he'd heard Bill and Willy having words about which ale was the best. A stupid argument and one for which there was no answer but Willy wouldn't let the matter drop – and in the end Bill just turned his back to him. Oh yes, he'd enjoy telling his mother all the news.

After the final piece of music, the audience attended a sumptuous buffet before climbing back into their carriages and making their ways home. It had been a lovely evening and lady Roberts was looking forward to her warm bed. The night was unpleasant with wind and rain beating against the horse and carriage when suddenly there was an almighty cracking sound and lady Roberts was thrown to one side. "Husband dear," she called out, "what on earth has come about?"

He climbed down from the river's seat and said, "Now, don't worry my dear – the wheel has come off the axle and the horse has run off across the fields. He'll go straight home so don't worry, he knows the route home very well. When Stewart sees him come into the yard, he'll know something has happened and he'll bring help. We just have to be patient and keep warm." He climbed inside the carriage and tried bot to look worried.

Back at the big house, Stewart did indeed see the horse return alone. He knew he must do something, but what? They could only have used one road so he could probably find them quite easily. *How to bring them back however – that was his dilemma? I know – I'll fetch the cart the head gardener uses and bring them back in that. If the carriage is damaged, it can be collected the next day and brought home. Yes, that's what I'll do. He had a pan!*

He remembered then that her Ladyship would be distressed by whatever had happened and that she'd probably need a maid to support her. He decided to take Mary with him – rather than Lizzie - and that way, he might be able to steal a secret kiss or two from the pretty young girl. Fate was playing right into his hands, he'd been wondering for a while how he could get her on her own. This was then the answer!

"Nay Mr Stewart, let it be me – or Lizzie. One of us can accompany you. Little Mary will be afeared." Cook didn't want the girl to go off into the dark with the butler, she knew she'd hate it. Stewart however, was adamant and instructed Mary to wrap up well as the master and mistress needed her. Reluctantly, she did as she was told. The rain was coming down even heavier and the branches of the trees were swinging about from side to side. It was not a night to be out in.

He brought the gardener's cart to the kitchen door and told Mary to climb aboard. She was well wrapped up but he wasn't even wearing an overcoat.

Cook called out to him, "You must wear something warmer Mr Stewart – shall I fetch your black raincoat and hat from your room? I know I can find it."

He brushed her suggestion aside, "I no longer have that coat Cook – please don't trouble yourself." And he was off in the rumbling cart, the little maid clinging to his side. This was more like it – he enjoyed her closeness. "Put your arms around me Mary – that way, you'll be quite safe." Mary was scared but she knew she had to hang onto him. He brought the cart to a sudden halt and turned to the maid.

"Come on now my dear, I don't bite. As your superior, I'm telling you to give me a kiss." His face was contorted and he looked quite unlike himself. She was petrified and pulled away from him but he held onto her and began to fumble with her clothes. She managed to slip from his grasp and actually fell to the ground. Picking herself up, she ran like the wind into the darkness and soon disappeared from his view. She ran and ran, not knowing what was ahead but she kept off the main road and kept to the line of hedgerows instead. Exhaustion caught up with her and she tripped and fell over a couple of times. Now she was tired, wet and very muddy but at least she was safe from Mr Stewart. Picking herself up, she started off again and ran right into a figure standing a few feet away.

"There now maid – don't take on so. It's only Joe. You know me – we met the other day. I'm the new footman at the house." She fell into the arms of the young man and knew she was safe at last.

"Why are you here Joe? How did you know I needed you?" She gasped.

"I didn't know you needed me, I was on my way to the pub for a pint of ale. I'm glad I was here to help. Where have you been and why are you in this state?" Joe was concerned and almost carried her back towards the big house where she fell into Cook's welcoming arms.

"Dearie me, what's happened to you?" And she sat the girl down in the rocking chair by the fire. "Don't try to talk yet, there'll be time enough for that." She hurriedly put the kettle on to boil. "Sit yourself down Joe – thank you for bringing her home."

With Mary tucked up in bed, she waited for the butler – and the master and mistress – to return home. They turned up about two hours later and Lady Roberts was in a terrible state. It wasn't possible to talk with her then, it would have to wait until the next day. The master was full of praise for the butler, who'd turn up like the guardian angel he was and rescued both his wife and himself.

Two days later when Lord Roberts, with his lawyer, had visited the police in town, young Willy Barbour was released and allowed home to his mother. Joe made sure he found the time to go and see him and arrived at his house the very next day.

"It's good of you to come and see our Willy, but I'm afraid he's still a bit confused about everything that's happened. If you want to chat to him, you'll find him at the bottom of the garden – you sit with him and I'll bring you both a cup of tea." Willy's mother was pleased to see Joe.

Sure enough, the young man was sitting on a bench whittling a wooden branch with a small knife. Joe called out, "Good to see you Willy, how are you feeling?"

"Why Joe, I'm fine. Why shouldn't I be?" Willy grinned.

"Oh, I just meant after your time in jail, that's all. Your Ma said I was to wait with you and she'll bring us a cup of tea." Joe reassured him,

"And some of her fresh biscuits too? I hope she doesn't forget them." Willy held the piece of wood up to the light, "It's taking shape Joe – can you see it?"

"Course I can Willy – it's a soldier, isn't it?" Willy was obsessed with soldiers and he was always whittling new soldiers for his collection - a collection that to some, may have looked like a load of twisted sticks, but to Willy, it was a fine regiment of brave soldiers.

They chatted for ten minutes about trivia and out of the blue, Willy asked, "How is Bill these days Joe? Is he well? I still think he's wrong about the best ale, you know." He found another piece of wood and started working on it. His mother appeared with two steaming mugs and thankfully, a plate of oatmeal biscuits.

Joe found it difficult but he couldn't let the boy go on thinking Bill was okay.

"Willy, Bill's no longer with us. Don't you remember he died?" He hid his awkwardness by slurping his tea.

"Dead, you say, well I never! I heard that he attacked someone in the woods?"

"No, what you heard was that someone attacked him in the woods - and killed him."

"Was that me Joe? Did I kill him? The police said I did, you know." He paused for a while and then, "Now you mention it, I remember a man 'ittin' Bill on the head. I didn't do it, Joe – honest, I didn't. The police were wrong."

Joe realised Willy's mind was still in a state of confusion and thought it best not to trouble him anymore. "I'll be off Willy, but I'll come to see you again in a few days. Is that all right?" Joe stood up to leave and then stopped in his tracks as Willy said quietly, "I.F.I.T.W. Joe – don't forget that, will you? Bill told me those letters when he visited me in my cell."

"Did he happen to tell you what the letters meant Willy? Did Bill tell you that?" Joe waited patiently for him to answer He hoped Willy knew what he was saying and wouldn't change his mind later.

"'Course he did Joe. Do you want to know? If I tell you though, you won't tell anyone else, will you? He said it was our secret." Suddenly Willy looked quite cunning and had a knowing smile on his face.

"It'll be our secret Willy – what do the letters mean?" Joe spoke gently, knowing he had to control his impatience or he'd scare the boy.

"Look further into the woods – that's what Bill says it means. Pass me another biscuit Joe." Joe did as he was told before hurrying off to speak to the police. He left Willy in complete ignorance of the bomb he'd just dropped.

This time the police listened to the 'message from beyond the grave.' They hadn't investigated further into the woods as they knew they'd already found Bill's grave. They had of course, but what if there was another grave – and that's where the little maid had ended up? Now perhaps, the secret would be revealed.

The local police asked for volunteers from other forces – and even from the local Army camp – they needed extra hands to cover the whole area of the wood. It took three whole days and about twenty workers to cover the ground not yet investigated. It turned out to be the young constable who'd earlier wanted to search the woods, who actually discovered the new burial place. The earth was slightly raised and he almost tripped over it. Fate must have played a part because it had actually been his day off, but he cancelled it when he heard the call for volunteers. When he saw the disturbed, uneven spot, he blew his whistle and other officers came running to join him. Before messing up the area, Forensics were brought in and they took over the exhumation of the bodies. Yes, bodies – not body. There were two corpses buried there, both women and both apparently quite young. One had been there for several years and was badly decomposed, whilst the other was still fresh, having been placed there not long ago. However, neither one was a pretty sight and the young constable vomited more than once that day to his embarrassment.

But there was more discovered in the grave than the women's bodies – they also found a black, heavy oilskin coat and a large sou'wester hat. The items were taken back to the station for examination and unfortunately for the owner, a name was found secreted under the lining of the collar – but even more unfortunately, it established who the killer actually was.

"Donald Stewart, we would like you to accompany us to the station for further questioning. We'd like you to come now." It wasn't an invitation, but an order and the butler asked if he could first speak with the master to acquaint him with what was happening. This was denied him as the police would do it for him. Donald Stewart was escorted from the house and suddenly looked much older than he had before. Cook and Mary watched him go but Lizzie wanted to run after him and scratch his eyes out. Although no formal identification of the bodies had yet been done, she knew beyond the shadow of a doubt that one of them was Mavis, her daughter.

Cook took young Mary into her arms and said, "It's all right Mary, the bad man's been taken away. You won't need to use that lock on your door quite so much now."

That afternoon, after tea and cake had been served to the master and mistress, Cook held court around the kitchen table. There was Lizzie, Mary and Joe, looking handsome in his footman's uniform – but they all seemed lost for words and stared silently at the table.

"But why? Why did he do such things? He had a good job, a nice home and good employers – why did he choose to hurt innocents in that way?" Joe looked as confused as he felt. Young Mary on the other hand, knew what had driven the butler to do the things he had. After all, she could have ended up in the woods along with the others, but thank God, she could out-run the butler – straight into the arms of Joe. Cook smiled at both of them, knowing that only good things were going to happen for the pair.

Lizzie suddenly spoke although she'd been silent until that moment. It was as though she'd just come out of a trance and looking straight at Joe, she blurted out, "You're going to be the butler here Joe – maybe not today and maybe not tomorrow – but sooner than you think. The house needs a butler!"

Joe started to say, "Don't be silly Lizzie………….." but the bell in the drawing room suddenly rang out. 'What could the master want?' Cook said, but Lizzie just smiled at the startled expressions around the table – especially the one on Joe's face.

DRUID OR NOT A DRUID – THAT IS THE QUESTION

She fingered the key in her pocket but still hesitated to bring it out, to put it into the lock. Standing there, she looked at the front of the cottage and *thought 'Twelve years Mother! Twelve years since I last stood here. And you couldn't wait to see the back of me, could you – yet, here I am with the key to your house in my pocket? But it's not your house now, is it – it's mine?'*

She sat on the front door step, nervous yet eager to move. She'd just come from the lawyer's office where he'd given her the details of her mother's death and also the key to the cottage, left to her only child – Marion Jennifer Parker. The child who'd left the home, the town, the mother so many years ago, swearing never to come back. And yet, here she was!

The cottage was one of a dozen similar homes, built in a circle so that the front windows all looked into each other – but they were quite far apart and generally hidden from the eyes across the way. They were very old but had been kept in good repair – all white-washed with roses or hydrangeas around each door. A chocolate box top she'd once heard them described and looking at them now, she realised the description was apt – they really were rather pretty. It was a small village with just one pub, one general store and one church – children had to travel to the nearby school for lessons. She'd once been one as one of those children – but that was a long time ago. Not a particularly happy time, she recalled.

On looking around, Marion could easily imagine her mother standing by the kitchen window of number twelve, but it was all in her imagination, she knew that.

When she'd first heard from the lawyer, she'd been determined to stay where she'd been settled for a number of years now – she'd made a life for herself there and she'd never missed the village – nor her mother. As the weeks passed however, her curiosity actually changed her mind and she found she wanted to know what had happened to the village in the time since she'd been gone. So, she took some annual leave from her boss at the library and bought her train ticket.

She was still sitting on the doorstep and thinking, *'She was a terrible mother, why do I care? She never cared whether I was happy or not, even when I was a child and yet here I am, a woman on the wrong side of thirty, coming to pay my last respects. Or am I actually doing that, or is it just curiosity? I do have a home of my own however and I don't have to stay here long – I'm a free agent after all.*

Finally, she took the key from her pocket and turned it in the lock. It was stiff and made a scraping sound. There was no-one around to watch her and she found the eerie silence Inside the cottage, quite disturbing. Everything smelt just as she remembered it and for a moment, she was a schoolgirl again, being screamed at by her mother. The smell wasn't unpleasant, it was an aroma of lavender but it made her think of the unhappiest times in her life.

Nothing looked different from how she last remembered it- she was eighteen at the time and the carpet, the drapes, the furniture – even the ornaments - all looked the same. She'd grown up here and been miserable here - she didn't remember being happy even once. She wandered around the ground floor, ending up in the kitchen where she took coffee and milk from her bag and set it on the table. Filling the kettle, she found the silence foreboding and looked around for a radio, just for some company, but of course there wasn't one. Her mother had never been one for anything as frivolous as a radio. Amazingly, it was the same patterned tablecloth – red and white checked - just the sort a cottage like this should have.

She caught sight of herself in a mirror and was shocked by her appearance. She'd expected to see the young girl she'd once been in that mirror, but instead there was a mature woman in a smart, tailored suit looking back at her. That young girl had long gone now. It was some time since she'd last admired herself in anything as daunting as a mirror. She wasn't a vain woman and didn't waste time worrying about her looks, but she was strong and healthy and positive about life. She'd inherited her mother's chestnut coloured hair and slim build, but she had her father's character and humour – thank God! A thought popped into her mind, 'Could she live here – even for a short time, where there was still so much evidence of her mother? Unfortunately, she barely remembered her father, who'd disappeared out of her life when she was only about twelve – she always said disappeared and not died, as she never really knew what happened to him. One day he was there and the next, he was gone – and her mother wouldn't tell her what had happened. However, she did remember his gentlemanly ways and his kindness – and most certainly, his humour. She'd often wondered how her parents had ever got together, they were so very different from each other.

The kettle boiled and she poured herself a mug of coffee. 'I wish I had some biscuits!' she thought and reached for her mother's biscuit tin – yes, there were some Kit-Kats there – there always had been. They were her mother's favourite. She made up her mind to stay for a couple of weeks at least, to sort everything out – only then, could she decide whether moving back to her home town was a good idea – or if it was not. She wandered upstairs and cautiously opened the bedroom door, the room that had once belonged to her. She was amazed, not a single thing had changed - her books, trinkets and even the bed was made up with a flowered quilt she remembered. *"My God,' she thought, 'I hope she's changed the sheets since I last slept here.'* Of course, she had – her mother had always been very careful about cleanliness – she'd been a slave to housework. In fact, that had been one of the reasons she'd left home all those years ago – everything was always too neat and tidy and it never felt like a home at all. Nothing was ever allowed to be out of place – and if it was, it would only be for a minute! It was uncanny! She remembered afresh, the many arguments they'd had about her untidiness.

She crossed to her mother's bedroom and of course, it too looked exactly the same. Neat as a new pin – quite unlived in! It didn't upset her standing in the room and looking at the familiar ornaments and personal bits and pieces. Nothing had changed. Marion was amazed by her own lack of emotion – but not surprised by it.

Outside the window, the garden was quite tidy, but then it was Spring time and everything was just beginning to wake up. It was just a patch of grass but along one side, the snowdrops were thrusting their heads above ground – a welcome sight of better weather to come. As the cottages were built in a circle, the back gardens met together in a point at the centre, giving each cottage a triangular-shaped plot. Of course, people had grown shrubs and trees to separate the gardens, but it still seemed like one huge plot of land. She went into the garden to have a better look around and was surprised to see a man cutting his grass just across the way. 'It seemed a bit early to be cutting the grass!' She kept in the shadow of the walls as she didn't feel like talking to anyone – especially a stranger. He looked about her age, but was probably married with four screaming kids and a dog.

She went back into the house; the front door bell was ringing. The sound reverberated around the empty rooms and made her jump. 'Who could it be? Who knew she was here?' She could see the figure of a man through the glass panel of the door and thought she recognised him. It was the lawyer – he'd probably forgotten to tell her something. *'I suppose I'll have to let him in, but I won't offer him coffee. He's not my friend, not even my lawyer – he was mother's lawyer.' She argued with herself.*

"Do come in, Mr Jenkins. Is there something you forgot to tell me?" She rudely kept him standing in the hall. Lawyers didn't impress her – she was a librarian after all and had read as much as he probably had.

'My God,' she thought, the lawyer was certainly no oil painting. He wasn't old, but dressed very conservatively, just as she did herself she had to concede, but her clothes had more joie-de-vivre. He looked old before his time and his hair was beginning to thin, with a decisive bald spot at the back. To complete the picture, he had an annoying way of wringing his hands together when he spoke.

Suddenly, she felt sorry for him and decided to offer him a coffee after all, which he gratefully accepted. She brought the drinks into the sitting room and waited for him to speak.

Remembering his mission, he produced a long, white envelope from his brief case, "When you were in my office, I forgot to give you this. Your Mother gave me clear instructions to hand it to you left on her death," and she saw her own name on the envelope, written in her mother's familiar hand.

"Why, thank you for taking the trouble to bring it." She knew she had to say something, but she didn't want to open the envelope whilst he was still there. She put it to one side.

"You hadn't seen your mother for some years, had you? She told me how you'd both fallen out many years ago and you'd left home when you were very young."

"She seems to have spoken more with you than she ever did with me. Mother and I were like chalk and cheese with absolutely nothing in common." Marian felt rather miffed that he knew so much about her.

He stood up to take his leave. "I'll go now, I've done what I came for, but if you need anything, you know where to find me. I actually live in the big house on the edge of the village - you can usually find me there or at my office in town." He was wringing his hands furiously as if he suddenly felt uncomfortable in her company. She had to admit she hadn't attempted to make him feel very comfortable - but then, why should she?

She made herself a fresh cup of coffee – one she could enjoy now that he'd gone – and settled down on the sofa to read the letter.

It started off rather ominously, saying that she would be dead when Marion read it. It pointed out the obvious, saying she hadn't seen her daughter for twenty years and that she hoped she was in good health. Since her daughter had left home, she'd lived at the cottage with only some neighbours for company but she'd continued to find comfort in her religious beliefs. Then significantly, she went on to say she'd left some secret messages hidden around the cottage which would help her daughter understand what was expected of her.

'I've left you clues so you can find them – it shouldn't be too difficult for someone as clever as you. *'Ah, Marian thought with a smile, 'There it was – sarcasm, something her mother had loved handing out. And what did she mean 'What was expected of me '– as usual, she was making presumptions on my behalf.'*

Folding the letter, she put it in her handbag, telling herself, she'd look around the place the next day. But before settling down for the night, she had to visit the village shop for some provisions. As she arrived there, her first thought *was 'My God, the woman behind the counter was someone she remembered,*

*older of course, but definitely the shop keeper she remembered
from her childhood.*

"Good Afternoon Miss, what can I get you?" It definitely was
her, she remembered her strong accent.

Marion bought some basic foods and before she knew it, a
bag had been filled with bread, butter, cheese, jam and ham. She
paid for the food and listened to Mrs Williams praising the
locally-produced ham. "You'll definitely enjoy that, or my
name's not Williams." She was right, she'd known her name
was Williams, yet it was twenty years since she was last here. *'I
must have a better memory than I thought.'*

As she was about to leave the shop, the woman leaned over
the counter, "Have you come to replace your mother then?
We're going to miss her from the group – and you'll be most
welcome."

"How do you know me?" she found herself asking.

"Oh, I know who you are all right – you're Marion Parker and
your mothers not long passed on. I remember you when you were
young – my, how you've grown!" Her words reminded Marion
of her, it held the same sarcasm and innuendo. This woman
however didn't speak with quite the same sting as her mother.

Marion asked, "And what group might that be, Mrs
Williams?"

"Oh, it's a group of local people who get together from time
to time to discuss what's been happening and what might happen
around the corner. If you plan to stay around for a while – and I
sincerely hope you do – you'll soon find out about our group
meetings." And she disappeared into the back of the shop,
making it clear she had finished chatting.

Oddly enough, Marion slept well, although it did feel strange
sleeping in the bed she'd last used when she was a teenager.
Despite her concerns, sleep came easily and she awoke refreshed
to a Spring morning full of sunshine. The daffodils were just
peeping above the ground in the back garden and she found
herself hoping they'd soon flower so she could have a vase full
of the bright, yellow magic. It was just what the kitchen needed.

As she was taking the food wrappers to the outside bin, she
saw the man again – the one who'd been cutting grass the day

before. He raised one hand in a gesture of 'Hello' and she had no option but to respond.

Hi," he shouted across the gardens, "I'm John and I knew your mother. One morning, you must come over for coffee so we can get to know each other."

'Well,' she thought, 'I hope your wife's all right with you inviting strange women into your home.' She just smiled and went back indoors. Although, the morning was Spring like, it was still rather chilly, and she decided to light a fire. She seen some coal and kindling sticks in the shed and so she got to work. As she bent to put the kindling in place, she noticed a piece of paper sticking out from beneath the clock on the mantlepiece. Very gingerly, she moved the clock - the words were in her mother's handwriting. *Was this the first of the promised secret messages left around the house? She believed it must be and sat down on the sofa.*

'Well Marion, you've found your first clue – it'll lead you to several others – so, be patient.' Below these words it continued,

'Use this as a stepping stone – what does the mantlepiece clock tell you now?'

What on earth did that mean – how could a clock tell her anything. She lifted it up and examined all around the case. There was nothing out of the ordinary and even when she opened it, there was nothing other than its winding key inside. She placed it back on the mantlepiece and got on with making up a fire. Soon, she was admiring the growing flames coming to life – and she felt better.

She took the note into the kitchen whilst she toasted some bread and boiled the kettle. Munching the buttered toast, she brought the clock into the kitchen, where she could study it more closely. She read the note again. Yes, it was something about the clock itself – but what could it be? She wound it and it began to tick loudly, then she noticed the pattern on its dial. It was an engraving pf some kind of flower – it was quite pretty and she recognised it as a Lily – a willowing, long-stemmed Lily.

'Lily! So, it was something to do with a Lily.' After breakfast, she began to wander around the rooms, looking for a Lily. Nothing, no matter how much she looked – there was nothing Lily-like in the cottage. She sat on her mother's bed to think.

What could it mean? What was her mother trying to tell her? Then she spotted it. At the edge of the bedside rug, there were some flowers worked into the carpet pile – and in the centre, a large Lily stood out from the other flowers. *But how could a rug hide a secret?* She lifted the rug and saw that one of the wooden floorboards was loose. Kneeling down, she pulled at the one crooked floorboard and there, hidden in its depth, was a wooden box with a cross burned into the lid. She lifted it out and tried to open it, but it was stuck tight.

Down in the kitchen, she found a tool box and using a file, she managed to prize the top from the box. At first sight, it looked like an old piece of cloth, but when she carefully lifted it out, she saw it was a hood – a hood, attached to a sort of collar. 'What a strange thing to hide in a secret place – an ordinary white hood. It was made out of cotton material – but a very soft cotton and it looked as if it had never been worn.

As she unfolded it, another scrap of paper fell to the floor and she smiled at herself for feeling excited – it had only taken a white hood and here she was, looking forward to her next find! She took the hood into her bedroom and put it in a drawer.

The second note also gave very little away. There were no words this time, just a drawing of what looked like a sword or a dagger. *It was very simply drawn but had a jewel encrusted in the hilt. At least, she supposed it was a jewel – slightly blue in colour and seemed to be set in a gold clasp.* 'A dagger' – what could it mean? 'Did she like this game – no, not especially. She took the paper and put it with the first one. 'She'd think more about it later.'

For the first time in twenty years, she walked the whole length of the back garden, reaching the point where all the gardens met. *My God, the tree that grew there was magnificent. She didn't remember it from before, but then it had been such a long time ago. Had it grown to this size since she'd left home? But no, it looked too old for that – it really was ancient, with a thick trunk and many branches – maybe she'd just not noticed it before. 'I think it's an oak tree,' she decided! Yes, it's definitely an oak tree.*

She felt, rather than saw someone approaching from behind the tree. It was the man she'd seen on her first day and he was carrying a spade. He obviously liked his gardening!

"Hello again." he smiled and she realised she liked his smile. He didn't look arrogant, just friendly. He was tall, with brown hair and eyes – not particularly handsome, but attractive in an unassuming way.

"A fine, old tree, isn't it? I can't imagine how old it must be." He leaned his spade against the trunk and turned towards her. "I really am sorry for your loss - I did know her, you know. We often used to chat just about here. Why have I never seen you before – you couldn't have visited very often."

'That's none of your business,' she thought and chose to ignore his question. "Well, I'm here now. My name is Marion Parker by the way." And she waited expectantly for him to introduce himself. properly.

"As you can imagine, I live next door – by myself, all by myself – and my name is John Reynolds." And he smiled ruefully as if trying to make a joke of his lonely status.

Tell you what," he continued, "How would you like to come for a drink in the one pub we have within walking distance? It's a pleasant place and the people are always friendly. You're obviously alone and it would make you feel welcome - do come, the first round's on me."

She had no option but to accept and as she turned to go back up the garden, she spotted another couple of neighbours wandering around their patch of garden. They seemed older, but looked friendly enough as they both waved their hands in 'a hello.'

In the pub that evening, she waited for him to arrive. The pub was old, he was right about that, and looked as if it hadn't changed since it was first built – probably in the Middle Ages! The wooden beams and the bar were cracked and split with age, but seemed solid enough. There was a large fireplace against one wall, and at its side, was a dog-turning spit. *I wonder how many meats have been roasted there – and how many little dogs lost their lives turning that wheel.'*

The landlord could have been King Henry V111 himself – he was a dead ringer for him and had offered Marion a drink while she waited for John. "Go on, my dear, he's always late – probably be late for his own funeral." He laughed at his own joke and began lighting candles along the old mantlepiece – and then the bigger ones in the two windows.

The window glass was so old, it had the bubbles in the centres, from a time when they were hand-made - centuries ago - the candlelight was fragmented in the reflections.

"Here I am Marian, sorry to be late, but then I suppose Fred here has told you I'm always late." He reached for the pint Fred had already placed on the bar. "I was just finishing off a chapter – if I don't do it when the writing juices are flowing, then I completely lose the thread."

"What kind of books do you write?" she asked, "Fact or Fiction?"

He told her he wrote Fantasy-cum-Fiction books, "I actually like the Occult and Druidism. It's a fascinating subject – have you read anything about it?"

She told him she'd read most genres – she was intrigued by reading, "I'm a librarian, so I have free access to all types. I don't think I've ever met anyone involved with Druidism before."

"Well, you have now – I often talk about it with Fred over there – he finds it fascinating too. Are you ready for a top-up?" and he lifted her empty glass.

The next hour and a half passed quite pleasantly and soon, she felt as though she'd known him for some time. He walked her back towards the cottages but as they approached Number 12, she pulled up short and reached for his arm. "There's a light in my house – I know I never left on any lights. I'm always very careful about things like that. Please, will you see me inside, I'm not used to the place yet?"

He took the door key from her hand and opened the door. There was a light in the small sitting room – one of the table lamps had been left on. "You must have missed it when you were leaving – as you say, you're not used to the place. Easily done!"

He was trying to reassure her, but she knew what she knew. She hadn't left that light switched on – but what other explanation could there be? *'Maybe I'm just being silly.'* She told herself and said goodnight to John.

When he'd gone, she sat in the armchair for a while, thinking of times when she used to live here. She'd never got on with her mother – they'd been two opposites. It was a good thing she could just about remember her father as there were no photos of him in the house. Mind you, there were none of herself either. Her mother certainly didn't reminisce about old times, in fact the only thing she'd ever been sentimental about, was her violin. She'd loved her violin and often said, had she had the right encouragement, she'd have become a talented, probably famous, violinist. Obviously, that encouragement hadn't been forthcoming – and as for Marion, she'd always been tone deaf!

When her father disappeared, her mother wouldn't allow his name to be mentioned ever again. She had often told Marion, "He's gone now from both our lives and that's all you have to know. Discussion over!"

Her thoughts were making her shiver and suddenly there was an atmosphere in the room She was cold. *'Bedtime,' she thought, 'At least, I can relax there.' But a little voice in her head whispered, 'Can you really?'*

She fell asleep quite quickly however, but was abruptly awakened by a horrendous peel of thunder. It was the middle of the night and flashes of lightening were darting around the room – one-minute dark, the next blindingly light. Something was moving about in the cottage – she could clearly hear footsteps. *'What did she do? Pull the covers over her head, or face the consequences and go downstairs – allegedly to fetch a cup of tea to help her sleep?' It had to be the latter – she couldn't lie there with her head under the covers, after all she was a mature woman of thirty-five and not a child!'*

Wrapped in her housecoat, she cautiously opened the door and peered along the corridor. There was no-one there. Whoever it was must be downstairs – waiting for her. *'Right – let's go Marion – best foot forward.'*

The stairs in the old place creaked as she crept downstairs. Whoever was there would definitely hear her coming – that was for sure. There was a light coming from under the sitting room door and she turned the handle slowly. The table lamp had been switched on again – she'd definitely turned it off this time. *The word 'Occult' popped unbidden into her mind – odd, but that was the second time she'd heard that word in the last few hours.*

Next day, she had the telephone re-connected, so she must be going to stay for a little while anyway. It made her feel safer, being connected to the outside world. There was no evidence of anyone having been in the cottage – she checked thoroughly but could find nothing. On the doormat, she found a notice, advertising a celebration to be held in the wood on the edge of the village. 'It sounded a bit like a picnic or a barbeque – it was April after all and the weather just might be a little kinder. It was to take place on 30 April and its name was Ostara in the Spring Equinox – funny, a picnic with a name. She'd once read an Ostara Festival was to celebrate fertility, a time when everything in Nature was coming alive.

She decided she'd go to the festival – after all, what harm could it do?

"A pity you missed our Yule Festival – it's a good one." The postman handed her a letter and saw the poster in her hand. "At that festival, we sit around all night waiting for sunrise and that's when we're all re-born." His matter-of-fact tone took her by surprise and having dropped the bombshell, he jauntily disappeared down the road to the next address.

'Yes, this certainly was an unusual place,' Marian decided, 'People said the oddest things. She decided to drive into the nearest town and find the library there. She wanted to find out what the Ostara Festival was really about.

She was still checking around the cottage to see if she could find some reference to the dagger – and then she saw it. How could she have missed it? It was fixed to the wall beside the fireplace and hung in a leather holster. It was the blue gem that caught her eye and she carefully lifted out the dagger. It was a rather beautiful object and was probably very old – but then, everything around the place was.

She heard the words clearly floating through the air and accompanied by the gentle sound of a violin in the background, *'Keep this precious dagger alongside the white hood – there is more to follow. You're moving towards your destiny now.'* There was no doubt *about the words – they were obviously intended for her – but who was speaking them? Could it be her mother, although it didn't sound like her – but then, she hadn't seen her for such a long time. And what destiny was she moving towards?*

A friendly librarian in town helped her find the books she needed and she was allowed to book them out – although she wasn't a local. It was that sort of area – trusting – her own library would never have allowed it.

That night she sat down with the books and began reading through them. She looked up the word that had first made her curious – the Ostara Spring Equinox Festival – and sure enough it was an official Druid celebration when prayers were offered to the God of Fertility. It sounded a bit ominous, but was most likely just a day of cake-selling and pint-pulling. A day to enjoy! 'I'll still go,' she said aloud.

Reading on, she learned about other festivals and about the clothes Druids wore – of how their different colours of robes signified their status in Druid society. It was quite an interesting subject but to Marion, it seemed like fantasy, rather than fact. Then she remembered the strange things that were happening around her – and she began to wonder!

When she'd put the dagger in the same drawer as the hood, she thought she noticed a slight change of colour in the cloth, it was now a bit more orangey-pink – just slightly, but noticeable. *What on earth could have affected it so quickly? It might have been being exposed to the air, but maybe she was just tired.*

A week passed and the weather was getting a little kinder. By this time, she'd found her way to the supermarket in town and filled her cupboards with every day essentials, but she still popped down to Mrs William's shop where there was also a little post office. It seemed a good way to become part of the community and Mrs Williams was always up for a chat and a gossip. She now knew that all the twelve cottages in the circle, were occupied by local people – some quite young and some on the far side of sixty or seventy. So, she and John were quite 'the youngsters' living there.

Despite looking, she'd found no other clue as to where the secret hiding places were. Standing at the bedroom window in her mother's room, the sun was low in the sky as the afternoon moved on, when she spotted two figures making their way to the middle of their back garden. The strange thing was, they were dressed in long, flowing robes – one in white and one in blue. They stopped at the great oak tree in the centre and wound their arms around its trunk. *'What on earth were they up to?* The blue figure had been carrying a large, black bag and together, the two began to hang bits and pieces on the branches – branches that were still quite bare, although there were tiny buds of new growth beginning to appear. Like everything else, the tree was wakening up after a long winter and in a few weeks, would proudly produce its own flowers.

She couldn't quite see what they were hanging on the tree, so she planned to go there after they'd gone home. She was sure one was a man and the other, a woman – the taller figure, the man, was dressed in blue and the shorter one was definitely a woman - she was all in white. They seemed to be talking to the tree – but that was just silly – however they certainly were caressing its trunk. What strange folk!

Much later, when they'd gone, she walked down to the tree and was amazed to find the small decorations hanging from the branches, were baby's mittens, baby's bootees and little baby rattles. 'What a strange choice of objects! Then she remembered what she'd recently read about the Ostara Festival. It was the festival to encourage fertility and of course, the first sign of that, was new and re- birth. It all fitted together – *'My God, there really were Druids around.'*

She had sudden, flashing memories come into her mind – memories of when she was young and of some strange behaviour she'd seen then, even by her own mother and father. She hurried back up the garden path as she suddenly felt cold and uneasy. *She thought, 'I can't go on living here – it's not natural.' And yet, part of her felt she had to remain to see what would happen next. It was as though the place had a hold on her. She must have witnessed Druid practices when she was young but hadn't understood what was going on.*

In the kitchen with a cup of hot tea, she picked up one of the books again and began to read. A piece of paper fell from the pages and she stared at it. *She knew it hadn't been there earlier, but who could have hidden it?* It was folded into a complicated shape, which was an eight-sided octagon. There were no words on the outside – just her name 'Marion'.

There was a sudden, sharp tap at the window and she saw John standing outside. He'd made her jump, so he mouthed 'Sorry,' although he didn't look like he was sorry. He came inside and she wasted no time in saying, "Was that you I saw putting baby things on the Oak tree – you were with a woman and were both dressed in coloured robes." She went straight for the jugular.

"I don't know what you mean – I've been in town all day – and why did they look so strange?" He was smiling, but seemed defensive. "Maybe your eyes were playing tricks on you." His excuse sounded lame.

"Oh no, they weren't. There was a man wearing a blue cloak and a woman in white and they hung baby objects on the branches of the tree. The sun was just going down, but I saw them clearly. And what strange things to hang there!" She poured him a cup of tea and refreshed her own cup.

"I don't know what to say Marion – but out of interest, what do you think they were doing?" He'd noticed her opened book on the table, with the word 'Druid' on the cover.

"It made me think of witches and warlocks – of the Occult, and I felt really uncomfortable," she said rather quickly.

"May I press you to be truthful?" She knew now something was afoot and he continued, first picking up the octagonal piece of paper and holding it out to her, "I think you should read this. I take it you've been finding messages hidden about the house – messages meant for just you? I have to admit your mother told me she was planning to do this."

She nodded and began to unfold the paper. There was one word written under each flap. She spread it flat on the table, and read the words aloud. The words were in italics and jet, black ink – only one word under each flap. 'Sun-*Moon- and -Stars-your-only-way-ahead.*'

"What on earth does that mean, John, I'd really like to know? I'm getting pretty tired of all these cryptic clues. All I've found so far is a silly hood and a jewelled dagger. What's that all about?" She felt both scared and exasperated.

His rejoinder to her outburst was, "Come to the Ostara Festival next week and all will be revealed." In the meantime, I want to take you around the cottages in our circle, so you can meet and get to know your neighbours. They're all lovely people, so you have nothing to fear."

Tell me just one thing first – is this all to do with Druidism?" And his silence gave her the answer.

"All you need to know at this point is that Druids are a gentle people who love all living things. We love the sun, the moon and the universe and allow them to control our lives – not so bad, is it? " He crossed to re-fill the kettle, "A hot, sweet drink is what you need." He was quite concerned about how worried and uptight she seemed and discreetly took a small phial from his jacket pocket. Surreptitiously, he put a few drops into her cup. It would calm her down and relax her. He was pleased she'd missed his use of the word 'we' when he spoke of the Druids – it was still too soon.

She went on accusingly, "It was you in the blue cloak, wasn't it? I knew it – I could tell. Are all of you witches and warlocks?" She knew she sounded paranoid, but couldn't help it.

"We're from an ancient culture and we have our own religion and the name we're given by ignoramuses, is cruel and completely untrue. When the sun rises, we worship it and revel in its power, when the earth bursts forth in Spring and the land comes alive again, we glory in its fruitfulness. We say thanks for the food it gives us – we owe so much to Nature and that's just about how devious the Celtic religion is."

"But you dress in queer clothes and chant, don't you? And, I've read you make sacrifices to your Gods – is that right?" She wasn't going to let him get away with just admiring the sun and a few shrubs and trees.

He held out his hand and said, "There's something I want to show you." And she went with him out of curiosity. Now, she was beginning to feel rather drowsy as they wandered off the path and into the woods outside the circle of houses. After two hundred yards, they came to a clearing where trees had obviously not been planted. It was a round piece of ground and had been used for many different purposes through the centuries. The surrounding trees were old and gnarled and yet, from their branches, new growth was beginning to appear.

He sat down on a log and beckoned for her to sit by him. "This is where we meet and join together in praise of all we hold dear. Through time, there have been sacrifices of course, as that was the way of the ancients. But that isn't as common a practice nowadays"

She looked up through the trees, just as the sun was going down and she experienced an incredible feeling of peace and contentment. In fact, her eyes began to close and she felt her head fall forwards. *My God, I feel tired. What's happening to me? Am I in a different world – it feels that way?*

Everything was suddenly black and when she came to, she was lying on the ground and there were voices murmuring around her. She tried to get up but a gentle hand pushed her back. Then she saw them, milling around her – some were in white robes, some in blue and some in brown or black. A strange mixture of colours and shapes. She lay there, listening to their voices.

One white-robed man was speaking, "We must do it – we must find another, or our community will fall apart. Why has she not come to us – we've been promised she would come and it's been a long time now since we've lost our Arch Druid?"

A white-robed figure spoke up – it was a woman this time, "It's the right time for re-birth too, so she should come to us now. She must know we're waiting for her." And she uttered a strange sound, like a loud moan. Some others joined her and their sounds of woe filled the centre of the woods. *'Who on earth were they waiting for – she, whoever she was, must be pretty special.'*

Marion heard a new sound then and realised it was the bleating of a sheep. *'Where had that come from and what were they going to do with it? ' Her mind began to imagine all kinds of things and somehow, she knew what was coming. ' 'Were they going to sacrifice the animal to their God of Re-birth? God, she hoped not. It was the right time of the year and why else had they gathered here and brought an animal? '*

The Green Man has always been our friend and we need him now more than ever. Our leader is lost to us and we have no-one to hold us together. It's been a long time since you took our last leader to personally support you." He repeated his beseech to the Green Man and the others joined his chant, crying for the Green Man to come to them.

He plunged the sharp knife into the sheep's neck and blood spurted onto the ground. Marion was hypnotised, almost comatose, and watched his actions as the blood seeped into the grass and turned the green to brown. Poor animal, one minute alive and the next dead. At least the creature was out of its misery now. The cloaked figures darted forward and dipped their hands into the sheep's warm blood – then held them up to some invisible God.

Through her misty eyes, she saw him! She actually saw the Green Man himself. He came from a break in the trees and stepped into the circle of moaning people, some of whom were already on their knees. Although afraid, she saw he was quite magnificent – very tall and broad shouldered, with lots of green coloured foliage for hair. The hair seemed to twist and turn around his head and fell onto his shoulders and down his arms. He had a swarthy complexion but was not unpleasant to look at – in fact he actually looked benevolent. His great strength was obvious and the people seemed to admire and fear him, both at once.

A deep, gruff voice boomed out of his chest. "There is one amongst you already, who will be your leader. You have no need to wait for the return of the previous Arch Druid, but you will have to be patient until your new leader understands her role in life." He said nothing else, but disappeared into a heavy mist, that carried him upwards into the clouds. He was gone, as suddenly as he'd appeared.

Marion felt a sudden icy chill grab hold of her and she saw the cloaked figures were beginning to walk away. She saw two blue-cloaked figures coming towards her and she blanked out completely, either from fear or exhaustion, she wasn't sure but she was grateful. She knew no more!

She awoke next morning with a splitting headache and desperately needed her coffee pick-me-up. God, she found she' run out of milk, so she dressed quickly and dashed to the shop, where Mrs Williams was standing as usual behind the counter. The woman was serving another customer and she had to wait patiently in the queue.

"What can I get you this fine morning, Marion?" Marian recognised the voice - she'd heard it recently and knew exactly where. Not in the shop but in the woods the previous night. She stared at the elderly woman and asked, "Do you live in one of the cottages in the circle – near mine?"

"I do my dear, for many a year! Why do you ask?" Whilst she was fetching the milk and eggs Marian had asked for, she looked over her shoulder, watching the young woman closely.

"I was just curious, that's all. Were you out last evening, I thought I heard your voice outside my house?" Marion was quite certain where she'd last seen the woman and could still hear that voice moaning and crying that they had no leader. She waited for the woman to reply.

"Why no, my dear – when I got settled in my comfy chair, I stayed in all night, watching television. There was a good documentary on BBC – did you see it?" She held out her hand for the money.

"No, I'm afraid I was otherwise engaged. I actually went for a walk in the woods just outside the cottages, so I missed the programme." She took her groceries and walked home, knowing full well the woman was lying.

Several people nodded their 'Good Mornings' to her and she thought how quickly she'd got to know the locals. 'It was almost as though they were eager to get to know her and she wondered how many of them had been in the woods last night.' But she said nothing.

She decided to visit John before she went home – perhaps she could scrounge a cup of coffee from him – he certainly owed her one.

"Morning Marion, come on in." He was his usual self as he closed the door behind her. His place was much as her own, but he had several deer antlers adorning the walls and several pictures of foxes and badgers.

"Have you enjoyed hunting in the past – it certainly looks like it?" She sat at his kitchen table and propped her groceries on the side.

"Not really. Many of these trophies belonged to my father and his father before him. I'm not really any sort of hunter, but I have lived here all my life and I admit to having changed my surroundings very little. I'm quite comfortable with the family trophies. Coffee?" And he rattled cups and saucers from the cupboard and put some Ginger Nut biscuits on a plate.

"How are you today?" he asked innocently.

She could hardly believe his nonchalant attitude, so she replied. "Not so good actually John – I've got a dreadful headache, mainly from my experiences in the woods last night, I should think."

"I'm sorry, what experiences are those? I didn't know there was anything going on last night." He poured the coffee and pushed hers forward.

"Don't play the naïve innocent with me John – it won't wash! You know exactly what went on there." She stared at him over the rim of the cup. 'God, the coffee was good, she could feel her headache begin to ease. But she fervently hoped there was nothing in it this time – she couldn't face that again!

"I'm sorry Marion, I really don't know what you're talking about. Tell me what happened." As he spoke, a pair of antlers suddenly fell off the wall and onto the stone floor – it was like a sign, reminding them they were never alone. The antler cracked and a piece actually broke right off.

"You've upset my family's trophies." He laughed and reverently laid the broken trophy on the side. "I wish I could help you, I really do, but I know nothing about you, the woods or the Green Man.

"I don't think I mentioned any Green Man John – no, I'm sure I didn't. Look, you as good as told me straight that you're a Druid and I know you wear a blue cloak because you're a writer. I've learned that Druids are colour-coordinated and wear certain colours, according to their skills and strengths."

"My, you've learned a lot, considering you knew nothing when you first arrived here. Been reading it up, have you? If you believe something happened in the woods – something that upset you – tell me what it was and I might be able to explain it. Before you do however, I want to tell you something. I did take you to the wood last night, just to show you where the Ostara Festival will be held, but early on, you seemed to become confused and actually passed out. You just sank onto the ground and lay there"

She grabbed her groceries, gulped the rest of her coffee although it was still hot and left his cottage. She knew she wasn't going to get anywhere with him in that mood. 'So, what was the point in flogging a dead horse?'

She knew she had to make a decision about whether she could stay here in the cottage – or leave and go back to her old life. A few weeks ago, there would have been no question – she would be going back – but something about the place was making her feel this had become her home again and also, an odd feeling that she was needed here. She couldn't explain but that's how she felt.

She hadn't heard her mother's voice since the last time with the violin, but she was sure she was still around the place. She could sense her presence, not an ominous presence but not a loving one either. The relationship she'd shared with her mother had never been a loving one – she had spent all of her young life being constantly criticised and it had affected her badly. And yet, here she was actually thinking of staying for good. She had the option of requesting a transfer from her library to another in this area – she was after all well qualified – but she wasn't quite ready to take that huge step.

She looked in the drawer again, just to make sure nothing unusual had happened. No, everything was as it had been – except the hood was becoming even more discoloured and was almost orange now. 'How strange, something must have affected it before it was put in its box. She closed the drawer and began to wonder about the sun, the moon and the constellations, all of which were supposed to control and decide her life. *'My God, she was beginning to think like a Druid. Enough of that nonsense, she told herself.'*

Back in the town library, she browsed through the other books on Druidism she could find – there were only three of them, but she read them all. It was an interesting subject and unlike what she'd seen in the woods, they seemed to have been – and still were – a reasonably gentle type of people. *'Had she really seen a sheep being killed – or was it the drug John had doped her with?' She no longer was sure!*

The books described them as a strange, very strange people but harmless. They'd first been recognised as early as 300BC, which unfortunately for them, was when the Roman Empire invaded and occupied the country.   Julius Caesar himself actually wrote a book on the Druids whom he'd first come across in Gaul in France – and when he found them here as well, he made a point of ridding the country of the odd culture – a culture for, whatever reason, he didn't trust. In the end, he successfully chased them away – but they'd obviously come back.

Driving home that day, she felt a little more relaxed and found she was actually happy at the thought of going home. Home! She'd used the word and that was obviously how she felt about the place now.

The fly in the ointment was, there was a presence of her mother around the cottage, but that was better than having her actual living there. Now, if that were true, she would really leave the village – no question about it.

She parked the car and waved to Mr and Mrs Thomas, whom she'd chatted with before – a really nice, but again elderly couple, who'd made a point of introducing themselves. 'I wonder if they meet in the woods as well, all dressed in their robes?' She couldn't help smiling at the thought.

She sat on the sofa in front of the fire and sipped a glass of wine. She'd made up her mind to go to the woods the next night for the Ostara Festival and see what that entailed.There was a soft tap on the door and she welcomed John in from the evening chill. She viewed him with a suspicion she couldn't help – she didn't quite trust him, but unfortunately, she did like him. 'Odd how I can feel both?'

She poured a glass of wine and handed it to him. "Don't worry," she smiled, "I haven't doped it, although I think you did put something in my coffee the time you last made it." She could see from the startled look on his face that she'd surprised him. He hadn't expected that! "How did you know?" he blurted out.

"My mother told me. You shouldn't find that difficult to understand, after all Druids believe in reincarnation. She visited me last night – well at least her spirit did - and told me everything I'd seen on that night was all in my imagination. You did that to me John – I saw and heard things that night that were horrific and upsetting. Why did you dope my drink?"

"You were over-wrought and bordering on hysteria. I was only trying to help you." He sipped his wine slowly. He had wanted to be her friend and as he strongly believed in the magic of nature's medicine, the small draught he put in her drink was meant only to calm her. Maybe he'd been a bit heavy handed!

The warmth of the fire made the room very cosy and the two of them sat there in companionable silence. It was odd but she felt she'd known him for a long time and not just the few weeks it had really been.

"If your mother comes to you in your dreams, why haven't you asked her what she wants of you?"

"I wasn't prepared for her – that was the first night she'd come and I just didn't think of it. By the way, how did I get back home after I'd passed out in the woods? I take it none of the things I saw really happened?"

He told her he'd carried her back –there was no alternative. "You're heavier than you look, that I can tell you. And before you ask, it was me who put you to bed – there was nothing else to be done. Will you ever trust me again?"

"I'll reserve judgement on that. Changing the subject, how is your writing coming along? What are you writing just now?" And they chatted on, until the fire dropped so low, that he realised it was time to leave and they agreed to go to the Festival together.

She took her time straightening the room before going upstairs to bed. She'd got into the habit of sensing a feeling of foreboding when it was this time – wondering what or who she'd meet in her sleep. 'If it was in her sleep!' Dreams or reality – they'd begun to merge since she'd come home and bedtime was the worst. Before climbing into bed, she looked into the drawer where she kept the secret clues – the dagger was the same, still beautiful and yet threatening. The hood on the other hand, had changed yet again – she was sure it had. Now, it was a brighter, yet deep orange, quite shiny – it wasn't imagination, of that she was sure. She closed the drawer and thought how strange everything was.

Sleep came easily that night but she woke with a start in the early hours of the morning. The first thing she thought was, 'Where's Dad? Where is he Mummy? I want him.' Then her mother's voice filled her head, "He's gone Marion, you've just got to accept it. He chose to leave us, although we needed him. But others apparently needed him more. He's in a much better place now where he'll be happy." *At the time, she'd thought her mother was trying to be kind – to tell her gently that he had died. But it struck her now that the word 'dead' had never been spoken – even all through the years as she became a teenager. 'I wonder where he went. Did he just leave us and she didn't want to tell me that? Or, did he go someplace else, someplace he couldn't come back from?' With that thought lingering in her mind, she finally went back to sleep and slept late the next morning.*

Out of the kitchen window, she saw the daffodils were almost over – they bloomed for such a short time despite their beauty. They'd still been in bud when she'd first come home and now, they were turning brown, their heads drooping towards the ground. How quickly the Seasons change – it'll soon be summer and the Druids will probably have another odd celebration to mark that.

The postman brought her a letter she'd been waiting for – her library had arranged her transfer to the nearby town, so the decision had been taken out of her hands – she was going to stay here. Part of her was sad, but mostly, she felt relief - now she knew the way forward. She would be busy, arranging to give up her old home and having her bits and pieces brought here, but it had to be done. She couldn't afford to run both places and it would be exciting starting a new job in town, although she had a whole month before that had to happen – plenty of time to sort things out.

She wandered down the garden path towards the Oak tree, whose branches were covered with the buds of new birth. Old Mr Thomas was there, pulling up some weeds

"Hello my dear, and how are you this fine morning?" He was such a nice old man, always happy to see people. He'd obviously lived here a long time, so she asked, "Mr Thomas, did you know my father?" He looked startled at her question and paused before saying, "Why yes, I knew him – Archie used to be a mate of mine, we'd often have a sly cigarette standing right here when the leaves were in full bloom and hid us from prying eyes." He smiled at the thought, "But he was too special to stay here – he had to go on to better things."

She felt her blood run cold. Somehow, she knew he wasn't referring to the Grim Reaper, but to something very different.

"I can just remember him, I was almost seven when he died." After all these years, she could still feel the tears come into her eyes.

"What do you mean, Marion – may I call you Marion – your father didn't die. He was chosen to serve the Green Man himself, an honour if ever there was one. It was at a time when it was known as a Celtic Pagan Festival, but once the Christians stole our beliefs for their own religion, we had to change it to All Hallow's Eve, sometimes called Halloween nowadays. That's when the veil between the living and the dead is at its thinnest and both sides can mingle with the other. Did your mother never tell you how special your father was? Well, I'll be – I'd have been so proud of him!"

Now things were becoming clearer. She'd never felt he had simply died – there was no memory of a funeral or a burial - so none of that had ever happened.

The old man was getting ready to go, but she had to keep him talking, "Can you tell me why my father was so special – why he was chosen by the Green Man and where he is now?"

"I can't answer all your questions, my dear, I'm not clever enough. All I know, is he was a remarkable man, whom everyone turned to in moments of crisis. He helped my wife and I through many disasters – and everyone else in the cottages around here – did you not know he was the Arch Druid, the leader of our community, who conducted all our special ceremonies? Surely, your mother told you that."

His wife appeared at the top of the path, calling for him to come home. "Coffee's ready." The words floated in the breeze and he turned to go, "See you at the Festival tonight – you'll be especially welcome."

'Oh my God, what did he mean by that? Should she feel afraid – or was he just being nice? Yes, that was it! He was just a nice old man, not a Pagan Druid uttering threats. Her imagination was getting out of control!'

In one of her books, it said the most important Druid Festival was 'Samhaim' and that was the All Hallow's Eve Mr Thomas had mentioned. That seemed to be the time when 'big things' took place - but that was still to come.

That day, she decided to empty her mother's closet, cupboards etc. It was something she'd been dreading, but it had to be done. Clothes and shoes, she just bundled together and put them in a black sack – she'd take that to the charity shop in town. The more personal items like jewellery were more difficult, as she could remember her mother wearing some of them, especially some Celtic brooches she'd had. They were unique in design and made from colourful, semi-precious stones – not especially valuable but rather beautiful. There were a few rings as well as necklaces – again, not valuable but obviously precious to her mother. She put some of them back in the drawer where she'd found them and put the rest in a box for the charity shop as well. Strangely, there was no wedding ring and yet she knew her mother had always worn one, even after her husband had left. *'Where was it now?   She decided it didn't really matter in the bigger picture of everything.'*

The wardrobe was empty now and she began to put some of her own things inside, but they only filled a small space as the bulk of her things were still at her old home. There was still a lot of her things back in her old home but she'd have them packed with the furniture and delivered here. She saw the back of the wardrobe was slightly loose at one side, leaving a gap. She'd have to get some tools and fix that.

As good as his word, John turned up at seven o'clock that evening. The ceremony was to begin on the half hour. She had dressed carefully in a cream coloured dress and white box-jacket. Flat white pumps finished off the ensemble and she was ready to go. She thought she looked rather special.

'I must just accept it.' She told herself. 'And act normally.' A fire had been built in the middle of the grounds and some brown and white cloaked people were forming a circle – all sitting on the grass. Marion had to admit they didn't look as though they were planning to sacrifice a sheep - or a person for that matter. There were more 'white cloaks' appearing from amongst the trees and in the end, there were about twenty people

all together. One tall white cloaked Druid seemed to be in charge and he gestured to everyone that they should now join the circle.

The sun had set and the light was fading, but the flames of the fire cast a soft glow on every face. John sat beside her and for a moment, she thought he was going to hold her hand, but he pulled back quickly. *'Maybe she'd imagined it.'* The tall man held up his hands and spoke loudly, "Welcome to all! Thank you for coming to this happy event."

He went on, "This is one of the most important and happiest ceremonies we hold and I am pleased that we will share it together." Marion had no idea who he was, but then there were still some people from the cottages she hadn't met yet.

Two brown-clad figures left the circle and walked towards him. Marion thought they were holding hands but then realised their wrists were actually tied together with a string of beads. John whispered, "They've been hand-fasted, you see – and are soon to be married."

The tall man said, "I call upon our Gods of Nature to bless this couple – the Sun, the Moon, the Stars, the Universe and all living things on the earth. Being Ostara, this is a particularly apt time for a wedding to take place – a time of new and re-birth, a time of joy at the awakening of the first Druid season on earth." He told the man and woman to kneel and hold up their hand-fasted wrists which he untied and allowed the beads to fall to the ground. He spoke to the man first and asked him to make his vows and promises to his intended, after which the woman did the same. Marian thought the things they said were similar to those spoken at normal weddings she'd attended – but then, why shouldn't they? People wanted the same things no matter their culture.

"You must now place the ring on your bride's finger." And when it was done, he placed crowns of flowers on both their heads – needless to say, they were Spring flowers. "I call upon the Gods to bless you and guide you through life according to Druid Law and customs. You are now husband and wife."

The newly-weds re-joined the circle and food and drink appeared as if from nowhere. Someone started to play a flute and then a violin and the night filled with shouts of 'Congratulations' and 'Well Done.' People began mixing and sharing food and Marion found herself with a drink in one hand and some food in the other. The atmosphere was electric and laughter was loud. Suddenly, the night light was gone and only the flames of the fire showed each person's expression. The tallest trees opened up and a path appeared, coming straight into the middle of the circle.

The tall man shouted, "Be still everyone. He comes to bless this ceremony. We are indeed honoured." And a booming sound heralded the magnificent figure of the Green Man – just like the one she'd seen in her dream, the night of the sacrifice. *Now, she doubted it had been a dream.* He wasn't alone this time however – there was a servant dressed in green, by his side. He was an ordinary man – a man, whom Marion thought she recognised. *'But how could she – that was just silly.'* His cloak was a soft silk and his robe swept across the grass silently - a gentle swishing sound as he followed his master.

It was him, although her childhood memory had faded over the years, there was something about him, even with his hood pulled over his head, that took her back to her childhood. All those around her were on their knees, showing how much they honoured the newcomers – even John had dropped to the ground – but Marion still stood exactly where she was.

The Green Man raised his arms and said, "Bless all that's here! Spring is all around us and I wanted to attend your special marriage ceremony. Step forward the bride and groom so I can put my hands on your heads and promise you a wonderful future together." And he did just that – touching both of them as they knelt before him. The man in the green cloak and hood stepped forward and did the same, then he let his gaze move to the young woman who was still on her feet.

He spoke simply, "My daughter! Blood of my blood and the most precious thing I ever had. I begged my Master to let me accompany him, once I learned you'd come home at last. I knew you'd never have come before – not while your mother was still alive. But you're here now and ready to fulfil your destiny." He took her hand and she was amazed at how normal it felt to hold the hand of a person who'd been gone for so many years. The tears began to run down her face and she couldn't find the right words. *'Were there any words in such circumstances? Probably not!'*

"I am only allowed to be here for a short time and must return with my master, but I needed to meet you to tell you something. I've been waiting for you to come for a long time now – but of course, I had to wait 'till you felt you could come home. You have come to take your rightful place in this community. Your mother never saw the point in my culture and was never a Druid, but I inherited the beliefs from my own father and was his direct descendant. I was the Arch Druid to these wonderful people and I loved every minute of it, but I've been waiting for you to hand over the crown. The privileged position can only be passed to a direct descendant – and so, I give it to you now. You see, your mother knew you were to be the next Arch Druid and it was something she'd never wanted. I believe that was the reason she chose to make your young life so miserable – in the hope that you'd leave. She did promise me however that if you ever came home, she'd try prepare you for the inevitable, but then she died so suddenly.

The Green Man was moving towards him – her father's time here was almost over, but he looked at John and said, "She's yours now – to treat like the queen she is, or I'll want to know the reason why." He laughed as he spoke, but John said nothing – he was still in awe of everything that was going on.

Very little to do with the Green Man could be done in silence and there was a sudden clash of thunder. The Green Man enveloped the smaller man in his arms and took him away from the woods. The fire had almost died and the people had drifted off - as Marian and John too made for home, without speaking

She stood by her kitchen door the next week. She hadn't seen any of the Druids since the night of the Festival, but that was because she'd hardly gone outside the cottage. She felt she couldn't trust John again – it seemed he'd known a lot more than he'd told her and had chosen to keep her in the dark. He hadn't even told her she was going to a Druid wedding that night – that would have been easy, yet he chose to keep the ceremony in a shroud of mystery, along with everything else.

He'd tried to see her several times, but she'd refused to answer the door. The last time, he'd actually called out to her,

"We've got to talk Marion, you know that. There's a lot to discuss – and explain." But she wasn't ready – her mind was still confused with Pagans and Druids, with green men and with meeting her dear father again. She was actually afraid of what was to come!

Her phone rang and it was Mr Jenkins, the lawyer she'd met on her first day here. He asked if he could call and see her the next day, or if she'd prefer to call on him.

"I'd rather come to you, if you don't mind – I need to get out of the house, it's been one 'hell of a week, as they say." And so here she was, walking along the main road towards the big house he'd told her about. It was a dark, dank day, not really one for a walk in the country. It was an impressive house and she realised her lawyer must be very comfortable.

A middle-aged woman opened the door, "Yes, can I help you?" Marion explained Mr Jenkins was expecting her and she was shown into the sitting room and offered tea. "Mr Jenkins will be with you shortly." And she left her alone.

Five minutes later, Paul Jenkins arrived, looking less officious this time, as though being at home had taken away some of his 'lawyer' stiffness' – and he wasn't wringing his hands this time either.

"Hello Miss Parker, nice to see you again. How have you been? Mary's just bringing the tea."

"Mr Jenkins, if I were to tell you the truth about how I've been, you'd never believe me, so I won't. I'm all right however and curious as to why you want to see me." Mary delivered a tray of tea and biscuits, making sure she gave Marian a look of 'thorough scrutiny' as she did so. It didn't look like she approved of her employer's visitor.

He poured out both cups and handed one to her, "When your late mother came to see me to draw up her Will, she gave me not one letter for you – but two. You've already got the first and I was instructed to hold the second back, until I was sure you were planning to stay in this area. Can you give me that assurance now – or do you plan to return to your old home?" He waited expectantly, adjusting his glasses which had become steamed up from the heat of the tea – not the most attractive look in the world. It struck her as funny and she couldn't help smiling –

only this man could manage to look awkward and steam up his glasses at the same time!

"Had you asked me that when I first arrived, I would have told you I was returning home as soon as possible – now, I feel rather different. The place – and the cottage have grown on me and I've already made up my mind to stay here. I've even arranged a job transfer to the library in town, so I've already taken the necessary steps." She took one of the biscuits – they were Kit-Kats after all. "Are you able to give me the second letter now?"

"I shall give it to you before you leave but, in the meantime, are you able to stay for a little while and enjoy your tea?"

'Well, I never,' she thought, 'That's a surprise – I didn't expect him to be so normal.'

If she was reading the situation correctly, he was 'coming onto her' as the young people say.

"I would welcome finishing my tea – I'm afraid it's been a rather exhausting time lately." She made herself more comfortable in the big, leather chair and crossed her ankles before surprising even herself by asking. "Are you a local man and may I call you Paul – Mr Jenkins sounds so stuffy?"

He answered 'yes' to both questions and poured them both a second cup. He was much more relaxed than when they'd first met, but she still thought 'he was no oil painting.' Perhaps she wasn't either, the thought jumped into her mind and she sat up straight again and uncrossed her ankles.

She stayed there for an hour and had to admit the time passed more quickly than she'd realised. He gave her an envelope and she could feel a small, hard object inside. "Do you know what's in here?" she asked.

"No, certainly not, but I don't have to be very clever to work out it's a ring – an easy shape to determine. Odd, isn't it that she didn't want you to have it until you'd made up your mind to stay here. I wonder why that was."

She had the same thought, but didn't open the envelope until she'd left his house. *She felt rather bemused at herself as she'd agreed to meet him for dinner in a restaurant in town. 'What was she doing? It was as though something was making the decision for her – she didn't find him attractive, but he was a nice man. Anyway, it was a long time since she'd been invited out for dinner.' And she needed to get away from 'all things Druid' for a while anyway.*

Actually, both she and Paul Jenkins had been wrong about the envelope contents. There was indeed a wedding ring – a plain gold band, but there was also a really tiny key which looked too small for any practical purposes. But that couldn't be or why would she have gone to the trouble of leaving it with the lawyer. *'Another search around the cottage would have to be done, but she'd do it another day when her energy levels were a bit higher.'*

A week later, she shared a delicious meal with Paul Jenkins in a rather nice restaurant in town – an expensive restaurant she was pleased to note. 'Better than a pint in a pub, which is all John had ever offered her.' It soon became a regular date, much to housekeeper Mary's annoyance. They had interests in common and were able to chat on various topics – and of course, the weekly treat of a dinner in town was most acceptable. She had kept a low profile around the cottages lately and hadn't been involved in any further Druid events. She saw John several times working in his garden, but they hadn't spoken for some time now.

On this particular day, she had spent a lot of time searching around her home, looking for a likely lock the key would fit. She had no luck though and felt quite disappointed by her lack of success. Her sleep pattern never quite came back to normal and she sometimes spent parts of the night sitting downstairs, reading the books she'd got into the habit of borrowing from Paul's wonderful library at the big house. He was very happy to allow her to use it and positively encouraged her to do so. In fact, he'd actually asked her if she would like to catalogue his books, which had got into rather a mess over the years. Her knowledge of such things was incredibly useful and he even offered to compensate her for her time. Being practical and sometimes short of cash, she took him up on the offer. Now, they had a friendly-cum-business relationship which suited them both. Romance between them was still a 'no-no', especially on Marion's part.

She had begun her new job, so she had to fit the cataloguing of Paul's books between her working hours. It wasn't hard and she was happy with how busy she'd become. She found she was settling well in the area – on a couple of occasions, she even met a couple of school friends whom she hadn't seen since they were all young. They struck up a friendship again and she visited them in their homes in town – neither of them lived in the hamlet, and especially not in the circle of cottages. As she got to know Melanie and Norma again – she was surprised to learn that they knew of the Pagans and Druids who were supposed to frequent the woods.

Over coffee one morning, Melanie was saying, "We always kept well away from them – they scared us. Did you not know about them when you were at school? I can't believe you lived in one of the cottages and never saw anything odd."

"Well, I didn't – I swear to you. My mother was a domineering woman and she kept me on a tight rope. She didn't mix much with neighbours and didn't allow me to do it either. How did you know about the Druids?"

"Everyone knew about the Druids, except you it seems. Even in the town here, they know about them. In fact, your boyfriend Paul, has probably always known as well. I don't see how he could live where he does and not know."

Norma added, "People just chose to ignore them as they never did any harm. They minded their own business – everyone just thought they were odd and creepy, believing in all those daft things. Do you know, they claim they can turn themselves into animals at certain times of the year – you know, like foxes or badgers? "

Marion was surprised to hear herself begin to defend them, "They're just like you and me – ordinary folk, who have some weird habits. Haven't we all? I've been to one of their ceremonies – and yes, they're pretty surreal but they keep their strangeness amongst their own. And I don't think Paul Jenkins can know of their existence." *'Why was she defending them? My God, did she feel an affinity with them?'*

"Well, next time you're invited to one of their festivals, let us know – we'd like a good laugh." Marion remembered now why she hadn't bothered with these women when they were girls. She hadn't liked them then and she didn't like them now. She said goodbye and left them in the café. *They weren't her kind of*

*people.' she decided, 'Did that mean the Druids were? Good
God, surely not.'*

Summer was in full bloom and she and Paul decided to go on
a cycle ride into the countryside. He had asked Mary to make
them a picnic lunch, which she reluctantly did. The Bluebells in
the wooded areas were passing now and the Poppies were
appearing in the fields. It was a lovely sunny day and the breeze
was gentle, keeping them cool as they cycled along. They didn't
go near 'the special woods' but stuck to the open countryside
where they soon found a lovely spot – with no cows or bulls.
Paul spread the food on a tablecloth and Marion stretched her
legs and enjoyed the warmth of the sun.

She leaned on one elbow and asked him outright, "Paul, have
you always known about the Druids and their ceremonies – about
their priests in white and their scholars in blue? My friends from
school were saying you had to know, considering how close you
live to where they meet." She waited for him to speak.

"I've always known about them, but they don't bother me, so
why should I bother them? At certain times, Mary has attended
their meetings – she has a certain sympathy for them. Why do
you ask about this just now – you've never mentioned the Druids
before?"

"I'm sorry, I don't mean to pry but I've experienced some
strange things since coming to the cottage – a bit surreal – in fact,
very surreal." She nibbled a sandwich as she spoke and he
offered her some cold milk.

"I don't mind talking about them, but that's all I want to do –
I have no wish to attend their meetings – or go to their seasonal
festivals, where I'm told 'strange things.' take place.

Perhaps now's the time to make it clear – I'm a regular,
normal Christian chap, no frills attached. I attend the C of E
church in the next town almost every Sunday and that's as
religious as I get." He paused as though considering whether he
should say more and then added, "I do know about your father
Marion and how he was the Arch Druid for the 'Village
Community of Druids' – your mother told me all about it, even
how you would be in line to inherit his role, being his only
descendant. So, you see, I do understand the strange world
you've found yourself in. She told me that was the reason she

370

chose to treat you so harshly when you were young – so that you'd want to leave home and have a life elsewhere. She didn't want you to be swallowed up by Druidism, especially the leading role with such an all-consuming responsibility. She did want you to come home, but that was because she wanted you to meet me – she thought you and I might get along very well together. Hence, the gift of the wedding ring left with me – it was supposed to spurn me on to propose to you, but I haven't found the right moment yet."

There, he'd told her at last, something he'd been suppressing for some time. He felt relieved too, as his confession might mean she now understood at last, why her mother had treated her so severely. She'd actually loved her daughter very much she'd said and had chosen to sacrifice her own happiness to set her daughter free. She'd told him that once – exactly in those words. He'd also managed to raise the subject of marriage at last, something he'd been meaning to do since he'd first met her.

Suddenly, they both heard a strange sound coming from the nearby hedge. The sound developed into a deep growl - an amazing sound in the usually quiet countryside. Paul quickly gathered the picnic into the tablecloth. He had no idea what was concealed in the hedge but it didn't sound too friendly. Marion stared towards the sound and saw two dark staring eyes glittering from the greenery. *'What on earth was it? A creature of some sort, but what? What kind of animal would threaten people like this?'*

Paul gestured that she should get up, it was time to move – fast. Before they could, the hedge pulled slowly apart and a head appeared – a rather beautiful head – the head of a fox. He was a handsome chap, golden brown in colour with bright highlights shining in the sun – but his jaws didn't look beautiful at all and they'd fallen apart to show sharp, white teeth. He wasn't smiling but rather grimacing and there was no doubt he was not their friend. He looked as if he was going to attack and moved forward, his belly slunk low and almost touching the ground. An ominous sight indeed. He stared at them very intently and then suddenly but slowly turned away and almost crawled along the line of the hedge, his bushy tail dragging along the ground. A few yards away, he again disappeared into the hedges and was lost from sight.

"Come along quickly Marian, we have to go. He might come back." And that's what they did, grabbing their bikes and disappearing as fast as they could along the lane towards the big house.

A couple of stiff whiskies later, they sat side by side in the sitting room. Mary had brought them the whiskies, having seen how distraught they both were. She didn't know what had happened but it had obviously shaken them up. She came in again, this time carrying a tray of sweet, hot chocolate drinks – Marion especially looked as if she needed something hot, as she was definitely shivering and it might have been with fear.

Mary did something unprecedented then and sat down in an armchair. She hadn't been invited to do so, but she was aware something bad had happened. She'd been his housekeeper for many years but was also his friend and could clearly see he'd had some sort of scare. "Tell me about it – what on earth has upset you like this? It's best to talk about it – it always helps."

Marian and Paul looked at each other. Neither wished to be the first to speak. The sighting of a fox didn't sound like much and therefore they were a bit embarrassed at their reactions. But it was not just any fox, it was the threat it posed and the evil in its eyes - and its horrible growl. It had intended them no good and so, they told the housekeeper about it.

"It was much more than just a fox, I mean we've all seen a fox before, but this particular fox with its threatening gaze, obviously had a message for us." He knew it sounded silly but she'd asked, hadn't she?

"That was no ordinary fox," Mary said, "That was a special one and it did have a message for you – for you both." She searched her memory for all she'd learned from her Druid knowledge. "What were you talking about just before it appeared?"

The time for privacy and diplomacy was over. He'd always known about Mary's interest in Druidism and he knew too of her quite obvious dislike of Marion. He said, "We were discussing her father's involvement and leadership of the local Druid community and I told her I was hoping she'd not accept her inheritance of the role of Arch Druid. That's the truth Mary, but what does that have to do with the fox?"

"That fox was warning you to keep out of Marion's business – she should be allowed to decide for herself whether she wants to be involved with the Druids. The fox was a Druid priest who'd turned himself into a wild animal to scare you into understanding. It was definitely a warning!"

Marion stood up and said, "I'm going home now, it's all become too much for me." She said nothing more, but left the house quickly.   Paul didn't try to stop her – it wasn't the right time. She had to have time to herself now – to consider her future.

Over the next few weeks, she went to work on most days. She missed her cataloguing duties at the big house which had really absorbed her, but it couldn't be helped. To fill the hours, she threw herself into re-decorating the cottage and enjoyed choosing different colours for the rooms. Indeed, the new décor encouraged her to change the furniture, the drapes, the carpets – in fact everything, except some small ornaments so obviously loved by her mother. Whilst doing all this, she used the changes to search for where the tiny key would fit. She knew now the ring was meant to encourage her to remain in the area and hopefully to marry Paul Jenkins, but what was the point of the key? It was an enigma!

John tried to speak with her more than once on the phone but she still wasn't sure how much she could trust him and told him she wasn't yet ready to see him. *'Had he been the fox?' Could she trust him?*

She hadn't been invited to any other Druid events, although she knew there'd be an important one when Summer finally arrived. The next and most important was when the dead were allowed to mix with the living, both sides coming together - spiritual and earthly people mixing together once more.

She also kept Paul at arms' length as she didn't want him to put pressure on her about marriage. *She often thought however, 'I could do a lot worse than marry the man in the grand house and the bottomless pockets, but do I love him? Do I need to love him – I like him and surely that would be enough.' It was a pity she'd decided to give her old school friends the cold shoulder – she could have done with someone her own age to talk with.*

In the village shop, Mrs Williams was pleased to see her come in the shop, "Why Hello my dear, how nice to see you. How have you been?" Marion looked at her and tried to imagine her in her Druid robes, wondering what colour she was allowed to wear. 'Probably white, she decided.' One thing she did admire about the Druid culture was that women and men were treated equally, one being regarded as important as the other.

There was one cane-backed chair by the counter, kept there for anyone who needed a little rest - or an excuse to gossip. She plonked herself down and asked Mrs Williams a direct question,

"Mrs Williams, you are a Druid, aren't you? I thought I saw you there on the night of the Ostara Festival - I did see you, didn't I? You were in white, weren't you?"

"I don't have a problem admitting that, I am a member of the Druid community and like to worship all aspects of nature, including the passing seasons and the stars and planets that guide them." She'd obviously used this speech before. "But what makes you ask the question now?" She'd sat down on her own chair on the other side of the counter.

"I just need someone to talk to, I suppose. It's very lonely up there at the cottage. It's lonely and yet sometimes, the atmosphere is strangely suffocating. I imagine my mother is there. You knew her, didn't you?"

"I did that – she was a fine woman. She wasn't one of us though – she didn't warm to Druidism and so, we left her to her own interests. She knew if she ever needed anything, we'd be there for her. Your father now, he was quite a different kettle of fish – and I liked him. I respected him too, you know – well I would, wouldn't I, he was the Arch Druid after all?"

"Sometimes I hear her playing the violin, you know. It's always gentle music and not at all scary, but I do wonder if she's trying to tell me something. I don't know how to find out what she wants to say."

Mrs Williams invited herself to Marion's home. "Let me come to your home and see if I can contact her. Although not a Druid, she was a friend and she would often sit just where you are right now, and we'd chew the cud between us. It did us both good."

She visited Marian that evening and told her how much she loved her new décor and furniture. "You've really changed the place, haven't you?" She settled on the plush sofa and asked for something that had belonged to Marion's mother.

A small padded pin cushion of red velvet was placed in her hands and she smoothed the soft cloth gently.

"Can you leave me alone for a while – perhaps you can make us some tea? I need to soak up the atmosphere and search for a wandering spirit. Spirits will soon be allowed to freely wander the earth, you know – All Hallow's Eve is only a week away." Marian did as she was asked and took her time preparing a tray. She mustn't rush Mrs Williams.

Standing in the kitchen, waiting for the kettle to boil, she looked out of the window and saw a pair of torch lights weaving their way down the garden path towards the old Oak tree.

'Now, who could that be at this time of night?' she wondered. She stepped out of the back door and saw it was John and another man. 'They're probably going to hang some stupid bits and pieces on the tree. I wonder what they'll hang to symbolise the dead walking. Well, it's nothing to do with me.' She completed her hospitality tray and returned to the sitting room. As she went into the room, she could hear the soft, violin music filling the air. Mrs Williams had fallen asleep on the sofa and her head was resting back against the cushion. She still held the pin cushion in her hand.

Quietly, she put down the tray and sat in a chair. If she woke the woman, she might scare her, so she decided to wait until she came back into the room. She allowed her own head to sink into the deep chair, it was so peaceful in the room and the music wasn't in the least scary. She was soon asleep and found she was a little girl again, playing with her dolls in front of the fire.

Her mother said, "Not too close to the fire Marion – you'll burn yourself." She was busily knitting. Marion remembered that jumper she'd made for her – it had been one of her favourites.

"Oh Mama – don't fuss, I'm quite safe. Papa lets me sit here." Marion the child spoke petulantly and moved just a little closer to the hearth.

Her mother's ball of wool dropped and rolled across the carpet. Marion moved quickly to catch it and returned it. In her mother's knitting basket, she spotted a tiny key that shone in the firelight. "What's that key for Mama, I've never seen it before?"

"Never you mind Miss, you're too nosey for your own good. It's my key, that's all you need to know."

Before the child could say more, Mrs Williams woke up and sat bolt upright. She and adult Marian were back in the room. The music was still playing and Mrs Williams reached for her cup of tea.

"It must have been the music – I thought I'd just close my eyes for a second and suddenly I was gone. Did your mother visit you as well? She did come to see me, you know." And she placed the pin cushion back on the table. "She's asked me to pass on a message to you – although why she couldn't tell you herself, I'll never know. She says it's time you made up your mind – if you don't marry soon, you'll probably not be able to have a child and she wants to see her grandchild before she finally has to leave this earth."

Marian was astounded. She hadn't expected that. 'A bit cheeky!' she thought and then found she had to smile. "And has she already chosen a husband for me?"

"Oh, there's no doubt in her mind about that. She chose the lawyer, Paul Jenkins for you a long time ago. She says she knows you have a soft spot for John Reynolds two doors along, but she thinks Paul is more suitable. Have you got any biscuits my dear, I find communing with the dead can be quite tiring, and I need some sugar?"

Before she left, Marion asked if her mother had mentioned the tiny key she'd left with Paul? "I've searched the house from top to bottom and can find nothing." she explained.

"Nothing to report on that, I'm afraid."And that was their first evening together – the first of many as it would turn out – Marian and the shop lady became quite close friends in the end.

The following week, she'd just finished work at the library, when she found Paul waiting on the doorstep. His office was in the same town so he hadn't come far. It was October though and the night quite chilly – in fact, he looked frozen half to death.

Why Paul, I wasn't expecting to find you here. Is anything wrong?" She was taken-aback by his sudden appearance and perhaps she wasn't as welcoming as she might have been.

"I need to talk to you Marian. Can we have a drink – there's a decent pub just around the corner."

At first, she was going to say no, but his face had such a sad expression, she couldn't do it. "Why yes Paul, that would be nice." And soon they were sitting in a booth of once-plush chairs, but now covered in worn patches. There were two Gin and Tonics placed on a chipped, marble table by a waitress – the table looked as though it had come from Ancient Greece. Not the most salubrious surroundings and certainly not a 'decent pub.'!

"I've waited for as long as I can Marion, I need to know your answer. Will you marry me and come to live in my big, lonely house? You know, it's something your mother always wanted." He came straight to the point.

"Oh yes, she always wanted to have things the way she wanted." Marion couldn't keep the bitterness from her voice. She knew she didn't love him, but she did like him. He'd always been kind to her and she knew he'd probably take good care of her. She thought quickly, 'What else do I have? A lonely cottage that sometimes gives me the creeps – and one man of my own age, who's never really shown me any sign of love? One time he seems interested and another, he keeps well away.

She looked at his pleading face and thought, 'He really does love me.' Maybe he'd make a good husband and she was certainly no Spring chicken. If she wanted to have a family of her own, she was fast running out of time.

And so, perhaps for the wrong reason, she held up her glass as though to make a toast and said,

"I will marry you Paul but not because I'm in love with you, but because you're a kind and decent man and I should be grateful for your interest. I'll do my utmost to make you happy – I know I'm being blunt but I want to be honest, or there'd be no good basis for a marriage."

Paul heard the words and understood what she was saying, but he loved her enough for both of them and he was delighted with her promise. "Thank you, Marion, I'll take good care of you, I promise."

And the evening ended then. They separated and went their separate ways – one full of hopeful expectation, the other worried that she was doing the right thing. But it was done and she knew she would keep her word. Sitting before the fire, she wondered what John would make of the news. She really thought there was something between them at one time, but that time had passed now and nothing had changed. She poured herself a Sherry and leaned back against the sofa and for no reason whatsoever, began to cry. Great, sad tears ran down her face and she didn't know why.

Another thing she didn't know was that Paul hadn't yet reached his own home. He'd reached his car with a spring in his step and a very excited feeling in his chest. It was dark and the rain was coming down heavily. One of his windscreen wipers had been broken off, probably by some juvenile delinquent who grudged him his nice car. The vision ahead wasn't great and he had to peer into the blackness and use some guess work to determine the tricky country bends in the road.

He had a couple of scares and was relieved he didn't have too far to go now. He hoped Marion's drive had been better than his – at least she'd have working windscreen wipers. The bend ahead came up faster than he'd anticipated and he stiffened. There in the middle of his path sat a large fox, who's glittering eyes shone in the car's headlights. It didn't move and he slammed on his breaks, swerving to avoid hitting it. He couldn't move quickly enough and crashed into the still figure, the car continuing at speed into a muddy skid. He'd completely lost control and crashed into a tree at the side of the road – it was a large Oak tree and he hit it at speed, the car turning over onto its side. Paul's head smashed against the side window and went right through it. He was dead before he knew it and suddenly everything in the lane was still, except for the sound of heavy rain on the mangled heap of a car. Ironically, the last thing to stop working was the one windscreen wiper. Paul had died before it had.

Of course, the fox had long gone – if it ever had been there. It certainly hadn't been hit. He'd believed he'd ploughed into it, but there was no trace of a body in the road. 'Had' *it been a fox or perhaps a spiritual manifestation of a Druid priest – a priest who wasn't happy about Paul and Marians' recent engagement?'* 'Had Paul been allowed to answer this question, he would have said emphatically, "Of course it was a fox – not this stupid Druid business again!" He'd never really believed his housekeeper's claims.

It was two days later before Marian heard what had happened. It was Mrs Williams at the shop who told her. She'd gone there for some bread and milk and had gone into the shop feeling happy and for the first time in her life, actually looking forward to the day ahead. She'd come around to Paul's way of thinking.

On hearing the news, she fell – rather than sat – on to the chair by the counter. She'd gone ashen white and couldn't speak. Her friend fetched her a glass of water. She didn't know what else to do – she hadn't realised the lawyer had been such a friend of Marian's.

Had she known, she'd have broken the news in a gentler way. But, the deed was done now and she busied herself tidying the counter, waiting for the young woman to pull herself together.

As luck would have it, John MacDonald chose that moment to come into the shop. He was shocked by the sight that met him and he looked quizzically at Mrs Williams, one eyebrow raised in question.

"She's had a bit of a shock John – will you be able to take her home? I can't leave the shop or I'd do it myself." She put Marion's bread and milk into a carrier bag and handed it to him. "Can I get something for you?"

He told her he'd come back later and took hold of Marion's arm. She went with him although she didn't really know what she was doing. He walked with her to her front door, "May I come in Marion, I'd like to make you a cup of tea – hot, sweet tea." And she nodded, still saying nothing. The hot drink made her aware of her surroundings and she looked at John.

"How could it have happened, John? It wasn't even a long distance. How on earth did he lose control?" She automatically assumed he knew what she was talking about – which of course, he did – news in such a small place got around fast.

"It was a pretty bad night – the rain was torrential and the roads slippery, he must have misjudged the bend. It's always been known as a tricky turn." He knew very little about what had actually happened – but apparently, Paul had died immediately, hopefully without knowing anything." He sat beside her and made to take one of her hands, but she pulled it away sharply.

"Please don't do that John. Did you know Paul and I had just agreed to marry – on the very night he died?" she asked.

"How could I have known that? But now I understand why you're so upset. I'm truly sorry for your loss." There was little else he could do for her and he was shocked by her news. He asked, "Will you be all right if I go now – perhaps a little sleep will help?" He stood up.

"Of course, you must go. Thank you for seeing me home. It was kind." She did feel suddenly very tired and decided just resting in bed might help.

At the door, he turned, "Marion, I don't know whether you know, but when someone has lost a person they were close to, they visit the old Oak tree in the middle of the gardens. If there's anyone they knew who's recently passed over– sometimes it helps to visit the tree and say how much they're missed - a card cut in the shape of a star should be hung on the Oak's branches. It should have their name on it and a message meant just for them. It might be something you'd like to do – I know, from experience it can help."

He closed the door behind him before Marion could say anything. It sounded like a Druid practice to her, but she might actually do it. In a way, it wasn't only Paul she mourned, it was her parents as well – her father might as well be dead, he was to her!

She did sleep the afternoon away and felt a little better when she woke up. She fetched some card, scissors and string – and cut out three star-shaped discs. She searched in her bag for a pen and also came across 'the little mystery key'. She promised herself she'd search for its lock just one more time and failing that, she'd throw it away. 'And yet, why did mother take the trouble to leave it with her wedding ring? As Alice in Wonderland said, 'Curiouser and Curiouser.' She wrote her mother and fathers' name on two cards and then Paul Jenkins on the third. Even if it did no good, it could do no harm! Then she heard it, soft and gentle, but clear as a bell. The violin music floated through the room and she knew her mother was near. *'Maybe I'm imagining things because I've just written her name.* Despite the cold, something made her get up and open the windows – she looked down the garden and saw old Mr and Mrs Thomas standing by the Oak tree. She took the cards, put on her coat and walked down the path towards the tree. She liked the couple and for whatever reason, trusted them. She knew they were both practising Druids but she suddenly felt the need to talk to them.

"Hello Marion Parker and how are you this fine, cold day?" He always had a twinkle in his eye that showed he was happy to see her. "We're just hanging our Star Wishes on this ancient tree – it's for our daughter. She died when she was young and we hang a card every All Hallow's Eve to let her know we're still thinking of her – and missing her. She's happy though, we know that, she's with our family who've gone on before."

Mrs Thomas interrupted her husband, "Let the girl do what she's come for Henry – don't you see she has some cards of her own? Here's an empty branch, just waiting for you." Like her husband, she seemed a warm, friendly person with a loving heart.

As she hung the cards on the tree, she couldn't stop herself from saying, "I know it's probably silly, but what harm can it do?"

Mr Thomas bristled and said, "There's nothing silly about it. You'll feel better once you've done it and within a couple of days, you'll see your lost ones – just once – but for long enough for them to reassure you they're happy. You mustn't mock what you don't understand, my dear." And he beckoned his wife to follow him and the old lady gently touched Marion's arm, "We're off to the warmth of the fireside now. We're old but we've lived long enough to know 'There's many a thing 'twixt Heaven and Earth that we don't understand.'" And the two of them, arm in arm, walked back up the path. She'd made her point although she may have mis-quoted Shakespeare's famous lines – but her meaning was clear. She believed the Star cards were worth doing!

The next night was All Hallow's Eve, or Halloween as she'd always thought of it. This was apparently the time when the dead could walk amongst the living – at least that's what she'd been told. Following American culture, it had become a 'Trick & Treat' night when children performed at people's doors, in the hope they'd have masses of sweets thrust upon them. However, should the people decide not to reward them with sweets, they'd have to face the consequences of toilet rolls thrown at their doors.

To the Druid religion however, it was a much more serious occasion. 'Would she go to the woods tonight? No, she told herself although it couldn't be creepier than staying alone in the cottage after everything that had happened. That decided her and shaking her chestnut curls in defiance, she grabbed her coat and walked down the lane. *'There's no need to be afraid.' She told herself, she'd know many of the people who'd be there.'*

It was a dark night without a threat of rain, and in the sky above the trees, she could see the sparks from a fire and quite a big fire it seemed. Around the circle, were many candles burning on iron tripods and most of the people had already gathered in a circle around the great bonfire, whose flames were now reaching high towards the stars.

White and blue clad figures dominated the crowd, but there were also brown and black robes as well. She'd learned those in white were priests who acted as judges and lawyers in their everyday activities - and they were very respected. The blue figures were scholars and artisans – people who were creative and intellectual, with some others being writers and teachers. John was one of those. The brown and black robed people were merely ordinary folk who acted as servants to the others. Despite their concealing white robes, Marion identified Mr and Mrs Thomas' plump figures – and felt reassured at seeing them there.

Marion of course, wore no such robes as she had not yet made up her mind about joining the community. She did notice however, there was no gold-robed Arch Druid – it seemed the position was still vacant. What surprised her more than anything was that some of them wore masks and even false, animal heads. With the bonfire and candles, the scene quite took her breath away and she looked around for John. Perhaps she'd welcome his company after all. On this occasion, she definitely saw two of the priests sacrifice a small pig. They'd had to chase it first, as though it knew what was coming, but at least they ended its life humanely, by holding an ether-filled rag over its mouth - before slitting its throat. Thankfully, there seemed no 'other' acts of barbarism planned that night.   Strong cider appeared as if from nowhere, accompanied by mounds of bread and several types of cheese. There was laughter and some dancing within the circle – and of course, a lot of singing. Strangely enough, there was no appearance of the Green Man himself yet and Marion found herself wondering if he'd even been real. In her head however, she knew he had!

The candles were burning low and the servants replaced them with fresh ones. The candles were an important part of the whole thing, as they apparently kept away evil spirits who could be lurking amongst the trees. There was a commotion just outside the circle and everyone moved to that spot. Several ethereal, wistful figures were appearing from a misty cloud and suddenly the light from the full moon added to the mysterious atmosphere. The shadowy figures moved forward and people began to recognise their departed relatives and friends. So, the star shaped cards on the Oak tree really did work.

John moved to her side and pointed out his mother and father, who seemed contented enough. They were smiling at their son and he blew them a kiss. No-one was allowed to touch any of the visitors as that would serve to damage their spirits.

Then she saw them. There was no doubt, it was her mother and father. They looked exactly as they had when she was young, except for their different skin tones, which wasn't too surprising, as one had actually passed over whilst the other still had a half-way life, being the Green Man's right-hand man. Her father was the first to raise his hand in recognition and then her mother did the same. They actually looked happier than she ever remembered them being and she copied John, and blew them a kiss.

Standing just behind them was Paul Jenkins, who looked well and fit and considering his tragic accident, reasonably content. He didn't look happy exactly – just content. Anyway, if anyone had the right to look fed up, it was him. She smiled at her old friend and he did the same. He mouthed the words, 'I miss you,' and she mouthed the same words to him.

Then, it was all over and the grey mist slowly disappeared into the night sky. The Druids settled back around the fire and John took his place beside Marion. She didn't object, so he took her hand – and she didn't pull away this time.

The next weeks and even the months passed – Christmas came and went. It was the first Christmas she'd spent in the cottage and it had been a quiet one. She'd stopped hearing the violin and the secret, hidden messages were no more. Everyone was apparently at peace now – and she knew the atmosphere in her home was much lighter. The mystery of the tiny key remained however, only now, it seemed to mover around the rooms and she never knew where she'd find it next.one thing that refused to change was the mystery of the tiny key. It seemed to move about the house of its own accord, but she could live with that, it wasn't a great problem.

And now she'd struck up a relationship with John MacDonald again, things were moving on nicely – slowly but nicely. She still suspected he'd been the fox who'd caused Paul's accident – but she could never prove it, so she decided to let it lie.

There was a loud knock at the door one afternoon and she found a stranger on her doorstep. She didn't know the man, but he was well dressed and carried a briefcase, so she invited him inside.

"May I help you?" she asked him politely, wondering, 'Whatever next?'

"I've come from town to see you, Miss Parker – I have some information for you which will be to your benefit. My name is Giles Thomson and Paul Jenkins was my colleague. We worked together in our shared chambers.'"

She fetched some tea and when she returned to the room, he was still sitting exactly where she'd left him. He must have been about seventy years old and looked exactly as a lawyer should look – very straight-backed and with a serious expression.

"I have been appointed as Paul Jenkins' Executor and sorting out his affairs has taken a little longer than I'd expected – he died unexpectedly, as you know and was still a young man. He thought he had plenty of time to put things in order, but then the unexpected happened.I'm sure you're aware of how he died – a cruel and evil twist of fate. He paused before opening his rather old and quite tatty briefcase.

"Paul had no relatives and having checked his family history, I am able to confirm there are no descendants. Therefore, I should tell you he has appointed you as his sole beneficiary."

Marion covered her mouth with her hand. She couldn't speak – she hadn't expected such a thing. She began to cry and found she couldn't stop the tears – in fact, it was a relief as she'd been keeping her distress to herself.

"Oh Paul, you actually thought of me in such a way?" She spoke as if Paul could hear her, "You may understand better when I tell you, that just before he was killed, we'd become engaged to be married." Telling him this, made more sense of his kind gesture towards her.

"What exactly has he left me?" She had to ask, then realised the question might sound greedy. "I'm sorry – that sounds a very mercenary question – I'm still in shock, I think."

"I have a copy of the Will for you, but in a nutshell, his beautiful home and all its contents are now yours. There is also a significant sum of money, which should make the rest of your life reasonably comfortable."

She heard him speak but thought she'd mis-heard the amount of money Paul had left her, *'It couldn't be that much. How could he have saved so much money?'* She asked him to say it again and when he did, she thought her head was going to explode. It was a life-changing amount! His love for her couldn't be denied and she suddenly felt sorry she'd told him she couldn't return that love.,

John visited her next day to say, "The Ostara Festival will be coming up soon, Marion – what do you say if we use it to marry? Priest David will conduct the service and all our acquaintances can help us celebrate."

She liked him and knew she was just a little in love with him and as she'd told herself before, she wasn't getting any younger. "Yes, I'll marry you John – we're both past the 'normal' age for a first wedding, so let's just get on with it."

She suggested they live in the big house as all the legal papers had been sorted out and it would be silly to hang onto two cottages, now the big house was available. In a week's time, she would be Mrs John Reynolds – that would take a bit of getting used to.

That evening, she was going through a catalogue, looking at formal dresses. Although she knew she'd have to wear a robe for the ceremony, a brand-new wedding dress was a 'must' for after the ceremony. She'd almost made up her mind, when an almighty crash made her jump to her feet. It had come from the kitchen and when she rushed through, she found a large rock lying on the floor, surrounded by shattered glass. It had come through the window and she could feel the cold draught. *'Who would have done something like that?'* She didn't have any *enemies, or so she thought. She racked her mind but couldn't think of anyone who'd do something like this.*

The rock was wrapped in a piece of paper and on the paper were the words:

'

To the Bitch in the Cottage

You took all he had, even his life – but you'll pay for your selfishness one day. I'll make sure you do.

From One Who Wishes You Only Bad Things

She sat at the table, paper in hand and knew exactly who had thrown the rock. It had to be Mary, Paul's housekeeper. She'd never liked Marion and resented her visits to the big house. *She wondered, 'What on earth was she thinking though? Why does she hate me so much? ' But she knew the answer really – she'd wanted Paul for herself.' She was almost twenty years older than he was, but what did that matter when you loved someone?*

She knew the lawyer had told Mary she must leave the big house as there was no longer a job there. It was like leaving her own home where she'd looked after Paul for almost ten years. No-one had been prepared for what happened to him, but Mary must have been absolutely devastated. She'd lost not only the man she'd loved, but her home as well.

She rang John and asked if he was any good at repairing broken windows.

"You should report this to the police, you know. She can't be allowed to do such things – you never know what she might do next. A word from the police would put a stop to her madness." He was both angry and worried.

"Why does she blame you for Paul Jenkin's death – you had nothing to do with it. The woman's obviously deranged." Marion realised he would never understand the frustration felt by a woman in Mary's position.

"Let it go John, maybe she's done her worst." He nailed a wooden board to the frame until a glazier could come with new glass. As he was about to come indoors, he noticed a fire burning down by the old Oak tree and set off down the path to investigate "I'll be back in a second Marion – I'll just see what this fire's about."

It wasn't a big fire, but enough to light up the sky. There seemed to be no-one around and he began throwing earth on the flames. Then he spotted the figure slumped just behind the trunk of the tree. Mary lay in a heap on the ground - she looked pitiful lying there with her plaid scarf hanging loose from her neck and her coat buttoned up wrongly. It made her look even more tragic.

He phoned for the police before he told Marion what he'd found in the garden. She was already shaken by the window incident and he thought seeing Mary's sad body would take her closer to the edge. The police found a bottle of pills lying on the ground beside the dead woman – it was empty now, she'd taken them all. The police surgeon said later that she'd taken enough pills to kill an elephant. In her handbag, there was a letter, which she'd placed neatly into an envelope and written on the front, 'To Whom it May Concern.' In it, she accused Marion of forcing her to take the pills – at the point of a sharp knife, in fact a dagger. She also wrote how Marion had hated her and blamed her again for Paul Jenkin's death. She'd tried very hard to point the finger of blame on the woman she hated.

The police of course, had to investigate her claims, ridiculous though they were. It was easy to discredit Mary's claims and so, Marion had no case to answer.

"But why did she choose to die at the Oak tree– what significance did the tree have for her?" Marion asked John, as she sat in her sitting room, which she hadn't left for three days. "Has all this happened because I came home – everything bad that's happened seems to have something to do with me. Paul Jenkins dying in a freak accident and now his housekeeper who hated me so much, she took her own life."

"You're just being ridiculous – these things happened to you and not because of you. You didn't want either of them to die, why would you?" He tried to comfort her.

"But I did gain so much from Paul's death and that must have upset Mary, I'm a very rich woman now and I own a beautiful house - almost a mansion. I'd say I benefitted from Paul's death – but not from Mary's suicide, that was all down to her."

On Sunday, it'll be the Ostara Festival again– the time for new and re-birth. We're going to be married – and put all of this behind us. Okay? We'll start a new, shared life together – a better life than you could imagine."

The plan was set and soon Marion, who'd thought she was destined to be a spinster, would be a married lady and if John agreed, she'd use her mother's wedding ring for the service. That night, as she was getting ready for bed, her bare foot touched something cold and hard and when she looked down, it was the tiny key on the floor, lying in front of the wardrobe. 'Where will I find this next time?' she smiled and bent down to pick it up. Someone was really trying to tell her something. The key had been in every room in the house!

Exasperated, she looked inside the wardrobe again and this time pushed all her clothes right to one side. She remembered the loose back panel that she'd never got around to repairing and she knelt down to see inside more clearly.

This time, she gingerly touched a piece of jagged wood and discovered a very small lock at one side. Now, she knew what such a small key was meant for. Lying flat on her stomach, she used the key. It worked! She'd obviously been meant to find the lock earlier, but of course, she never had. The back wall of the wardrobe swung slowly open and she realised it had a hidden compartment beside a false wall. What would she find inside?

Whatever was hidden there, it was bright and shiny. She could see the shining glint quite clearly and when she stood up again, she reached deep inside and touched it. It was the most beautiful thing she'd ever seen. It was a long, flowing robe made from a sparkling gold material - its skirt fell in folds all the way to the floor. She knew immediately what it was and it scared her. In his day, her father must have worn it – and now, it had been given to her. She was after all his descendant and therefore the only one entitled to wear it – she was to be the village's Arch Druid. This was her destiny it seemed and there was no escaping it.

She hung the robe on a hanger and opened the drawer where she kept the hood and dagger. And there it was – the hood was now a brilliant gold and matched the robe exactly. She made up her mind to wear her finds to the Ostara Festival and the robe could actually be her wedding dress now.

The night of the festival arrived and she dressed carefully, attaching the hood to the collar of the robe. She used one of her own belts and hung the dagger there with the blue gem facing outwards. She knew she looked the part and felt more than ever this was her destiny. She walked to the clearing in the woods by herself and in the shimmering gold costume, she knew she made an impressive figure. The Druid community had already gathered and were standing around the fire. A ripple of applause broke out when they saw her– this was the person whom they'd been expecting for a very long time. She couldn't have been more welcome.

The white-robed priest gestured that she and John should approach. It was his honour to marry the two, willing Druids. He conducted the service beautifully and Marion Parker and John Reynolds became husband and wife. The celebrations began after the service and as always, food and drink were produced at just the right moment. Singing and dancing around the fire broke out and everyone joined in, including the bride and groom. The pipes of Pan filled the air and they called for their God, the Green Man to come and bless the couple.

And he did! In his usual way, he appeared in a thunderous flash of lightening, his long green tendrils of hair hanging loose to his shoulders. His green garb was wonderful to behold and the Druids fell to their knees, shouting out their praises into the night air. Then -it was all over and the Green Man disappeared from the festivities as suddenly as he'd arrived. The celebrations began to slow down, but as with all good parties, some party-goers hung on to the very end.

Not long after their marriage, the time arrived for Marian and John to leave their cottages and move to the big house. The whole thing was very exciting and going there made them feel just like the lord and lady of the manor. They were lucky however, not to hear the hushed whispers of the locals, some of whom believed the couple's good luck had depended too much on the tragedy of other people. But then, it was always thus!

The first evening in their new home was spent in front of the huge fireplace. Drinks in hand, they talked about how they hoped to spend the rest of their lives. Marion felt more content, now she'd made the decision to embrace the life of a Druid and for the first time in her life, she felt that she was respected and hopefully loved by those around her.

The house was very quiet with just the loud ticking of the mantlepiece clock and the odd piece of coal falling over in the fire. John sat back and heaved a relaxed sigh and Marion reached for his hand and held it in hers. They knew they were probably happier than they deserved to be but that was life and they couldn't change it.

In the high-ceilinged hall outside the sitting room, the heavy, velvet drapes had been pulled across the front door and now, even the hall was cosy. Everything in the house smelt of money and contentment. What the man and woman on the sofa didn't know however, was that two other figures were also sitting on the winding stairs that led up to the bedrooms. One was a man and the other, a woman!

The man spoke, "Well Mary, now you've joined me, I feel so much better – two ghosts are better than one, I always say. It would be too much work for me on my own but not now that I have you." Paul Jenkins looked just as he had when he was alive – and so did Mary, his housekeeper. They were both dressed in their usual clothes and if possible, looked healthier than how they'd looked when they were alive.

"What shall we do first to annoy them? He went on and rubbed his hands together in a very familiar way. "Moving curtains and strange sounds are all very well, but we've got to be more inventive than that. We'll have to move things around in the house, so they think they're losing their minds – but that'll be easy. We must bang doors in their faces and when they're asleep, we'll float around their bedroom and make ghostly sounds - that'll soon wake them up."

Mary joined in excitedly, "And we'll leave windows and doors open just after they've closed them. We'll have to devise a plan so they know who we actually are and that we're not just any old ghosts. I think that would scare them even more, don't you? Knowing it's us will make it more personal and hopefully, their consciences will suffer and they'll eventually become nervous wrecks. We should reveal ourselves every so often though but then, disappear right before their eyes. I think we're going to enjoy ourselves, don't you?"

Paul nodded his head, "You know, I'd never have left her the house if I'd known she was going to marry John Reynolds – a man I never cared for. And I wouldn't have left her all my money either - now he'll fritter it all away and it'll run through his hands like water." He fell quiet for a few moments, obviously thinking of how the couple had 'benefitted' from his frugal ways, then he said, "You know the night I died, I know now he *was* the fox in the middle of the road. the one that made me crash into the trees. I died because of him Mary and I wonder just how much of all this, he'd actually planned. Ah well, they're both welcome to each other now!"

"And as for her, I always knew she was no good – just a money-grabbing tart." Mary looked angry – an odd expression for a ghost.

"Well, we both have our reasons to make their lives a misery now, so let's get on with it, shall we?

"Yes please – what's first on the agenda? Why don't we go upstairs and throw back their bedcovers – it's a freezing night so everything will get good and cold. "She was already on her feet, eager to begin.

"And when they discover the disturbed bed, we'll make the lights fuse and they'll be plunged into darkness – he'll panic because he won't yet have discovered where the fuse box is. Yes, that'll be good. And while they get what little sleep we'll allow them; you and I can be planning new tricks for tomorrow. Paul too stood up – he was even more keen than Mary to begin the torture.

The two ghosts flew up the stairs and Marion and John in the cosy sitting room, remained oblivious to their uninvited guests and to their plans. In fact, they had another Gin and Tonic before damping down the fire and making their way upstairs. Paul and Mary had worked hard on the room by this time and everything looked as if a tornado had hit the room.

"Do you realise Mary, people will stop calling this place 'The Big House' – from tonight onwards, they'll call it 'The Haunted House.'? And between us, we'll make it the most haunted house in the whole county. In fact, when All Hallow's Eve comes around again, we'll invite all the dead spirits walking the earth on that night - and we'll have a Druid ghostly party right here.

Mary smiled her agreement, "That's sure to 'spook' the dear newlyweds!"

Deja-Vu - Again and Again and Again

The service was over and the vicar was closing his bible. Elizabeth turned from the graveside and reached for her husband's strong arm – but it wasn't there and for a moment, she wondered where he'd gone. Then it all came flooding back and she remembered exactly where he was. He was lying at the bottom of the hole in the ground in a solid wooden box, that's where he was. Her precious Richard was dead despite being only 35 years old. Without his support, she stumbled and was grateful for her father's comforting arm.

"Come my dear, let's get you home to the warmth of the fire. It's been a very long day." And he led her up the grassy slope towards the waiting carriage.

He was right, the house was warm but without Richard, it wasn't welcoming. The maid took her mistress's cloak and told her a tea tray was waiting in the parlour. She was only 28 years old but already a widow – a widow with two young children, who now depended on her and her alone. She settled in the chair closest to the hearth and her father sat opposite, first pouring tea into the cups.

"Thank you, Papa, you've been most kind – I couldn't have coped without you."

"Nonsense my dear, I'm sure you could have – but you don't have to as I'll always be here for you." Bernard was an elderly man with a shock of white hair and he walked with the use of a cane. He loved his only child very much and offered his support eagerly.

Elizabeth smiled, "That's what Richard told me once, but he was wrong, wasn't he? Oh Papa, I miss him terribly. Three weeks ago, he was fine but the pneumonia was too much for him. I don't think he ever had a day's illness in his life until that thundery night when he arrived home, soaked to the skin. A simple cold he thought at first, but a severe chest infection soon followed – he was wrong yet again about the cold - now the children are without their father.”

Bernard wished again that he’d insisted on holding a proper wake at the house, but Elizabeth was so against it, he had no option but to obey her wishes. Having people around her at a wake might have helped, but it was too late now and it was up to him to do what he could to see his daughter through this terrible time.

There was a timid knock at the door and the children’s Nanny hesitated before coming into the room. “Would you like to see the children now Ma’am? They’re asking for you.”

Bernard intervened, ready to say his daughter wasn’t yet up to that yet, but Elizabeth stood up and said, “Yes Mary, I’d like that. Have they behaved since I’ve been away?”

“Oh yes Ma’am, they’ve been good as gold, but they’ve been wondering where you are.”

“Come Mary, let’s go upstairs. I’ll be back in a short time Papa, just sit there and enjoy your tea.” And she closed the parlour door behind her.

Next day Bernard had spent the morning shut away in the study going through piles of Richard’s papers and accounts. The young man had worked in the city and should have been able to keep his affairs in order, but alas Bernard discovered it wasn’t so. Richard’s affairs were in a bit of a mess and something had to be done quickly to wipe out his debts.

“I’m afraid the house will have to be sold Elizabeth, there’s no other way. Although I’m not a poor man, I just don’t have the resources to deal with Richard’s outstanding debts.” Bernard knew this had to be said, yes it was hard but Elizabeth needed to know the truth.

“When the house eventually sells, you and the children will come home to live with me. I have the room and would make you most welcome.” He put his arm around her shoulders and looked down into her tear-filled eyes.

“I understand Papa but I know very little about our finances – Richard always protected me from such things. Now I wish he hadn’t, but things are as they are and I must accept whatever the situation is.” She’d always been a strong young woman but this was bigger than anything she’d had to face before - she dropped her head into her hands. "I'll be all right Papa, with you to help me. I must think of the children and I will do it! I'll just need a little time to come to terms with everything that's happened."

And that's what she did! She spoke first with the family lawyer and arranged for the house to go on the market. She knew she was lucky to have such a supportive father who was willing to put a roof over her own and the children's heads. When she came home from the lawyer's office, she sat by the warmth of the fire and in her hands, she held a framed photo of Richard. She'd loved him so much and he'd been a good husband, except perhaps where money was concerned. She stared into his smiling face and knew she'd never forget him – and after all, she had his children to remind her. Nanny brought her wards into the room and Elizabeth spent the next hour playing with them – her precious boy already had a look of his dead father and the girl had a cheerful and happy disposition.

The next week was spent gathering together the things needed to live at her papa's house. She and Nanny were to travel ahead of the belongings in a hired carriage and so they took with them just the things needed for a day or two. Although this Christmas would be a sad one, at least they'd all be together at Papa's house. She knew she had to make Christmas merry for the children's sake, although it wouldn't be easy, but not impossible.

"Now Mary, have you packed everything you'll need for a couple of days? And of course, what the children will need?" Elizabeth was fussing around everyone.

"Yes Ma'am, I believe I have and they're both very excited at the thought of the journey. Have you got your things together Ma'am or is there anything you'd like me to do for you?" Mary was anxious to please her mistress who'd always been kind to her. "And by the way Ma'am, I've been saving for a couple of years now and I won't be needing any wages until you're back on your feet." She'd rehearsed the words several times and blurted them out as quickly as she could, before rushing off in case Elizabeth wanted to argue. She wouldn't let Nanny go short of anything, she promised herself – especially after such a kind offer.

It was still a few weeks 'till Christmas when the hired carriage drew up at the front door. The little family were waiting on the doorstep and ran to the carriage through heavy falling rain. In fact, it was the heaviest rain they'd seen for a long time and the skies promised a storm ahead if the driver was to be believed. He told Elizabeth, "I think it'll be pretty localised so we should be able to run ahead of it."

Unfortunately, he was wrong. After an hour they were right in the thick of it and the young girl Victoria began to cry. "Make it stop Mummy – please make it stop." Nanny Mary comforted her as best she could, but the terrible winds were blowing so hard, even she was afraid. The driver was finding it difficult to keep the carriage stable and it swayed from side to side, throwing its passengers against each other. It was an incredible storm and because they'd been on the road for some time, they were already deep in the countryside – in fact, no-one knew where they actually were – including the driver.

Suddenly the horse cried out – it didn't neigh, but shrieked instead. The carriage came to an abrupt halt and the children were thrown on top of Elizabeth and Mary. Everyone was topsy-turvy and the carriage was lying on its side. The poor horse was trying to struggle to its feet.

Amazingly, no-one was actually hurt and the driver's face appeared at the carriage window, "It's bad ma'am – I'm afraid it's really bad. The horse was struck by a broken branch and we've ended up in a ditch."

"Can't we get the carriage out of the ditch? If we all pulled together, it might work." Elizabeth asked but the driver looked dubious. And then the lightening came, followed a few moments later by a horrendous crash as the thunder boomed close by loudly. It was like a death knoll and for a moment, Elizabeth wondered if it might be the end of the world.

"The horse is back on its feet and doesn't seem to have broken anything, so that's good. The only thing I can do is mount him and ride back to the town for help. You ladies and children should stay inside the coach – at least that way, you'll be sheltered from the storm – well, almost sheltered."

There were no lights anywhere to be seen – they really were in the back of beyond with no possibility of any help. Elizabeth agreed with him and on her words, he mounted the frightened beast and rode off through the torrential rain. More lightening lit up the sky and the booming sounds of thunder scared the children even more. Inside the carriage, they all cuddled into each other and Nanny told them the driver would soon be back – although she wasn't sure of this.

"It's all right Mary, it'll pass – and the driver won't desert us, I'm sure!" Elizabeth wasn't as confident as her words implied – in fact it even crossed her mind that the driver might choose to desert them – after all, he hardly knew them. "The storm can't last much longer, so we'll just cuddle up and wait. Perhaps we could sing to keep up our spirits." Nanny suggested, but no-one felt like singing unfortunately and the gusts of wind continued to shake the carriage from side to side.

Amazingly, in the midst of such chaos, the children managed to fall asleep and Elizabeth and Mary sat very still, so as not to waken them. Sleep was a Godsend at such a time and whilst blaming God for the storm, they also thanked him for keeping the children asleep. The thunder and lightning were getting less and less and the sound of the heavy rain was drumming less on the roof. Elizabeth started to say, "You see, it's passing." But she saw Mary was asleep as well and so she sat there alone and missing Richard more than ever. *If he'd been here, he would have taken care of us, but I mustn't think like that – he wasn't there and I've got to get used to it.*

It must have been 2 or 3 hours later when Elizabeth noticed the sky was brightening to a pale grey. It still looked threatening, but at least there was no more thunder and lightning. Mary stirred and sat bolt upright, obviously wondering where on earth she was.

"Oh Ma'am. I'm so sorry, I fell sleep and left you all alone. Are you all right – I wish I could do something for you Ma'am, but there's nothing I can do. Has there been any sign of the driver?" She woke up very fast.

Elizabeth shook her head, "Afraid not Mary – it's not a good sign I fear. He should have had time to bring help by now, but we're all alone I'm afraid. It's up to me to try and get help, so I'm going to leave the carriage and try to find my way to some local house – even if it's just a small cottage, I'm sure they'd offer shelter, especially when they hear there's children involved. You must remain here with them – I know they'll wake up soon and be afraid, but I have no option." She pulled her shawl tightly around her shoulders and gingerly opened the carriage door. At least the door wasn't damaged and opened easily. She did it as quietly as she could and stepped out onto the ground – the soggy, wet ground which was just a sea of mud. "I'll be back as soon as I can – don't worry, you know I won't desert you - you've got two of the most precious things I have left, so I'll be sure and come back." And she slid through the mud, her little bootees soaking up the slippery ooze, which came right up over their top.

She slipped and fell several times but made sure she knew her bearings so she could direct help towards her family. She felt as though she'd been walking for hours, but of course she hadn't. It was just the difficulty of each step that made it all so laborious. *Please God, let me find somewhere soon.*

In the greyness ahead, she thought she could hear cows in a field – and then she saw it – not a cottage or a farm house, but an imposing manor house with bright lights in all the windows. Her feet suddenly felt lighter and soon she was on the drive and walking on gravel - much easier than the muddy fields. She stopped at the front door and realised it would be wiser to go around the back – she'd be sure to find servants there. She knocked on the door of what she hoped was the kitchen – at least there was a light in the window.

A rosy-cheeked, plump woman opened the door just a little and peered outside. "An' what be you after? We don't like beggars 'ere – now you get on yer way afore I call for 'elp." Elizabeth suddenly realised how she must look after her ordeal – a tramp, a proper tramp and no mistake, so she pulled herself up to her full height and said in her best tone,

"I am not a beggar, I'm a lady and the carriage in which I was travelling fell into a ditch in the storm, breaking its axle. I've been walking for miles and I 'm looking for help. Are you a good Christian soul who'll help a lady in distress? I've had to leave my two children with their nanny in the carriage."

Luckily for her, the cook was indeed a good Christian soul and she opened the door wider. Elizabeth could feel the warmth of the stove and in her eagerness, she almost fell in the door.

When she stumbled, Cook grabbed her arm and placed her in front of an enormous fireplace, filled with fresh logs.

"Sit yersel' down 'ere an' I'll fetch ye some 'ot tea." And that was the start of Elizabeth's relationship with the kindly cook, who immediately called for the footman and sent him off to find the broken carriage. "Take the 'ores an' cart – it'll be easier than the carriage on the damaged roads. In the meantime, I'll tell 'is Lordship and Lady what's been 'appenin 'ere." And she left Elizabeth supping a welcome cup of tea and went off upstairs.

Fifteen minutes later, she reappeared with a tall, elegant gentleman by her side. He was an elderly man with long, white hair and was dressed in the very latest fashion. He introduced himself as Lord Winship and explained this was his home. "Would you like to tell me your story? Cook has made me aware of the misfortune you've suffered and I know John the footman, has been sent off to collect the rest of your party. I would like you to tell me your story again." And she did. He was patient and actually pulled up a stool from the fireside and sat down beside her. He listened, saying nothing until she'd finished. It was odd, but he seemed so caring, she went back even further in her story and told him of the recent loss of her husband.

"Dear me, you have been in the wars, haven't you? I'm going upstairs now to have my breakfast with my dear wife, but the maid will take care of you and find you some dry clothes. Once you've bathed and dressed, perhaps you'd be good enough to join me in the parlour, where you can meet my wife."

Elizabeth couldn't believe such kindness from total strangers, but was very grateful for it.Jenny the maid did as his Lordship had promised. She filled a hot bath in a guest bedroom and provided some clothes, which miraculously seemed quite a good fit. *God, she felt better now – and when the footman finally returned with Mary and the children, she would feel even better.*

Soon the footman returned with the horse and cart and bouncing around in the back amongst small pieces of luggage, were Nanny Mary, Victoria and Albert. Although their appearances were bedraggled, they seemed happy enough – just being rescued after the night from Hell must have cheered them. The maid Jenny was waiting by the back door with a pile of blankets which she immediately wrapped around the children and their nanny. Cook served hot soup and watched with satisfaction, as they all wolfed it down. It was good to have folk in the house who appreciated her cooking, so she took a thick, creamy rice pudding from the larder and served it as 'afters'.

Jenny told the newcomers to follow her into the room next door, where a hot bath was waiting for them and then onto a nice, cosy bed. Elizabeth tucked the children under the blankets and before she'd even left the room, both were sound asleep. The hot soup and hot bath had worked their miracle. Elizabeth crossed the landing and went to her own room to tidy her hair – she'd been invited to dine with the master and mistress and was really looking forward to it. It would give her the opportunity to thank them for such kindness and hospitality.

Lord and Lady Winship were sitting at each end of a long, highly polished table and between them, a row of candles in holders reflected their glow on the surface. No-one was speaking when she came into the room and immediately felt an atmosphere which she could have cut with the proverbial knife. Luckily, the footman appeared at that moment and served the first course. As the guest at the table, she should have been addressed by at least one of the people there, but it was not to be and Elizabeth drank her soup in silence.

It was all so very strange. Earlier, she'd been made most welcome, and yet now it felt as if she was being shut out. The main course was again served by John the footman and she couldn't resist catching his eye and raising a quizzical eyebrow. He said nothing however - it wasn't his place. Soon, dinner was over and not one word had been uttered throughout the entire meal. Elizabeth made to rise from the table, when Lady Arabella suddenly burst out with, "Come my dear and we'll adjourn to the withdrawing room. His Lordship will want to smoke his cigar." She spoke with a definite air of superiority and the white hair piled on top of her head, made her seem even more in control. A tall lady who carried a lorgnette, through which she peered regularly and her gown was of the best quality material.

Using her fan to cool her cheeks, she waved it to and for, seeming agitated to Elizabeth, who wondered what to say next. The lady Arabella suddenly plonked herself down on a sofa and started to cry, harsh, bitter tears. Now Elizabeth really didn't know what to say.

She stuttered, "May I help you your Ladyship? Is there something or someone I can fetch to help you? Your husband perhaps?"

"You mustn't bring him in here – he's out there waiting for me to make a mistake. He's told me he's going to kill me but he won't say exactly when. He likes to keep me dangling, you know. I don't know how he plans to do it – but I know it won't be pleasant. He's a cruel, vicious man." She laid her head against the cushion, her breath coming in short, sharp gasps. "Help me please – will you help me, my dear? I know you're a stranger in my home, but if you have a Christian spirit, you'll feel pity for my position." Her guest was confused – did she stay or did she go?

"I'll leave you now your ladyship, but first I must tell your husband of your distress." She quickly left the drawing room and headed back to where Lord Winship was enjoying his cigar. *I don't believe for a moment that the woman is in any danger from this kind man.*

"Ah here you are – I wondered how soon you'd be back. I suppose she's told you I'm going to kill her. She has told you that, hasn't she?" Elizabeth could only nod her head.

"Well, now I'm going to surprise you even more. The truth is that she's the one with murderous intent – she's sworn more than once that she'll end my life. She won't tell me how she's going to do it – she likes to keep me on tenterhooks, wondering when she's going to strike. I've lived in fear for my life for some time now and I don't know how much longer I can go on." He placed his arms on the table and rested his head on top of them. He looked up at her with a stricken expression, "You'll help me, won't you? You're a good lady and I know you won't turn your back on me." *My God, what is going on – he was even more distressed than his wife? Who was the killer and who was the victim? She had no idea!*

Gently, she touched his shoulder before scurrying from the room and running up the wide staircase to her bedroom. Before disrobing, she looked in on the children and was grateful to hear their gentle snores.

Elizabeth pulled the bed covers around her body and pressed her face into the pillow. *She told herself she'd speak with Cook the next morning – and find out how much the woman knew about what was going on between her master and mistress. Yes, that's what she'd do, even if it wasn't strict etiquette to speak so with a servant. But needs must, she told herself.*

At one point, she found herself awake and listening for what she didn't know, but something was troubling her. She slipped out of bed and quietly crept downstairs. Luckily, there were a couple of gas holders still alight on the ground floor, so she was able to find the withdrawing room. Something had drawn her to that particular room where she knew – and feared – she'd find something unpleasant. And there it was! Helped by the gas lights, she saw two figures lying on the sofa. They lay at either end and both had a deep, bloody gash across their heads. Lord and Lady Winship had done what they'd said they would – they'd murdered each other. She tentatively checked both pulses and could feel nothing. They'd truly done for each other! *What do I do? Who do I tell? I'm a stranger in this house and this is none of my business. She glanced out of the window and saw dawn was breaking. I won't do anything, she decided, I won't get involved in this catastrophe. I have my children to think of and after losing their father, this would be one drama too many.The house was deadly quiet and she'd leave it that way. The bodies would be found next morning, probably by the footman - and he'd know what to do. She tried to sleep again, but found she couldn't.*

`Next morning, she was exhausted. Jenny knocked and came into her room, carrying an early morning cup of tea. She went back outside to fetch a coal scuttle. "I'll just light your fire Ma'am – it's a chilly morning and no mistake. When you're ready, so will breakfast be – all laid out in the breakfast room." And she dropped to her knees by the hearth and without waiting for an answer, got on with the job. *Okay, Elizabeth thought, why is there not an uproar with people running hither and thither after discovering the dead couple downstairs? Jenny was as cool as a cucumber*

So, she dressed quickly and made sure Nanny and the children were okay before she went downstairs. Everything was uncannily quiet and she could hear Cook singing some religious song in the kitchen. *She wondered what kind of house this was! Had no-one discovered the bodies yet? They must have done - but she could smell food being prepared for breakfast as though everything was normal.*

"The breakfast room is this one Ma'am," John came along the corridor and indicated the correct door. "If you'll take a seat, I'll make sure Cook knows you're here. Oh, by the way, the master and mistress are up early today and have already begun their own breakfasts." He too, was behaving as if nothing had happened.

'What? A voice inside her head cried out – no way can that be! I saw both of them lying dead last night.' She went towards the breakfast room and froze in the doorway.

"Good Morning my dear. I hope you had a good night's sleep. We certainly did." Lord Winship was helping himself to more eggs from the sideboard.

"No more for me dear, I've had quite sufficient." Lady Arabella replied and smiled at Elizabeth. "Do sit down my dear – Cook will be fixing you some fresh tea, if I'm not mistaken."

Elizabeth was completely mesmerised and just stood there with her mouth open. She stuttered, "But…but you were…". Then she paused and said "Good Morning," before staggering to the nearest chair and sitting there dumbfounded. She tried to compose herself by thinking, *'This can't be. I saw them last night and felt for their pulses. I saw the red gashes on their foreheads where the blood was beginning to congeal. Yet here they are, hale and hearty and tucking into a tasty breakfast.'*

Lord Winship told her the roads were still very bad and that she mustn't even think of trying to continue her journey. "John will keep checking and will let me know when things are looking better. And you must think of the children and their safety."

Lady Arabella was nodding her head in agreement. "It's a pleasure to have you here, my dear – perhaps you'd like to join me in the warm parlour this afternoon and help with my embroidery. Wouldn't that be nice?"

Elizabeth just nodded and said how pleasant it would be. She looked from one to the other and couldn't believe this was the same man and woman who'd separately complained they were going to kill each other. And she'd seen with her very own eyes that that's exactly what they did. Except they didn't. It was all too much for her and she excused herself to go and check on the children – yes, that would allow her to visit Cook in the kitchen and ask if she knew what was going on. It really was an enigma.

She found Nanny Mary and both children settled comfortably around the big table in the kitchen. "Use your napkin Albert you've got porridge all down your chin." And the boy immediately wiped his chin with the sleeve of his clean shirt.

"Has it all gone now, Mummy?" He asked innocently and then remembered she'd told him to use his napkin, but it was too late.

Jenny the maid was busy at a side table, cleaning copper pans. She directed a question to Mary, "When I've finished this lot to Cook's satisfaction of course – may I take the children to the playroom? There's lots of great toys there – old toys but good ones. They belonged to Master Philip." Then she caught sight of Cook's warning glance and stopped talking.

"Who's Master Philip?" Little Victoria wanted to know. No-one answered so she asked again, "Who's Master Philip? I haven't seen a little boy in this house. Have you Albert?" Her brother said he hadn't and looked at Jenny for an answer.

Cook spoke up instead, "Master Philip was a little boy who used to live here but 'e died when 'e was just 18 years old. We don't speak of 'mi because it upsets the master and mistress. 'E was their only son ye see an' they never got over losin' 'im. ''E decided one day to ride we' the local 'unto and 'is Ma didn't want 'mi to go cause 'e wasn't a great rider, but 'is Pa said 'e could an' that was that. 'E fell from 'is 'ores an' broke 'is young neck. 'Is Ma and' Pa blamed one another for what 'appended."

Both the children looked sad at the story. It seemed dreadful that his toys were still in the playroom but he couldn't play with them anymore. "Poor boy," Victoria said between mouthfuls and Albert added "Absolutely."

To cheer them up, Cook said, "But 'e wouldn't mind you playin' wi' 'is toys. I know because I remember 'mi well. Now then children, both o' you should go we' Jenny 'ere an' find those toys." Her usual red and cheery face had taken on a greyish hue and she crossed the room to the sink where she wiped tears from her eyes. She turned abruptly and said, "This carry-on will never get the lunch ready, now will it?" And she began peeling potatoes with great gusto. The children went off with Jenny and Mary went upstairs to mend some of the children's clothes. A little respite from looking after the children was always welcome.

Elizabeth and Cook were left alone together. She didn't know how to broach the subject and Cook just blurted out, "Is there somethin' ye want to ask me Ma'am? It would be best if ye just asked an' if I know the answer, I'll tell ye."

Hesitantly, Elizabeth began to describe the events of the previous night, leaving nothing out. Cook listened but went right on peeling vegetables. She kept her face turned away,

before finally putting the potatoes in a large saucepan. She turned then, to face Elizabeth and sat down on a chair. She reached for the coffee pot and poured them both a cup.

"What ye saw Ma'am, wasn't real? It must 'aver been a figment o' year imagination. The master and mistress are fine – ye've seen them for Yertle' this morning'. I don't know what ye want me to say." She spooned lots of sugar into her cup.

"Cook, please don't do this – I know what I saw. And they both told me the other was planning their death. They spoke to me separately and blamed the other, saying it was a long-time plan. It was quite clear they hated each other." Elizabeth was almost pleading for cook to believe her.

"It's a pity ye came to this 'Ouse – it's not a place for the likes of' ye – or yer children. I know what yer sayin' be true - cause it's 'appened afore. I can't explain it – I think it's cause they 'ate each other so much." And she looked sad at the thought. "I can only advise ye accept what ye can't change – and be on year way as soon as ye can. That's my advice an' the roads will soon be clear."

She knew that was all she was going to get, so she gave up and left the kitchen. *No use flogging a dead horse, she thought. Cook's going to spill no more beans!*

Later in the afternoon, she did join Lady Arabella and offered to help with the fire-screen she was embroidering. It was a beautiful piece of work with every possible colour of silk thread. She chose a soft pink and began working on a corner of the material. A delicate rose would look just right there – and Lady Arabella approved her choice.

"My, what lovely stitching, my dear – you're doing them quite exquisitely. I wish I had your artistic ways – but then, I'm old and clumsy. By the way, have I told you my husband is planning to murder me? I shouldn't think I have as we've only recently met – but he is, you know. He's a wicked man who wishes me harm. What do you think I should do?" And she went on stitching as though she'd just mentioned the weather or a new headscarf.

It was all too silly for words and after spending an hour with Arabella, she sought out Lord Winship who was ensconced in his study. She asked him if it would be possible to borrow the family carriage to continue her journey to her father's house – about 100 miles away. She knew it was a big ask, but she had to get away.

"Of course, my dear – that won't be a problem, but not just yet. You know the roads are unpassable in parts and the same thing that happened the other night, could happen again. I can't allow you to take that chance, especially with the children. I could hear the little dears laughing when I passed the playroom just then – they seemed to be having a great time with our maid. You can't spoil that for them, now can you?" And he went back to his book and sherry, obviously dismissing the woman who had entered – uninvited – into his inner sanctum. As her hand was on the door handle, he added the devastating words, "And please watch out for that damned woman, she's still intent on ending my life. She knows not to disturb me in my study but if you see her creeping around anywhere else in the house, you'll let me know, won't you?" And there it was again!

Joining the children in the playroom, she found Nanny there, sitting beside a small pile of mending. Victoria was playing with a spinning top which hummed very pleasantly every time she spun it. Albert had found a partially completed colouring book and some crayons and was diligently working to finish off a picture someone had already begun. Elizabeth settled herself on the window seat and thought how resilient children could be. Events of the last few weeks had been too much to bear and the young widow rested her head against the window, thanking God they'd all soon be with Papa. She crouched down on the floor beside her son and admired his picture.

"What lovely colours Albert – you've made some good choices – but why have you added that little boy with crutches – the one in the corner?"

" He was already in the corner Mummy, I didn't put him there." He's in the corner so he can watch the others playing. He has a broken leg, you see and he can't join in their game." Albert had obviously thought the whole thing through.

"I see – poor, little boy! Although he is quite a lot bigger than the other children in the picture, so maybe he's stronger and will get better soon." She wanted to encourage him in his imagination and had joined in with the story. Then she turned to Victoria and her spinning top. The girl didn't seem to get tired of doing the same thing again and again. *Bless her, she's only six – sometimes I forget that. And Albert was only 2 years older, although sometimes he seemed quite grown up.* No-one needed her there, so she told Mary she was going to her room for a short nap before dinner.

As she lay fully-clothed on top of the bed, she thought of Albert's drawing of a crippled boy and how he couldn't join in and play with the other children. It was such a sad story for him to makeup. Soon, she fell asleep but in a very disturbed way. She knew she'd be expected to go down to dinner, but she dreaded the thought. The clock said ten minutes before eight and at 8 o'clock the gong would sound and she'd have to go. She thought of pleading a headache, but knew the excuse sounded feeble. There it was - the sound of the gong ringing throughout the house. Elizabeth thought it sounded like a death knoll. In the hall, she met John and realised she was a little late. She dreaded what was to come next.

"Ah, Mistress Elizabeth and looking as lovely as ever." His Lordship was on top form tonight. Lady Arabella just smiled and started to sup her soup. It was delicious – Cook really was clever, she was thinking. Starter over, John appeared with the fish course and had just set it on the table, when Lady Arabella suddenly shouted, "John, I need music. You know I like my fish course served with music. Kindly see to it at once." Unperturbed, the footman opened the sideboard and lifted out a wooden box and when he raised its top, the beautiful tinkling sound of the well-known tune 'Shenandoah' filled the room.

Elizabeth was pleasantly surprised and the song immediately took her mind back to her days in the schoolroom. She remembered the words well and wondered if the others knew them too.

"It's so beautiful, isn't it? I love the music and it's all about a meandering river- so restful." Arabella had a dreamy look on her long face whilst her husband tutted and said something about 'Damned music every time we eat fish – I ask you!'

Elizabeth brought the conversation back to the tune, "Actually, it's not about a meandering river at all but about a love story of an American man and his love for a Red Indian princess."

Arabella was immediately 'all ears' and asked her to continue. Even his Lordship seemed to pick up his ears. Elizabeth found she liked to be the peacemaker between them, so she went on, "Well, it was written many years ago and no-one ever learned who the composer was. The American man was not a Red Indian but his love was. The young couple planned to go away from Missouri and settle in his homeland and the song is about them telling her father, the Indian Chief, what they planned to do. Her father didn't want to lose his daughter but the girl was strong-minded and had made up her mind. Shenandoah was actually Chief Shenandoah and the words of the song are directed at him. It's a very sad story, isn't it – not so much for the couple, but for the old Indian chief?" She stopped speaking and looked at the couple. *I'm gabbling – I know I'm gabbling! But someone had to say something. I don't know what else to say to keep them from killing each other - again.*

"Well, I never did!" Arabella was the first to speak, "I never knew that – I thought it was about a river called Shenandoah. It's a lovely tale, my dear – thank you for sharing it with us. By this time, all the dinner courses had been served and the music box had been rewound several times.

Arabella stood up and invited Elizabeth to join her in the withdrawing room whilst her husband enjoyed his cigar. Everything was just like the night before.

As soon as the door closed, Arabella started the same conversation, "He's going to kill me. Did you see the look in his eyes – I've seen that look before? He hates me you know." And so, she went on until Elizabeth could stand it no longer and begged to be excused, claiming she had a headache.

He was waiting for her in the corridor however and grabbed her arm, "What has my wife been saying to you? She's quite mad you know and determined to take my life. She tells people I'm the one with malicious intent, but it's her – I tell you, it's her." Elizabeth pulled away from him and ran upstairs. She knew for definite she had to get out of this house, and soon or she'd be the mad one. She waited until it was quiet downstairs and she crept back down again going straight to the kitchen where she found John helping Cook put dishes away.

"John, I must leave tomorrow – my father is expecting me and will be worried because I haven't tuned up. Are you able to drive the carriage, the way you did the cart? The master said it would be okay and we could use the carriage." She kept her fingers crossed as the lie left her lips.

"'Course I can drive the carriage – as long as you've cleared it with the master, I'll have it ready at 8 o'clock tomorrow morning. I'll have to set off early so I can get back to my duties here – can you and the children be ready to leave first thing." He suddenly paused and looked at Cook, "What do you think Cook? It'll be all right, won't it?" Elizabeth waited with baited breath, hoping Cook wouldn't put a spanner in the works now.

Cook just nodded however. If anything, she seemed relieved it was going to happen. She knew it was the safest thing to do.

Finding Mary upstairs, she told her of the plan and stressed that the children must be kept quiet as the master and mistress would still be sleeping 8 o'clock and they mustn't be disturbed. Mary understood the urgency and immediately started packing their things. Before going to her own room, Elizabeth was sorely tempted to go back downstairs and see what her hosts were up to. Then she realised she didn't really want to know and tried to talk herself out of the idea. Curiosity won the day however and she slipped off her shoes and crept back downstairs. All the doors were open except one – the withdrawing room, where she'd found the two bodies the previous night. She needed to know whether she was the mad one – or they were. *Had she really seen the dead bodies before and yet they were both alive by the next morning – or had she imagined the whole thing?*

She stood outside the door and knew she had to open it. The couple were probably sitting together, chatting away about the Shenandoah story. She peered around the door and this time, there was no-one on the sofa – but lying in front of the fireplace were the same two bodies she'd seen before. She couldn't see the wounds this time but the figures were in a crumpled heap, one lying at an angle to the other. It looked as if they'd been struggling. Quietly she crossed the room and again felt for pulses – but again, there was no sign of life. They were stone cold dead just as before. The whole situation was impossible and yet it was real enough. This time, she wasn't surprised at what she'd found but just turned and climbed the stairs again to the safety of her own room. She didn't bother to tell Cook – what was the point? She would just have nodded and got on with her work. What would the morning bring, she wondered?

John was as good as his word and next morning, he was waiting at the back door ready to leave. Mary brought the children through the kitchen and Cook kissed them both goodbye. Elizabeth slipped the woman two gold sovereigns - she'd been so welcoming and kind to all of them. Cook had tears in her eyes and she turned away quickly, saying, "I hear the master and mistress going into the breakfast room, so I must hurry with their food."

So, it was just as it had been before and Lord Winship and his dear wife were alive and kicking – despite what Elizabeth had seen the night before. The carriage sped off and everyone sat comfortably back for the journey. My God, it felt good!

Despite taking the wrong road a couple of times, John soon drew up outside Elizabeth's old home and Papa came out onto the doorstep, to welcome them. The children were excited and happy to see their Grandpa and he cuddled them both in turn. My God, he was glad to see them all – he'd been so worried something bad had happened during the storm, but here they were, hale and hearty – and safe. Bernard ordered his stable boy to see to the horse with fresh water and hay and to take John to the kitchen for some warm food. After that, he could be back on the road home, but not before the horse was rested.

It was lovely to be back in familiar surroundings and Elizabeth felt she could relax. So much had happened since

Richard's death and the bizarre happenings at Lord Winship's that she felt completely drained. "Oh Papa. It is good to see you. We've had an odd time because of the storm and all the roads closing but at least we're here now." She looked at her father closely and thought how grey and washed out he looked. "Have you been ill Papa, you don't look so well?"

Bernard told her not to fuss – he was fine! But she thought differently and vowed to care for him now she was home. But her plan never reached fruition because Bernard died in his sleep a few days later and yet again, Elizabeth found herself in mourning. It had been so unexpected and both children were devastated. Again, there was again so much to settle and she could have been forgiven for thinking God had deserted her. But she had the children to think of.

The funeral took place just before Christmas and what should have been a happy time, was doubly miserable. Elizabeth seemed always to be dressed in black these days and she hated it. The children on the other hand, were a Godsend and no mistake. They forced her to be positive and Albert especially, tried to cheer her up.

"Mummy, look at my book of drawings – they'll cheer you up, I know it. Look at this one you admired before when we lived in that other house with Cook. I liked Cook – she was always kind and baked lovely cakes. Grandpa would have liked her I think." He held out his picture book.

"Why Albert, did you take this drawing book from that house? You shouldn't have done that – it didn't belong to you." She knew she was being trivial, but he had to learn not to take things that didn't belong to him.

"But he said I could – he said, 'Take it and welcome Boy.'" He thought she was telling him off and he looked upset. "He came into the playroom and showed me some of his soldiers. I've got some of those as well – he told me to take them, he didn't want them

anymore." Now, there were tears in his eyes. *Was Mummy cross with him? But why, he hadn't done anything wrong? The strange boy was crippled but much older than Albert and so friendly. He'd said he liked me – I was good company. He'd said he was lonely and had been for a very long time and I was a breath of fresh air in the musty old house. He'd not mixed with young people for a very long time. Albert's mind was once more back in the playroom in the old house.*

He told Elizabeth everything the strange boy had said, but she just cuddled him and held him tight. He felt he was suffocating and pushed her away, "Why Mummy, you're crying just like me. What's wrong?" She just cuddled him again and said, "There wasn't any boy was there – you just liked his toys, didn't you?" *He'd just made up that story so she'd let him keep the book and soldiers – he'd been through so much lately, it wasn't really surprising.*

"I'm not telling lies Mummy – he came into the playroom more than once and he always used his crutch. He couldn't walk without it, you see. Look, I'm crossing my heart cause I'm telling the truth."

"What was this boy called, Albert? He must have told you his name." She wanted to believe him, but it was hard.

Philip – his name was Philip Winship and he used to live in the house, but one day he was out hunting and fell off his horse. That's how he broke his leg and had to stay in bed for a long time. He said they thought at first, he'd broken his neck, but it was just his leg. Then his chest went all funny and he got 'Monia' – at least I think that's what he called it."

My God, there was a son! She remembered Cook telling her about him and how he'd died in a hunting accident. His parents had never got over it and from that day on, they'd become more and more strange. Albert could be telling the truth after all. The young man's spirit must have stayed in the house and it was only when there were children around, he felt he could come out in the open. And she'd doubted her own son and as good as accused him of both lying and stealing. 'Shame on me!'

"Albert, how would you like to call Victoria down and we'll have big bowls of ice cream? I know Grandpa told the housekeeper to buy lots of different flavours because he knew you were coming to stay."Tears forgotten, he did what he was told and ran out of the room to find his sister. Elizabeth picked up the picture from the floor and carefully put it back inside the book

Days later, she had an appointment with her father's solicitor. It was Christmas Eve and she was surprised he wanted to see her on such a special day but he'd been more than just a solicitor to Bernard, he'd been a friend as well. Mr Matthews' secretary showed her in to his office and he asked her to fetch some tea for his client. In good lawyer fashion, he shuffled some papers on his desk and cleared his throat – rather pompously. When he told her how much her father had left her, she was amazed. She'd expected he would leave her his home, but she had no idea he had so much capital as well.

"It's perplexing Mr Matthews, when my husband died, he told me he couldn't help me financially and I'd have to live with him. He was always such a kind man, I find this very confusing." Elizabeth felt hurt by her father's concealment of his healthy finances.

The lawyer had been prepared for this and started to explain, "My dear, your father loved you very much but when your husband died, he wanted you to come home to him so he could keep an eye on you and the children. If anything, he cared too much and if he'd just handed you money, you would most likely have stayed right where you were. That was something he didn't want – he wanted you home with him. I assure you his motive was purely altruistic because he loved and missed all of you – he wanted you back in his life."

"Did he leave something for his servants – I'd like to know they'll be rewarded for their years of loyalty? If he hasn't, I know he'd like me to do it." So much unexpected information in such a short time was too much for her and caused her hands to shake and her cup rattle in its saucer.

"You don't have to worry about that – he's remembered everyone – and I'll see to it all. What I want you to do now is to take a little time to yourself and decide what you're going to do. Will you stay here and live in your old home, or would you prefer to return to your home in London? I realise you have the children to think of, but I'm sure, after deliberation, you'll make the right decision." The tea pot was empty and the papers re-shuffled. He stood up and escorted her to the door. "I'll call on you in two weeks and you can give me my instructions. I shall do whatever you want, but if you want to return to London, I'll have to act quickly and put a stop to the marketing of your house. If it were to sell in the meantime, there won't be a decision to make."

She chose to walk home, rather than call for a carriage. It was a chilly afternoon but she was well wrapped up against the cold. She looked in the shop windows – all decorated for Christmas – but actually saw nothing. Her mind was in turmoil - what should she do? What was the wisest thing? But she had time to think about it and was touched to learn just how much Papa had loved both her and the children. She'd think about it over the next few days.

When she arrived home, Nanny Mary and the children were helping Mrs Smithers the housekeepe, to dress the house with evergreens and berries. The decorations made her address the fact it was Christmas next day. She'd been ignoring the festive season because of her father's death, but the housekeeper and Nanny had put her to shame by making some jolly changes to the house and keeping Christmas alive.

She turned on her heels at the front door, "Mrs Smithers, I have to go back out again – there's a few things I need to get. Everything is looking lovely – please don't stop and I'll help when I get back. Straight back into the shops, she found several things the children would love. She found a lovely silk scarf for Nanny and a box of embroidered handkerchiefs for Mrs Smithers. She even bought some pretty hair ribbons for the little maid – the girl would love them. She had so little time and it was Christmas Eve already, but she was lucky and found most of the things she wanted. This time, she had to call for a carriage as her bags were more than she could manage. She couldn't resist sampling one of the bonbons she'd bought. Scrumptious! Albert would love them. The thought of her son, made her think of her late husband. *I miss Richard so much and always will but my job now is to look after his children and Papa has made that easy for me.* His generosity had made her a very wealthy woman. *But why did the two men she loved so much have to die – one after the other?*

In the large sitting room the three servants – the maid, housekeeper and cook had joined the family - and Nanny, of course. The children were so excited, they couldn't sit still.

A roaring fire and many candles gave a pleasant glow to the room and the greenery tucked behind every picture glistened and shone, reminding everyone it was Christmas night, the night the baby Jesus was born. Candle light was so soothing and warm, the room couldn't have looked better. The children had opened their gifts and Victoria was holding her baby doll, refusing to put her down even for a moment. Now the man of the family, Albert had carefully taken his train set to his bedroom so he could admire it later from the comfort of his bed. They looked like two lucky and happy children, despite all they'd just been through.

"Right, what shall we play now? Blind Man's Bluff has quite exhausted me and I need something less strenuous." Elizabeth paused for breath and threw herself onto the sofa where Nanny was already sitting.

Mrs Smithers said tentatively, "I know a game we haven't played yet. I used to play it when I was a child. It's called Snapdragon and it's good fun but we'd have to be very careful, especially with the children, as it can be quite dangerous. It is exciting though." She looked shyly at her hands, wondering if she'd gone too far. Was it her place to suggest such a thing?

"Oh yes, I know the game you mean." Cook looked quite excited at the thought and her usually red cook's cheeks shone even more in the candle light. "As long as we watch the children carefully, I think it would be a great game." She was almost bouncing on her chair at the mere thought of Snapdragon.

"Tell us what we have to do?" Elizabeth asked.

"Well," Mrs Smithers said, "we need a shallow bowl filled with candied fruit – raisins, sultanas and nuts – we then fill the bowl with brandy and set it alight. But first we have to blow out all the candles and put a spoonful of salt in the bowl as well. The salt makes our faces glow deathly white in the dark. We then take turns of bravely – and quickly - snatching the fruit from the blue flames of the fire – the quicker you snatch, the less chance of being burned. The winner is the one who gets the most fruit – and the prize is eating all the fruit you get."

Betty the maid, jumped up and said she'd go to the kitchen and get what was needed. In the meantime, the others blew out the candles and the room had only the bright glow of the fire. The children couldn't help sniggering and laughing but Elizabeth stressed it was a dangerous game and they mustn't allow their fingers to dawdle in the flames. "Or you'll pay for it by burning your fingers."

Betty returned and put the bowl on the table in the middle of the room. Mrs Smithers poured a large helping of brandy into the bowl. Amazingly, the salt did its work and everyone's faces turned a ghostly white colour. Cook said she'd go first as she'd played it before and that was the cue for lots of laughter and some tears, from those whose hands lingered too long in the flames. Albert was especially good at winning fruits and he didn't burn himself once – well, he said he didn't. Victoria refused to try and just squealed with delight as everyone else grabbed the fruit.

"Has anyone noticed that all the candles have come alight again – now that we've finished playing the Snapdragon. How could that be? "They all looked accusingly at each other but no-one owned up.

"It's like a miracle." Nanny said, "A real miracle."

"Or a visit from the occult perhaps – some passing witch did it." Albert preferred the occult theory and not the miracle one.

Everyone sat in silence as the flames in the bowl flickered and eventually died. Elizabeth said, "I know a game we haven't played yet. Have you heard of Squeak Piggy Squeak?"

No-one had so she explained. It wasn't a dangerous game like Snapdragon but it was exciting. "We all sit on our chairs with a cushion on our lap. The farmer stands in the centre – one of us has to be the farmer - and he makes a note of where everyone is sitting. He is then blindfolded and turned around ten times whilst all of us silently change seats. He then feels his way to one of the cushions and sits on it, saying, 'Squeak Piggy Squeak'. That person then squeaks or grunts like a pig and the farmer has to guess who it is. Well, what do you think?"

"It's not as exciting as Snapdragon, but at least you don't get burned. I think it sounds like fun." Betty the maid was feeling braver now although she wasn't used to being in the sitting room with the mistress. It was Christmas however and the mistress was so nice.

And so, the game was played and, in the end, everyone was snorting like pigs and laughing fit to burst. The children were then chased to bed by Nanny and Mrs Smithers promised

Elizabeth she'd come down extra early next morning to clear away the 'debris.' The mistress was still too excited to go to bed yet, so she sat by the dying embers of the fire and stared at it. She suddenly felt quite tired and didn't know whether she'd fallen asleep or not, but suddenly she found herself wide awake. Papa was sitting opposite her and smoking his old pipe. He looked very comfortable and she was delighted to see him. "Why Papa, I hadn't realised you were here."

The lovely, familiar voice floated through the air, "Ah yes my daughter, I've always been here. As long as you're in this house, so will I be. I promised to keep you safe and I intend to keep my word." Bernard sounded just like his old self.

"You don't have to worry about me Papa, I'm all right." She replied quietly, less she frighten him away. "Are you happy where you are now? Please say you are, I couldn't bear if it wasn't so."

"I'm happy enough daughter, but I would have liked to spend this last Christmas with you and the children before I left. Actually, I suppose I have spent it with you all and a grand Christmas it was. I especially liked Squeak Piggy Squeak. I laughed quietly so I didn't scare anyone – but I forgot myself and almost gave my presence away when re-lit all the candles."

"Was that you papa, we did wonder?" She made to cross to his chair, but he raised a hand, "Don't approach me Elizabeth, I've not yet fully passed over and human contact at this stage could prevent it." He paused before continuing, " I know you're thinking about whether to stay in this house or to go back to the one in London." In fact, I believe you've already made up your mind – is that not so?" Papa's figure seemed more indistinct than when she'd first seen him.

"Yes, I have Papa, I'm going to take the children back to the home they've always known – and I'm going to ask the staff here if they'd like to join me. Your generous legacy has made it possible. I can't thank you enough for that."

"That's what I thought and I wish you well. You don't have to worry about me – once my spirit has fully passed over, I won't be here any longer – but I'll always look after you and the children." He paused again and she knew something more was coming, " But what I have to tell you is this – you are about to undergo some further experiences of 'Deja-Vu' - they will surprise you greatly." Whatever you have to face, you must remember you are the only support the children now have and you must protect them accordingly."

He was barely visible now and Elizabeth had to lean forward to hear, "Papa, where are you going? You seem to be fading."

"I must go now daughter, my spirit is weakening and coming to see you has drained my strength. I may not be able to come again, but remember I will always love you and the children." He was gone and once more, she was just a woman sitting in a room beside a dying fire. Her dear, lovely father had disappeared and might never return.

She sat bolt upright, her precious dream fading away. *But had it been a dream – had she really been asleep? No, she told herself, that was no dream – Papa had really been here.* She stumbled upstairs and fell fully dressed, on the bed. Sleep immediately came and she slept soundly until the morning light came through the unclosed curtains and shocked her awake.

Now that Papa's unexpected visit had helped with her decision, she made an appointment to see the solicitor and instructed him to ask his London office to remove her home from the market. Now she needed him to put Papa's house on the market instead. Mr Matthews said he would act on her instructions immediately and Elizabeth left his office with more of a spring in her step than she'd had for ages. Making decisions was good for the soul!

Amazingly, the housekeeper and the cook said they'd love to work in London – Betty, on the other hand, said she couldn't leave the area as she had a sweetheart living close by and he wouldn't like if she moved so far away.

"Perfectly understandable my dear, of course you must stay here." Elizabeth knew she'd have no problem finding a replacement maid in London. She first began going through Papa's bits and pieces in his study before asking Mrs Smithers if she would help her clear out the attic. There were lots of memories everywhere. Papa had obviously thrown nothing away, especially things that had belonged to her mother. As usual at times like this, her mind travelled back to when she was young. She selected papers, photos and personal bits and pieces, planning to pass them onto the children in due course. It was a sad time but it had to be done and the housekeeper was a great help.

The day soon arrived when Betty left her employment and Cook and Mrs Smithers were sent ahead of the family, to prepare the London house for their arrival. Their carriage was packed to the gills with household items as Cook swore she couldn't do without her special pans and baking tins. As her baking was so wonderful, Elizabeth didn't want to jeopardise things by reminding her there were plenty of such things in London. Nanny Mary travelled with them as well, in order to prepare the children's rooms but she was squashed into a small corner of the carriage and all thanks to Cook's special pots and pans.

Two days later, Elizabeth and the children started their journey in another hired carriage. Although it was the end of January, the day was bright but cold - no rainy clouds however and very different from when they'd travelled here a few weeks ago. She'd often thought about the Winship family and of the strange things she'd experienced in their house. It was incredible to think of the repeated arguments and traumas between husband and wife – and how the staff just accepted the shocking, every day events – and murders - as if they were normal.

"Children, I plan to make one stop before we reach home. It won't take long but I think it's the right thing to do. Do you remember the short time we stayed at the mansion in the countryside – after the dreadful storm when the carriage ended in a ditch?"

Albert looked thoughtful before saying, "Perhaps I'll be able to see the crippled boy again – the one who gave me his drawing book and soldiers. I'd like that Mummy because I liked him." Elizabeth explained he'd just have to wait and see. She knew she had to humour her son.

The first few miles passed without incident until the countryside became familiar again. *Yes, I remember this area although John the footman had rushed us through it. Yes, she remembered it well! She had to smile as she wondered how many more times the master and mistress had murdered each other since she'd seen them last.*

The carriage turned a final corner in the lane and Elizabeth saw a house – a large house, or at least a house that had once been large. Now it was merely a shell with its rafters showing to the elements. The walls were blackened and broken, the windows were shattered and filthy and there were various pieces of furniture lying around the building. There was no sign of life and Elizabeth could only sit and stare from the carriage window. Slowly she climbed down and told the children to stay inside, "I won't be long," she told the driver and walked around the burnt-out mansion. *How had it happened – it must have been very recent as she'd been there only a few weeks earlier. Was anyone hurt in the fire, she wondered? What had happened to the servants and had Lord and Lady Winship survived? So many questions filled her mind as she sat down on a broken chair that seemed less blackened than the others.*

She suddenly heard men's voices and she turned to look at the carriage. The driver was talking to an elderly man dressed all in black – a vicar she thought. She walked back to the carriage and introduced herself to the stranger.

He shook her hand and bowed, "A sad sight, isn't it? Even the trees have never grown back. It was a devastating fire and no mistake."

"Do you know what caused it, Sir? And do you know what happened to the servants – and of course to the master and mistress? I met them all only a few weeks ago and everyone was hale and hearty then."

"Oh no my dear, I don't think that could have happened. Perhaps you're mistaking the house for another in the area?" The vicar seemed quite certain that Elizabeth was wrong. After all, he thought it was quite easy to mistake one house for another – especially in the wilds of the countryside.

"No Vicar, this is the house I knew – there's no mistake. It was Lord and Lady Winship's' home and I met all the servants as well. Everyone was so kind to my children and to me the night we were caught in a terrible storm and our carriage broke down. They took us in and we stayed with them for a couple of days. No, there's no mistake about it, it was this very house."

He felt very sorry for the confused young woman and asked if she'd like to come to the vicarage for some hot tea, "And then I can tell you the story of what happened here."

Elizabeth accepted with gratitude. The children would welcome a hot drink and so would the driver – and it need only take a half hour or so.

The vicarage was only 5 minutes away and the driver followed behind the vicar's smaller carriage. A sweet cottage soon appeared, right beside the church itself which sat in the middle of a graveyard where there were some very old tombstones. The whole sight was idyllic and looked just as it should. The old vicar climbed down from his carriage and tied the horse to a fence post just outside the front door.

"Do come in – and the children of course. Your driver can go straight to the kitchen where I'm sure Cook will spoil him atrociously. She loves visitors and always treats them like long lost friends." He took them into a small sitting room where a welcoming fire was burning in the grate. There were plump cushions on the sofa and several comfortable armchairs dotted around the room. In one of the chairs sat a little, round darling of a woman who smiled at the newcomers as though she'd been expecting them. Her husband often turned up with strangers for tea and she always catered for extra people, just in case.

"Do please make yourselves comfortable and I'll ring for tea. You must help yourselves to the goodies on the table there – all freshly baked and prepared by Cook's light fingers. After that, I'm sure my husband will want to show you around his church – he's very proud of his church, you know." She reached over and rang the bell-pull.

Whilst they waited, the vicar told his wife that the lady and her children were looking at the burnt-out mansion when he found them. "The day was cold and they looked tired so of course I invited them here. Miss Elizabeth here was surprised to find the mansion was now derelict – a burnt-out shell in fact. She knew the Winships and the house itself. I must admit she seems young to have known them but she insists that she did."

"It was sad when the fire happened – it took hold of the house very quickly and the results are what you've seen today. The Winships died in the fire, you know – as did all the servants who were at home that night. How long ago did it happen Husband?" she asked the vicar.

"All of 20 years my dear – in fact slightly longer than that, I think. One day, the building stood there proudly and by the next night, it was no more. Years of history wiped out by a single act. When examined later, it was discovered the fire had begun in the master's bedroom when a candle was knocked over and left burning. The fire soon spread up the curtains and then it was like a tinder-box, igniting every flammable thing in sight. The smoke apparently overcame everyone in the house – and I'm afraid that was that. God works in mysterious ways but it is his will of course."

"I'm sorry Sir, but it couldn't have happened so long ago – I stayed there myself only a few months ago and met the Winships and their staff." She turned to Albert and asked, "You remember Lord Winship, don't you Albert?" And of course, the boy nodded his agreement, adding "I remember the smashing playroom and all the toys as well."

"And so do I." Victoria shyly backed her brother's words.

There was an awkward silence in the room, only broken by a young maid carrying a silver tray of tea things. It seemed wiser to drop the subject of the mansion – for the time being only – it could be revived after sharing Cook's goodies. The different stories however, hung in the air as they differed so much from one other.

However, the mood soon changed as the children munched their way through the spread of delicacies. Elizabeth too was surprised at how hungry she felt, but then it had been a long time since breakfast. Meal over, little Victoria fell asleep from a full stomach and from the warmth of the fire. The vicar again brought up the subject of the burnt-out mansion, something that had to be done, considering the huge discrepancies in either story. He fetched a heavy notebook from a desk and opened it on the table. His finger ran down several lists before stopping at one in particular. "There you are my dear, that's my recording of the funeral services I performed when the Winships died." And there on the paper clear as crystal, were the names of the Lord and his Lady with a date 22 years before. There was no argument with that and Elizabeth bit her lower lip, feeling really confused.

"How can it be?" was all she said. *What else could she say – she couldn't argue with the man who had performed the service. And why would he lie – or produce falsified documents to prove his assertion? He hadn't known she was coming here today. On the face of the evidence, she realised she must accept what he was saying – although it all seemed impossible.*

"Come my dear, let the children rest here and I'll show you my little church, as well as the graves of the people who died in the fire." His wife placed a shawl over the sleeping child and held her finger to her lips for Albert to be quiet. She found him a book about far-away lands and he settled down on the floor.

The church was just as she'd expected – very old and full of memories of those who'd gone before. It was cold as all old churches were, but it did have a large and beautiful stained-glass window, which cast warming colours of red, green, blue and orange all around the walls. So very pretty!

"How beautiful!" was Elizabeth's first remark, which clearly pleased the old vicar. "The air is cold but the colours warm it so, I can almost feel the heat." She touched the ancient, stone font where numerous babies must have been christened and marvelled at the carvings at the base of the plinth.

Now I want you to brace yourself as we're coming to where Lord and Lady Winship are buried. " And there it was – a beautiful stone slab covered in stylish, gold script, 'Here lies Edwin Winship Lord of this Parish and his Lady wife, Arabella, both of whom perished in a terrible fire at their nearby home. God Bless These Two Souls.' The date was plain and clear and it was 22 years before.

"I understand your shock my dear but I had to remove your delusion for your own sake. It might help however, if I were to tell you of the numerous sightings people have experienced throughout the years – sometimes local people and sometimes passers-by who don't know the area. They've individually claimed that on certain nights, the mansion appears intact and as splendid as it was before – there are lights at all the windows and laughter can be heard inside. The local people just turn and run away, knowing full well the building had been totally destroyed and the vision was some sort of visitation from the occult. The passers-by knew no better and just passed on away from the house, thinking what a charming building it was. Does this perhaps help with what you might have experienced a few weeks ago?"

Elizabeth agreed it made some sense but she'd actually stayed there and met everyone. The occult couldn't have been part of her experiencer – and yet – the strange things that occurred between the master and mistress were not exactly normal. She told him, "But after killing each other, they were both well and healthy the next morning – and then it all started up again. I'm honestly not mad – it really did happen. Are you sure none of the servants survived the fire? "

"One servant did – John, the footman and he now works for the village blacksmith. It would do no good to search him out though, he wouldn't be able to confirm your story – since he was saved from the fire, he's been unable to see and I'm afraid his mind is quite deranged. I'm truly sorry, but I might be able to offer you some explanation – have you ever heard the phrase 'Deja Vu?"   She told him she hadn't, but that she knew it translated in French to 'Already Seen'.

"Exactly my dear – I'm afraid you've been a victim of Déjà Vu. I can't explain any of it as I don't understand it myself, but it suggests that, were you to return to the mansion at some future date, you might find the house and its occupants living there just as you experienced before. With the repeated murders of the Winship's and their return to life the very next day, it was another example of her chronic Déjà Vu. Some people believe it and that it's part of the paranormal and some scientists suggest it's like a prophesy which occurs over and over again – but only to certain people with the right gift. It seems likely my dear that you may be one of those people."

And the conversation could go no further – neither the vicar nor Elizabeth understood the phenomenon and truth to tell, both looked quite scared by it. The vicar's last words to her as she climbed back into her carriage were, "There are more things in Heaven and Earth Horatio, than are dreamt of in your philosophy.' Shakespeare really knew what he was talking about, didn't he?"

The carriage eventually rolled away from the vicarage, where the vicar and his wife stood to wave goodbye – a loving couple, if ever Elizabeth had seen one. "Driver, could we take one last detour before setting off for home? It'll only take a short time and I'll happily pay you if our journey is made longer." Th driver agreed and she told him to drive into the nearby village to the blacksmith's stables. She knew full well the vicar had told her seeing John would be pointless as he was now in no fit state to remember anything, but a feeling inside her said she couldn't be this close and not go to see him. After all, he was the one person alive who knew exactly what had gone on in that house. The one person who might be able to make her feel she wasn't mad.

She saw the blacksmith and asked where John was. "'E be in the stables feedin' the 'orses." Was the reply from a thick, heavy-set man who didn't even trouble to look at her. The inside of the stables was dark, lit only by a tallow candle, but she could see the figure of a man shovelling hay into a trough. She recognised him immediately, but when he turned to face her, she saw a middle-aged man with strange staring eyes that obviously couldn't see her.

"John, don't be afraid. It's Elizabeth – the lady who stayed at the mansion a few weeks ago – the lady you drove to her father's house. The one who said she had to get away from the house. Do you remember?" She waited with baited breath and at last he moved closer. "If it were only a few weeks ago ma'am, it must 'ave 'appened on one o' the occasions when the 'ouse would've come alive again. Were that it? Were it when the ghosts walked?"

"I think it must have been John but you do remember myself and my children, don't you? We'd been caught in a storm and the carriage had gone off the road so we stayed at the mansion for a few days."

"Yep, that were it! It were one o' the special times when that 'appened – and I 'ad to go and fetch yer luggage, didn't I?"

"You did John and you brought it safely to the house. I've heard about the fire and how everyone but you, died. For my own sanity, do you agree your master and mistress repeatedly murdered each other but came back to life each morning? It happened twice whilst I was there. Am I talking sense John – I need your reassurance that I am?"

"Aye that be true Ma'am," and his voice dropped to a whisper as if he didn't want anyone else to hear. "Every time the 'ousel comes back t' life, so do the people – even me when I was a young man. I'm part of them, you see. At first, I tried to tell people the truth, but no-one believed me an' now they call me Mad John. But I'm not mad, am I Ma'am? It all 'appened just as I said an' now only you know it's true."

That was it – she'd heard it from his own lips – and he certainly wasn't mad – maybe a bit slow, but not mad. She wished she could change things for him but with the passage of so much time, the villagers had obviously made up their minds. *Poor John! What strange memories he must have.* She searched her reticule and brought out 5 gold sovereigns

which she pressed into his hands. "That'll last you some time John – it's just a thank you for how kind you were to me. Goodbye and take care of yourself – you're certainly not mad and just ignore those who say you are. You and I know the truth!"

She left him then, climbed aboard the carriage, feeling completely exonerated. It all

had happened just as she said it had. *'I'm not mad either!'* *she thought.*

The children were sound asleep in the carriage and she took care not to waken them.

"One other favour driver – and remember I'll recompense you for the time I've wasted – could we return once again to the burnt-out house we passed earlier? There's something I have to do before going home." Th driver just nodded. He was getting used to the eccentric woman and as she'd promised to pay him, why should he care?

Ten minutes later, they turned into the driveway that led to the mansion. "I'll get out here driver and walk the rest of the way – I promise I'll not linger. Now I know what actually happened at the house, I just want to say good-bye to some people I knew there." He gave her a strange look but said nothing.

She started walking along the drive. The day was getting darker but as she reached the bend, she sensed things were going to be different from last time. She saw no burnt-out mansion now, just a solid house with welcoming lights shining from every window. Everything was just as she remembered when she and the children had stayed there before. She could clearly see the dining room through the large window and along the table, were the usual line of candlesticks. The whole room was ablaze with light. She stepped closer to the window and saw Lord Winship and Lady Arabella sitting at opposite ends of the table. They seemed to be laughing at something and looked unusually genial towards each other.

Creeping around to the back of the house, she had to jump backwards as the kitchen door was suddenly thrown open and rosy-cheeked Cook came into the yard. She carried a pail of soapy water which she poured down a drain in the yard. Everything seemed quite normal and everyone was acting as they'd always done. There was no sight nor smell of blackened walls and she realised this must be 'one of the special nights' John had spoken of – the nights when everything reverted to what it had once been.

Cook had looked so familiar and friendly that she wished she could speak to her, but she mustn't do that as the woman was only a mirage – something unreal and a trick of her mind, in fact an example of her Déjà Vu powers. She gave a heavy sigh and knew she must leave as quietly as she'd arrived. It was all so familiar to her but she knew she was experiencing nothing more than a case of Déjà Vu yet again, something she'd have to get used to as it was bound to happen again.

She took one last look at the blazing lights in the windows and began to walk back down the drive. The driver had brought the carriage to meet her as it was properly dark by then. She stopped by the horse and looked up at him, "Isn't it a wonderful sight? A bit different from when you saw it last, isn't it? Every window exudes happiness and warmth, doesn't it?"

"I'm sure it's as you say Ma'am – everything looks as it should." She climbed into the carriage, into the company of the sleeping children who hadn't even stirred. The driver's thoughts were, *'Cor blimey, the gentry really is sixpence short o' a shillin'*

*an' no mistake. The place look as bad as it did earlier today –
can't imagine what she's lookin' at.'* And he told the horse to
'giddy-up' and they'd soon be home.

Meanwhile at the London house, Cook and Mrs Smithers had
already opened up the house and aired all the rooms, ready for
when Elizabeth and the children arrived. Neither had ever visited
the house before so it took more effort than usual – they had also
been instructed to advertise for a general maid and one for the
scullery. When Elizabeth finally arrived home, the maids were
being already being interviewed in the kitchen.

"Well done ladies – you managed everything nicely – let's
hope you find someone suitable. The children and I can manage
as we don't want to disturb your interviews – the carriage driver
has offered to take our valises upstairs, so don't give us another
thought for the present."

It felt odd being here again – she'd made up her mind that
when she'd left, it would be for good, but things don't always
work out as planned. She took the children to their old rooms
and as expected, they soon settled as if they'd never been away.

"Mummy, now that we're home again, do you think daddy
will come back?" Victoria would have preferred everything to
be exactly as it had been before.

"Now darling, you're too big a girl to ask such a thing. You
know Daddy's in Heaven with God and that he's quite happy."
She lifted the little girl onto her lap.

"Are you sure about that Mummy?" Albert joined the
conversation. "Sometimes people come back after they die –
remember the boy in the mansion, the boy who used crutches?
He told me he'd died and yet I saw him as plainly as I see you. I
liked him too, although he was older than me – he told me it was
his death that caused his parents to row all the time. His father
told him to ride with the Hunt but his mother told him not to. He
obeyed his father and unfortunately fell from his horse and hurt
himself badly – he had to stay in bed for a long time and then he
died – so his mother blamed his father. It's a sad story, isn't it?"
He seemed to need to tell the story again and he was actually
holding the soldiers he said the boy had given him. She nodded
her head, but didn't know what to say. She'd actually seen the
anger between the boy's mother and father for herself.

"I'm just going downstairs to see how Mrs Smithers is getting on. Nanny is in the room next door sorting out your clothes, so if you want anything, go see her." And she disappeared into the corridor where, for the first time ever, she felt an intense cold that wrapped around her whole body. She was shivering and yet the housekeeper had made sure a fire burned in every room, so why was this particular spot so cold? Shrugging her shoulders, she went downstairs and told herself not to be so silly. It was just a draught.

"Yes Ma'am, we've found two girls we believe will be suitable. They're both young and have clean hair and finger nails – a sure way to judge their suitability." Mrs Smithers had obviously done this type of thing before.

Everyone slept well that night – everyone except Elizabeth, that is. She'd looked forward to sleeping in her own bed, the one she'd shared with her husband but more than once, she found herself reaching for the reassuring presence of her husband. *That isn't going to happen again Elizabeth. I'm afraid, you'll just have to get used to it.* And she turned onto her side, praying that sleep would soon claim her.

It took a couple of days for everything to be just so - but soon, she found the time to visit the London solicitor, a colleague of Mr Matthews. She'd never been responsible for paying bills and dealing with tradesmen – Richard had seen to all that - so now she needed advice from someone who could help her. "Do sit down Mrs Lawrence – my colleague Mr Matthews has already made me aware of your situation and I am only too pleased to offer what assistance I can. Should you have any problems you must come to me and I will endeavour to help." He spoke rather pompously but had a kind face - she liked him from the start. As Mr Matthews had done, he had his secretary bring in some tea things, then he sat back in his chair, ready to listen. She found she could speak easily to him.

When their conversation was over, he hesitated before saying, "Mrs Lawrence, there is something I have to tell you - a couple of weeks following your husband's death, I received a letter from a gentleman, a gentleman who'd lived in New Zealand until recently. He'd heard about Mr Lawrence's death from a mutual friend and asked me if I felt he you were ready to receive friends

– he wanted to offer you his condolences. At the time, you were in the first stages of bereavement and I asked if he could leave it for a little while. Then I never heard from him again and I assume he never did contact you. You left London then to visit with your father and that was that. I felt however I should tell you now – his name was Robert Thompson. Is that name known to you?"

She thought for a moment before saying she'd never heard of him. "Perhaps he knew my husband when he was younger but I don't recall him mentioning such a person – and do remember, we were married for almost 10 years. But no, I've never heard of a Robert Thompson." He told her it didn't matter and perhaps it was a case of mistaken identity.

On the way home, she imagined someone was following her – when she stopped to look at a shop window, so did her follower. When she finally turned into her Square, she saw there was no-one there. Anyway, why should anyone be following her?

The house was warm and cosy now with everything working as normal and she went straight to the back hall and into the kitchen, where Cook was asleep in her rocking chair. She tip-toed so as not to scare her, but the woman sensed she was there and abruptly sat bolt upright. "Why Ma'am, you're back – you should have rung for me and I'd have come. You shouldn't have to come to me."

"Don't be silly Cook – it's no trouble. I just wanted to go over tomorrow's meals with you – to see if you needed anything." She flopped herself down on a chair and waited for the sleepy woman to become fully awake.

Rather surprisingly, Cook said, "By the way Ma'am, I know the house has heated up warmly now but have you noticed that cold spot just outside the study door. Mrs Smithers remarked on it only today and I went to see. Sure enough, it was uncannily cold there for no obvious reason."

Elizabeth was surprised at such a question, "Strangely enough I have noticed a cold spot upstairs outside the blue bedroom. You've found one outside the study now – but no, I haven't noticed but I will check now."

Sure enough, it was similar to what she'd felt upstairs – icy cold air in just a small area. Mrs Smithers came upon her and asked if she needed anything. Elizabeth told her what she was doing and the housekeeper agreed she could feel it too. "If the cold spots don't disappear and there's nothing obvious causing them, perhaps we'll have to ask the local vicar to call – it could be a spirit unwilling to leave this place and in need of a little encouragement."

Elizabeth couldn't help smiling at the housekeeper's dramatic interpretation of the chilly air and promised her she would look into it. Mrs Smithers went off to investigate the cold spot outside the bedroom door and Elizabeth returned to the warm parlour. Everything was nice and cosy and she settled on the sofa with a book she was thoroughly enjoying.

After a few pages, she woke up and felt cold. The fire had gone out, which shouldn't have happened as there'd been a huge burning log there just a short time before. She sat up and for some reason, was reminded of the time Papa's spirit had visited her. Sitting in his favourite armchair was Richard, her dead husband – he seemed solid and substantial. She didn't move or speak – she had no idea what to do next. He stood with his back to the fireplace and rested his arm on the mantlepiece – just as he always did.

"You look surprised my darling – why is that?" He looked just as he always had and the tears welled up in her eyes.

"Oh Richard, I have missed you. So much has happened in the last few weeks, I don't know where to begin." He reassured her he already knew everything she'd been through and he'd only come to make sure she was alright.

"I'm all right Husband, but being without you has been a nightmare."

Just as she was about to say something else, the parlour door opened and the new maid came in, carrying a tea tray. "Cook sent you this madam, she said you looked as though you needed it – and she said to put lots of sugar in your cup – good for what ails you, she said."

"Why thank you Maisie – tell Cook she's very kind. She raised a hand towards Richard and said, "This is the master Maisie, although you've never met him."

The maid looked puzzled and looked around the room, "Why Madam, there's no-one else here – perhaps you've been dreaming." And when Elizabeth looked towards the fire, which was burning again, Richard had gone. *Had he been there? She was so sure he had! But she couldn't argue with Maisie, could she?*

"Thank you anyway Maisie and you are right, I must have fallen asleep and was dreaming." She dismissed the girl and the room returned to normal. Richard was of course nowhere to be seen. *It must have been all that rubbish Mrs Smithers had spoken – about asking the vicar to carry out some kind of exorcism. Whatever next!*

Next morning, Nanny took the children to the park and when she brought them back, they were rosy-cheeked and giggling. She told them "Say hello to your mother children and then I'll take you upstairs where I'm sure Cook will have left out milk and biscuits." Mary was glad to be home again – she was used to this house and she was a true Londoner after all.

"Mary, do leave them with me for a few moments and I promise to bring them up in 10 minutes. We three conspirators need to have a chat." And she winked at the children, which she knew wasn't very ladylike.

Albert waited for Nanny to disappear before saying excitedly, "We met a man in the park Mummy. He spoke to us and was very nice and do you know the strangest thing – he looked exactly like daddy. He did, didn't he Victoria? "

"Yes, he did Mummy – he really did. But he sounded different though – he didn't sound like daddy."

"Where was Nanny when he was talking to you?" Elizabeth didn't like the idea of a strange man accosting her children. On hearing Nanny had been sitting on a bench nearby and had watched them all the time, she felt reassured and let the subject drop.

The January weather was pretty atrocious with the rain becoming heavier and heavier and the wind whipping up into some proper storms. In fact, it reminded her of the night they'd set off to visit Papa – the night of the worst storm in years. Tonight, seemed just as bad and Mrs Smithers made sure everything was securely locked up before asking if she could retire early – it seemed storms gave her bad headaches. Nanny had tucked the children in bed and was dozing in a chair in her own bedroom. Elizabeth felt quite safe – she knew Cook and Maisie were in the house, so she didn't feel alone. She was working on a new piece of embroidery and was busy choosing different silks, when she heard a sound in the hall. If she hadn't known better, she'd have sworn it was the sound of the front door closing – but that was just silly – no-one would go out in this weather.

The parlour door opened and a man stepped inside. The rain was dripping from him and he looked soaked to the skin. He removed his hat and outer coat and put them in the hall. There stood Richard – a very wet and agitated Richard who'd obviously come through the worst of the storm. Elizabeth gasped and placed her hand to her throat. She knew she wasn't dreaming this time – her late husband was actually standing there, dripping rain onto the carpet. *Déjà Vu! It's Déjà Vu! This is just like the night he came home before – but this time he's soaked to the skin!*

"Richard, is it really you? I'm not dreaming this time, am I?"

"Don't be silly woman, of course it's me. I've just come through the worst storm in years – I left the office and I knew something was coming, but I never imagined it would get this bad." He shook his dripping hair and crouched down in front of the fireplace.

"I'm going straight upstairs darling – I need to feel warm blankets around me. I don't even feel like eating tonight, so I'll miss dinner if you don't mind. You'll tell Cook, won't you?" And before she could answer, he climbed the stairs, leaving wet marks on the stairs as he went.

Now this really was Deja-Vu. She'd known every word before he said it – it was exactly what he'd said the night he'd come home and then developed the pneumonia that killed him. But what did it mean? And why was it happening again? How long would this feeling of Déjà vu last – would she have to watch him becoming more and more ill and finally succumbing to the pneumonia? Please God, don't make me live through that again – I don't think I could bear it. I'm afraid to go upstairs now – what will I find there? Will he have gone to bed, not knowing it would be the last thing he ever did?

She climbed the stairs, relieved to find his wet footprints were no longer there. She arrived at the cold spot on the landing and placed her hand on the bedroom door handle. *Come on Elizabeth, you can do it. If he's not there, you've experienced another weird phenomenon – if he is there, you're no worse off than you were a few minutes ago.*

The bedroom was dark, with only the soft glow of the gas lamps out in the street shining through the window. She moved towards the bed and saw it was empty. Richard wasn't there – in fact, he was nowhere in the room. Again, she'd suffered from a delusion – had he come home as he did on the night of the last storm – or had the torrential rain and atrocious weather reminded her of that time. She left the room quickly and went to the cosy kitchen where Cook would make her welcome.

Two days later, Maisie answered a ring at the front door and there on the doorstep stood Nanny Mary, the two children and a man she'd never seen before. She'd never met the old master, so she didn't find his doppelganger surprising. Nanny Mary however had seen the similarity immediately.

"We've brought Mr Robert to see mother, Maisie. Let us in and we'll take him to her." The boy was so excited he could hardly contain himself.

"No Master Albert, you must let me announce your visitor to the mistress – you know that's the right thing to do." Nanny nodded, the maid was quite right.

"There is a gentleman caller Madam who's asking to see you. May I show him in – or shall I send him on his way?" Maisie wanted to impress the mistress with her knowledge of the correct etiquette.

"Is he a respectable gentleman, Maisie?" And on being told he was, she told the maid to show him in. "The children are with him Madam – and they want to show him in themselves. Is that all right?"

Albert and Victoria came in, each holding the gentleman's hand. Nanny had disappeared to tell Cook what was happening. She'd quickly learned that Cook liked to keep an eye on everything that was going on in the house.

Elizabeth froze when she looked at the stranger. This was no apparition – this man was clearly flesh and blood – and was also

434

visible to the children. But for the style of his clothes, he could have been her late husband and she didn't know what to say.

He made it easy for her and said, "Madam, you must forgive my sudden appearance in your home, but your children were adamant that you wouldn't mind. Should that not be the case, you only have to say and I will be gone. But before I do, may I introduce myself and state my business? My name is Robert Thompson, by the way." He had a pleasant voice with a slight accent – he'd obviously lived overseas for a while.

"If my children have brought you, then you are most assuredly welcome. Do please take a seat." What else could she say? The children were delighted to have him there and she couldn't refuse them anything. But his likeness to Richard was uncanny and disturbed her a lot.

Mummy, can he have a glass of milk with us – and perhaps some of Cook's special cake?" The boy obviously admired the stranger and was as proud as punch to have found him.

She told the children to run along to Cook and ask for the milk and cake – and to be sure to include Mr Robert in the refreshments.

"You do like milk I hope Mr Robert Thompson?" She asked with a smile. "I usually offer my visitors tea or coffee, but in your case, the children have already decided for you."

"Milk and cake would be excellent Madam." And Albert and Victoria ran off to give Cook her instructions.

"Well Sir, perhaps you'll tell me your business now? In fairness, I should tell you that your appearance has shocked me – you bear a remarkable resemblance to my late husband – and that may be the reason the children are so taken with you." She felt, it would have been wrong not to have mentioned this at the outset. It was the honest thing to do.

Strangely, he chose to sit in the chair that had always been Richard's favourite. He explained he'd already contacted her solicitor some time ago, but had been advised it wasn't the right time to approach her. "He was right of course, it was just the beginning of your bereavement, so I left it for a while and then I spotted you'd come back to the house to live. The place had been in darkness for several weeks and I saw a 'For Sale' sign in the garden, so I thought I'd never be able to meet you – but the lights in the windows told me otherwise – and here I am, courtesy of your children."

"But why was it so important for you to meet me, Sir?" she asked,

"Please call me Robert and may I call you Elizabeth – you see, I happen to know we're related. In fact, I believe you are my sister-in-law." He went on, "I have lived in New Zealand all my life – my adoptive parents took me there when I was just a baby. They adopted me from a country vicar whose wife had just died in childbirth. She'd given birth to twin boys, for whom he was now the sole provider. He lived in a very poor parish and didn't have the where-with-all to raise both children. And that's when he made the decision - which I'm sure wasn't an easy one – to give up one of the boys for adoption. The charity he used was a religious one and so he felt sure any potential parents would be more than suitable. And that's where I come in as I can confirm they were very suitable, kind and supportive. They raised me as an only son, but never hid the fact from me that I was adopted. They emigrated to New Zealand as they believed it would be a country of opportunity and they spent their frugal means on providing me with an excellent education – hence the lawyer status I have attained."

The man actually looked exhausted after his long speech – it was easy to see he wanted to get everything off his chest. The children however, chose that moment to burst into the room, followed closely by Cook herself.

"They said you wanted cake and milk for four people. An unusual request, so I thought I'd better come along and check if it was true." It was easy to tell the children had been harassing her in the kitchen as she looked quite flustered.

"Yes, thank you Cook, that's what they were supposed to tell you." Elizabeth smiled her gratitude to the woman.

The next half hour passed in a flurry of excited chatter – Albert in particular was beside himself with excitement. The creamy cake was soon demolished and the glasses emptied, when Elizabeth told the youngsters to go upstairs and ask Nanny if she would wash their sticky faces and hands. Of course, they objected but Elizabeth insisted – she wanted to hear the rest of

Robert's story. Alone, she waited for him to pick up where he'd left off – and he did.

"Thank you for the refreshments Elizabeth – I feel much better now. To get back to my story however - until quite recently, I had no wish to leave New Zealand – but then something happened a little while ago, that made me change my mind. I was sitting by my fireside one evening when I had an odd experience. Everything suddenly went dark and very cold. I had no idea what was going on and when the fire in the grate went out and the room became even colder, I began to feel afraid. I felt as though I'd suffered a great loss and that someone close to me had died. My parents, who have now passed on, were always open with me – they told me I'd been born one of twins and the other had been a boy as well. I knew then who had died and that he'd wanted me to know. I felt more alone than I'd ever felt before and yet, I'd never known nor met him – I knew however that he existed and that had always been enough. In my head, I clearly heard a voice telling me I must come to England and seek you out." He paused then, waiting for her to speak and maybe tell him he was being ridiculous - but she didn't. She just sat and stared at him.

"And here I am Ma'am, at your service." He added, hoping she would speak now.

"You're going to have to give me some time to digest what you've just said. Until now, I'd never known of your existence – my husband never told me he was one of twins, but perhaps his father – who by the way, was a vicar – never told him he'd given away his brother. I honestly don't know that but this is too much for me to take in at once." She genuinely sounded upset. "Will you leave me now please – I've learned a lot in the last few minutes – so much to take in?"

"Certainly, but you should know you've also taught me something I knew nothing about. I never knew my brother and I were identical twins – just twins. Maybe you've just explained why I knew he'd died, he really was half of me, wasn't he?" And since that night when I learned of his death, I've felt both lonely and very alone. I'll go now but thank you for your hospitality. Should you need me, here's my card – the address there is some rooms I've rented at Charing Cross." And he left the house quietly.

The next few days passed in a flurry of activity for the household. Elizbeth had decided about the children's education and rather than employ a tutor, she searched out a good school which was quite close by. She had to persuade Albert it would be a good thing – and he'd learn so much – but the boy didn't warm to the idea. Victoria, on the other hand, was very enthusiastic – she would be able to show off her new dresses to other little girls – make new friends which would be a plus for her – and of course the learning, in that order.

With the children attending day school, Elizabeth found she had time to herself. Her husband hadn't appeared to her again – perhaps the recent incidents had been his way of preparing her for the shock of his twin brother. Mr Robert's sudden appearance had been quite a bombshell after all.

The next months, February and March were dark and dank and Elizabeth found she often thought of her new brother-in-law – but she couldn't bring herself to contact him. His card was on the mantlepiece – but she tried not to look at it. *I'm not sure what he wants of me. Perhaps he genuinely wants to support me – but I don't need support, I believe I've managed quite well since both Richard and Papa died. Perhaps he wants something from me – perhaps he's lonely and wants to be part of the family. The thought made her feel she should be more generous to him – and perhaps invite him to dinner or something. The children would have to be present as he obviously liked them, so perhaps it should be lunch – and not on a school day. I'll send Maisie to his address with an invitation – that's what I'll do.*

He turned up on the doorstep a week later. Now he was dressed more like an English gentleman and looked even more like his twin brother. It was an odd situation and she found it difficult.

"Do sit down Robert – I'm sorry it took so long to contact you, but we had a few things to sort out – the children's schooling for example." She offered him a pre-lunch sherry.

Thank you and don't worry about the time, I've been rather busy myself. I'm in the process of buying a large house in the countryside. When I sold my business in New Zealand, I made quite a bit of money and I want to put it to good use. I intend to remain in this country and make it my home now." He gulped, rather than sipped his sherry and she quickly refilled his glass.

"That sounds very exciting. Where exactly is it?" She asked.

"Well, I'm being a bit premature I suppose. I'm actually buying the land on which it stands – the house itself is derelict and in a dreadful state of repair. Buying the land is the cheaper part of the deal – the rebuilding of the house is what will swallow up the money. I'm excited about it however – it's the sort of undertaking I've always wanted and I know I'm going to enjoy it." He sounded eager to get started.

But when he told her where in the countryside the house actually was, she felt her blood run cold and she began to shiver. She asked hesitantly, "Was the house destroyed in a fire by any chance?"

"Why yes it was – but I'm going to undo all the damage – it'll be like a Phoenix rising from the ashes. Perhaps you and the children would like to drive out with me to see it. I'd appreciate your opinion as to the location – it's about a hundred miles from here and my money will go a lot further than if I bought in London. I realise it'll take some time to get there, but I know there's an hotel in the nearby village where we could all stay for the night. What do you say – it would be an adventure and I'm sure the children would love it? Do say you'll come Elizabeth." His eagerness was infectious and he was right, the children would love the adventure.

"Very well Robert – that would be exciting and I'm very curious about the house's location." She hoped very much she was wrong and it wasn't the mansion she knew – but she had to find out.

One week later, a smart coach and driver drew up outside Elizabeth's front door and she and the children came eagerly down the steps. Seated comfortably, Robert tapped the carriage roof with his cane and their journey began. It was a lovely drive and the passengers felt not a bump – until they left the outskirts of London that is and ventured into the countryside.

Elizabeth began to recognise the passing scenery and eventually they'd reached the village Robert had spoken of.

As he'd promised, the hotel was very suitable – small, but suitable- and there was a coach house where the driver could bed down the horses – and as he was used to doing, he would just sleep in the hay loft. It was a driver's lot in life.

Before eating, they decided to take a short walk around the village. The weather was fair and it wasn't yet dark, so they wandered on for a while before Elizabeth saw a man coming towards them. He seemed familiar and then she recognised him. He was dressed much smarter than when she'd seen him last, but it was definitely John, the footman – she'd have known him anywhere. He still used a white stick of course, but she could see a quickness in his step that hadn't been there before.

Ma'am, is it really you?" He spoke first and stopped in the road. He obviously could see better than before.

"John, how lovely to see you – and looking so well. What a transformation!"

She introduced Robert and added with a smile, "You already know these two ruffians, don't you?"

He greeted the children – shook Albert's hand and kissed Victoria's. "Now, what are ye doin' in this part o' the world?" But before she could answer, he told her how his fortunes had changed and all because of the five gold sovereigns she'd given him. He'd gone straight to the bank and asked how he could make it grow. As simple as that! 'Invest in the right stocks and shares." I were told,'and so I did just that Ma'am – and do ye know, 'e was right. I may not be rich but I'm comfortable an' I don't work at the blacksmiths any longer – instead I be the pot man at the Risin' Sun in't village. What do ye think o' that?"

I think that's wonderful John – well done!" Elizabeth was touched by his gratitude and was glad he'd done so well for himself. From little acorns, great oak trees grow – and that's exactly what he did with his money.

"I must be off now Ma'am – Sir – and children. I'm due at tavern now, but before I go, I just wanted t'ask - Yer not goin' near that ol' 'ouse, are ye? I've no wish t'be impertinent, but ye know it's a bad place an' not for the likes of ye. To this day, I've never gone back." And without another word, he was off to his duties as pot man. Needless to say, Robert looked puzzled and asked what the man had meant – in fact he actually asked if the man was mad. "He certainly looked mad when he was talking about the house."

"Don't worry Robert, John's always been a little strange and sometimes he says things he doesn't mean. He gets confused, you see and his disability is the result of working at the house you're interested in – he was caught in the fire that burnt it down and he can't get over it. He blames the house, you see." She didn't want to go into how she knew John or how she'd once stayed at the house in question – and that only some months ago. It was all too complicated! And would he believe her anyway?

Albert and Victoria thought it great fun to dine like grown-ups in the hotel that night and Robert raised an eyebrow to Elizabeth at the children's obvious enjoyment in the event.

Next morning and after a hearty breakfast, the coach was again waiting for them in the courtyard. After just ten minutes they turned into a drive Elizabeth recognised. Yes, she'd been right all along – there stood the same burnt-out shell of a house she now knew so well. It had been tidied up a bit by the builders but it was still shambolic.

In Albert's enthusiasm he burst out with, "Mummy, we know this place, don't we? But we remember it before it burnt down. Do you remember it Victoria?" He turned to Uncle Robert, as he'd begun to call him and asked, "Is this the house you're going to buy?"

"It is indeed young man, but it'll look very different when I'm finished with it." He helped them down from the coach and gazed at the house. "See how much land it has – it'll make an enormous garden. Most of it will need tearing down but not all of it, I'm sure the foundations are intact. I'm just going to take a stroll around – would you like to come?"

The children grabbed one hand each and went off, but Elizabeth stood where she was for a while, before moving slowly around the house. The coachman had fallen asleep with his arms folded across his chest – his night's sleep had obviously not been good.

The strangeness of the situation made the hairs on her neck stand on end. She felt nervous and wondered what Albert would be telling his uncle. What on earth was she doing here, she'd sworn she'd never come back? As she wandered around, she was careful not to get too close to the black, jarred wood and stones. She knew she was just outside where the kitchen had once stood and she thought she saw a light inside. She could hear the children laughing in the distance. She knew she must be imagining the light, but on closer inspection, found she wasn't.

There was a distinct glow inside and she could see Cook banging her pots and pans onto the stove. The little maid servant was running around the kitchen, trying to obey ten orders at once. She heard Cook, "Get yer lazy backside over 'ere an' 'elp peel these spuds." Yes, that sounded just like the cook she remembered, but her bark had always been was worse than her bite. There was no mistaking the people – they looked just like before and she felt sad at knowing they weren't really there - they'd all died in the fire.

The light in the kitchen dimmed and then disappeared completely. She moved on towards the front of what had once been the house and there were the large blackened windows of the dining room – she remembered how it had once looked. The children were still laughing and suddenly there it was - a light appearing in the dining room and suddenly, there were velvet drapes at the windows and a roaring fire in the grate beyond. She moved closer and peered inside - there, sitting in pride of place at each end of the table, were Lord Winship and Lady Arabella. As usual, they seemed to be bickering with each other. *They're probably arguing about who will murder the other first and maybe if I stood here long enough, I'd see them do it. In spite of the venom she could see in both faces, she had to smile – she knew, even if they died that night, they'd be fine in the morning.*

She stepped back from the window and the light inside dimmed, disappearing completely. And the house was once again a burnt-out shell. Robert and the children were coming towards her and she turned to meet them. She knew not to ask if they'd seen the lights in the house because of course they hadn't – that was her privilege alone. Her continuing powers of Deja-Vu were just as strong as ever and not for the first time, she thought of it as a curse – and not a privilege.

"Let's go home now Robert – we've seen what we came for – at least I certainly have. Look, the driver's still asleep – poor chap, he must be exhausted." She made a point of slamming the carriage door which woke him from his pleasant slumber and stopped his embarrassment.

That night, when she was tucking Albert in bed, Elizabeth noticed that he had something clutched tightly in his hand. "Darling what do you have there? Would you like me to put it on your bedside table until morning?"

"Oh no Mummy, I'd like to keep hold of it. He gave it to me today you know, and told me to take good care of it. It belongs with the other soldiers he gave me." He opened his hand and showed her a small metal gun carriage – a bit charred but quite intact.

She knew she had to ask the question but dreaded the answer, "Who gave it to you Albert?"

"Why Philip Mummy – Philip gave it to me. When I was investigating the burnt rubble, he suddenly appeared and picked it up from the ground. He was still using crutches to get around – he doesn't seem to have got much better. Poor boy." Albert obviously thought a lot of the young man, the young man who didn't really exist – although he certainly did to Albert.

"Did Uncle Robert talk to him too?" she asked innocently and was told Robert didn't even see him.

Albert looked thoughtful, " I don't know why he said he couldn't see Philip because the boy was standing right there! I told him who Philip was and that I'd met him before when we stayed at his house, but Uncle Robert didn't seem to believe me."

She left him clutching the small gun carriage and went towards the door, "Just before I go Albert, may I ask you another question? When you were walking around the house today, did you happen to see any lights in the rubble?"

He looked puzzled and said sleepily, "No Mummy - no lights, just Philip. She switched off the lamp and closed the door quietly. *So, it was only me – I'm the only one with the special powers. Thank God the children don't have it! I saw the lights and the sounds of voices from the past so clearly – and the people actually looked as though they were flesh and blood. When will this end for me – will it ever end? At least my son doesn't seem to have it – or does he, after all he has no difficulty in seeing the lame young man? It was a dilemma!*

The weeks and months passed – Spring, Summer and now it was Autumn again when the glorious oranges and reds were bursting out everywhere. Robert had become a regular visitor and often dropped in for afternoon tea, hoping to be asked to stay for dinner of course. The whole household was fond of him and Nanny Mary in particular thought him a reincarnation of her old master. Elizabeth was guilty of calling him Richard on occasion, but he took it well and never contradicted her.

There had been considerable progress on the Winship house and Robert worked hard to oversee the architect and then, the builders. It had almost become his life's work and he was determined to complete it. Now and again, he'd made it apparent that he intended to ask Elizabeth to marry him one day, but he knew it was just too soon to broach that subject. Elizabeth in turn, never gave any indication of what her answer would be – in fact, she remained quite aloof from his attempts to get close to her. At one time, he'd suggested that he give up his rented rooms and perhaps move into her house – it was costly to maintain the rooms at a time when his money was needed for the house - but Elizabeth wouldn't even consider such a thing. After all, she had been a widow for one year only – far too soon for such a close relationship with her late husband's brother – if ever at all.

It was six months later and Robert had been working on the house spending equal amounts of time in the countryside and in London. Every time he came to visit, Elizabeth noticed him becoming more stooped than before - he wasn't an old man and yet his bowed appearance made him look so. Working on the house was obviously harder than he'd expected. She noticed too that he seemed to have developed a nagging cough which left him breathless. He ignored her suggestion to see a doctor, saying he must complete the house first before spending time on himself.

One day he turned up unexpectedly and found only Nanny and the children at home. Elizabeth had gone to the dress maker. Nanny fluttered around him, making him sit by the fire and removing his overcoat – Albert and Victoria came down from the playroom to sit by his side. He really looked quite ill with skin an ashen grey colour.

"My rooms are cold Nanny, so I've really come for a heat." He tried to make light of it. "This house is always so cosy and warm and I'm always made to feel welcome." He smiled at the nanny's fussing. "How's about I just sit here by the fire and you read your old uncle a story Albert? Mummy tells me you're very good at reading."

Victoria added, "He's very good Uncle Robert – he reads to me now and again, but I'm getting better too, so soon I'll be able to read to you as well."

And when Elizabeth walked into the parlour, she found the small family group, completely in tune with one other. "How is the house coming on Robert?" she asked.

"It's right at the point of completion, my dear. I think you'll be absolutely amazed when you see it. You will come to see it soon, won't you?"

Two days later, the doorbell rang and Maisie opened the door. A woman she didn't know stood there looking quite awkward. "Is the mistress at home please?" And the maid went to enquire.

"Come inside and wait in the hall – she'll be out soon." Maisie sniffed loudly to show she was a cut above the woman.

"Oh Ma'am, I've come with bad news I'm afraid. Mr Robert is in his sick bed and is asking for you – he's too poorly to even get up." The woman was the landlady of the apartments where her brother-in-law lived and he'd begged her to fetch Elizabeth, who grabbed her coat and went immediately with the woman.

Although the woman had looked quite dowdy, the apartment block was smart and fashionable and they were soon climbing the stairs to Robert's rooms. "I'll leave you now Ma'am – the doctor's still with him – and I don't mind telling you the struggle it was to let me call him."

She gently knocked the door and a man answered. He was tall and rather gaunt and had a stethoscope around his neck. He was looking very serious.

"I am his sister-in-law Doctor – how is he?" The doctor kept his voice low and took her into the small sitting room. "I'm afraid it's a bad case of pneumonia Madam – his chest is completely congested and his breathing is very shallow. May I ask if he's been like this for long – I should have been called sooner, you know? He has asked to see you however so please do go into the bedroom - but be prepared for what you find there."

Robert was ashen and he seemed to be shivering and sweating both at once. His eyes were staring and he was plucking at the bedcover with his fingers. He tried to talk when he saw her but his voice was weak and she had to bend down to hear his whisper.

"Dear Elizabeth, I'm afraid I'm undone. But I feel better for seeing you." She could just make out his words.

"Oh Robert, come now - you'll soon be on your feet again. You've just caught a nasty cold, that's all." She tried to sound positive and smiled at him. She knew however his days were numbered – perhaps even his hours. *How can this have happened so quickly? I had no idea he was this ill. He must have a weak chest like his brother – they were twins after all. What will I tell the children – first their father and now their beloved uncle. The words Deja-Vu jumped into her mind – she was at the death bed of a man who looked just like her husband – it was happening all over again and she could do nothing to stop it.*

He died the next day although the doctor had tried to help him, but there was nothing more he could do. Robert had actually died in the night and Elizabeth was told next morning – her house was once again in mourning and the children were bereft at the loss of another loved one. As she stood by the graveside, she waited for the vicar to close his bible – just as she'd done at Richard's burial – she wondered how many more funerals she would have to attend. This really was the worst Deja-Vu she'd experienced and she turned to go to her carriage, when an impeccably dressed man quietly approached her. She recognised him as the lawyer, whose office she'd once visited when she 'd returned to London.

"Madam, may I offer you my condolences? Life has been rather unkind to you of late but I have news that may give you some cheer. Your late brother-in-law also undertook of my services when I helped him with the legal work needed for the house he was rebuilding. He was of course a lawyer himself, but needed my objective advice. May I call on you at your convenience, in order to read his will? As a precursor however, I thought you should hear something positive – your brother-in-law has left everything to you , that is his entire estate, including the country house he'd just rebuilt. You are his sole beneficiary and will be an even richer young woman than you are now." Having said his piece, he disappeared amongst the other mourners, leaving behind a distraught Elizabeth.

My God – please don't do this to me. There is nothing on earth I want less than Robert's house. The very thought of it distresses me and I know for a fact it could never bring happiness to me or mine. It was built on the foundations of a house I'd once known - a house full of despair and misery. I swore I would never live there again – nor shall I !

She passed a weeping willow tree whose branches swept along the ground and something made her turn around for one last look at the graveside. Now the people had gone, there were only the grave diggers there, waiting to do their work. Beyond them and under another tree, two well-dressed gentlemen stood side by side. She stared hard and realised what she was seeing. Two identical men, both of whom she recognised – Richard was one and the other was Robert – both as alike as two peas in a pod. They were together at last – born at the same moment and now joined in death. They were both watching her as she stood there, clearly saying their final goodbye.

She pressed her gloved-hand to her mouth in a gesture of both love and goodbye. She blew them a soft kiss. Her eyes however were not filled with tears, but with a fiery light of determination. Sweet, gentle Elizabeth looked straight at the two men and spoke softly the words, "Never! I shall never live in that damned awful house! Any future Deja-Vu will have to come looking for me – I'm certainly not going there to look for it! You two should go there however – you'd fit in perfectly with all the other souls who just refuse to leave this world!" And although she never knew it, that's exactly what Richard and Robert did!